EVERMORE ACADEMY: WINTER

YEAR ONE

AUDREY GREY

STARFALL PRESS

To Savannah and Jack, my two great loves.

The darkly beautiful beings that rule the western half of my world call themselves the Evermore, but we have other names for them.

Invaders.

Cruel folk.

Tricksters.

Sidhe.

Fae.

My favorite is pointy-eared dickwads, but that's a mouthful so I usually stick with Fae.

They came eighteen years ago in a bright wave of magic that demolished half the North American continent. They claimed the explosion—now cleverly termed the Lightmare by the media—was an accident . . . as if wiping out half a country is a simple mistake.

No apologies, no real explanation beyond a Fae war that got out of hand.

Just oopsie, we effed up. But since we're here and the space is unoccupied, mind if we move in?

Typical Fae logic.

My younger sister, Jane, claims she saw one once on the edge of the forest. Her depiction was only slightly terrifying. Daggerish, elongated ears. Sharp, angular faces. Huge, inhuman eyes. Craploads of magic oozing out of their pores.

Her words, not mine, and probably not true. She has a flair for the dramatic.

My brain refuses to believe the more creative tales. That the Fae have horns and wings and hooves and predatory fangs made for ripping our flesh to ribbons.

Either way, I honestly didn't think about them much. It's hard to focus on mythological boogiemen when we have very real, very human monsters to deal with.

And Cal Miller is the worst of the worst.

Which makes my close proximity to him unsettling, at best. Lucky me. Wiping a sweat-damp strand of pale blonde hair from my eyes, I peer at the man-child where he sits on a giant stash of baby products—formula, diapers, wipes—his reddish brown Cavender boots propped up on green barrels of drinking water.

As if he knows he's being appraised, he tips back a Coors Light can, drains it, and crushes it inside his hand.

Here we have the redneck in his natural habitat, I think in a terrible British accent. But my running commentary on Cal and his disgusting habits is running dry.

I've been here way too long.

With a belch that could wake the dead, he chucks the can into a trash bin dangerously close to where I hide. As he laughs at his own amazingness, his man-belly jiggles.

Someone hasn't missed a meal in a while.

Sweat beads down my forehead. The warehouse is hot as the Summer realm, and the tiny fan whirring in the corner barely keeps the flies away. I would have opened one of the doors to let in a breeze . . . but it isn't my warehouse. It belongs to the Millers, aka worst humans on the planet, aka ass-hats.

Did I mention I'm not supposed to be here?

I peek my head from the two crates of potatoes I'm wedged between, barely breathing for fear Cal will hear me. My neck has a crick, the girls are smashed against my chest, and my butt has lost all feeling.

Who thought this was a good idea?

Oh, right. Me.

Cal leans over and grabs another beer from a red ice chest. Then he walks over to the garage door, lifts the heavy metal with a loud crank, and pisses into the bushes.

Disgusting.

Cal's twenty-one, just three years older than me, but it's hard to remember that sometimes. Especially when he's guzzling beer like it's orange Gatorade and overseeing his family's illegal smuggling operation.

The muscles inside Cal's flannel shirt bulge as he returns, his wrangler jeans about two sizes too small, which doesn't help the beer gut that's formed since he graduated high school. A Glock pistol is tucked into his jeans just above his right hip.

I'm hoping he's drunk enough that his aim is crap. Actually, I'm hoping he never sees me at all. I mean, who's crazy enough to hide in the Millers' warehouse with him in it?

This girl right here. I'm either smart or crazy-dead.

Not for the first time, I question my sanity. This is madness. Hiding in plain sight. All Cal has to do is squint real hard while looking to his left and he'll see me.

What the hell am I doing?

In my defense, I thought there would be more places to hide . . .

Pushing strands of my hair from my eyes, I take a calming breath and busy myself cataloging the necessities—only the necessities—like this is a trip to Walmart. I can't take much, a few armloads at most, so I'll have to be picky.

Stacks and stacks of packaged food are everywhere. Cans of spaghettiOs, boxes of fruit loops, and sacks of flour. Bags of rice line the shelves to my left, canned yams and green beans to my right.

A knife edge of hope cuts through me, sharp and dangerous. This one score could feed everyone back at the farmhouse for days. My stomach clenches with need, but I somehow keep it from growling.

Voices draw my focus outside. It's nearly dark, the sun a sliver of gold on the horizon. Three men in camo shorts and tight green T-shirts have stopped their Polaris ATV to chat with Cal. They've increased their patrols recently, and now a girl can't break into a simple barn around here without taking desperate risks.

"C'mon, a-holes," I whisper.

Usually about this time, Cal is tanked. Enough to leave the warehouse and ride with his patrol around the grounds blaring Willy Nelson and waving their rifles while shooting everything that moves.

Not that they're using game for target practice. All the animals are long gone, either poisoned from the scourge seeping into our lands, killed by the darklings, or overhunted by the Millers and their hired thugs.

Cal's solution to my string of thefts was to hire a mini army. An overreaction, if you ask me. But I suppose he's trying to send a message.

Most of the new hires are former officers from the now defunct police force, although a few are Cal's former teammates from the football team who graduated a couple months ago. Far as jobs go, this is the best they'll find in the borderlands.

It's hard to fault them for that.

But I do fault them for protecting merchandise stolen from the people, which is why I give zero fracks about stealing it back.

At least, what I can fit inside the wheelbarrow I have stashed behind the barn.

"All right, boys," Cal calls, his voice sloppy and loud. "Time to hunt some Fae bastards!"

They throw up a cheer, and I rest my head against the cans of mandarin oranges with a thunk. *Finally.*

How such an idiot can lead the largest smuggling organization in the borderlands is beyond me.

As everyone piles into the Polaris, Cal slings a bolt action rifle over his shoulder and then lugs the ice chest over to the vehicle.

My gaze slides to his weapon. For a moment, I imagine Cal peering through his scope at me. Imagine what a bullet feels like as it rips through my flesh.

They have guns. Big ass freaking guns. This is stupid.

But I can't turn back now. For better or worse, I'm stealing this food.

My motto: Better stupid and fed than smart and starving.

As they strap the big red freezer onto the back, they make more jokes about killing Fae.

A girl can hope. We could only be so lucky to have the a-holes of this world and the Fae cancel each other out.

One of the guards yanks the garage door down, flooding the warehouse in darkness. But the merciless West Texas sun, never one to admit defeat, slants through the dusty windows at the top, providing all the light I need.

Quieting my breathing, I pop to my feet and ready my mind for what must come next. My heart plays a steady tune against my sternum.

Thump.

Thump.

A mewling noise nearly knocks me out of my skin. I whip around, my boots slipping on the sawdust-covered concrete. A yellow tomcat slinks around the corner and then sits on his hindquarters, staring at me with suspicion. His ribs stick out beneath his mangy fur, and it's obvious he hasn't had a meal in a while either.

Bastards. The Millers probably have him just to keep the rats away. If he doesn't hunt, he doesn't eat.

"Do they not feed you, buddy?" I whisper, trying to ignore the tug on my heart.

Remember, you're a badass thief. Now act like one.

The cat pauses, his lime-green eyes wide. Then he cocks his head and meows and oh my God he's so friggin cute I want to take him home right now.

My heart puddles into a pile of goo. Animals for me are like Louboutins for most girls.

Dogs are better, of course. No debate there.

As if the cat can hear my thoughts, he suddenly hisses.

I didn't mean it! I mentally think. *You're better than a dumb dog, probably smarter too.*

The cat stops growling and licks its white paw, watching me intently. There's judgement in his eyes.

"Technically this isn't stealing," I whisper to the cat.

Honest to God, the cat rolls its eyes.

What am I doing? I should be elbows-deep in fruit loops and spaghettiOs right now, not chatting it up with a friggin cat.

Summer, you are officially the worst thief ever.

"Okay," I admit. "I'm about to steal from your dickwad master. But I have four hungry kids to feed. Man, kids eat a lot. And you look like you would sympathize with that . . . anyway. This food was supposed to go to them in the first place, so I'm just reclaiming it."

The animal goes completely still, as if he understands me. Sometimes I trick myself into thinking they actually can.

"You might be wondering how I ended up responsible for four children," I continue like the lunatic I am. Man, I should probably get out more.

The cat's ears point in my direction, and it makes a tiny chirping noise I pretend is a response.

"Long story short, I was homeless on the streets of Dallas. You would not like it there. . . anyway, two wonderful women rescued me, and I've been doing the same ever since. Rescuing kids orphaned by the Fae. Only once they're here, I have to find a way to feed them. That's where this food comes in."

The animal and I lock eyes and I swear something passes between us. An understanding.

Then the tomcat pads over to me and rubs against my leg. After stroking his back for a sec, I get to work.

Everything on my mental list gets hefted or lugged to a pile near the back door.

When I'm done, I'm breathing hard and sweat drenches the top of my tank top. I tick off the list to make sure I have the important things, because after this break-in—or break out, if we're being technical—this place will turn into Fort Knox.

Powdered milk. Check.

Ramen noodles. Check.

Three crates of eggs. Check.

Giant bag of pinto beans (yuck). Check.

Cheetos (for Jane). Check.

Tampons (for me). Check.

Charms lollipops with gum in the center. (Because they make life better.) Check.

A few items, like toilet paper and razors, are impulse grabs.

My loot ends up being twenty items total. The pallets are sent by the government outside the tainted borderlands, so everything is family size.

I glance over my wimpy arm muscles. This could take a while.

A quick check outside the window above the door shows the coast is clear. The light is fading, the world outside a silvery-gray.

I laugh at the new deadbolt as I unlock the door and prop it open with a rock. *Deadbolt, Cal? Really? That's all you got?*

I would give almost anything to see Cal's face when he realizes I was inside this whole time.

It takes five trips to haul everything to my wheelbarrow, and when I'm done, I'm sucking humid Texas air like it's the sugar inside pixie straws.

Right before I leave, a mental image of the cat, his ribs sticking out, flashes across my mind.

No. I will not go back for the cat. I will not . . .

I go back for the damned cat. The poor guy practically throws himself into my arms, yowling so loud my aunts can probably hear it back at the farmhouse. His legs clasp around my neck, his claws digging into my flesh.

"Shh," I whisper-scold. "Chatty Cat, if you're coming with me, you have to be quiet."

Thank God he stops making his crazy noises, and I grab a twenty-pack of canned tuna before we head outside.

Chatty Cat is practically glommed onto my face. With a little effort, and a lot of cursing, I peel him off. The cat and the tuna go in the wheelbarrow. He settles on top of the packages of ramen, curls up, and immediately begins to purr.

I pick my compound bow up and toss it onto the pile. Pretty sure Cal's arsenal of guns trumps my one bow, but the weapon's not for humans.

This close to the Shimmer—the magical veil that separates

our world from the Fae's—everyone needs to be armed. The things that seep from the other side are inhuman, and it's not just the Fae.

When their magical war made everything go *kablooey*, the same magic transformed the nearest people into monsters we call darklings.

The Shimmer isn't just for keeping us out of their lands; it's for keeping the darklings out.

But sometimes they find their way into the borderlands anyway. And lately, the killings have increased. My heart spikes as I recall how, for the last week, tracks from something inhuman have appeared outside my house. The paw prints definitely canine but too large to be normal wolves.

Pushing the thought from my mind, I snatch a lollipop from the wheelbarrow and pocket five more, savoring the sour-apple flavor that explodes on my tongue. After nearly a day of nothing to eat, my body jerks as the sugar enters my bloodstream.

An owl hoots from the roof, reminding me I need to hurry. The creature perches right above us, his amber eyes seeming to glow, his orchid-white feathers bright against the dark sky. For reasons I can't really explain, the owl shows up nearly everywhere.

And his presence has gotten even more persistent in the last week too.

"Wouldn't be a party without you," I mutter before refocusing on the task.

I glance over my bow, the string close to snapping. A gun would be better, but ammo's expensive. Especially iron-coated bullets, which are the only type that can put a Fae or darkling down.

In the Tainted Zone, iron is worth more than gold.

Chatty Cat suddenly begins to growl. At the same time, the white owl takes to the sky, his shadow flickering over the lawn and drawing my attention to movement behind me.

My heart slams into my throat as I whip around to see a light coming from my right, the bright orb bouncing over the lawn.

Flashlight.

Which means someone is attached to that flashlight.

2

Hell *fire.* I grab the splintery ends of the wheelbarrow handles and shove it across the lumpy grass, my boots digging into the soil for traction.

Heavy. It's too heavy!

I aim for the woods twenty yards away. Every bump nearly topples the wheelbarrow as it careens all over the damn place.

A male voice yells behind me. "Stop!"

Yeah right. Does any criminal actually stop when they're told?

I break into a sprint. Chatty Cat's eyes are saucers, his claws dug into the ramen for dear life. My package of tampons straight up bounces out of my wheelbarrow.

Damn.

I barely hesitate before plunging into the dark woods. I'm hoping the guard won't follow me. Most are terrified of the forest at night, especially this close to the Shimmer.

I crane my neck back, only to see the guard standing at the edge of the tree line. He lifts his pistol, squints, and then a red flash lights up his gun's muzzle. At the same time, a loud pop splits the air.

The bullet hits the tree next to me, leaving a quarter-sized hole in the bark and propelling wood splinters into my jeans.

"You mother cracker!" I growl, sending my lollipop tumbling from my lips as I plunge deeper into the forest. My heart is lodged in my throat and I'm breathing so loud I can't hear anything else. My too-loose jeans sag low on my sharp hip bones. My belt is fixed at the last hole, but still it's not tight enough.

Yanking my jeans up, I blindly burrow deeper and deeper into the forest.

Once upon a time I could run a fairly decent mile, even in this infernal heat. But we had a herd of cattle then, a couple good dairy cows, some chickens, plus the biggest garden this side of Texas.

Hard to make your muscles obey when you have nothing to entice them with but saltine crackers and gruel.

Staggering across the carpet of underbrush, I fight the darkness nibbling my vision to jagged crumbs. Limbs claw at my bare arms and rip my tank top.

Panic strangles my heart, and I blindly punch farther into the woods. If I'm caught, my family will suffer.

Since they cordoned off our lands and closed the last of our trade routes, everyone in the Tainted Zone—the long four-hundred mile wide border zone that goes vertical from North Dakota to the tip of Texas—is struggling.

The government from the Untouched Zone in the East sends us food and water, but the Millers confiscate everything that arrives. For safekeeping, they promise.

Not sure when safekeeping something turned into selling it back to the people for five times what it's worth, but when you're as rich and powerful as Cal and his family, you get to make shit up.

Righteous fury steels my resolve. I tug my lips between my teeth until sharp pain punches away the dizziness. Coppery warmth pools beneath my tongue as I pause to get my bearings.

Surely the guy didn't follow me this far.

A yellow disc of light sweeps over the trunk of a huge oak ten feet to my right.

Oberon's luck!

Dragging in a lungful of air, I try to force the now half-deflated wheelbarrow tire over a fallen tree, sending the rickety contraption reeling sideways. I watch in horror as the contents spill out onto the forest floor.

Chatty Cat lands on his feet. Ears flattened, he pins me with a look of supreme annoyance.

I so feel you, Chatty.

Before I have time to process what this means for my family, my gaze locks onto something even more dangerous than the man behind me.

The Shimmer. It sweeps across the forest a few steps away, an undulating wall of iridescent magic. Compared to the muddy-brown of the trees, it burns bright and metallic and beautiful. The kind of beautiful that takes your breath away and makes you feel both hollow and full inside.

On the other side is the Everwilde, which is just a fancy name for the realm of the Fae. Or, as I like to call it, the place you should never ever visit unless you want to die.

I crane my neck, trailing the twinkling curtain up up up into the moonlit sky.

"Hands up!" the guard calls from behind me. His voice is shaky and quick. He sees the Shimmer too.

A warning prickle scrapes down my spine, but it has nothing to do with the guard or the gun pointed at my back.

Everything goes still, as if, this near to the Everwilde, there is no sound. No life. Nothing.

I should turn around and give myself up. Being this close to *their* world is madness. I can feel the danger of it sweeping over me like a drug, ramping up my pulse, my breathing.

One roided-out guard with a gun is child's play compared to what awaits me on the other side.

"Don't make me shoot you," the guard growls. His voice is closer; he's no more than seven feet away.

I glance over my shoulder and immediately recognize the guard. Bryce Hawkins, a heavyweight wrestler a year ahead of me in school.

"Summer?" he barks, spitting my name out like a curse. "What the hell are you doing?"

I whip around, hoping to hide my face, but it's too late. He's already seen me.

Craptastic. No way Cal lets this go.

Reminder to self: criminals wear disguises for a reason.

In my mind's eye, I picture the white farmhouse in the distance. The dark shapes bobbing around the lawn could be goats or even cows—if any of those were around anymore. But I know that each blob is a child. An orphan, like me. Rescued from horrible situations I can't bear to revisit.

I can't leave them. If Cal or his father catch me . . . there is no law here. No courts or justice. In the borderlands, the Millers are the law—which means I'm screwed.

Unless . . .

I take a step toward the Shimmer, heart thundering in my chest.

It's mesmerizing. Completely, utterly wonderful in its strangeness. The way the rainbow surface seems to move and slide like the shell of a bubble. A breeze emanates from the other side, cool and biting against my bare arms. A few fluffy snowflakes break through and cling to my cheek where they immediately turn to water.

In this infernal heat, it seems impossible that only a few

feet away lies a place of frost and magic and strange, dangerous beings. A place where day is night and summer is winter and the ordinary is extraordinary.

I place a hand on the wall. It's frigid and smooth and gelatinous, not at all solid like I imagined.

"Wait." Bryce's nervous voice marks him only a few feet away. "Please don't go any farther, I'm warning you."

My fingertips indent the slippery surface. The idea that if I push real hard I could break through comes over me in a wave of impossibility.

This wall is supposed to be impenetrable.

The only time something goes into the world of the Fae is when they want it to. Usually a foolish mortal who bartered with a Fae and then couldn't pay the price, or let a Fae give them something without understanding the consequences.

An Evermore never gives anything for free.

"Come to me before—before I'm forced to shoot you." Bryce is terrified, his voice pleading. He refuses to draw any nearer. "Please, Summer. If Cal knows I let you get away . . ."

Chatty Cat brushes against my leg. Then he disappears through the Shimmer like it's mist. Holy shit.

If Chatty Cat can do it . . .

Clutching my bow tight, I say a prayer and lunge through the Shimmer, straight into the Everwilde.

That was easy. Probably too easy.

Bryce yells at me on the other side, but it's warbled and hard to make out. Then the mofo shoots at the wall a few times. The gunfire sounds like those little fireworks you throw onto the ground.

The bullets don't pierce the Shimmer. They don't even *indent* it.

After that, everything goes quiet.

3

The moment I pass through the Shimmer, a blast of icy air envelops me, and it takes a second to make my lungs work again. When they finally do, I watch in wonder as my breath spews on in a milky cloud and spreads through the forest.

Huge winter trees with winding trunks and silver leaves rise from the icy ground. The branches all grow in one direction, making the trees appear to reach toward the heavens at an angle.

Bright red bark clings to the trees, peeling away to reveal grayish skin beneath, and strange fruit peeks between the leaves. Each perfect golden teardrop shimmers with ice.

And the frost—it's everywhere. Dusting the foliage, the soil, the leaves. Near the Shimmer the snowfall is thin, exposing thick green grass. Each blade is frozen solid, and when I walk, my boots crunch the delicate strands, the sound like shards of glass ground together.

A screech pierces the crisp air, and I duck just as the snowy owl from earlier swoops onto a crooked red branch.

His snow colored feathers fluff out as he watches me with amber, unblinking eyes too sentient for my liking.

This world is alive with animals. Two white rabbits hop between the trees, and a squirrel with black tufts above his ears scampers over a branch. Chatty Cat flicks a glance at the squirrel and then slides his lazy gaze to me and yawns.

No wonder you're starving.

A red cardinal drops from above and lands near us, pecking at the snow.

My jaw clenches. Perhaps the Fae are purposefully keeping us out because they want us to starve. First they took half our land, then they poisoned the earth along the tainted borderlands so those of us trapped here have nothing. They decimated our population, made orphans of the children, and expect us to obey their laws.

And now they get to sit behind some faulty, pretend wall in their stolen lands and watch us die?

Anger rushes through me, hot and pungent as a newly tarred highway in the middle of summer.

Stop sightseeing like this is the Dollar General, Summer.

Lungs aching, I reach for my bow with numb fingers. By now my hands have lost all sensation. Plus I'm having trouble getting used to the way my breath clouds my vision every time I exhale.

This is not the place to let my guard down.

Drawing an arrow along the bow, I sight down the squirrel first. I hate killing animals, but I have to bring something home to eat. My fingers are red and achy.

What are the stages of frostbite? Is red first or is that a later, fingers-fall-off stage?

"Who needs fingers anyway?" I say conversationally to the squirrel. "You do just fine without them—at least, you did until I came along."

Only I can't shoot him. *Pretend he's a cheeseburger, Summer.*

I try, but he's so cute with his fluffy black ears and spastic tail. I want to take him home and cuddle, not eat him.

Sighing, I sling my bow over my shoulder, slip the arrow into my back jean's pocket, and then pull out another lollipop, this one cherry-flavored.

For a moment, as the sugary goodness rushes over me, all seems right with the world.

Then I remember it's freezing, and I'm still a good twenty minutes from home. I can't re-enter our world in the same spot, in case Bryce is still waiting for me. And the guards are probably all looking for me now.

If I follow the Shimmer for about a mile to the north, I'll be out of the Millers' territory and near the woods close to our property.

"Time to jog, Summer. You can do it." My little pep-talk falls flat. My arms shake, and I'm so tired that even taking three steps seems impossible, let alone a freaking mile.

Yet I don't have a choice. Story of my life.

Promising myself the rest of the candy in my pocket when I'm done, I break into a half-run half-lurch. Bribery is an underrated act, especially when bribing oneself. Chatty Cat follows, swerving in and out of my legs as he bounds across the snow and makes weird mewling noises.

My breath plumes around me as I parallel the Shimmer, pushing my body hard, my boots slogging through the snow. My arms are frozen, and my sweat has formed a thin layer of ice that encrusts my body.

When I'm done, I can hardly stand. My body completely numb. But I'm incredibly proud of myself, and I demolish another lollipop, crunching straight to the gum this time.

As the sour juice from the gum trickles down my throat, I let out a cloudy sigh and then sweep my gaze over this forbidden world one last time. The beauty of it is haunting. The way nothing is dead, as if a winter storm blew in one fine summer day and froze everything just so. Even the moon seems covered in a layer of hoarfrost, the air honeyed with whatever fruit hangs from the trees.

Fruit. My tongue prickles with moisture. I haven't tasted any real produce beyond a few expired cans of mandarin oranges in months, and the artificial cherry flavor on my tongue suddenly pales in comparison to the real thing.

The golden spheres taunt me from where they hang, swollen and ripe, begging to be picked and eaten.

I can almost feel my teeth breaking their skin. Almost taste what I imagine is a semi-soft inside, like a firm pear. The promise of fresh fruit sends a surge of energy into my body. The promise of not going home empty-handed?

Even more alluring.

Everyone knows not to steal from the Fae. But this is wild fruit, growing from trees that were once our trees, in a land that was once our land. Which, technically, makes it our fruit.

The logic seems pretty legit to me.

My hands are no good for climbing, but I find a tree on the very edge of the forest with branches bent low enough to pick its fruit. Using my shirt like a basket, I fill the bottom of my tank top with nine of the golden fruits.

Up close, their skin is a greenish-gold, the curved stems dark eggplant-purple.

I lug them to the Shimmer, say a prayer the magical fence goes both ways, then prepare to leap back to my world. From this side, the wall is completely transparent, and I take in the rolling prairie and sparse forest.

Even covered in a layer of ice, the world on this side feels so much more *alive*.

Resituating my bow on my shoulder, I hold the shirt with the fruit in one hand, splay my other hand on the Shimmer, and go to push—

Something clamps down on my left arm and spins me

around. I cry out on instinct as fear floods me. The fruit goes tumbling into the frozen grass. I try to plant my feet to keep from flying, but whatever has me in its grip is too strong and I'm knocked sideways to my hands and knees.

Chatty Cat snarls before letting out a low, terrifying growl. He's crouched beside me, glaring up at my assaulter.

"Thief," a male voice hisses. A man stands over me, blocking my path to the Shimmer. . .

No, not a man. A Fae. He's surprisingly tall, or maybe that's because I'm on my knees, thanks to this dickwad.

Gritting my teeth, I lift my gaze to assess him, my eyes trailing up the finely-tailored black leather boots that rise to his knees, the thick sword belt and ornate long sword. The silver guard is fashioned into a dragon that wraps around the hilt. One gloved hand rests casually around the handle. White fur from some creature I can't place lines a silver cloak embroidered with indigo and dotted with crystals.

The ostentatious ensemble is finished off with two silver owl cloak pins on either side of his collar.

Next to him, my thrift store jeans and three-day-old tank top feel rather lacking.

Curious to what an actual Fae looks like, I move my focus to his face, only to be disappointed. The hood of his cloak casts a deep shadow over his features. But I can feel predatory eyes staring down at me, searching for . . . something. The sharp apex of his ears rise on either side of his hood, the exotic tips sticking up like swords.

Hells bells. I'm standing next to an actual Fae.

That genius realization is followed by two more epiphanies. I made a terrible, stupid mistake, and now I'm in danger.

All these years avoiding the Shimmer and playing it safe, and one promise of fruit is all it took to ruin everything. I'm not prepared to meet a Fae. I'm not wearing any of the safe-guards that protect humans from them.

My rowan-berry charm is somewhere inside my night-stand, and the little packets of salt I usually carry in my pockets are somewhere on the kitchen table. My clothes aren't even inside out.

"Rise," he orders, "and face the consequences of your crime."

Who talks like that? I would laugh, but the hatred in his voice makes me shiver instead.

It's not over yet, Summer. Now move!

"Happily," I snarl.

Shoving my hands deep into the snow for support, I dart to my feet and lunge for my bow . . . only to watch the sleek steel weapon turn to ice that shatters at my touch. *No.*

Shards of the only thing that's kept me fed and alive for years pelt my cheeks and then splatter the snow next to my lollipops.

I needed that bow to live. *We* needed it.

A pallor of desperation comes over me, but I shake it off. Where are my other weapons? My hunting knife! The folding blade sits at my waistband, nearly forgotten, and I fumble at it with clumsy, frozen fingers while the dickwad watches me quietly, probably grinning.

"I'll destroy that too," the Fae promises in a smarmy voice.

Ignoring his warning, I drag my thumb over the blade to open it—

The dagger breaks apart in my fingers in an explosion of snow. For a stunned moment, I stare at my empty fingers, unable to process the events unfolding. Both of those weapons were worth more than gold in my world.

Everything is spinning out of control so fast. I need to stop and think, but I don't have time.

Magic—only magic could have done *that*. Real magic.

The fact this creature can use magic shouldn't surprise me, but it does. Fear and anger churn into a whirlwind of emotion inside me. My chest aches.

With a desperate growl, I whip around to face the Fae. "Neat party trick. Does that impress all the mortals?"

The biting sarcasm in my voice does nothing to mask my fear. If anything, it makes me sound more desperate.

"It wasn't meant to impress you."

The coldness in his voice cuts to my core.

Squeezing my hands into fists, I try a different tact. "Put away your magic so we can fight fair."

A wicked laugh fills the forest. "Fight? With what?"

"With my bare hands . . . if I have to." I hold up my frozen fingers to drive home my point, hoping they look lethal instead of halfway frozen. "Or you could just move and avoid all that unpleasantness."

A spurt of icy breeze lifts the hood of his cloak back, just enough to draw the shadow up and reveal his lips: soft, cruel things bowed at the top and perfectly full at the bottom. Lips meant for smirking and taunting and kissing.

Another joyless chuckle drifts from the offending lips. "Try it and I'll turn you to ice too, mortal girl, and rest you in my winter garden, chipping away at you piece by piece. When only your heart is left, I'll crush it between my fingers and spread the remains among the snowdrops, so that nothing of you is here to mourn."

Wow. This guy is a bundle of rainbows and unicorns. The horrible cruelness of his words pierces deep into my heart, his voice a snow-driven shard of ice. What could cause such terrible darkness inside someone?

Or perhaps all the Fae are this twisted and hateful.

Shivers wrack my body, and I'm suddenly all too aware of the cold seeping into my bare flesh. I'm turning into a human popsicle. Riotous waves of my hair has escaped its braided prison and tumbles around me, the sweatier strands frozen at odd angles. The color is just a shade creamier than the snow.

"That sounds fun . . . but messy," I say. "I vote you just let me go home." I lift my arms above my head in the universal sign of surrender. If I can't scare him, perhaps looking weak and innocent will conjure pity. "Let me go and I promise, you will never see me again."

Another cruel laugh dispels that foolish hope. "The hubris of your kind never fails. You've stolen, an offense punishable by death, yet you ask to go home?"

Was he watching me earlier? "The food I stole is ours anyway," I say quietly. "I'm just taking it back."

"And the neverapple fruit you plucked from the Winter Prince's orchard?" he responds just as softly. "Does that also belong to you?"

Oh. Right. Somehow I just assumed the apples were, I don't know, wild or something. My gaze falls to the golden fruits strewn across the frosted grass, and I know denying his accusation is pointless.

Why did I have to be so greedy?

"We're . . . we're starving. The scourge has been seeping through your broken wall for years and it's poisoned every-thing in the borderlands. We have nothing to eat. You know"—I put my fingers to my mouth and mime eating —"that thing mortals must do to live?"

I peer through the shadowy haze surrounding his face, desperate for a shred of humanity. Of kindness. Instead I'm met with the faint glow of pale silver-blue eyes. They're not as big or as inhuman as I was led to believe. The rest of his features are indiscernible.

An icy hatred too dark to be human brims inside his strange irises. "You poisoned your lands, so now all your animals flee to our side. How, exactly, is that our fault?"

For a moment, I stare at him, aghast at his apathy. "Why are you so cruel?"

"I may be cruel," he admits. "But is that not the order of things? That bow you nearly used on me, how many animals have you killed so that you can live? Living and dying are two sides of the same blade. Call it cruelty or call it fate, I care not."

I roll my eyes. "Typical pointy-eared dickwa—Fae jargon. Using cryptic words in place of sense. Just tell me what I owe this Winter Prince and I'll find a way to pay him."

How much can nine neverapples cost?

"The price for stealing just one neverapple from the prince is death." My mouth falls open and his smug grin becomes wicked. *He's enjoying this.* "How do you expect to pay for nine?" he continues. "Do you have nine lives like the pixie to bargain with?"

"You're kidding." But of course he's not kidding. He doesn't even seem capable of cracking a joke. "What kind of monsters grow such a precious fruit right next to starving people? Is that your thing? Starve us and then taunt us with forbidden fruit?"

When he doesn't answer, desperation takes hold. "I haven't touched them. Can't you just, I don't know, put them back with your magic or something?"

I can feel his glare behind his hood. "Put them back? You've touched them with your human fingers, meaning now the revered fruit is tainted."

You mother cracker.

I would have laughed at the injustice of it, but his knuckles tighten over the hilt of his fine sword and suddenly I can't breathe.

The scrape of the blade exiting its scabbard sends my heart ramming into my breastbone, my strangled breaths

punching out in violent ivory bursts. The curved metal glimmers softly in the moonlight.

"On your knees," he says casually. Icily. As if executions of
starving mortals are an everyday occurrence.

That's when I know, without a doubt, he's going to
kill me.

4

I jut out my chin, cramming every bit of my rage into my expression as I glare at the Fae. "Screw you, dickwad. If you're going to kill me for taking a few stupid neverapples, I'm not making it easy for you."

Maybe I should run. I should definitely run. *Move!* I order my legs, who straight up refuse to budge. Either from fear or shock or the freezing cold. My bet is all three.

"Have it your way."

I'm working on coaxing my stubborn thighs into action when a flicker of white above calls my attention. We both glance up at the distraction to see a swarm of white moths fluttering down from the trees like giant drops of snowfall. They move as one, a cloud of sparkling wings that shimmer and glow.

I'm so in awe of their beauty that I nearly forget about the Fae and the blade he holds, or that I'm supposed to be fleeing.

Nearly.

One by one, they gather around my head. A few alight along my brow, the rest hovering a few inches above my messy, half-fallen topknot.

Like a crown.

One of the moths breaks from the others and alights on the tip of the Fae's sword. Its gossamer wings open and close as we stare on in stunned silence, the creature's ethereal beauty in stark contrast to the murderous blade and the monster holding it.

All at once, the moths take to the air and ascend into the darkness as quickly as they came, and my dark reality comes crashing down again.

"What is your name?" he asks.

"Why?" I scoff. "Do you need it to scratch into a murder notebook?"

Suddenly, I feel his focus flit behind me at something. A peek over my shoulder shows a young girl in worn overalls with bright red pigtail braids and freckles bounding up the hill on the other side of the Shimmer.

Jane. She's calling my name and she has a flashlight.

Should have known she'd come looking for me. As the second oldest, she acts like an adult when she's barely fourteen. Half the time she's arguing with me; the other half she's trying to be like me. Not two days ago I caught her shooting my bow into moldy hay bales.

Only instead of wild game, her target was black paint made into a long face with sharp, pointy ears.

Give her a couple years and she'll be a fine shot, better than me. Not that I'd ever tell her as much.

After a few moments of staring at the Shimmer, she begins to draw close, ignoring every single warning and rule I've ever told her about the Everwilde.

"Don't hurt her," I blurt, looking from her to him. "She has nothing to do with this. She's just a—a kid."

The Fae says nothing as he watches her. She's all gangly limbs and freckles as she peers into the Shimmer, her face covered in dirt and oil. Her thin lips are pursed, her brown eyes bright with the anger of someone just old enough to understand her world isn't fair.

I watch her too, willing her away with my thoughts. Internally screaming all the ways I'll punish her if she enters.

"Doesn't your kind follow any rules?" he demands. "Stay away from our land. Why is that so hard for you mortals to obey?"

All the things I want to scream burn on the tip of my tongue. Because it used to be our land. Because we're starving. Because we're pissed. Because people we knew and loved died here.

But for once in my life, I manage to hold back my smart tongue, instead pointing out, "She hasn't entered."

Yet, but she will. She's Jane.

A cloud of panic falls over me. When she's barely two feet from the wall, she points the flashlight into the Shimmer and squints her eyes, trying to see through the veil. If she spots me, she'll surely pass through.

"Do it," I blurt, my words tumbling out faster than I can think. "Kill me before she crosses over. I'll kneel for you . . . if that's your thing. Whatever floats your murdery boat. Just *don't* hurt her."

His head tilts so that now it's me he's watching. Studying me. The intensity of his gaze like a razor-edged blade dragging across my skin, splitting me open for all to see. Something in his demeanor shifts, and I can't help but feel I've surprised him somehow.

"You would die to protect her?" His voice is the soft tumble of snowflakes drifting in the wind.

"Yes." There's no hesitation in my voice because it's true. "I would die to protect all of them."

Quiet descends. I can hear Jane yelling louder, the idiot. Screaming at the top of her lungs like a banshee. She must have tracked me here.

Must somehow know I'm in trouble . . .

He lifts a hand and frost begins to grow over the Shimmer. I watch the frost crackle and pop across the wall, spider-webbing until the wall is no longer transparent.

When I'm convinced she won't be able to come through, I turn to face my tormentor turned executioner.

His gaze slides to the neverapples strewn over the snowy ground. "The stolen fruit was for your family?"

Perhaps I'm wrong, but his voice has lost some of its iciness.

I nod and drag a hand over my eyes, unshed tears pricking my throat. I have an embarrassing habit of crying when angry. "Sort of. I mean, yes. Not by blood, but that doesn't matter. There are—there are four kids, plus me."

Not sure why I add that last detail. If one starving human fails to sway his dark heart, four will hardly make a difference.

Without a word, he buries his steel back into the silver scabbard at his waist. At the sound, my blood rushes back into my toes and I release a ragged breath.

"What is your name, mortal girl?" This time his dark tone leaves no room for denying his request.

I clear my throat. "Summer. Summer . . . Solstice."

In East Texas, my name gets a lot of attention, along with musings about hippy parents and too many drugs. Not everyone names their kids for the day of the year they were born.

But apparently such names aren't odd to my tormentor, because he hardly blinks. He does, however, stare at me for what seems like minutes, seemingly torn on how to proceed.

"And *your* name?" I ask carefully. For the Fae, names have power, and just asking implies an intimacy we don't have. Actually, I'm not sure why I asked, except to keep this conversation going as long as possible.

Pretty sure I read somewhere that if I'm ever taken by a murderer, talking to them helps humanize me.

He ignores my request entirely and dives straight into a speech. "Summer Solstice, for the crime of thievery against the Winter Prince you are hereby enslaved to the Evermore." Another pause. "Your punishment will be carried out at Evermore Academy for four mortal years, or until your heart no longer beats. Whichever comes first. After the four years, you may buy your freedom."

"I'm sorry, what?" My mind races to understand. Words like *punishment* and *years* tumble around my skull. "Enslaved at your stupid Fae Academy? For . . . *years*? Over apples?"

I try to remember everything I've heard about this academy. Humans can serve there, but they're typically from families outside the Tainted Zone. Families with money, who hail from the most elite echelons of our society.

Basically, not me.

They go. Some come back. Some don't. It's all very hush-hush.

"Consider it a mercy." His voice has once again regained its gruff, icy exterior.

"A mercy? What planet do you live on?"

Ignoring my outburst, he sweeps a hand toward the Shimmer. "Arrive back here at midnight, by the time the moon crests the ridge. Even a second past, and I promise, you will not like the consequences that befall you."

"Be punctual, got it." I sound torn between laughing and crying, and my skull feels wrapped in bubble wrap. The shock and the terrible cold make a dangerous combination. "Any other advice before I head off to my prison? What to pack, perhaps?"

There's no emotion in his voice as he says, "You're allowed to bring only the clothes you wear. Preferably warmer than your current attire, if you value your fingers and toes."

I go to argue when a searing heat bites my right arm. I fling it up to examine, desperate to find the source. Metallic lines of gold and black appear over my forearm, twisting and crossing. I watch, horrified, as they snake up my elbow, claiming my flesh all the way to my shoulder.

The pain is unreal.

With a scream, I fall to my knees and gouge my arm into the snow, trying desperately to cool the flames. But the fiery ribbons keep unfurling, claiming more and more of my aching flesh.

Devouring and devouring and . . .

Oh, God, the pain.

Darkness consumes me. I blink, trying to keep hold of my wits. I'm sure my arm is gone, sure whatever is ripping chunks from my flesh will devour me whole. I feel my body rolling around trying to buck out the torment, and I don't even care how silly I look.

Hot bile slaps the back of my throat.

Right before I hurl, the ravaging pain stops, like water thrown on a fire. My cries become whimpers as I double over, holding my ruined arm close to my body. Snow presses into my cheek; tears wash down my face.

I don't want to look, but I have to look.

Unscrunching my eyes, I force myself to assess my arm. Because of the otherworldly pain, I'm one hundred percent positive I'll be met with a mess of blistered, ruined flesh.

Instead, a meshwork of metallic lines crisscross my otherwise perfect skin like a tattoo.

"You're branded now," he says, casually, as if the agony I just lived through means nothing. As if I'm *livestock.* "There's nowhere you can hide where we cannot find you, so don't even think about running."

I drag my gaze from my arm to his face, making sure the disgust and hatred in my expression is clear. "You're a monster. You could have at least warned me."

"If you think I'm bad, just wait until the academy." There's something about the way he says this that rubs under my skin. Like this is all some big joke.

"Looking forward to it," I assert. Even though I am definitely *not* looking forward to it. "Will you be there?"

There's no way to tell his age behind his shadowy mask. Even if I could make out his face, Evermore are immortal.

"Why?" There's a whisper of amusement in his gruff voice. "Looking forward to that, too?"

"Looking forward to repaying your unkindness. And if I find this Winter Prince, well, he should pray I never do." As soon as the words leave my big mouth, I cringe.

Yes, Summer, threaten a magical being who could turn you to ice and then melt you for fun. Grand idea. Better yet, threaten a Fae prince.

The Fae seems to agree. "I promise, you do not want to see me again. Keep your head down and your mortal lips shut, if that's even possible, and you might just survive us."

With that ominous warning, he bends down, plucks my lollipops from the ground—*bastard!*—and then turns on his heels and strides away.

Wrapped in a layer of shock, I watch him go. Watch his ice-blue cloak drag quietly over the snow, his tall form framed by the snow-heavy trees and illuminated by the too-big moon.

The moment I lose sight of him, reality bursts my nice little bubble and smacks me in the face. My anger, too, has faded with my tormentor. Stripped of that powerful emotion, my physical condition becomes impossible to ignore. Violent tremors thrash my body, my jaw locked together like a steel trap.

A brave look informs me my fingers are an alarming shade of purple.

Purple is way worse than red.

Staggering to my feet, I somehow make myself walk as the pain in my frostbitten limbs explodes, nearly overtaking my senses.

But it's nothing compared to the pain in my heart.

Four years? I'm supposed to survive four whole years with the Fae, and then somehow pay for my freedom . . . with what, exactly?

More importantly, how will my family survive without me?

A potent mixture of horror and dread floods my slushy veins, and for a moment . . . a single frosty breath, I imagine laying down and giving myself to the cold and fear and frustration.

A snowy tomb seems better than what awaits me at this academy.

Something bumps into my leg, hard, and begins to purr. Chatty Cat. He meows up at me with a look like, *c'mon already, let's blow this joint.*

Chatty Cat yanks me out of my pity party so hard I get whiplash.

Pity is for fools and beggars, and you are neither, Summer. I grind my jaw and picture my parents, the years I spent on the streets. The icy Fae bastard thinks I can't survive one over-hyped academy of puffed-up immortals, but he doesn't know all I've already overcome.

Whatever happens, whatever they do to me, I can withstand it. I have to.

Determined to ignore the pain, I go back to the business of collecting the neverapples. My hungry, frozen body complains, but the promise of bringing real food home spurs me on.

My life might have just ended, but no reason the others have to starve.

5

A unt Zinnia hums the tune for *Dynasty* as she bends over a baking pan, testing the doneness of her cornbread. Despite the heat, she wears a fuzzy pink and blue robe with cat faces. Her frizzy honey-gold curls are captured in a clawed clip, but a few have escaped and stick out at weird angles.

The window above the sink is open, the chorus of insect chirps mixing with the low static hum of the TV. Moths and June bugs swarm over the outdated brass light fixture centered on the water-stained ceiling.

The local news blares from the microwave-sized TV on the counter. "This grandfather from Briar county claims his granddaughter grew fangs while he held her in his lap, then bit him before escaping out a window. Could another darkling infestation be on the rise?"

Not wanting the story to alarm the children, I rush over and switch the channel to national news.

It's easier to tune out the newscasters from the other side as they speak of the newest bill that's supposed to help those in the Tainted Zone.

Yeah, right.

There's also a huge concert for our benefit. All the biggest celebrities and Fae have gotten together to raise money that will undoubtedly end up in the Millers' pockets. Sometimes I feel like we're the most forgotten place on earth.

"And where did the cat come from again?" Aunt Zinnia asks. Luckily she's too busy overbaking her cornbread to notice I'm wearing long-sleeves in the middle of summer, or that I keep rubbing my tattooed arm.

I shrug. "He just sort of showed up?"

"Well, can he just *sort of* go away?"

"Shh," I scold. "He can hear you. Besides, look how friendly and adorable he is."

Aunt Zinnia throws a dubious glance over her shoulder at Chatty Cat, who's made himself right at home on the kitchen island and is busy hissing at any kid who gets close. "I might be able to explain him to Vi, but"—she nods her head at the neverapples—"those will need more of an explanation. Where did you find them anyway?"

"Can't we just say they came from the same place the fresh eggs and milk needed for that cornbread came from?" I ask hopefully, eyeing the basket of large brown eggs on the table.

Any hope that Cal didn't know who the blonde thief was evaporated the moment I got home and discovered the wheelbarrow on the front porch. Cal personally delivered everything I stole to our house, plus a few extras.

For a block-headed idiot, his sense of irony is razor-sharp.

"Summer, you know the Miller boy would never trade in . . . well, whatever those are." She waves a hand at the neverapples, piled high in an old bucket near the sink.

"Right," I scoff. "Cal and his family have no problem stealing the pallets of aid sent from the other side and then selling them on the black market, but handling goods from Everwilde are way beyond their moral code."

More like, they have to keep up appearances. The Fae have grown popular in the big cities outside the borderlands. And why not? They have the money, magic, and influence to hire huge PR firms and throw lavish benefits for us: the humans caught in a no-man's land they swear is still tainted by magic.

While we're unable to leave this little slice of hell on earth, the Fae have influenced their way into every echelon of society on the other side. But here, where we see their evil up close and feel the sting of their crimes, they're reviled.

"So, did Cal say anything when he delivered all this?" I ask, trying to sound nonchalant.

Aunt Zinnia tugs at the fuzzy strings of her robe. "Only that you would know how to repay him."

The thought turns my stomach. Owing Cal is nearly as bad as being bound to the Evermore. At least once I'm there, I'll be out of Cal's reach.

Cal Miller has had a crush on me since ninth grade. He's a walking, muscled-up cliché. The high school quarterback, prom king, and eldest son to the wealthiest family in town, he's had everything in life handed to him.

Everything but me.

I had no idea he liked me. Not until he shoved his tongue down my throat after gym class.

I wasn't the first girl he's swapped spit with, but I was the first one who turned him down. That's before I understood that guys like Cal Miller don't get rejected.

At least, not by "orphan girls named Summer Solstice, who shop at goodwill and whose boobs aren't even *that* big."

His words, not mine. He said them right before pushing me against my locker and trying to touch said boobs.

So I informed him of the other rule. The one that states

don't-effing-touch-me-without permission. A well-timed knee to his man onions followed up by a right hook to his thick jaw made that clear.

Or should have. But some guys have rocks where their brain's supposed to go, and his obsession has only gotten stronger.

No more Cal, I think as I lug one of the blue gallon water jugs over to the pantry. *Silver linings, Summer. Focus on the silver linings.*

The kids gather around the bar countertop, helping prep the influx of goods. Cal and his guards must have gotten lucky hunting because there's fresh meat, too, although I don't dare ask what kind.

Between that, the stolen goods, and the neverapples, we're looking at three full meals a day for weeks.

"So," Aunt Zinnia persists. "Are you going to tell me where they came from, Summer Solstice, or should we wait for Vi to come make a ruckus?"

"Near the Shimmer," I admit, averting my gaze.

Not a lie; I just don't specify *which* side.

Aunt Zinnia snaps her head up. "Darling, what have I said about going near that place? What if there are darklings roaming the woods? Or, worse. Faeries?"

"The sightings are overblown," I assure her. "No one has seen a darkling or a Fae around here in months."

No one but me. But he was on the other side, so it still counts.

The others are watching me, especially Jane. Her hazel eyes narrow, but she just keeps rolling the bright red strips of meat into the seasoning. *Too smart for her own good, that one.* At one point, Chatty Cat pads over to where she works, watches her for a moment, then tries to snag one of the strips of meat.

Jane hisses at him—hisses, for Fae's sake—sending Chatty Cat to skulk in the corner.

Yep, they're going to get along gloriously.

Aunt Violet comes bursting in the front door, the hem of her lilac-printed duster she wears over her jeans and camisole nipping at her cowgirl boots.

Compared to her sister, she's tall and lean, all angles and ropy muscle, her face worn from years beneath an unforgiving sun. She wears her gray hair in a practical braid that snakes to her mid-back.

"What's this?" she asks in her sharp, no-nonsense voice. She smells of feed and hay from her job at the feed store. I still can't understand why she continues showing up to work. Money is nearly worthless, and a month's wages could barely cover a package of toilet-paper.

"Summer brought home a feast, that's what," Aunt Zinnia calls in her sing-song voice, totally omitting the part about Cal or the neverapples. "Now get down here and help me, Vi."

Aunt Violet breezes into the kitchen. "I was talking about that furry beast shredding my silk drapes . . ."

Her words abruptly cut off as her gaze finds the neverapples, piled high in an old bucket near the sink.

"What are *those*?" she demands, eyes wide with terror, as if I'd brought home the heads of my enemies instead of perfectly ripe fruit.

"Summer found them near the border," Aunt Zinnia explains, shooting me an I'll-handle-this look.

Aunt Violet's light brown eyes darken to coffee with a dash of cream. "You know how I feel about anything related to *them* in our house."

Aunt Zinnia pauses from cutting perfect little squares of cornbread. "Oh, Violet. Can't we make an exception?"

"I looked neverapples up," I offer carefully. "They're safe."

Aunt Violet pinches the bridge of her hawkish nose and

gives me one of her famous stares. "If they're not of this world, I refuse to keep them in my house."

"Please, Aunt Violet. I've already promised everyone an apple tonight."

Her lips press together, causing the lines around her mouth to deepen. "Summer, you know the rules of living here. Nothing from those creatures inside my house."

Her hard gaze flicks to the portrait in the living room above the dusty beige couch. A family wearing denim and shiny boots smiles against a white background. It's the kind of picture done at a department store, but that does nothing to cheapen the emotion I feel whenever I stare at the family she lost. Two strapping teenage boys and a husband.

I only lost my parents, and sometimes that grief is enough to swallow me whole. I can't imagine children. What it would feel like to have them stripped away one day without a trace.

Aunt Violet strides into the pantry where she keeps the secret stash of cigarettes she doesn't know I know about. As soon as she disappears somewhere on the back porch, the jar of moonshine she hoards clutched beneath her arm, Aunt Zinnia takes me aside.

"Don't you worry," she says. "Vi will come around. No reason to waste precious fruit such as this, even if it does come from . . . them. Now get washed up. You've done enough for today, Summer."

My throat aches as I imagine not seeing Aunt Zinnia again. Will she hate me for leaving without saying goodbye? If only I could talk to her, tell her what happened. I rub my arm, the mark embedded in my flesh aching.

Midnight. When the moon crests the ridge. I have roughly five hours until my life ends.

My secret bubbles up my throat, begging for release. But if I told Aunt Zinnia, she would never let me leave. The scars from losing her family, while not as visible as Aunt Violet's, run just as deep.

She would fight like a lioness for me.

I can't let that happen. The Fae's warning not to make him wait replays in my head, and I know I'm making the right choice.

Aunt Zinnia will be hurt, but she'll live. That's more than can be said for me.

6

I cross the peeling linoleum floor and inspect the neverapples. According to the few articles I could find before our internet crapped out, one bite of the golden fruit has more vitamins than a serving of spinach.

More importantly, they replenish themselves. You eat the apple, set the core on the windowsill at night, and in the morning it's good as new.

Magic is *so* cool.

One apple a day, plus anything Jane can find from the traps I have set up around the land, and they might be okay. Upstairs is a scribbled list of instructions on everything they'll need to know when I'm gone.

I hope it's enough. It has to be.

The back screen door slams shut as Aunt Violet reappears, the tinny smell of smoke clinging to her. The furrows trenched across her weathered forehead have softened, and she quietly makes herself some sweet tea, her spoon tinkling against the glass.

After she takes two sips, she begins washing the dishes left by Aunt Zinnia.

"Cal came by today," Aunt Zinnia says carefully, glancing up from her cornbread.

Aunt Violet stops scrubbing a heavy cast iron skillet and glances over her shoulder at her sister. "You let that boy enter this house?"

"Vi, I'd let the devil in this house if he came with the gifts Cal did."

"Huh." Aunt Violet slams the pan onto the drying rack and begins assaulting a cup. "And what did it take to buy you off?"

Aunt Zinnia stares down at her hands, a flush creeping over her cheeks as she lists off the items. Way more than what I fit in the wheelbarrow. "Oh, there might have been some slims in there too, for when you *don't* go outside and smoke."

Aunt Violet whips around, soapy bubbles dribbling from her purple dish-gloves onto the floor. "Are you saying *I* can be bought?"

"Well, you certainly didn't hesitate to fill your tea with the sugar Cal brought."

Vi stares death at her sister.

"I'm saying," Aunt Zinnia amends, her gaze flitting to the kids around the island, "we do what we do to survive."

If I don't distract them, they'll fight until one storms off, usually Aunt Violet. Then they won't talk for a week and the tension will be awful.

So I grab a hot pad shaped like a donut and bravely jump into the mix.

"I hate Cal more than anyone," I say, punctuating the word hate. "But if he wants to give us what's technically ours, anyway, why not let him?"

"Don't sell yourself short, Summer," Aunt Violet snaps. "You would have sent that boy running back to his farm with his tail between his legs and his ass peppered with buckshot."

God, she knows me too well.

AUDREY GREY

"Language, Vi!" Aunt Zinnia scolds.

"Well it's true. The Millers don't give away nothing for free. He thinks Summer can be bought just like his daddy and granddaddy when they bullied Dad into selling the back half of the property, remember, Zinnia? Well she isn't for sale and that's that."

I nod my head. *That's right, Cal. Not. For. Sale.*

"Do you see a for sale sign on her?" Aunt Zinnia barks.

Aunt Violet rolls her eyes. "That wasn't literal, Z."

I raise my hand. "Right here, guys."

They ignore me. They've locked horns like two old bulls, and only bloodshed will break them apart.

Aunt Zinnia huffs as she throws a towel over the cornbread pan and shoves it across the Formica counter. "Fine. I'll just go throw this out."

"Don't be dramatic, Z. We can eat the damned cornbread . . . as dry as I imagine it is."

Zinnia's face flushes red. "No, I will not have you saying I sold Summer like some dried up dairy cow. And . . . another thing. I'll have you know this cornbread is the best I've ever made."

"Oh, you are something else." Aunt Violet violently stirs the spoon inside her tea. "How the creator decided we were sisters, I'll never know."

If only I'd been here when Cal came, this could have all been avoided. I spare a glance at the 12 gauge shotgun propped by the door.

I would have totally peppered his ass.

"Stop," I order. Both sisters look over at me like they forgot I was still here. "Next time Cal comes, let him bring whatever he wants."

I won't be here anyway, I almost add.

The sisters go silent, and I take the moment to check the

roasted haunch browning in the oven so they can't see the hurt in my eyes.

When I'm done, I turn around to Aunt Zinnia wringing her hands in front of me. Her gray eyes shine. "Summer, I'm sorry if I somehow implied—well, you know. With you and Cal's history, well I shouldn't have taken anything from him. Not without asking you first."

After my assault on Cal, I was expelled from school. I thought my aunts were going to murder the principal with their bare hands, but I didn't blame him; he didn't stand a chance against the Millers.

Still, they both knew how important graduating was to me . . . if only because, somewhere deep down, I knew my parents would have wanted that. For me to find a job that changes the world for the better.

"No, Aunt Z." I brush a hand over her shoulder. "I'm glad you did. Otherwise . . ."

My words trail away as we stare at the kids at the counter. Their too-thin arms, the way their collarbones trap the shadows and cheekbones protrude, all of it convinces me she did the right thing.

"I like Cal okay," Tanner chimes in. The seven-year-old scampers across the floor and tries to grab a square of corn-bread, barely ducking Aunt Violet's swat. "He gives me twizzlers."

"Cal's a shithead," Jane announces loudly, sauntering in beside him.

"You can't say shithead," Tanner informs Jane, his blond eyebrows scrunched sternly.

"You just said it," Jane retorts. "Now go add a quarter to the swear jar, shithead."

"Both of you shitheads need to pay up," I order, conjuring priceless laughs from Tanner and Jane.

All of this is pretty pointless when money means nothing —but it's tradition, after all.

"Enough," Aunt Violet says. One gray-shot eyebrow lifts high above her forehead, the final warning rattle before she strikes. "Unless this house is a family full of heathens, I expect manners and clean language. Understood?"

Jane glares at her boots, but she nods along with Tanner.

"Good," Aunt Violet continues. "Now go set the table."

Every night without exception, Aunt Violet has everyone dress the cherrywood dining table with the gilded china from her walnut curio cabinet. Even when there's nothing to eat but bullion flavored broth, we drink that out of the china tea set passed down from her mother-in-law.

Aunt Zinnia is the last to sit. She comes sweeping in with a vase full of sunflowers picked near the road, smiling ear to ear.

Gosh, I love that woman.

I drink everything in. The loud chatter as everyone talks over each other. The way Julia and Gabe, both five-year-olds rescued from Houston, fight over who set the table better (definitely Julia). The way Aunt Violet primly cuts her meat into tiny cubes, and Jane only eats half her meal before sharing with Julia, who's given up her fork in favor of her fingers.

I'm going to miss this.

The thought hits me square in the gut. I don't have the words to tell them this is my last dinner. I've already decided to write out the letters to both Aunts, plus one to Jane. I'm afraid she'll try to come after me. To save me . . . or to avenge me, I can't be sure.

The other children are young enough that they'll soon forget I ever existed. That truth hurts more than I thought it would.

Perhaps my tormentor did exactly what he said: turned me into a girl of ice, to whittle down at his pleasure.

And when he's done, there will be nothing left for anyone to remember.

7

A sudden panic quells my appetite. I swallow down the last bite of (admittedly dry) cornbread and quickly excuse myself, my mind on making my abrupt absence as seamless as possible for everyone. There's so much that could go wrong with me gone, and I need to ensure they'll be okay.

Julia and Gabe try to follow me. Usually I read them a story after dinner—or five—but Aunt Zinnia grabs them before they can follow.

She must sense something's off with me. If only she knew the horrible truth.

My room is hot as the Summer Court, and I quickly open a window. As the oldest, I'm the only one with a private room, even if, technically, it's the attic. Usually by morning I find Jane curled in a pile of quilts by the desk in the corner, and Julia and Gabe nestled at the foot of my brass-framed bed.

Tonight, I let in Chatty Cat, who's been following me from a distance like he's too cool, and then lock my door. The little ones could sleep through a four alarm fire, but Jane's like me. A troubled sleeper.

I can't take any chance that she'll follow me into Everwilde.

While Chatty busies himself chasing the dust devils across my wooden floor, I slide into the red wooden chair at my desk and flip open my laptop. It's nearly ten years old and takes forever to load our crappy internet, but I wait.

I need to know more about the place I'm going. I nearly looked it up earlier when I checked out the neverapples, but then I lost my nerve.

What if I discover the Fae torture us for kicks, or find human flesh a tasty snack? It's not like I can choose *not* to go.

My homepage finally loads. Before I can stop myself, I scan the first article at the top. The headline reads: "She Lost Her Daughter Because of the Fae, Now She's Forced to Live Next to One."

I don't bother reading the article; my stress level is high enough, and the last thing I need is to be reminded that the Fae destroyed half our world, trapped me here in this cesspool, then somehow talked our government into giving them temporary visas to stay in the Untouched Zone.

How is that even remotely fair? Especially when we're stuck here, slowly starving to death.

Grimacing, I focus on the task and type in *Evermore Academy*. Then I hold my breath as the cursor makes the rainbow swirly disc . . . only to be disappointed with one result.

I stare in disbelief at the old Wikipedia page. Which I've already visited like a million times.

How can I find literally ten pages of information on a piece of magical fruit, but almost nothing on an infamous academy?

The first paragraph tells me nothing new. The noble sons

and daughters of all ten Seelie and Unseelie Courts go through its hallowed grounds, blah blah. The next paragraph is more interesting, but still too brief.

Sources say every year children from the most esteemed families travel to Evermore Academy to serve the Fae students and further the diplomacy between humans and Fae.

Huh. Something tells me diplomacy has nothing to do with it, but what do I know?

The rest of the summary describes how the mortal students at the academy are trained to protect their Fae keepers from the darklings. Upon graduation, most usually go into service as shadow guardians who protect high-ranking Evermore Fae from darklings.

After retirement, a shadow can ask any favor of their Fae; many go on to be incredibly powerful influencers on the other side.

Just for kicks, I click on the link over the word *darkling* and am rewarded by a terrifying photo. All-black eyes stare wildly at me above bared incisors. Once human ears rise sharply into points.

The darkling in the photo, taken God knows where, still wears her human clothes: an orange-and-blue flannel and ripped jeans.

Bad fashion sense aside, the wild, hungry look in the darkling's twisted expression scares me more than the way her back has hunched and her bones have malformed so that she runs on all fours. The way her body has grown larger even as her muscles and flesh have withered.

I skim the words below. *Infested with the residual dark magic that seeps daily into the tainted borderland, this used to be a happy, seventeen-year-old girl named Samantha Stevens.*

More pictures of turned darklings fill the page, and I quickly close the tab.

The Wiki for the Fae themselves is much more thorough,

with everything from their appearance (super good looking,) lifespan (immortal, duh,) and weaknesses (iron, ash, rowan berries, salt,) to conspiracies on why they came.

Annoyed at the lack of any real information, I push my laptop away. I need to focus on my letters, anyway.

I feel especially guilty for not telling Aunt Zinnia. Ever since she rescued me from a human trafficking ring in Dallas, she's been nothing but amazing. Treating me like the daughter she lost.

When the Fae arrived and took over the west, the Shimmer was erected almost immediately.

Anyone on the other side was just gone. The Fae sent a few of their leaders to talk to our side, and they quickly confirmed that not a single mortal survived what they called a terrible accident of magic.

It wasn't until later that we were told the truth: The twisted magic from the explosion turned the humans who didn't die into darklings. And the residue from that same polluted darkness was present everywhere in the borderlands.

The attacks began shortly afterward. Some of the darklings came from breaches in the Shimmer. Some spontaneously transformed in public places. A girl even changed in my high school. I didn't see it, but they said horns sprouted from her head and her bones twisted and bent, her body growing into some grotesque monster not quite Fae, and not quite human.

She escaped out a window. Most darklings only attack humans if they're cornered, injured, or starving. They prefer Fae flesh.

Still, the human government erected borders between the borderlands and the outside world as they worked to contain the spread of tainted magic.

Both Aunts were home during the Lightmare, waiting for

their families to come back from an auction near Denton. When Aunt Zinnia rescued me in Dallas, she was there looking for her daughter, Grace. Someone had called to say they spotted Grace, but it ended up being a false lead.

Instead, she found me. Not that I could ever replace her daughter. That was obvious. But somewhere in mending my wounds, physical and mental, she'd helped heal her own.

And now I'm about to break her heart again. The thought makes me sick. I grab my favorite pen and start her note. It takes nearly all evening to properly convey how grateful I am that she first saved me and then adopted me all those years ago.

More than once, I have to blink back tears.

For Aunt Violet, I write a more practical letter with the information I've found on the neverapples, plus a detailed account of the area of the Shimmer to avoid. I mention Chatty Cat too, begging her to keep him for the kids' sake. Every kid needs a pet, even a feral, mangy one.

I also detail everything I can recall about the Fae who harassed me in the woods, along with a description of the brand on my arm.

I don't think for a second the police will do anything. They've pretty much disbanded in the borderlands anyway. Taken over by prominent families like Cal's who pretend to maintain law and order while really just consolidating their power.

But, in case I just disappear, never to be heard from again . . . I want there to be an account of my story.

By the time I get to Jane's letter, the gibbous moon has already peaked over the ridge, and my clock says 11:20 p.m. An owl hoots nearby. Probably the same one I saw earlier.

I'm starting to wonder if he's a spy for the Fae.

Remembering the Evermore's warning, I scribble out a haphazard note on the location of my traps, the best places to find edible berries and best rivers to fish. I add in useful tips on stuff I'd always thought I had time to teach her—how to cut up cotton flannel to use for pads, making a tincture of fennel, ginger, and cinnamon for cramps—but that brings tears to my eyes.

I should be here for her. Aunt Zinnia will try, but she disappears for days on end sometimes, hiding in her sewing room or whatever chore she can throw herself into to forget her lost daughter. And Aunt Violet can be helpful, but she's trapped behind a prison of grief that no one can break through.

Jane is about to go through the toughest, most confusing years of her life, and I won't be there.

There's no time to really say what's in my heart, the sorrow and guilt I feel for leaving her without a proper good-bye, so I simply scrawl:

I'm so sorry. Please don't hate me, and understand that I had no choice. Don't come looking for me. And remember, mind Aunt Z and Aunt Vi.

Also, don't pick on Tanner. Or Julia or Gabe. Or anyone.

Also, ALSO. I love you. See you in four years. That's a promise.

I almost don't write that last bit. What if I don't return? Is it fair to give her false hope?

But if I don't make myself believe that I can survive, then I won't. From this moment forward, I have to cling to that hope, have to believe it with everything I have.

"I'm coming back home," I say aloud, breathing my own sort of magic into the words. Then I fold the three letters and place them on top of my made bed for them to find.

The house has gone completely quiet, the only sound the owl hooting near my window.

I throw on a huge blue-and-gray Dallas Cowboys hoodie, a pair of heavy jeans a size too big, and two pairs of inside out wool socks that cramp my old work boots. The rowan-berry charm goes in my pocket.

Finally, the hideous lilac and chartreuse scarf and mittens Aunt Zinnia knitted for me last Christmas add a pop of color.

I'm a hot mess and a half.

The girl in the cracked dresser mirror agrees. My snowy-white hair tangles around me in chaotic waves, branches and leaves caught in the knots. My cheekbones come up at sharp angles and cast deep shadows in craterous dimples below. Even tinted by the sun from days outside, my skin carries an unhealthy pallor from months of living off canned goods.

And Fae's teeth, my clothes . . .

Not my most fashionable ensemble—and, for me, that's saying a lot. But it will have to do until I can figure out something better.

Surely they have clothes in Everwilde? Something to help me fit in?

Lord knows I didn't even do that here in our human high school, which makes my chances of fitting in at this new immortal academy slim to none.

Panic lances my chest. I know so little about the school/prison, or what to expect, and what I gleaned from my tormentor yesterday is not comforting.

They will hate me because I am a mortal. They will despise me because they are cruel, merciless, beautiful things and I am weak and plain in comparison.

Oh, God, Summer. What have you gotten yourself into?

For a moment, fear roots me to my bedroom floor. I haven't had time to mourn the loss of my future properly. Haven't had time to mentally prepare.

I'm not ready.

The tattoo on my arm begins to burn, and I drag my gaze to the window. The moon is halfway over the rise.

I need to go, but I'm frozen with fear.

Nerves in a jumble, I collapse to my knees and drag a shoebox out from beneath my bed. My small ruby necklace sits on the top. The silver charm is shaped like a wolf's head holding a pea-sized ruby inside its fangs.

The details are painstakingly etched to perfection, right down to the gleam of the beast's large nose and his thick, shaggy fur. There's no denying this was made by the best silversmiths in Everwilde.

The second the cold pendant slips over my head and rests against my breastbone, I breathe a sigh of relief. Before taking a few choice items off Cal's hands earlier, I'd removed my pendant—just in case.

But I never feel right without it. It holds the memory of my parents, and is the only thing connecting me to them besides their picture.

That's harder to find. It sits at the very bottom, beneath my adoption paperwork.

I rub a thumb over the faces in the photo; a man dressed smartly in a brown corduroy jacket next to a Christmas tree, his arm around a pretty woman with dark hair pulled into a bun and an easy smile. Their happy eyes fill me with courage.

"I can't leave you guys," I say to my parents.

With the photo stored safely in my jean pocket, and the pendant around my neck, a hidden well of strength bubbles to the surface. My boots clop softly over the wood floor as I tiptoe to my open window, carefully push the screen out, and duck through.

Chatty Cat tries to follow, but I shake my head. "Stay. Watch over Jane and the others."

As if he understands, Chatty Cat jumps down to the floor and sits on his haunches, watching me with those too-bright lime-green eyes.

From the roof to the ground is a ten-foot drop. I manage to

lower myself and then jump, landing hard on the scratchy rose bushes near the front porch.

An army of stars march across the indigo sky. I make sure to leave no tracks as I slip across the prairie toward the Shimmer. When I'm close enough to see the spot from yesterday where I entered, a distant voice calls my name.

Jane. Somehow she suspected. But she's too late.

"See you in four years," I promise, ignoring the throb of my heart.

Then, for the second time in twenty-four hours, I pass into Everwilde.

8

The first thing I notice when I cross the Shimmer to Everwilde is that I didn't dress warmly enough. At all. Somehow it's even colder than before. A blizzard rages. The icy breeze piercing my flimsy clothes and taking up permanent residence in my bones.

And where the heck is the sun? Night still clings to everything, the moon in exactly the same spot as before. As if time is frozen here like everything else.

I'm not meant for wintry, dark worlds. I need sunlight on my face and a warm summer breeze. I need flowers and sunburns and the clink of ice cubes against a sweating glass of iced tea so sweet it'll rot your teeth right out of your head.

By my admittedly limited experience, the Everwilde is the opposite of that.

As if taunting me, a snowflake lands on the tip of my nose. I sigh, my annoyance growing. My tormentor demanded I be here at exactly midnight, yet now he's the late one and I'm freezing my lady balls off.

The second that thought hits me, something moves between the trees.

I peer through the flurry of snow and make out a man on a moon-white horse lurking near the base of the closest tree. Actually, not a man—I need to remember that—and he's not on a horse.

He is a horse, sort of.

"Centaur," I breathe, sure I'm still dreaming as I watch my breath crystallize in front of me.

The Evermore glares. I stare up at him, too enamored to care that he obviously finds retrieving me an insult. From the waist up, he appears completely normal. Or as normal as a Fae can look.

His features resemble a human's, but brighter somehow, like he's been painted with chromatic pigment deeper and richer than anything used on us. Large moss-green eyes watch me, set deep in a proud bronzed face. Vibrant red hair falls to his mid-back, twisted and braided with silver ribbons.

"Done staring?" he drawls, but the proud tug of his lips tells me part of him enjoys the attention. "You mortals always stare, in the beginning."

I nod, but I'm not done ogling him. How could I be? From the navel down, he's a horse. A mother-freaking horse.

Then there's the line of humans strung out behind him. They're linked together in pairs, their wrists restrained by chains. Another delicate chain connects the entire human line to part of the centaur's armor.

By their slack faces and distant, glassy stares, they're glamoured.

He holds out a hand and shifts toward me, the powerful muscles of his hindquarters trembling beneath his soft ivory fur.

"Who are they?" I ask.

"Recruits. They're going to the front to fight the scourge."

Cutting my eyes at the poor humans, I try to hide my

skepticism, in case there's a part of them that can still see. They do *not* look ready to fight an army of darklings.

He jerks his chin at me. "Hop on."

Yeah, that's not going to happen. I plant my silly, mittened hands on my hips. "I'm good, but thanks. I can walk like the rest."

He grins. "Unless you want to freeze your butt off here, I'd suggest doing what I say." When I still hesitate, he adds, "By the laws of the academy, I can't glamour you to obey. But those rules also don't specify I have to bring you to the academy *alive*."

Touché. Stupid Fae reasoning.

Frowning, I reach out a hand and let him help me onto his wide back.

He's warm, at least. I shift, trying to get comfortable. *Pretend this is a real horse.* "Is this okay?" I ask, flexing my fingers. "I'm not . . . hurting you?"

I've never thought to ask such a thing to an actual horse, but they've never been able to talk back, either.

An equine ear flicks back, and the rumble of his laughter seeps into my thighs. "You, hurt me? Is that an attempt at a joke?"

Impatience quickens his voice, but his laughter has nothing of my tormentor's cruel edge, and I make a mental note.

If I'm going to survive this place, everyone I meet has to go in one of two boxes: potential friend or enemy.

He waves his hand in the air. A moment later, a fiery blue and orange circle erupts, growing until it's as tall as my ride. Another world of ice coalesces inside the flames. Red-tipped mushrooms sprout beneath the circle, the magic seemingly drawing them from the snow.

"What is that?" I ask.

"A portal. You didn't think we'd walk all the way there?"

I shrug, having no idea where *there* is.

Apparently deciding I'm hopelessly ignorant, he says, "Look. This is Winter Court land. If we were to walk to Evermore Academy from here, that would take us weeks. Plus, the Winter Court frowns upon members of the other courts wandering through their territory so . . . we take a portal."

"Got it." I hold up a thumb, hidden beneath my mitten.

"Good. Now hold on," he orders.

"To what?" I scour his back for reins or something else to grab, but come up short. And no way am I grabbing his hair.

Before I can find a suitable alternative, he kicks off his hindquarters, plunging us straight into the fiery portal.

9

The glamoured recruits behind us all break into a sprint, that blank expression never leaving their faces.

I squeeze my legs for balance and throw a hand over my eyes.

Blinding light fills the cracks between my fingers, delicious warmth kissing my cheeks. When the light fades to a dull haze, so does the heat. Sighing, I remove my hand—and nearly fall off the centaur.

We're in a valley with nothing but snow and rocks. A three-story tall wall of stone looms behind us, covered in frost-bound ivy. The sky is a winter haze of fat, gauzy clouds that hide the moon. But my gaze is fixed on the pale cliffs in the distance. An enormous castle of ice and snow has been carved into the top, the monstrosity reaching so high it pierces the clouds.

The centaur catches my stare and laughs. "Welcome to Evermore Academy."

"It's . . . so big."

"That's only the back. Wait till you see the front."

"How far does the wall go?" I ask, shuddering at the thought. I hate walls of any kind; they bring to mind being trapped.

"All the way around the Island."

"Island?" I sweep my gaze over the land, searching for any hint of water.

"Yeah. Of course. The academy sits on the Island of Evernell, the most protected place in Everwilde."

I wrap my arms around my chest as he trots through the snowy valley toward the cliffs. "Any chance this is like, a fluke weather event, and it's really spring here?"

"This is actually warm for winter in Everwilde," he mutters.

"Winter? For how long?" My voice comes out a tad strangled.

"Forever."

"Forever?" I repeat, praying I misheard him.

He throws me an annoyed glance. "Kidding. Only a year. Winter started a week ago, along with the first day of the academy."

Only a year? Three hundred and fifty nine more days of this? A sinking feeling comes over me. "Are there any other mortal students showing up today, or . . . am I the only one?"

Please don't let me be the only—

"Only you."

"Wonderful," I murmur. Showing up a week late is sure to draw unwanted attention, and that's the last thing I need right now.

"Which is rare," he adds conversationally, "considering most of the mortal first years were chosen years in advance from the pool of mortals who owe us service. There's an entire process to ensure only the best, most beautiful mortals serve here. And you're . . . well . . ."

Apparently, unable to think of a word to describe me, his

words trail away. Am I really that different than the other students?

Shoving my mittens in my jeans pocket, I brush my fingers over my hair, wishing I'd thought to comb it.

Alarm pulses through me. Somewhere between this morning and now my hair has knotted itself into a matted, unmanageable mess.

Why didn't I think to take a shower? Or for that matter, brush my teeth? I run my tongue over my teeth, wincing at the fuzzy texture. Who knows when I'll get another chance.

"Just curious," I say. "Half-starved mortals who look like they're homeless aren't the fashion in Everwilde, are they?"

"No." His gaze flicks from me to the procession of humans happily marching behind us. The meaning in his glance is clear—that's where I belong. With them. The poor, glamoured recruits who smile dazedly in my direction.

Do they know they're going off to fight monsters who used to be human?

It makes me sick thinking that soon, these poor, happy fools will be fighting the darklings. From what I've seen of the darklings, these people don't stand a chance.

"How do you keep the darklings out of academy grounds?" I ask. "Other than the giant wall over there."

"Wards, mainly . . ." Again his gaze shifts to the poor, happy humans bumbling behind us. Pity flashes in his eyes, and he looks away.

Before I can ask more questions, voices trickle across the crisp air. I sink low on his back as we pass Fae students milling around the grounds. They throw strange glances our way. I'm guessing most students don't arrive on a centaur shepherding human prisoners-soldiers to the scourge lands.

I don't bother to hide my own curiosity as I stare back. The watery darkness is broken by golden orbs that float above the students. The magical light isn't enough to reveal their features, only that they are all different sizes. Some larger than mortals, some smaller.

We pass close to a group near the base of the mountain, and the heat from their orbs chases away the chill, if only briefly.

"Any chance the sun might come up, say, in the next century?" I call out to the centaur.

He cranes his neck to glance at the starry sky. Longing flickers in his mossy eyes. "That all depends on the Winter Prince's mood. If he's happy we might get a nice bright day, but experience tells me we're in for weeks of this."

That does not sound promising.

"Just curious. How many mortal students come from the Tainted Zone?"

"None." He shakes his head for emphasis, his ears twitching back and forth.

Although his answer isn't surprising—anyone with power and influence bribed themselves across the borders right after the magical apocalypse happened—I still wish I'd known all this beforehand.

"Stupid luck," I mutter. "Stealing from the Winter Prince."

He stops so suddenly I nearly fall off his back. "What did you say?"

"I stole some neverapples and . . ." The intensity in his voice makes me nervous, and I brush back a knotted rope of hair before continuing. "Apparently they belonged to a Winter Prince."

The silence that follows is nearly as cold as the frigid air. Does this Winter Prince control tongues now, too?

But it's obvious his shadow—and his brand—taint me much like the dark magic does the darklings. Until I sever this bond between us somehow, I'm untouchable.

As if the Winter Prince knows I'm thinking of him, the snow begins to drizzle down in wet, annoying bursts. I focus on the campus. It's huge, and I imagine in the springtime the land around us bubbles with life and beauty.

But now . . . now the sloping lawn leading up to the main campus building is blanched with snow. As are the conical evergreens and waist-high wall of shrubs leading to a massive gate. Two-foot tall droughts of snow line the top of the stone fence.

A huge diamond-shaped crest sits in the center of the wrought iron gate, half-covered in snow. Engraved into the surface around the letters EA are all manner of creatures: fawns, sprites, ogres, and strange animals I've never seen before.

With a twist of the centaur's wrist, the door parts, revealing a long gravel path cleared of snow. Flames of green magic flicker from ivory columns on either side.

I slide off the centaur's back without being told. His gaze hovers somewhere on the mountains in the distance.

For some stupid reason, my eyes prickle with tears.

"If something happens to you . . . I will let your family know," he offers kindly.

My throat aches. I hadn't truly realized until now how much I fear my family never knowing my fate.

But I made myself a promise. Straightening, I force my chin high. "Thank you, but that won't be necessary. I'll see them in four years."

The corners of the centaur's lips tug upward. "I hope that's the case . . . what did you say your name was?"

"Summer Solstice." I throw out my hand to shake his before remembering he's Fae, after all.

He regards my hand for a moment before tentatively offering his much larger one.

I give a good, firm pump while he frowns down at the whole thing.

"And you are?" I prod.

"Magus," he answers, retrieving his hand and then inspecting it. "Good luck inside." There's something in his tone that bothers me, a warning. But before I can dig further, he crowds me toward the door with his bulky body. "Go to the headmistress's office. It's on the tenth floor. And . . . try not to speak or do anything that grabs attention."

That's my new motto. Stay quiet and blend in. How hard can it be?

10

Surprisingly, the inside of the main building isn't as dark and dreary as I was expecting. A strangely comforting mixture of pine cleaner and sage permeate the air. Pendulum lights filled with magical orbs hang from the mahogany ceiling beams, and flickering sconces line the stone walls.

Maps are neatly stacked at an unoccupied helpdesk near an atrium. When I grab one, I catch sight of two guards near a door. Their ears are round—they're human. Their sharp gaze falls over me and I quicken my pace, my boots hardly making a sound against the parquet wood floor's polished surface.

On the third floor, I pass by a commons area where Fae students lounge on sofas that could have come from Ikea. MacBooks and iPads fill their laps, and a few have headphones on.

From a distance, most could pass as human—if not for their slender ears that end in delicate points.

The door to the headmistress's office is parted. A gold plaque on the door reads, *Headmistress Luna Lepidonis*.

Inside, I find an imposing Fae woman with stern features

and silver-gray hair pulled into a severe bun. She sits ramrod straight behind a neat mahogany desk, her inhumanly long fingers splayed out in front of her. Her face, like all the Fae, is smooth and poreless, with high cheekbones and large dark eyes.

She could be forty . . . or four-hundred.

Behind her, three heavily arched stained glass windows rise, the colorful panes made into a woodland scene filled with exotic creatures.

When I near, two powdery beige moth wings unfurl from her back. They're soft looking, like crushed velvet, a large mint-green spot adorning the apex of each wing.

She lifts an eyebrow as her sharp gaze takes in first my attire, then my hair. "Ah. You must be the new . . . shadow recruit. Come in."

There's a Fae male standing beside her . . . no, his ears are round, so he's human. Already that's the first thing I check. Ears pointed or curved?

He regards me with a grim smile as I stare. By his salt-and-pepper hair, matching mustache, and weathered face, he's at least fifty, with the body of a man who works out regularly.

The red-and-black uniform he wears fits snug around his muscular arms and thighs.

"This is the head Shadow Guardian for the entire academy, Mr. Willis," the headmistress says. "If you graduate in four years, he'll also be responsible for your placement with a keeper."

He gives me a curt nod as he leaves. Slipping into the black leather chair in front of her desk, I watch quietly while the headmistress shuffles around papers until finding the one she's looking for. She reminds me a bit of Aunt Vi, but I can't tell yet if that's a good thing or a bad thing.

Lips tight, she pushes a document across her desk. "All we need is your signature and then you can go."

That was quick. I stare at the paper, my heart pounding. "If I don't sign?"

Her dark brown eyes narrow. "Do you know how many mortals would love to be in your position? Mortals who have been training to come here since birth, whose parents came here before them. Mortals with means and influence. Mortals who can benefit this school and Fae-kind after graduation."

Well then. "And I'm not that kind of mortal?"

She doesn't even try to hide her disdain as she says, "You . . . are a special exception. Made by a very powerful student. But there is no reason to hide the truth: I do not think you belong here. Moreover, I do not think you will *survive* here."

Heat flares up my neck and into my face. "And I think you'll be surprised at how resilient I can be."

"Resilient?" The word spits from her lips like it's poison. "As a shadow, your job is to train beside an Evermore, the highest, most promising Fae heirs from each court. They rely on you for many things, but your most important job at this school is protecting your Fae keeper with your life." Pressing her hands together, she leans forward. "If a darkling breaks through our wards, are you prepared to kill it to protect your keeper?"

I open my mouth to answer, but the truth is, I'm not. And I'm not even sad about it.

"As I thought. You are untrained, undisciplined, and uneducated. If it were up to me, you would be drafted to fight the darklings outside the wards. Maybe then your death would mean something." Her lip curls. "But it isn't up to me, so here"—she slides the document even closer—"make your mark and this charade will be over."

For some reason, her words cut deep. I understand being annoyed with having someone basically foisted on them last minute, but I didn't choose this path. And I had nothing to do with my placement here, which I'm starting to realize is my tormentor's form of a cruel practical joke.

Biting the inside of my cheek to hide the hurt, I focus on the form. It's basically a declaration that I now belong to the academy, and that they aren't responsible for my safety, nor liable monetarily or otherwise.

There's also a clause at the end that stipulates after my training here, I will give four years of service to shadowing a Fae, or buy my freedom.

When I'm done reading, I scribble my signature and shove the document away.

"See," she says in a deceptively sweet voice. "That wasn't so hard, was it? Now, we have a temporary room available for you on this floor in the visitor's wing. Last room on your left. We'll know soon which court you belong to, and I'll have your books and schedule delivered to your court's mortal dormitory."

She hands me a pamphlet titled, *Rulebook for Shadow Guardian Students*, and sends me on my way. Right before I get to the door, she calls out, "Miss Solstice?"

I glance over my shoulder. *What now?*

Maybe I'm just imagining it, but the hard line of her lips has softened. "Your files are sealed, meaning no one knows about your slave-mark . . . or *who* requested your presence here. I highly recommend you keep it that way."

"Noted, thank you."

I'm halfway down the first flight of stairs when I remember I left my handbook in the office. Crap. When I get to the door of her office, I pause. Mr. Willis, the head Shadow Guardian, leans against the side of the desk, deep in conversation with the headmistress.

". . . cannot have another student death at our school," the headmistress is saying. "You saw her! She has no idea what awaits her inside this academy."

Willis's bushy eyebrows mash together, and he places a large hand on the headmistress's much smaller one. "I'll keep an eye on her. Make sure she gets extra attention from Richter and extra training."

"It's not enough." Lepidonis's gaze drifts to the window. "You know what they're like here. I doubt she'll make it through the Selection."

"I could inform King Sylverfrost about her presence."

"No. You know what he would do with her." The headmistress's words tumble out quickly, and I detect more than a hint of fear in them. "I cannot imagine why, but the girl is here. Now, let's just hope she understands the danger she faces."

11

My boots slap loudly against the metal stairs as I try to find where I'm supposed to go next. But my mind keeps drifting to the words I over-heard, and cold sweat trickles between my shoulder blades.

Why does everyone make this school sound terrifying?

Unfortunately, according to my handy little map, the visi-tor's wing is on the other side of the building. It takes me five tries to find the right place. The visitor's hall is ancient, cobwebs hanging from dusty corners and a faded gold rug lining the dim corridor.

When I get to the last room on the left, I balk at the tiny apartment. There's a cot, a nightstand, and a circular window barely the size of my head.

I need air. Space. Sunshine. A place to comfortably freak out.

As luck would have it, there's a stairwell at the end of the hall that leads to the roof. The moment I breathe in fresh air, I feel some of the tension bleed from my body. My boots crunch across the flat gravel roof that looks out over the campus as I make my way to the wrought iron railing.

I run my hand over the sharp finials and cast my gaze over the white world beyond, squinting in the hazy half-dark.

The campus is everything I thought it would be: ethereal, magical, and horrifying.

A wintry forest spreads to my left, curving to fill the entire eastern half. Directly below, a courtyard sits, nearly unoccupied. I'd guess it's around four in the morning, and the campus seems to be finally winding down.

I've read the Fae are nocturnal, but eventually, even they have to sleep.

In the far distance, starlight shimmers over the surface of a large frozen lake. And the cold. Oh, God, the cold is like nothing I've ever felt.

All of that alone is enough to take my breath away. But it's the ancient, primordial feel of this place that stipples my skin and settles in my gut. The promise of monsters and magic and a beautiful, lethal world beyond my comprehension.

I'm not sure what makes me turn around. A sound, perhaps. A feeling. When I do, my breath catches in my chest and I retreat a step, back pressed into the hard railing.

"You're not going to jump, are you?" a Fae male says.

He stands a few feet from me. He's tall, imposing, power coming off him in waves. And sweet Baby Jesus he's gorgeous. The kind of beautiful you feel in your belly. Maybe it's the way the silvery light falls over his features. Or the confidence exuding from his every pore. Or just the fact that his mouth is bowed at the top and full at the bottom.

But I suddenly can't breathe.

"No, of course not," I gasp, trying to mask the effect he has on me.

By the glimmer in his eyes, I'm pretty sure that he's aware. Since he seems to already read me like an open book, and since I'm terrible at hiding my feelings, I don't even bother masking my curiosity as I study him.

Despite the cold, he wears black jogger pants and a soft white T-shirt, both impeccably made and undoubtedly expensive. My gaze falls to his arms.

I never thought I would find this part of someone beautiful, but his arms seem carved from marble. Sinewy muscle curves and twists, trapping shadows. His flesh is smooth and pale and seemingly impervious to the bone-aching chill.

Winter Court Fae. Has to be. That also explains his icy demeanor.

I move my assessment to his face, taking in his features carefully. The way you savor a bite of rich cheesecake or swirl wine around your mouth first before swallowing it. Piercing silver-blue eyes glow softly, rimmed by dark blue lashes. Jagged cheekbones form deep hollows that end at a jaw you could slice apples on. His nose is straight, almost severe, but it somehow makes his inhumanly large eyes and soft, swollen lips work.

"How many Fae have you seen up close before?"

I startle at his voice. A deep, elegant voice tinged with an accent I can't place and a whole lot of amusement.

"You're my third—no, fourth."

"You can stare. All humans do." His lips curl up into a smile that doesn't quite reach his eyes. "Your bodies naturally react to our strangeness. You'll get used to it."

Heat flares across my frozen cheeks, but I accept his invitation . . . even if I feel like a total creeper.

I move my focus to his hair. It's cropped shorter on the sides and a little longer on top, showcasing wavy, tousled locks. They're a shade darker than his eyelashes, a startling midnight blue. I once saw a show about ice caves in Iceland and his hair is the exact color of the darkest part of the ice.

I shiver before remembering that I've just been standing here ogling him like a statue. But he's not a statue, because statues don't usually have lips that twitch at the corners or eyes that pierce your soul.

Is he about to smile or about to frown? I feel like that's important to my survival.

He crosses to the railing and peers at something in the distance. I watch him, stunned by how smooth and graceful his movements are. Every muscle, every tendon working in concert to make something as simple as walking seem like a dance.

Maybe it is. Maybe this is how the Fae mesmerize you into their power, like some magical, sexy voodoo. Maybe I should leave and go back to my pathetic little room.

But I don't *want* to.

"What are you doing out here?" he drawls, turning to face me. His gaze goes to the army of goosebumps amassed over my skin. His voice is syrupy and slow, but there's a demand there.

I tug my sleeves down to cover my mark. "I needed air."

"It's below freezing," he points out.

"I'm aware. But fresh air is better than the broom closet they put me in, even if it's cold as balls."

His expression shifts, moving in the same fluid way his body does, but I can't quite read it.

Amusement? Puzzlement? Annoyance? A lovely mix of all three?

"What are you doing on the roof?" I ask like the nosy girl I am.

He half turns to regard me. "It's quiet here." He seems to think about his answer for a moment before adding, "No one knows about this place."

Except me, I almost, but don't, say. "Are you hiding from someone?"

He blinks, his features hard and cold. This guy really knows how to play it cool. "Perhaps I just like the stars."

The gravel crunches softly beneath my feet as I shift from boot to boot. "There are no stars, if you haven't noticed."

"Pity," he says without glancing up.

Why am I so close to him? I've been inching across the roof toward the very thing I despise, caught in some weird magical Fae orbit.

What is wrong with me? I despise the cold almost as much as I despise the Fae. Yet here I am, in the cold, creeping closer to a Fae like some lunatic.

Am I smiling? Yeah—I'm totally grinning. This Fae must have some powerful magic, something that makes me feel comfortable with him. Is that even a thing? It must be.

I clamp my cold fingers into fists, wincing at the pain. I really *should* go inside. Instead I say, "Are you a student here?"

He nods, his eyes crinkling at the corners.

"I'm a shadow," I add.

"I'm aware."

My heart flutters at his voice, and it takes a second to understand he's turning my words back on me. It also takes a moment to notice that he's staring at me differently now. And there's a stillness to him that makes me uneasy. An intensity to his focus that wasn't there before.

I feel something snap between us. A sharp prickle of electricity. He must feel it too because his eyes widen. Only slightly, but enough to know.

I swallow, the air frosting in front of my lips as I struggle to breathe.

He takes a step closer.

A memory surfaces. Before everything really turned to crap, there was this exotic animal park an hour's drive from my house. Aunt Zinnia took me when I was thirteen because she knew how much I loved anything with fur. Looking back now I realize how sad it was, but back then, I remember the thrill when the man working there sat me next to this full grown lion.

The lion basically ignored me as I posed for pictures. But there was a moment near the end where the lion looked at me and something passed between us. An understanding. That with minimal effort, he could kill me.

That's exactly what I'm feeling now as I stare into this Fae's eyes. Not that he wants to kill me, exactly—but the shared knowledge that he *could.*

And there's something else. A familiarity I can't place.

A spark of remembrance flickers inside my heart. The shock like seeing a loved one you think is dead. I clutch my chest as an invisible tether snaps taut between us. The reaction to his presence visceral and raw. What is happening?

I know you. I know you. I know—

My skin goes clammy. "I . . . I should go."

His gaze chills my back as I hurry across the rooftop, and it doesn't stop burning until the door to my room slams shut.

Morning comes too soon. Clad in everything I own, I wheeze and lunge my way down a dark, endless stairwell to another door of marble that leads to an outdoor courtyard. Someone knocked this morning to inform me that I was needed for . . . something. I'm still not sure what.

I must have been tired because I slept way past noon. I think. There are no clocks in my room, and the sun is imprisoned behind a layer of dirty winter clouds so deep I'm not even sure it's there.

As soon as the door opens to the courtyard, cold air slaps me in the face, knocking every bit of sleep from my body along with my soul.

Lord, I hate the cold.

I inhale sharply. The space is big enough to fit two football fields. English primroses and winter jasmine decorate the grounds, crystal waters from countless fountains sparkle, frozen mid-spurt, and hedge mazes crisscross the paver stones, dusted white. Snow drizzles the many statues and forms mounds in the corners.

I barely have time to take in the place before a noise catches my attention.

"Hurry up!" a female orders in a tinkling tone.

I whip left to right, pulse pounding as I search for the voice. A ginormous magenta butterfly swoops at my head.

On instinct, I swipe at the papery, iridescent wings.

"Hey!" the voice screeches. And that's when I realize the butterfly is not a butterfly, but a miniscule person with abnormally large lungs. She screeches at me again, the sound earsplitting, buzzing around my head so fast I can't make out her features.

Suddenly she hovers in place, her eyes traveling over my clothes. "Fae hells. You're a weird one."

Curiosity gets the better of me, and I snatch the creature from the air, holding her gently around the waist. My fingers cover her entire body. She wriggles and kicks, and I can't stop staring at the tiny clothes she wears. The shoes made out of bean pods and soft dress spun from spider silk.

She's like the Barbies Julia plays with, only her hair isn't colored with crayons, but a deep, beautiful magenta, and she's warm and *alive*.

"What do you think you're doing?" she demands. Her wings beat the air in a blur, sending cold puffs of wind at my face.

"What are you?" I ask.

She gives up on trying to pry my pointer finger back with her hands and glares up at me, arms crossed. "I'm a sprite, and your escort for the next four years. And if you make any Tinkerbell jokes—any at all—I will cast a spell to give you hemorrhoids so bad you'll never sit down again."

Well, that sounds horrible.

She bares her ruby lips, revealing razor-sharp teeth. I think I recall something about sprites carrying a toxin, so I release her before she can bite me.

The moment she's free, she buzzes around my head, a string of curses spewing from her little mouth.

Then she says in her tinkling voice, "Follow me. We're already late for the Shadow Selection."

"The what?" I call. But she zooms so fast over the courtyard that I have no choice but to run to keep up. I zigzag around a statue of a faun and lunge over hedges, my boots slipping and sliding on the gravel.

Why did I ever love running?

Her sparkling form disappears through a propped open door into another building, this one tall and spiky. I follow. Those orb thingies from before spin inside delicate glass bulbs affixed to the walls, casting light over marble hallways and warming the air.

Soon I'm sweating. My hair plastered to my face and mouth hanging open in a pant.

The sprite ducks into an open door of deep mahogany, and I burst after her, swearing under my breath . . . into a giant auditorium full of people.

Crap.

Not people. Fae. Note to self. I suck at remembering that.

Hundreds of Fae eyes pin me to the spot, the air in the room heavy with a sense of magic.

I freeze, suddenly recalling my overwhelming hatred of crowds and attention. Perhaps if I hadn't slammed the door open I could have snuck in unnoticed . . .

Shoving my fear down deep, I force my legs to move, shuffling forward.

Why can't I breathe?

One of the Fae near the back calls out, "Who's the fresh meat?"

My gaze darts around the crowd, the exoticness of their features spinning my heart into overdrive. Some are wild-looking, with beaks and hooves and claws. Some only come up to my waist and are strange colors. Varying shades of mauve and teal and chartreuse.

But most look like versions of us, just with pointy ears, expensively tailored clothes that are a mix between modern fashion and a renaissance fair, and like a million times the hot factor.

In contrast, my frumpy, spaghettiOs stained hoodie, clunky Salvation Army boots, and unattractive jeans feel like a prison yard uniform.

I take a few more tentative steps, scouring the room for my sprite guide, whom I've already developed a love/hate relationship with.

Where are you, tiny person?

Instead I find massive chandeliers in the shape of vines hanging from high, arched ceilings. Magical orbs drip from their golden branches, each orb of light a little sun that illuminates the room. A layer of shimmery frost covers the entire thing.

Wooden bleachers filled with students surround the chamber, looking down upon a marble floor that appears to be a giant map, segmented into seven distinct locations. Great leafy mosaic trees of orange and yellow and red spread across the section I stand on . . .

I suddenly get what each segment represents. The Fae Courts. This area is Autumn. The one next to it, Winter.

The crowd on the floor is smaller, less than a hundred Fae, all dressed in extravagant clothes beyond imagining. Headdresses made of gold-spun leaves; cloaks weaved from spider silk and butterfly wings; armor carved from ice.

The clothes match the theme of the floor each Fae stands on, and I quickly realize these students are split up by court, meaning everyone has their place.

Everyone but me.

Desperately, I search for an indication of where to go.

A dais of obsidian rises in the center of the room. As I take in the black pedestal and the very human, very terrified group that huddles there inside a silver cage, I answer my own question.

That's where I belong.

A pang of dread pierces my gut.

They're inside a cage. A Mother. Freaking. Cage.

My nostrils flare as I try to pull in air, panic tightening my chest. I don't do well in tight, enclosed spaces.

The sprite that led me here flits over, an anxious look scrunching her face. "What are you doing, weird one? Get up there with your people."

"No!" I didn't plan on yelling my refusal, but the combination of acoustics and fear amplify my voice and it reverberates through the room, even echoing for dramatic affect.

Oh. My. God.

A collective gasp goes through the crowd. *Hide. Where can I hide?*

A few of the closest Fae gape at me, obviously not used to anyone disobeying. But most stare at me with a mixture of curiosity and disgust.

A Fae girl breaks off from the crowd on Winter's side, her clear ice heels clacking loudly as she marches toward me, two other girls in tow. Everyone she passes cowers a little.

Great. Resident mean girl incoming.

Why am I not surprised? Mean girls tend to target me, probably because I can't just fall in line like everyone else. It's not in my nature. At my high school there was Mary Louise, homecoming queen and sometimes girlfriend of Cal and half the football team.

But compared to the Fae girl and two others stalking toward me, Mary Louise is a nun.

Crap on a stick. This is not going the way I planned at *all*.

The sprite hisses in fear and starts tugging at my earlobe.

"Oberon's teeth, girl. That's Inara Winterspell. I suggest you move your ass, now."

But her words have no effect. My brain has already decided I won't go inside the cage—bad things are going to happen there—and even someone as intimidating as Inara Winterspell can't break me out of my terror.

"No," I spit through clenched teeth. "I . . . can't."

Memories flood my brain like poison. I was only ten when my parents died. Instead of letting the government throw me into foster care, I took to the streets. But ten was way too young to fend for myself, and I was caught up in the human trafficking that runs rampant in the Tainted Zone, especially the bigger cities.

If not for Aunt Zinnia's help, I would have been sold to the Fae years ago.

A shiver begins deep in my torso. I cross my arms over my chest. I can still feel the bars from the cramped dog cage they shoved me in cutting my skin. Can remember screaming and thrashing and crying to get out. I half lost my mind between those steely bars.

Bile slams into my throat. No way in hell I'm going back in a cage. Any cage.

The sprite yanks hard on my ear, and I try to swat her away. She's strong, though, and fast.

I'm so focused on struggling with this pint-sized bundle of aggression that I miss Inara and the two girls until they're right next to me.

The sprite releases my ear and drops into a dramatic bow, her beautiful magenta hair falling over her shoulder and to her waist.

But Inara doesn't even look at the sprite. Her icy gaze sweeps over me with disgust, her lips curled into a sneer. She's model-tall with porcelain skin over delicate features, long silky ultramarine blue hair that tumbles artfully over one shoulder, and legs for days that end in seven-inch crystal pumps.

But it's her eyes that chill me to the bone; her irises are an ashy-white hue, like frost.

"We have held the Selection ceremony for thousands of years," she snarls through lips as blue as her hair, "and never once has a shadow recruit acted with as much disrespect as you do now." She cuts her strange eyes at the sprite. "Why haven't you glamoured her into submission?"

"I apologize, oh good and wise Evermore," the sprite begins, giving me the side-eye. "But she just arrived moments ago and according to the new rules this year . . . we are only allowed to glamour them if they try to flee."

"What do you mean, just arrived?"

The poor sprite is trembling. "All I know is I was ordered to make sure she made it to the Selection."

"Ordered by *whom?*" Inara demands in a soft, horrible tone that scrapes down every knob of my spine.

The sprite's petrified gaze drifts from Inara to someone near the Winter Court's side, although I can't see who. Whoever it is, she must find them more terrifying than Inara because she says in a quiet voice, "I don't think I should tell you."

Inara glares at the sprite. "Stupid sprite! I should freeze you for a couple hundred years and see if your tiny idiot brain grows any smarter."

My sprite guide darts behind my head and nestles into the back of my neck. She's trying to hide. We're not exactly buddies, but I feel a sudden urge to protect her.

She's tiny, after all. An easy target.

"Wow," I say, forgetting where I am or *what* I'm talking to. "Picking on creatures smaller than you must make you feel really big and strong."

For a split second, Inara is too stunned to say anything.

Her impossibly blue lips part, a look of outrage slowly twisting them into a sneer as her friends tighten the circle around me. The sprite has gone completely still, as has the entire room.

I catch sight of Magus near the doorway. His horrified expression sends my heart into a tailspin.

Way to not grab attention.

A menacing grin flashes across Inara's jaw. She holds a manicured hand up between us to reveal blue and white magic crackling between her delicate fingers.

"This is going to be fun," she purrs, turning to her two friends. "Which part should I freeze first?"

"Her tongue," the first girl suggests behind a deceptively sweet smile. She's athletic with a thick head of beautiful caramel brown hair streaked blonde, piercing honey-brown eyes, and tawny skin.

The second girl, the smallest of the three, shakes her head at the idea, sending her chin-length black hair swaying around a delicate chin. Strange golden eyes more animalistic than human cut a sharp contrast against her bone-white skin. "Then she can't scream. Why not freeze her feet to the ground so she can't run, but can still cry out?"

Holy hell. They're sociopaths. All of them.

"Fabulous idea, Kimber," Inara purrs, her praise making the black-haired girl beam. "Just for that, I might let you drink from her before I kill her."

Despite my fear, for a moment, I give the dark-haired girl a second look as my curiosity surpasses my survival instincts. She's a real-life vampire, a member of the Mortal Beast's court.

Welcome to Everwilde, Summer.

My awe takes a backseat as the pack of murderous girls close in, adrenaline flooding my veins. I fight the overwhelming urge to recoil. To run.

Too late. A blast of unimaginable cold bites my skin.

With a cry, I fall to one knee as frost crackles over my flesh and a marrow-deep chill fills my bones. At the same time, horrible, aching pressure begins to build in my skull like a brain freeze times a million.

I can't move. Can't call out. Helpless—I feel so helpless.

My sprite suddenly darts over my shoulder, putting her tiny body between me and Inara. Her papery wings flutter wildly as she holds up a tiny hand. "Wait! She will go . . . won't you, human?"

The cold eases, if only a bit. Both sprite and Evermore glare at me. My sprite is nodding her head in an effort to convince me this is the best option. Magus, too, frantically nods his head as he tries to coax me into agreeing.

The rational part of me *does* agrees, but my body has entered fight-or-flight mode, and it's determined not to enter that cage even if that means freezing to death.

I have a choice: let fear control me and refuse, in which case Inara will turn both the sprite and me into popsicles.

Or overcome my terror and let myself be caged.

I glance to my right at the Winter Court crowd and lock eyes with a lithe, beautiful Fae male. Even standing in a crowd of gorgeous beings, his arresting looks draw the eye. The hood of the silver cloak he wears covers most of his head. White fur lines the cloak like snow. And two owl pins glitter on each shoulder.

Still, I can make out short, messy hair the deepest blue I've ever seen tumbling over his forehead. Rich silver-blue eyes strike a stark contrast to his pale, almost bloodless skin.

The terrifyingly beautiful Fae from last night.

A tremor reverberates straight to my core. As if he can feel it, he smirks at me, and something about the tilt of his totally kissable lips dredges up the memory of not just the roof, but the forest . . .

The cloak. The owl pins. The smarmy expression. That explains the crazy reaction I had last night. I'm staring at my tormentor, the one who condemned me to this prison under the name of the Winter Prince.

And he's smirking at me. *Smirking.*

Fury overrides my attraction to him. Fury and shame. I should have known last night who he was. Did he laugh with his Fae buddies over my stupidity? What if he felt my strange attraction to him?

I groan internally, but my anger numbs any embarrassment I feel. He thinks I'm here for his enjoyment. He thinks I'm already beaten. Well screw him. I'm a fighter, and I refuse to go down like this. I refuse to give him one more second of pleasure watching me struggle.

Drawing upon every ounce of willpower, I stand, the thin layer of ice cracking, and look Inara straight in the eyes. "I'll go in the cage."

A disappointed sigh flees Inara's lips, but she steps out of the way, waving a slender hand with silver-lacquered fingernails at the cage.

"Run along, little human. I'll see you again soon . . . if you manage to survive until the Selection."

Her tone makes it clear she doesn't think I will. Just like the headmistress. Just like every single Fae in this room.

Time to prove her wrong. Time to prove them *all* wrong.

Only once I'm away from Inara and her friends does the air warm to a tolerable level. My veil of frost becomes water dampening my skin and clothes. Red carpeted walkways divide each court's side. With my head held high, I find the closest walkway and stride toward the cage.

My former tormentor's icy gaze bores into my back, and once again I get the feeling he gets off on this. My struggle, my embarrassment and pain.

Annoyingly, there's also that strange bond connecting us, as if an invisible thread travels from his heart to mine.

Magic. Has to be.

I shake my head to dislodge the bizarre feeling and push on. Each step closer makes it harder to pull in air. But, between my sprite literally shoving between my shoulder blades, my embarrassment, and my resolve, I keep moving forward until my boots clop over the dais.

There are countless people packed inside the golden, bell-shaped cage. White jasmine and ivy cord around the bars and scent the air. A Fae with long tufted ears and a donkey tail grins at me as he pulls open the closest door, the hinges creaking. It's one of seven doors.

See? Seven doors means seven ways to escape at the first sign of being trapped.

My mind seems to accept this fact just fine, but my body is paranoid. It's been inside a cage before and it hasn't forgotten. Cold sweat slithers down my spine, my heart twerking to its own panicky song. A pit of terror slices open inside me.

I'm about to bolt when a pretty girl rushes past the guard and grabs me by the elbow, guiding me into the cage. Her fingers are warm and gentle as they press into my flesh, and something about her easy confidence and beaming smile calm me.

As I pass some of the other humans, they snicker under their breath. A gorgeous girl with long curly chestnut hair and enough makeup on to stock a Sephora says, "Who let Trailer Park in?"

She has the air of someone who's never even seen a trailer park, much less lived in one. If she had she'd know they're convenient, economical, and can be moved when necessary.

A boy winks at me, but his lips twist hatefully as he does it. His friend makes a lewd gesture I won't even deign to describe.

"I'll help you win if you promise to come by my room later," he says.

My jaw grinds, but I ignore them. Compared to the Fae, who can *actually* freeze me with magic, their words barely even sting.

What's the saying? Ice and snow may freeze my toe, but words will never hurt me. I totally just made that up, but it fits and I'm keeping it.

"It's not so bad," my hero says, squeezing my arm. She's curvy and short, maybe five-two, with a body that makes mine feel boyish in comparison and plump lips meant for smiling. "This is all for show. The Evermore do like their cere-monies." She gives my arm a nice pat. "Didn't your parents prepare you for what's to come?"

I shake my head, hiding the wince from her touch. My tattooed flesh is still a bit tender.

She must see that I'm still really close to panicking, because she says, "Here. Don't look at the bars. Focus on me."

I do. *Wow. She's really pretty.*

Deep-set cornflower-blue eyes. Thick chocolate-brown hair cut chin-length and streaked hot pink and purple. On either side of a pert nose, a smattering of freckles dust her tawny cheeks.

"I'm a legacy." Her face beams with pride. "My parents actually met here twenty years ago."

My eyes widen. "And they . . . bargained your life for a wish?"

She shrugs. "They couldn't get pregnant, and their . . . circumstances made adopting nearly impossible, at least back then. So they summoned a Fae and, well, the rest is history."

I don't dare point out the irony of wishing for a baby only to bargain it away as a slave.

She must see the expression on my face because she adds, "It's only for four years. Plus, they both survived so there's no reason to think we won't. And there are perks, if you can look past the Evermore's superiority complex."

"That's a no from me," I mutter. I'm one-hundred percent positive I will never be able to overlook the Evermore's asshole tendencies.

"A few are okay . . ." she offers.

"Really? Which ones?"

She glances around. "I've heard those from the Summer Court are nice."

I raise a dubious eyebrow. "Nice? Or just not serial killers? Because there's a difference."

She laughs. "You're right, they all suck." She juts out a slim hand. "My name's Mackenzie Fairchild, by the way. Everyone calls me Mack."

I do the same. "Summer Solstice."

"Summer Solstice?" A grin shows off her perfectly straight white teeth. "Your parents really got creative, huh?"

"Yeah . . ." I look away.

The problem with having dead parents—aside from the obvious—is explaining that in conversation. Most people either get really quiet or really talkative, but it's *always* awkward.

Time to change the subject. "So," I say. "What are we doing inside the cage, other than being ogled like fresh meat?"

"That's basically it." She tucks a hot-pink strand behind her ear. "Although I prefer the word 'appraised' to ogled."

Appraised?

As my gaze travels over the others, I discover they're all dressed in luxurious cool-toned clothes similar to the Winter Court attire. Even Mack. She sports a gorgeous ensemble of silver pants and a low-cut ivory blouse, dark blue embroidery lining the hem of her bodice. A royal blue jacket of expensive velvet tapers to accentuate her slim waist and curvy hips, and knee-high white Jimmy Choo boots pull everything together.

I pluck subconsciously at my dirty sweatshirt. Guess I didn't get the Fae-inspired wardrobe memo . . . thanks, Evermore dickwad. Not that I'd ever be able to match their style with my goodwill inspired closet, but he didn't know that.

She notices me looking and says, "I ordered my outfit from Barneys. Dressing like the Evermore is all the rage in Manhattan. We follow their seasons and everything, and winter fashion is my favorite." I must be making a face because she adds, "I mean, it's a bit overdone, in my opinion . . . but when in Everwilde . . ."

"Right." I grin, her peppy mood contagious. "We don't have a Barney's in Amarillo."

She laughs, a hearty sound that lifts my spirits. "You know, Dallas Cowboys, I think I'm going to like you. Depending on who chooses you at the Shadow Selection, maybe we can be bunk mates."

"Shadow Selection?" Could there be a more ominous sounding name?

"Yeah," Mack answers, sounding way less panicky than I feel. "The ceremony where basically our entire next four years are decided." I must look confused because she adds, "Each Fae chooses a human shadow to train under them at school. I mean, we also fetch them things a lot and do trivial errands and stuff. Especially first year."

Oh—that's what the headmistress was talking about. The thought brings to mind cattle yards and auctioneers, but it also explains why the Evermore have drawn around our cage. They're assessing us like bugs under a microscope. And most eyes seem to be on me.

Before I can question her further, the dais begins to *move.*

We're sinking. Fast. Another round of panic lodges deep in my chest, and I clamp the iron bars of my cage, flexing my hands over the cool metal and spreading my legs for balance.

"Mack," I call. "Which part of the ceremony is this?"

Her eyes go wide. "Did no one prepare you for this?" There's incredulity in her voice, along with pity, an emotion I despise.

"I think you should just assume I know nothing." The last few words come out two octaves higher as the floor lurches faster and faster into the ground. I barely have time to glimpse the Fae cheer, hooting and jeering, before the dais sinks into the earth.

Into the earth, for frack's sake. This is totally how I die.

Mack sweeps a concerned look over me. "I don't have

time to explain all of it . . . you know how to swim, right?"

"Swim?" Dear Lord, my voice is squeaky. Why do I have to hate tight, enclosed spaces? "Sure. Why?"

I used to love it, but swimming requires enormous amounts of calories . . .

"They're dropping us into a river system below the academy. We have to make it to the lake of sorrows." Of course it's called the lake of sorrows. "We're supposed to be scared of the selkies that live there, but my parents told me they secretly feed the selkies a huge meal right beforehand and then drug them with magic."

Selkies . . . what are those again? My brain supplies endless images of mermaid creatures with rows of pointy teeth.

Killer mermaids. They're throwing us into water with killer mermaids. "So they're . . . harmless?"

"Supposedly." She shrugs. "The biggest threat, of course, is drowning. There were two during my parents' Selection." She shrugs again, but the conditioned response is unable to hide the way her mouth puckers at the corners. "Other than making sure we don't die, we just have to be one of the first fifty to arrive."

This just keeps getting better. "What happens if we're not?"

"We lose our spot in the academy."

A spark of hope blossoms inside my chest. So there's a way to get kicked out of this place? "Is that a . . . bad thing?"

Her eyes widen, and she shakes her head. "I still cannot get over how little you know about how this all works. Yes, that's a bad thing. A very bad thing. Once we entered Everwilde, we belong to them. Any human who loses their spot at Evermore Academy goes to work as a slave in the Unseelie Courts, or worse . . . fighting the darklings in the scourge."

An image of those poor souls trudging mindlessly behind

Magus flashes in my mind, and newfound fear pierces my core. I cannot let that happen. God only knows what life in the Unseelie Courts would be like.

And the scourge . . .

My hands clench the bars as we're plunged lower. The Fae students peer down at us. Inara's face is gleeful as she calls out, "Watch out for the hungry selkies, little humans." Her cruel gaze flicks to me. "I hear they eat the ugly mortals first."

I can't quite catch my breath. I should have expected something like this in the beginning—the Fae are vicious jerks —but still, I'm caught off guard, and I hate the feeling.

Someone is crying—a tall girl with lavender -dyed hair wrangled into a tight knot. In between sobs she blurts out that she can't swim.

"We should help her," I say, but Mack puts a hand on my arm and shakes her head.

"No. She's already panicking. In the water she'll drown anyone who tries."

I feel sick. This isn't right. But I don't have time to come up with a plan. In a few moments, we'll have to swim.

Swim . . . with shoes. I lose my scarf and sweatshirt, pocket my mittens, then I bend down and rip my boots off. Mack catches on immediately and does the same, wincing as she has to get rid of her expensive Jimmy Choo's.

Together we chuck our stuff through the cage bars. Mine barely miss a blond Fae boy's head before disappearing above.

I'll have to come back for those later.

The others follow our lead and shoes fly through the air, a few missing the dwindling ledge above and raining back down on us.

A giant greenish-yellow orb hangs from the top of the cage, illuminating tiny streams of water rivering down dirt walls as we're dragged deep into the earth. The circle of light from above grows smaller and smaller, the faces of the Fae watching us becoming nondescript.

The others inside the cage are starting to group into packs of three to four.

"Here's the deal," Mack says, turning me to face her. "There are seven tunnels leading out from here to the lake, each with magical reeds placed along their length to let us breathe. But there aren't enough of the breathing devices for all of us."

A mixture of anger and fear roils my gut. "Why would they do that? Give us less than we need?"

"Because they're the Evermore, and we're their entertainment. The sooner you get used to that fact, the better."

My jaw locks as anger pours through me. I'll never get used to that idea. Never.

The trembling beneath my feet stills as the floor stops moving. Water begins to fill the space, lapping at my socks. It's surprisingly warm. The stagnant odor fills my nose and turns my stomach.

"So how do we make sure we get a breathing device?" I ask, my eyes glued to the brackish water now swirling around my calves. Now my knees . . . my thighs . . .

The cavern is filling fast.

"Swim like hell?" She gives a nervous laugh. "Everyone knows the shortest route is that tunnel"—she nods to her left —"so we just need to be the first ones inside."

Already, a crowd blocks that door, waiting to be first. Frowning, I scan our surroundings. A small cavern hardly larger than our cage greets me. I can just barely make out the tops of the tunnels. They must be low to the ground because they're already underwater. Golden light flickers from each entrance, brightening the water enough to highlight its clarity.

At least there's light to guide us. It could be worse.

Silver linings and all.

"Which one is the longest tunnel?" I ask.

She raises an eyebrow and nods behind me. "The one directly at your back. But no one takes that one . . ."

"And you're a good swimmer?" I ask as water reaches my armpits. My long hair swirls around my body, and I regret not pulling it up out of my face before we came.

She winks. "State champion two years running."

For some reason, that's not surprising. I grin. "Good, then let's take the long tunnel."

Her eyes narrow as she works out my thinking. "It won't be crowded . . . so we won't have to fight for oxygen reeds."

"Exactly. And we're both excellent swimmers, so the extra distance won't make that much difference."

Her eyes light up. "Genius."

We wade together to the door nearest the unpopular tunnel. Just as I suspected, we're the only ones. Although I also suspect everyone is avoiding me.

When the water reaches so high I can't touch the bottom, the cage doors spring open and swing out, and everyone surges through the doors to a tunnel.

Go time.

I dive for the door—

But right before I slip out, the pretty girl who laughed at me earlier slams into the door from the outside, the clang of metal on metal loud inside the chamber. She sneers at me. "Your kind doesn't belong here."

Aw hell no.

I lunge for another door but two other boys are working with her and they've locked them. All of them.

Murder. I would murder them with my bare hands if I could get out.

"Good luck with that, Trailer Park!" the girl calls out before diving under the water.

I'm so screwed. I grab the handle to the closest door just as Mack's head pops up from the water.

"What are you waiting—" Her eyes go huge as she takes in the doors. "They're all locked?"

I nod, gritting my teeth to keep from freaking out.

"Did Reina do this? That bitch! I'll kill her."

"It's okay," I lie, shoving with all my might on the iron door. "Go without me."

"No," she says immediately, although her voice wavers, and her gaze keeps flicking to the tunnel.

"Go!" I insist, sagging against the door, which is now completely under water. My mind spins wildly, my heart smashing against my ribcage as I do the same, throwing myself at the iron bars.

I'm trapped. I'm trapped. I'm trapped. The words swirl around my skull, a mantra of panic. This is my worst nightmare. Trapped in a cage. A cage that's slowly filling with water.

Think, Summer. Desperation will only get you killed.

Thrusting my arm through the bars, I reach around the

door and grab the lock. It's solid, so I can't break it, and there's no key to be found . . .

I yank it anyway. A zip of electricity shocks my fingers.

Ow. What the Fae?

I reach for the lock again . . . only to discover it's somehow been broken.

How did that happen?

Not one to dwell on the unimportant, I smash into the door with my shoulder, popping it open. Mack's face softens with relief, and then we both grab a lungful of air and dive, swimming toward the closest opening.

Nebulous orbs of gold light our path, revealing a seven-foot wide tunnel. River grass sways at the bottom and tickles my arms. The precious air in our lungs bubbles out of our lips and tinkles faintly in the water.

Because I was forced to exert energy breaking out of the cage—assholes!—my lungs burn and ache almost immediately. Where are the oxygen reeds? Not sure what I'm supposed to be looking for, I follow Mack's lead, trying super hard not to panic because I'm underwater. Without a plan.

Seconds away from drowning.

Just when my chest feels like it will explode, she points to something nestled in the grass below. Two wooden flute-looking things sit inside a shell. She grabs one and hands me the other. Her dark hair floats around her face like a muddy cloud. Then she brings the reed to her lips and nods for me to do the same.

The moment the reed touches my lips, I drag in oxygen.

I can breathe again. The feeling is wonderful. Clamping the reed between my teeth, I take two more breaths and then we keep going, swimming hard toward a pinpoint of light in the distance.

Every time my reed starts to lose oxygen, we discover two more planted below. I can't imagine what it's like in the tunnels where five or six people are fighting for these life-saving devices.

Everything about this infuriates me, but I focus on swimming and conserving my energy. My outrage can come later.

Finally we grab another set of reeds just as the tunnel empties into a large body of water. The flow of water drags my white-blonde hair in front of my face. Kicking like mad, I swim into what I assume is the lake of sorrows. Strings of lanterns glowing with golden magic are all around us, providing more than enough light to see everything.

As we come out near the bottom, slimy reeds of grass tickling my arms, a flash of silver catches my eye. I assume it's a fish until a semi-translucent tailfin slides across the sand, undulating gently in the current.

Selkie. Sucking on my oxygen reed, I take slow steady breaths and try not to freak out. If my heart pumps too fast, I'll use the oxygen too soon, and the surface of the water is at least fifty feet above.

Mack sees the selkie too. She points, nodding her head. Her dark hair floats around her face like a shadowy halo, and bubbles stream from her nostrils.

Other students begin trickling from the holes all around the lake floor. Most don't have reeds. Some are clutching their throat, their eyes wide, and I'm glad we took the long tunnel.

Mack pushes off the sandy bottom, torpedoing toward the surface. I follow, kicking hard and fast as I savor the last dregs of my oxygen, forcing myself to take a breath every twenty seconds.

My lungs burn, and I know I can make the surface with oxygen to spare, but the cautious miser living inside me refuses to use up the last of my oxygen until I'm sure I won't need it.

Excitement amps up my heart. We're going to be one of the first ones to surface. *Take that, mean girl who locked me in.*

She and I were going to have words soon. Once I break the surface and take my place beside Mack, who has just now breached the water. Thin patches of ice float beside her. The lanterns must also warm the water.

Something makes me glance down. As my eyes adjust to what I'm seeing, injustice overwhelms my senses.

The girl with the lavender hair, the one who couldn't swim, struggles near the sandy bottom. When she said she couldn't swim, she must have meant she couldn't swim *well*, because she's managed to claw and fight her way into the lake.

And she could probably paddle her way to the surface . . . except the mean girl who trapped me in the cage swims by, same two boys in tow, and rips the oxygen reed from the other girl's lips as I watch.

Lavender hair grabs at her throat and flails, her eyes all-white saucers.

No way in hell I'm going to watch her drown. Without a second's hesitation, I dive, shooting straight for her. The others are now all passing me on the way to the surface, and my heart sinks. I'm going to lose.

But I'd rather lose than let someone die.

By the time I get to her, the girl is entangled near the bottom in the long red and green sea-grass. The girl's eyes lock onto mine. I rip the reed from my lips and shove it into her mouth. Then I grab a fistful of her sleeve and give a hard kick, propelling us to the surface.

I make it maybe two feet when a shadow passes over us. Before I can look up, something slams into me from above, knocking every bit of air from my chest.

The impact yanks the girl from my grasp and sends me tumbling end over end into the sand. I fling my arms straight out and wave them for stability as I try to get my bearings. Dirt and silt cloud the water, camouflaging whatever hit me.

But I already know what it is. Selkie.

The word shoots straight terror into my veins. A flash of silver and red to my right. One glance and my heart stops, a scream dying in my throat.

The creature is hideous, a strange blend of fish and human. Overly large inhuman onyx eyes are set inside a white face with two holes where the nose should be and gills under the jaw. Reddish-translucent fins stick straight out over her ears, her thick tail covered in silver and blue scales and ending in blood-red plumage.

But I'm focused on the huge gaping mouth set with rows and rows of serrated teeth.

Grinning, the selkie shoots straight for me. I try to punch her but underwater I can't get any real force, and my fists glance harmlessly over her slick flesh. Her mouth yawns wide as she plunges her teeth straight for my throat—

Suddenly bright red light blooms between us. The selkie halts, peering with those big oily-black eyes at something on my chest. I glance down, shocked to see my pendant emanating radiant red light.

The selkie drags her gaze from the pendant to my face. I take advantage of her pause and strike out, the heel of my bare foot glancing off her tail. The action startles her and she darts into the maze of grasses before disappearing.

My lungs are on fire as I shove off the ground toward the surface, kicking as hard and fast as I can. I find Lavender haired girl floating ten feet from the surface, and my heart clenches. She's motionless. Eyes closed. Shafts of light from above highlight the vibrancy of her hair swirling around her slack face.

Using every bit of energy I have left, I grab her arm and drag her to the surface. She doesn't move, doesn't kick or struggle or anything.

Not good.

Cold air stings my face, steam from the warm water curling around my head. Clutching the girl to my chest, I struggle to keep her head above water, but it flops lifelessly side to side.

Crap. I need to help her.

Someone calls out, and I manage to yell back, taking deep lungfuls of frigid air. Every exhalation sends a milky cloud shooting from my shivering lips.

A wooden rowboat with peeling brown paint drifts over and someone tugs us over the side. As soon as we're both in the boat, I turn the girl on her side to get any water out of her lungs. I feel for her pulse, but my fingers are too numb to be of much help.

Is she breathing? Her chest isn't moving.

Head spinning, I position her on her back and start compressing her chest like I've seen on TV.

After a few minutes, I stop, unsure if what I'm doing is even helping.

Oh, God. I stare up at the stars and try to catch my breath as we near the shore, pieces of ice smacking the hull.

It's not exactly light outside, but a strange mixture of dusk and moonlight reflects off the snow and brightens the land.

The person rowing—a huge, muscular faun with goat legs covered in white fur and large ram horns protruding from short red hair—hands me a blanket. Wrapping the scratchy wool around my body like a burrito, I sit up in time to see Mack sprinting toward our boat, followed closely by the blond Evermore I nearly brained earlier with my shoes. He's holding my boots and grinning.

My sprite, on the other hand, is not grinning as she flutters through the air clutching my sweatshirt. It's too heavy for her tiny wings, and she keeps dipping and weaving in the air, dragging my poor sweatshirt through the snow.

The curses spewing from her lips could fill ten swear jars.

A crowd gathers on the snowy lawn a little way ahead. Beyond that, the academy rises impossibly high, the most beautiful building I've ever seen. Carved from white marble, the spires and towers glimmer faintly under the moonlight. Blue and gold orbs of magic pulse from thousands of lanterns that sparkle like the stars above. A flag flies from the middle tower, the silver and blue colors definitely from the Winter Court.

For a moment, a breath, I have the odd feeling that I've been here before. Or dreamed about this place. Or read about it, even. In much more detail than that tiny Wikipedia article.

Then the bottom of the boat scrapes on the shore, and I'm dodging the sweatshirt being thrown at my face.

After I slip my sweatshirt and boots on, the blond male Evermore who carried my boots helps me off the boat. I accept his hand, startled by the warmth of his fingers. He grins and I suddenly realize how strikingly handsome he is.

I mean, all the Evermore are unbelievably gorgeous, but he surpasses even the normal Fae standard. In our world, he would be a movie star or a model . . . or both.

He wears the green and gold of the Summer Court, the colors matching his gold-flecked green eyes. His hair, too, is gold, and pulled back in a half-knot that would make any other man look ridiculous. Golden cuffs shaped like ivy wind up his pointed ears, capping the tips.

"Are you okay?" he asks, flashing perfect teeth.

He's running his hands over my body, an orange-gold light flickering out from his palms and seeping into my flesh. Each pass fills me with delicious heat and dries my clothes. Once he's done with that, he waves his fingers and creates a bubble of warmth that covers my entire body.

"Yes, I'm fine." I nod and glance back at the girl I saved. "But she needs—"

My words trail away into silence. The girl hasn't moved from where I positioned her.

The Summer Evermore's expression goes dark, and he looks to the Faun. "Basil, is she alive?"

The Faun shakes his head, and I can't help but notice how he genuinely seems sad about her death.

Tears spring to my eyes before I can help it. I try to blink them away, but then I remember that I'm now disqualified from staying at this cursed school, which means I don't have to pretend to be strong. So I let the tears fall.

And with them, my anger grows.

"A selkie attacked us," I say to no one in particular.

The Summer Evermore frowns. "No, they were all fed and sedated."

"Well someone forgot this selkie. She almost killed me but . . ." My hand goes to where my necklace rests, hidden beneath my shirt. "I scared her away."

Basil steps from the boat, carrying the drowned girl in his arms. "If the selkie wasn't drugged, you would be dead. I promise."

Mack wraps her arms around me. "I didn't know you'd gone back for her until I was in the boat . . . and then . . ."

"It's okay." I rub the last tear away with the heel of my hand and glance at the crowd in the distance. As my gaze falls on first Inara, then Reina, and finally my tormentor, I feel a potent rage spark inside my chest.

They're to blame. Not Mack. Not the poor drowned girl. Them.

We walk toward the crowd, the bubble of warm magic the Summer Evermore gave me melting the snow at my bare feet. They're grouped into two sides: Seelie and Unseelie.

A shrill voice I immediately recognize as Inara's calls out, "How did you like the selkies? Guess they thought you were too ugly to eat."

A thought comes to mind that I can't shake. She's responsible. She somehow made sure that one selkie wasn't drugged.

If not for the selkie, I would have had time to get the girl to the surface before she died.

If I were staying, I'd recognize the uncontrollable rage and tamp it down. Even I'm not stupid enough to make powerful enemies when I don't have an escape plan.

But I'm not staying, and I don't care if they all want to murder me.

I'll be long gone soon, out of their reach.

Fists balled at my side, I throw off my blanket and march the rest of the way toward them before Mack or the Summer Evermore can stop me.

15

"**H**ey a-holes!" I yell at the Unseelie court gathered to the right.

The mean girl who locked me in the cage, Reina, is the first to acknowledge my words, followed by a gorgeous male Fae who, with his spiky snow-white hair, deep lavender eyes, and sneer, has to be related to Inara.

Speaking of, Inara gives an incredulous gasp, her murderous gaze sliding to me.

I match her scowl with one of my own. What can she do anyway? What can *any* of them do? I'm about to get shipped off to somewhere far from her reach.

"I guess in your world, killing someone innocent is fine," I say, crossing my arms over my chest. "But where I come from, that makes you cowards."

Mack has caught up to me and gives a hard yank on my arm, nearly popping it out of socket.

"What are you doing?" she whisper-yells, her voice shaky.

"Go," I order, "unless you want to be associated with this train wreck."

Before Mack can respond, I prowl over to the trio. Anger

seeps from my every pore. "Did you really think you could lock me in that cage and not face consequences?"

Reina shrugs. "Yeah, actually, I did. You weren't supposed to make it to the surface."

The way she talks of my death so casually fills me with uncontrollable rage. Despite the cold, prickly heat flashes over my cheeks and chest. "Like the other girl?"

The two mortal boys that helped Reina in the cage stroll over. One of the boys whispers something to Reina, and then they all burst out laughing. But there's no mirth in Reina's eyes as they lock on me.

Her sprite, a dark-haired female with a dour face, hisses at me. My sprite, who I didn't notice until now flying above me, hisses back. Her tiny pinprick teeth bare in a snarl as she hurls a string of what I assume are insults in another language at the dark-haired sprite.

She's definitely growing on me.

"Too bad you didn't take the hint and die too," Reina purrs. "She was just in the wrong place at the wrong time, but you . . . you I definitely meant to drown. Your kind don't belong here. You're too weak, too ugly, too *poor*. Just like the dead girl. I say good riddance."

Something inside me snaps.

Before I can think about what I'm doing, I swing my fist at her smug face, every ounce of my indignation concentrated in my right hook.

Obviously not expecting me to hit her, she doesn't even try to defend herself as my knuckles catch her square on her perfect nose with a loud, satisfying crack. In shock, she crumples to her knees, her eyes wide and hand covering her nose.

Blood dribbles between her fingers.

"That's for locking me inside the cage," I snarl.

Holy Fae. I just punched her.

"You—you hit me!" she screeches, coming to the same

genius realization. The two boys flock around her. One has already ripped off his shirt and is pressing it to her face. Inara and her look-alike male Fae are just staring at me in shock. As if, they literally cannot believe I hit her.

That makes three of us.

A wide grin spreads across my face as I shake out my hand, playing it cool. "Yeah, someone should have done that a long time ago."

God that felt good. At least I get to leave this place with the memory of my fist connecting with her now-not-so-perfect nose.

Mack has come back to rein me in, and she finally succeeds in dragging me away. She plants us behind the Summer Evermore that helped me out of the boat. The Seelie and Unseelie react, the Seelie cheering while the Unseelie boo and hiss.

It's only then that I realize how big our audience was.

I glance over my shoulder at Reina, who's still on her knees, being tended to by her two male bodyguards. Inara has her arms crossed over her chest and a murderous look twists her face into something truly terrifying.

"That was crazy-wicked," Mack whispers. "She's had her nose done three times already; I bet she's livid, along with half the Fae Courts. Now get ready."

The panicky tone of her voice puts me on edge. "Ready? For what?"

Reina is the typical bully who can dish it out but can't take it. She's still crumpled on the ground in dramatic fashion. No way she comes after me in that state.

Mack shakes her head at me. "Inara has already unofficially chosen Reina as her shadow, so she's under the protection of the Elite Six."

The elite who? Nope. I don't even want to know. The less I know about this pretentious school before I leave, the better.

"I didn't mean to piss off the *Elite Six*. I just thought, since I wouldn't be here . . ."

Mack's eyes go wide. "Who told you that?"

"You . . . did?" *Uh oh.* A pit of dread forms in my gut. "You said I had to be one of the first fifty students out of the lake or . . . they would kick me out?"

The Summer Evermore comes up beside me, one side of his mouth quirked. His gold ear cuff glints along his pointed ears. "That's true, but we also have a bravery clause. If any of the participants show extreme and selfless acts of courage, a court may petition to have them stay."

Shit. My mouth goes dry as Mack says, "Rhaegar petitioned for you to enter the Selection." She nods at the Summer Evermore before turning back to me. "You're still a shadow candidate . . . although anyone who chooses you now will risk the wrath of the Six."

There's that stupid name again. I barely keep from rolling my eyes as I say, "What's the Elite Six?"

She lets out an exasperated sigh that blows her pink and brown bangs away from her forehead. "This school is ruled by six incredibly powerful Unseelie: Inara Winterspell, her twin brother, Bane Winterspell, and the Winter Prince, all Winter Court. And . . . see that girl?"

I follow her gaze to a beautiful Fae girl near the edge of the Unseelie crowd. She wears a gorgeous sable-black tunic embedded with diamonds in the shape of half-moons, her silver hair pulled back into an elaborate nest of braids. Half-moon earrings hang from her pointy ears, and a similar jewel sparkles from between her silver eyebrows.

"That's Eclipsa Skywell from the Lunar Court. And that boy there"—she points to a big Fae with dark brown hair that falls to his shoulders and huge moss-green eyes—"is Asher Grayscale, a dragon shifter and the prince's best friend."

I swallow as I watch Inara's two friends from earlier

whisper with her. "Let me guess; those two psycho girls I met earlier with Inara are part of the Elite Six?"

Mack nods as she flicks a quick, fearful glance toward the pack. "Only one, the vamp from the Mortal Beasts Court, Kimber Bloodstone. The other, a lycan girl named Lyra, isn't technically a member . . . but she's currently dating Bane, so they let her hang out with them. She'd love to make it the Elite Seven, but that will never happen."

An overwhelming mixture of conflicting emotions surges through me as I scan the rest of the Unseelie side. On one hand, I'm thankful I get to stay at the academy and not slave away in the Unseelie Courts. But I've also basically pissed off all the Unseelie, by the way they're all staring daggers into me.

Especially the Elite Six.

Fae-freaking-tastic. I'm so screwed.

But screwed or not, Aunt Vi would die if she knew I wasn't using manners. So I turn to Rhaegar and say, "Thank you for making sure I don't get kicked out."

He smiles, a nice, warm grin that somehow makes him even more beautiful. "It was nothing. Besides, I'm interested to see how you shake things up."

I raise a confused eyebrow, and Mack jumps in to explain. "This part is the official Selection, but most of us have already been claimed, unofficially, by an Evermore." She tilts her head to Basil, the Faun who was in the boat earlier. "Basil has already promised to claim me. But you . . . you're the wild card. You haven't been claimed, and no one really knows anything about you."

I release a nervous breath and sweep my gaze over the crowd. Thankfully, the Selection ceremony is well underway, and attention has drifted from me to the shadow candidates, who mill nervously near the front. I follow Mack to a spot near the back of the group.

When our names are called, we go stand on a small stage in a circle of crystals. A dark blue Fae, who introduces himself as Cronus, the Master of Ceremonies, reads out a little spiel on our lives. I try to focus on his words and not the deer antlers rising high above his head.

Unsurprisingly, the Unseelie choose the humans they deem cruel or cunning. I study their ranks, trying to catalogue the different courts. According to Wikipedia, the Unseelie are made up of Winter Court, Autumn Court, Lunar Court, Dusk Court, and the Mortal Beasts Court.

The Winter and Autumn students are easy to recognize; Winter wears silvers and blues and ivories and loads of fur, their hair varying shades of the same. Autumn Fae dress in Fall colors, orange and brown and red.

The Lunar and Dusk Courts are harder to pinpoint because the students dress similarly.

On our side, the Seelie side, the courts are what you would expect. Summer, who wear loads of green and gold, Spring, clad in vibrant pinks and yellows and purples. The Star Court wears light, gauzy clothes that sparkle under even minimal light. The Dawn Court sport colors of the sunrise, mainly orange and red, and Mythological Creatures Court have adopted earthy colors like juniper and coffee-brown.

The Mythological Creatures are fascinating. Along with centaurs and fauns, there are countless beasts from the storybooks like orcs, pixies, and even mermaids.

It's interesting, and if I wasn't about to be chosen like a slab of meat, I'd probably enjoy this part more.

When Mack enters the stage, several Seelie look interested in choosing her, but just as she predicted, she ends up with Basil. He smiles kindly at her during the process, running a hand through his short red hair. A pang of disappointment sweeps over me knowing I may not be as lucky.

I'm a loose cannon, a bad bet, and I'll be surprised if *anyone* selects me.

Still . . . my generally optimistic nature makes me hope. Maybe I'll be lucky enough to end up with an Evermore like Basil instead of Inara. Someone who thought to cover me with a blanket and actually looked sad when a human drowned.

I don't think that's asking too much from the universe to match me with someone who isn't spawned from Satan and surrounded by a pack of beautiful mean-girl sociopaths.

A girl can dream.

My name gets called near the end. As I walk up to take my place in the circle, the crowd goes silent. The bubble of heat still protects me from the wintry air, but goosebumps ridge my flesh anyway as the cruel gaze of the Evermore scrapes over me.

The boos start right away as Cronus calls out, "Who claims this mortal as their shadow?"

He has a flair for the dramatic, all grins and bows, but I can feel his anxiety all the way from here.

Right there with you, guy. I shift on my feet, nerves making it hard to stand still. My gut twists, and I wrap my arms around my chest to keep my arms from shaking. Now I know how cattle feel when they're auctioned off at livestock shows.

Maybe no one will choose me? What happens then?

My sprite zips above my head and hands off a tiny scroll to Cronus.

The Master of Ceremonies squints down at the scroll, held between his delicate blue fingers, and begins to read from it. "This human female is eighteen years old. She hails from the Tainted Zone. Her hobbies include hunting and stealing, and she was kicked out of her high school for assault. She's thin, but with proper food she could look decent."

I glare up at the sprite. Who made this bio?

"Although untrained in the fighting arts, she's feisty, mean, and prone to violence. All useful traits when you need your shadow to travel to the scourge lands for rare herbs, or desire protection from a darkling."

Feisty and mean? *Pfft.* I roll my eyes.

Cronus peers down at the scroll for a breath, frowns, and then rolls it up. "Any takers for this human?"

Wow. This is sad. Worse than all those times I was chosen last in gym class.

Compared to the illustrious bios of the other humans— private schools, numerous awards, speaks five languages, already accepted into Ivy League colleges—mine is pitiful, and if I didn't recognize how lacking my life was before, I'm all too aware now.

I'm tugging at my hoodie when a voice rings out . . . no, make that two voices.

"I claim her," both voices say.

Sure I misheard, I whip my head up to see who spoke . . . as does the rest of the crowd. The second I take in the Summer Evermore, Rhaegar, striding toward the stage, my face breaks into a sloppy grin.

The other Evermore walks on the opposite side of Rhaegar. She's the Lunar Court girl I admired earlier, the one with the crescent jewelry and beautiful silver hair.

Someone wants me. Two people, in fact. I barely manage to keep from fist pumping the air in triumph.

I. Am. Wanted.

I've already decided that if I get to choose, I'm going with the Summer Evermore. But I have no idea how this works. None of the other candidates had more than one Fae claim them.

"I claim this mortal for the Winter Prince," a *third* male voice chimes in.

Whoa. I glance to my left and nearly die of shock. My

former tormentor and rooftop crush stalks to the stage, his silver cloak rippling out across the snow behind him.

Where did *he* come from?

Everyone has gone completely still. I recognize the emotion tightening their faces: fear.

Everyone but Inara, who somehow manages to look even more homicidal than before as she watches him approach me. Maybe she has a thing for the Winter Prince's lackey.

For his part, he seems oblivious to the effect his presence has on the crowd.

Those arresting eyes lock onto mine and another strange shock carves up my spine, similar to what I felt when I touched the lock earlier and somehow broke it. A raw emotion burns through me, expectation and something . . . else.

Something so close to desire that I take the inside of my cheek between my molars and bite, hard, just to make it disappear.

When the metallic taste of blood chases away all emotions except loathing, I allow my gaze back on the offending Fae. He's still watching me as he strides up to the stage.

I match his glower with one of my own. *I'm not afraid of you.*

But my heart hammering in my chest says otherwise, and I'm ninety-nine percent sure he can hear it because a menacing grin carves his sharp jaw.

The cruel lilt of his lips chills my blood.

Cronus is looking from my potential Fae masters to me, his ears flickering back and forth. His expression a mixture of confusion and shock that undoubtedly matches my own.

Cronus waits until all three of the Fae are standing in front of me before he says, "We've never had three claimants before. I need to check with the sprites on what the academy guidelines state."

As Cronus confers with a swarm of sprites who yell over each other, I wait for my future to be decided.

Rhaegar cuts his eyes at my tormentor. "I thought the Winter Prince didn't lower himself to have mortal shadows."

My tormentor shrugs without tearing his gaze from my face. "The Winter Prince thinks having a mortal shadow might be fun."

Fun? I grind my jaw to keep from saying something stupid. I've already pissed off enough Fae today. Last thing I need is to publicly antagonize the emissary to the Winter Prince, or whatever title my tormentor carries.

"More like he wants to present his mate with a human plaything," the Lunar Court girl points out, glancing back at Inara, who looks ready to traipse up here and murder me with her bare hands.

Mate? For some reason this shocks me. I've never met this Winter Prince, but I already know he's just as cruel and hateful as Inara. Who else would have rules demanding death for stealing a single apple?

It's hard to imagine either of them finding someone to love. But I guess dark attracts dark.

"So why do you want her, Eclipsa?" Rhaegar asks. "I thought you said owning shadows was stupid?"

I study the Lunar Girl. She's one of the Elite Six, but she doesn't have the same cruel look as the rest.

Lunar Girl doesn't even acknowledge me as she says, "I like her spirit."

I hate the way they're talking around me as if I'm not here, but I'm playing nice so I ignore the urge to wave my hand and remind them.

Finally, Cronus shoos the sprites away and announces my fate. "I believe the rules state in this case, the human chooses who they want to shadow."

Thank. God.

My shoulders sag as relief pours through me. Well that makes this easy. I step forward, ready to shout Rhaegar's name, when my tormentor interrupts.

"That may be the rules of the Selection," he says, his unsettling silver-blue eyes never leaving mine. "But Evermore law dictates, technically, everything in the academy belongs to the prince from the ruling court."

Mother cracker.

I glare at him. Unlike last night, he wears all the finery of what I imagine an elite Fae wears, right down to the silver ceremonial armor that fits his lithe form and the sleek leather gloves covering his long fingers. And holy hell it's hot.

But the most luxurious clothes in the world couldn't hide the horrible soul beneath.

Then he turns to me and winks. The bastard *winks*. His blue-black eyelashes brushing his sharp cheekbones. And any bit of willpower I had left to play nice disappears.

"Don't you ever get tired of being ordered around?" I blurt. "Do this. Do that. Ruin this innocent human's life. You're . . . you're basically the Winter Prince's bitch."

I swear to God, the entire assembly goes dead quiet. The Lunar Court girl starts to grin, but then thinks better of it and slaps a hand over her mouth. Rhaegar's green eyes are twice their normal size, his pretty mouth gaping open.

My tormentor's nostrils flare, a muscle twitching beneath his clenched jaw.

Take that truth bomb and shove it where the sun don't shine.

With one last icy glance my direction, he turns to Rhaegar. "She's mine, and that's final."

Mine? Rhaegar turns to face the Winter Evermore, his jaw set. "I invoke the right of Nocturus."

A collective gasp from the crowd stirs the air.

"What's Nocturus?" I whisper to Cronus, who's too busy conferring with the sprites to hear me.

A moment later, he turns to the three Fae vying for me. "Nocturus has been invoked. Because Rhaegar was the first to claim this mortal, he keeps her as his shadow until Samhain, when the battle will be held under the full moon." *Keep me? Battle?* He turns to the Lunar Court Fae. "Eclipsa Skywell, do you claim Nocturus as well?"

My heartbeat jackhammers against my skull. What's happening? What's Nocturus? It sounds horrible, if I'm being honest with myself.

Eclipsa shakes her head, a sly look on her face. "It wouldn't be fair to either of them if they had to fight me."

Despite my panic, her bravado makes me smile.

A sudden blizzard begins to rage, giant snowflakes dumping from the sky and pummeling the bubble of warmth that's been basically keeping me alive. I watch in horror as one snowflake pierces the shell, then another, until a bitter cold forces itself into my wet clothes and penetrates my bones.

Rhaegar rushes me off stage and hands me off to Mack, with a quick warning to go straight to our dorms.

"I'd go to hell right now if it was warm," I mutter, conjuring a tight smile from Rhaegar. Rhaegar does another warmth spell on me, but the weather is so bad that it has little effect this time.

"What's Nocturus?" I ask Mack, desperate for someone to tell me what the heck is happening.

Apparently still in shock, Mack takes a few seconds to compose herself enough to answer. "It's a magical battle held during Samhain."

By brain is reeling. Do I dare ask what Samhain is?

She must read my confusion because she says, "The holiday celebrating the start of winter? No? Not ringing a bell?"

I shrug hopelessly, and then a thought occurs to me. "How do they decide a winner?"

"No, they . . ." She brushes a hot pink strand of hair behind her ear. "They fight until one of the combatants yields . . . or dies."

"Do the Fae ever choose the death option?" I ask, glancing over at Rhaegar.

"They do if they want to keep their honor."

My heart sinks. The last thing I want, the last thing I *need*, is some Evermore dying for me in a stupid magical battle.

This is decidedly *not* a good start to my first day.

"What about the other girl?" I ask. "From the Lunar Court?"

A wry smile tugs on Mack's lips. "You mean the renowned Lunar Court assassin, Eclipsa Skywell?"

I swallow. "Assassin?"

"Yep. I heard every half-moon jewel on her body stands for a kill. You should probably be glad she's no longer in the running to be your keeper."

I groan. Today is quickly becoming the worst day ever. And I say that as someone who's been kidnapped, caged, and nearly sold.

With my sprite guide in tow, shrieking every Fae curse word in the book, we follow the rest of the group around the academy and to our dorms.

When we're far enough away from the Fae students that their supernatural hearing won't pick up our conversation, I say, "Guess the Winter Prince, wherever he's hiding, is having a bad day. Can someone please go cheer him up so we can have some sun?"

Mack halts.

"Do you really not know who the Winter Prince is?" she asks, concern etched across her face.

Dickwad supreme? But the serious tone of her voice makes me swallow the sarcastic retort on my tongue.

"The Evermore you were taunting back there isn't the Winter Prince's bitch," she continues, exasperation making her voice raise an octave. "He *is* the Winter Prince, the most powerful and wicked Evermore in this school, and you just publicly insulted him."

No, no, no. This can't be happening. "But . . . he talked about himself in third person, for Fae's sake! Who does that?"

"The Winter Prince and heir to the Winter Court," she replies. "He does that."

As we trudge after the group, our boots crunching the snow, one thought echoes through my mind.

Worst. Day. Ever.

16

By the time we make it to the mortal dormitory, the blizzard has made visibility less than two feet. *Thanks moody Winter Prince.* I'm still having trouble believing the Fae I met in the forest is the Winter Prince, but it makes sense.

It also means I've not only pissed off the entire Unseelie side of the academy, but I've publicly humiliated their leader. And something tells me they won't let that stand.

Way to kick off this dumpster fire properly, Summer. And on the very first day. I should win an award for self-sabotage.

The Seelie mortal dormitory sits just over a hill near the main academy building. A well-kept castle that looks like it was taken straight from the University of Oxford, the building is hedged in by forest on three sides and overlooks a frozen pond.

Despite the snow icing the roof and lining the windowsills, green ivy covers the stonework, and violets fill the gardens, a burst of purple and yellow color against the bleached world. Smoke curls from several chimneys and trickles lazily into the cloudy sky.

The plaque above the steel-gray painted door reads *Hall of Shadows*.

Quaint.

"There's another Seelie mortal dorm close by," Mack explains. "This one houses mainly shadows under the Summer and Mythological Creatures Courts' protection."

Inside, we're handed stylish silver cuff bracelets with the Seelie sigil, a sun held by two harpies. Mack explains we don't take the true sigil of the Evermore we shadow until second year, since we can be traded between Evermore in the same court. It's less complicated this way.

"Being traded isn't ideal, but it's not that bad," Mack adds as I follow her up a winding set of stairs and pretend not to be winded. "If it happens, it's usually within the first month."

She says that a lot. It's not that bad. They're not that bad. Meanwhile, I think the idea of being passed around like Pokémon cards is demeaning, but whatev.

"But," she continues, her tone lowering as she grows serious. "Never, ever sleep with your Fae keeper, or any Fae, for that matter. Once you do, you're expelled."

"Why do they care?"

"I don't know, but that's been drilled into my head since the moment my parents gave me their awkward speech on sex. It was all, hey, Mack, here's a packet of condoms and five different forms of birth control. Keep a harem of human men, or women, or both for all we care. But never, under any circumstances, let a Fae male seduce you."

"Your parents sound . . . not like my aunts at all."

"Yeah, they're cool when it comes to that stuff." She shrugs. "Just remember what I said. The Evermore males lay bets on all of us. Don't fall for one no matter how charming."

"That's *so* not going to be a problem," I promise. I don't point out how unfair that rule is. A girl sleeps with a male and *she's* the one who's bad?

Then again, everything here is unfair to humans in some way.

"That's why I'm glad my keeper is Basil," Mack adds. "If the Winter Prince had chosen me, my panties would *accidentally* drop every time we were alone together." A wicked grin brightens her face. "You know what they say about male Fae? The longer the ears . . ."

I snort, although I get the feeling she'll do whatever it takes to keep her place here. Including resisting the prince's magnetic good looks and long . . . *ears*.

Mack's dorm room is on the third floor. Every tiny apartment has a fireplace with a magically fed fire that never dies —they don't want their human slaves freezing to death—and delicious warmth assails me as soon as we enter Mack's room.

"This cold is sapping away what's left of my soul," I groan, rubbing my frozen fingers together.

Mack glances sideways at me. "Just wait. Ever seen snow so thick it's like an avalanche from the sky? I have."

Fantastic.

Mack does a twirl around the room, showing off the tiny chamber. I wiggle my nose. It reeks of mothballs and magic— a metallic, cloying scent, like lilies and copper. Now that I've been around magic, I'm starting to recognize its smell.

A brass bunk bed presses against the far wall. Her previous roommate, a dour girl with both her ears surgically enhanced to look Fae, she explains, has already moved her stuff to one of the two Unseelie dorms on campus.

Twin cedar nightstands, a matching dresser, and a desk crowd the room. Aged, peeling wallpaper with a pattern of beautiful centaur females frolicking in a meadow covers the walls.

We take a moment to warm up. While I swaddle myself in every blanket available and then position myself close to the fire, she examines my tattoo. Apparently none of the other shadows have one, at least not a full sleeve marking. Her eyes grow wide as she points out the Winter Prince's personal emblem—an owl with two daggers—swirled inside the intricate lines.

Another thing to make me stand out from the crowd. Yay.

Before, I couldn't muster the courage to look at the tattoo. Now I take in the dark swirls running down my right arm. The moment my gaze slides over the gold and black lines, the Winter Prince's words ring through my skull.

She's mine.

A surge of bitterness blasts up my middle. I've been branded as his, and even if Rhaegar wins the Nocturus and I stay his shadow, this mark will claim me as property of the Winter Prince until I graduate.

Mack must read my upset expression because she frowns. Then her face brightens. "When I visit my parents in a few months I can ask them if there's a way to hide the prince's brand. You won't be able to erase it, but you shouldn't have to see it all the time."

"Wait? We can go home?" Hope makes my voice squeaky.

She bites her lip. "Some of us can leave Everwilde. But most . . ." Her gaze darts to my marked arm. "I have a pass because my parents are legacies, and they're still in touch with their Evermore benefactors. But a pass home is rare."

I pretend to rearrange my burrito blanket to hide my disappointment. "That's okay. I'm not sure what I would say to my family if I could go back."

She squeezes my hand. "I'll have my parents talk to their benefactors and see if they might be able to secure you a pass home."

For some reason, her kindness tightens my throat until I realize I'm one more hand squeeze away from crying.

Before I can embarrass myself, she marches across the floor, hands on her hips.

"On to the important stuff." She drags a Louis Vuitton suitcase across the hardwood floor and flops it open. "We need to educate you on everything Evermore over the weekend."

I'd nearly forgotten it was Friday. Usually I spent the weekends hunting, watching the kids, or occasionally working at the feed store with Vi. "Educate me?"

"Yep. Our sole purpose, aside from learning to protect the Evermore, is to shadow the students and make sure all their wants are taken care of. And since you somehow landed the two most sought after Evermore in school, your life here depends on being helpful. Next Friday is the first academic test."

Test? I release a long, ragged sigh. Friday is supposed to be a happy day. "You said the first. Does that mean there are more?"

"Yep. The first one is basically like an entrance exam to make sure we know the fundamental stuff. But we attend classes like regular school in the morning, and then shadow our keepers in the afternoon classes. And we're tested just like regular school."

Splendid.

As if Mack can sense my panic, she adds, "Not to put the fear of Oberon in you, but you need to take this first test seriously. The rest are for a grade, but this one is pass or fail. Meaning you're one slip-up away from being sent to the scourge. And kids that go there . . . they never return."

"I did okay in high school," I point out, purposefully omitting that one ridiculous algebra test . . .

"Know what the darkening ceremony is? How about the difference between a fiddler mushroom and a fennick mushroom? Because they sound similar, but one will enhance a potion, and the other releases spores that poison everyone within thirty feet."

I shake my head. *Way out of my element here.*

She pats the floor next to where she sits, a MacBook with pink and teal leopard skin open on her lap. "Then come. Time to cram a year's worth of studies into your brain. All of the other students attended a 'Summer camp' every year run by the Evermore where we learned most of the basic stuff. But I brought along some materials as a refresher. We can use those until your books show up."

I grin; I can already tell Mack is a great student. I'd bet anything she was top of her class in high school.

My heart clenches as I remember how much I used to love school. I wasn't a next-level-overachiever like Mack, but I liked learning about worlds outside our small little town.

"I can help you study this weekend and then in the off hours this week," she continues, all business. "We shadow our keepers from after lunch to sundown, then an hour of fight training. After that, the rest of the time is ours."

"How generous," I mutter. "Wait, back up. Fight training?"

"Yeah. That's what we do as shadows. Protect our charge."

"But, they're Fae, basically gods. Why do they need *us* to protect *them*?"

"Obviously you've never seen darklings around Fae," she says. "Something about the Fae's magic makes the darklings go into a feeding frenzy."

"Yeah, but the Fae have magic, and they're infinitely stronger than us."

"True, but darklings are incredibly hard to kill, and only one thing can finish them off. Know what that is?"

I shrug.

"Here's a hint: it kills Fae too."

"Iron?" I offer.

"Exactly. A Fae can't get within ten feet of the stuff. But guess who can?"

"Us."

She nods. "And infused with oils from rowan berries and the ash tree? Absolutely lethal. So . . ." She stretches her arms as a proud smile splits her lips. "In short, they may be gods, but they need us."

"Could have fooled me." Resigned to enduring a weekend of studying, I sit cross-legged beside her on the floor and eye the clothes inside her suitcase. "Wait, I thought we couldn't bring anything but the clothes on our backs?"

She snorts. "We were allowed to send our bags months ago to be inspected and approved. You didn't . . ." The truth dawns in her eyes, and she bites her lip. "Of course you didn't have time. So that means you have . . . nothing?"

I sweep a hand over my outfit. "Just my lucky hoody, my ass-kicking boots, and my awesome self."

Her gaze slides to the mound of clothes in her suitcase. "I would let you borrow an outfit, but I don't think it would fit."

She's right. She's short and curvy; I'm tall and one lost meal away from withering into full-blown starvation.

"Anyway," she continues. "That's at the bottom of our priorities. First thing we need to do is give you the rundown on this place and the rules."

I watch as she pulls out a manila envelope with glossy 8x10 photos from the nearby desk. When she hands me the first picture and I spy the face of Inara grinning menacingly at me, I nearly recoil, fighting the urge to rip the picture into tiny shreds.

It doesn't help that the pictures are imbued with some sort of magic so that Inara's face actually changes from a smile to a sneer inside my hands.

"Be gone, Satan," I whisper, flipping Inara's face onto the ground.

"Here." Mack slides an entire stack of portraits toward me. "Memorize these. They have every Evermore student in the school, along with their court, ranking, and powers on the back."

"This will take years," I grumble.

"You don't have years. You have ten minutes."

I glare at my bossy new roommate overlord as she hops up, rifles through her clothes, and then pulls out a Nespresso coffee maker. "Technically we're not supposed to bring any modern technology that isn't school related to the academy, but everyone does it. Memorize those bios and you get one of these bad boys."

She waggles a shiny orange espresso pod in my face.

Hell. Yes. I haven't had coffee in years, and the chance of a fresh cup fills me with motivation. After making her show me how it works—to make sure it indeed can make coffee—I blow through the photos, carefully repeating details in my head until I'm pretty sure I know them by heart.

When I set the stack down, Mack flicks up her eyebrows. "You still have a minute."

"I don't need a minute. I need some of that bean juice you're hoarding. So test me and then let's get over-caffeinated in this *beotch*."

"Okay, hot shot. Give me Rhaegar Moorland's story."

"Pointy ears, super gorgeous, enjoys strutting around being ogled and saving damsels in distress?" Her eyes narrow and I laugh, adding, "Member of the Summer Court, his father is hand of the Summer King, who has no heirs, by the way, making Rhaegar presumptive heir to the Summer Throne."

Her nose crinkles. "Anything else?"

"His elemental powers include fire and earth magic, his

shifter form is a hawk, his best friend is your keeper, Basil, his mortal enemy is the Winter Prince . . . and you can bounce a coin off his ass."

Mack laughs, a deep, beautiful belly laugh that solidifies my adoration for her. Then she takes a pink sharpie from a ziplock baggie of pens and actually writes that on the back of Rhaegar's photo.

How in the world I landed one of the coolest humans in Everwilde as a roommate and friend is beyond me. I keep waiting for the other shoe to drop. For her to yell surprise and then dump sheep's blood or something on me.

Girls like Mack don't befriend people like me. It just doesn't happen. Except, apparently, in Everwilde.

I slay the rest of the quiz, impressing even myself. When we get to the Winter Prince, I hesitate. My anger messes with my memory as I try to recall the details listed on the back of his picture.

Then something occurs to me. "Wait. His last name is listed—Sylverfrost. But there's no first name."

"In Everwilde, names have immense power. No one knows the prince's true first name. And he's never told anyone." She's whispering as if he can hear us. "Now—" She snaps her fingers. "Stop stalling and give me his deets."

"Heir to the Winter Throne, and leader of the Elite Unseelie Six," I begin, wracking my brain for the rest. His list of magical skills was longer than most. "Powers include turning me into a popsicle and shifting into winter animals, elemental powers include ice, storms, and wind. Best friend is Asher Grayscale, a dragon shifter, and his familiar is a snowy owl. It's rumored the prince can fly, has healing powers, and he's mated to the daughter of the Winter Court's general, Inara Winterspell. What am I missing?"

I pretend to think for a moment. "Oh, right. Total douche canoe."

Mack picks up his photo and shivers, making a face. "I am not going to write that on the back, in case he's watching. I've heard his powers are so strong and volatile that even his father is scared of him."

Rolling my eyes, I snatch his picture away.

Admittedly, he looks hot in his portrait. A crown of jagged ice sits atop a mop of blue-black hair, a few dark curls falling around sharp ears. Dark lashes frame serious blue eyes ringed with silver, and a snow-white owl, similar to the one that shadows me on the other side, perches on his shoulder.

Frowning, I stick out my tongue. I swear one corner of his lips quirk.

Why do you want me as your shadow? I think, wishing he could answer. *Why me?*

Instead of responding, his magical picture smirks cruelly at me. A moment later, the owl takes off, disappearing from the picture altogether and sending a single feather floating to the dusty floor.

A *real* feather. On our floor. What the eff?

Dread coils around my gut, and I crumple the photo into a ball and then toss it into the trash bin.

Not long after, a white owl lands in the tree outside our window where a blizzard still rages. Fluffing out its wings, the owl stares into our room until I stomp over and rip the emerald-green drapes closed.

Suddenly, magic isn't so cool anymore.

"All right," I growl as Mack carries over a steaming cup of coffee. "What next?"

I'm ready to slay my studies so when Rhaegar wins the Nocturus, I'll be the best shadow to him in Everwilde. It's the least I can do for Rhaegar saving me from Mr. Douche Canoe.

And Rhaegar has to win. If he doesn't . . .

Nope. Not even imagining my future then.

17

"**M**y brain can't take anymore," I mumble, kneading my knuckles into my temples. We're entrenched on Mack's bottom bunk, surrounded by empty Sour Patch Kids packages, Pringle cans, and a near-empty liter of orange Crush.

Thank God, her parents sent a care package full of her favorite treats, which we've managed to nearly demolish over the weekend.

We've also slammed a kajillion cups of coffee and my heart twitches weirdly in my chest.

"Almost done for tonight," Mack promises.

I glare at the windowpanes being pelted by relentless snow. "Are you sure it's night time? It could be midday for all we know."

Mack turns her wrist to flash a hot-pink watch. "It's set to Everwilde time."

The watch face shows just after midnight.

We've already blown through elemental magic and soul magic, the two main types used by the Evermore, and are deep into the history of the Fae courts. It feels like months have passed, not days.

"Besides," I continue, talking through a yawn. "What more is there to know? Summer hates Winter; Winter hates Summer. They've basically started every single war between Seelie and Unseelie since the dawn of time."

"And the upcoming Nocturus may start another war," Mack adds nonchalantly.

"Kill me now," I moan.

Mack laughs. Then her expression gets all serious, and she flips the screen of her laptop to face me, pointing at the map of what used to be the western half of the United States but is now Everwilde territory. "Name the courts and their territories."

I spout off the courts in each location as she watches proudly. The academy sits in the center of all the territories, a neutral Island surrounded by a magical sea.

In addition to the huge wall and wards surrounding the academy, the waters are enchanted with protection spells. All meant to keep the darklings out.

There are neutral cities, as well, off the nearby coasts, but first year Evermore students rarely leave campus.

With an impressed grin, Mack shuts her MacBook. "Enough for tonight. Don't want your brain exploding all over the room. You need to be fresh for your first day of school tomorrow."

Ugh. That. I've never felt so nervous about starting school before, and the knot of anxiety I've had since I arrived tightens at the thought.

Despite my nerves, I fall asleep almost immediately. I wake up a few hours later. Mack snores above me, tiny snorts that make me grin.

Too restless to fall back asleep, I pull out the photo of my parents from where I stashed it under my mattress. The light is too dim to see much, so I pad to the window until moon-light washes over the picture.

Fingerprints streak the glossy surface. I stare down at the people I'm supposed to remember, a ragged sigh escaping my lips. It took five years after my parents were murdered to finally look at their faces without reliving the night they died.

And that's only because I ran away from the farm and found someone in Fort Worth, a woman who specialized in forbidden Everwilde artifacts. I had nothing to pay her, but she took pity on me and gave me the necklace around my neck to draw the tragic memory of my parents' death away.

Only, the ruby stripped all my memories of them, right down to what they looked like, what their voices sounded like, how they smiled. I realized my mistake immediately, but when I returned to look for the woman, she was gone.

The owner of the diner next door told me she was a dirty-blood, a half-Fae half-human, and that a crowd had gathered around her apartment above her shop while she slept and scared her away.

Then he spit at her blue door and said, "Good riddance."

Dirty-bloods don't last long in the Tainted Zone. By law they're not supposed to live in human lands, and the Fae pay handsomely in magical artifacts for information that leads to the capture and deportation of one back to Everwilde.

Meanwhile, full-blooded Fae with visas live in the Untouched Zone where they're treated like celebrities.

"Gosh, I'm glad you guys aren't alive to see how far we've fallen," I say to the picture, waving it back and forth as I try to conjure a memory—any memory—of them.

But just like every other time, nothing surfaces. I touch my necklace, cool and hard between my breasts. I've pushed aside what happened in the lake because the memory is too painful, but now, I can't help but wonder if there's something to my pendant beyond the stored memory.

Setting the photo on the windowsill, I press my hands over the glass, the pane startlingly cold. Outside, snow drizzles the air, but there's something almost peaceful about it. In the distance, the half-moon glints off the frozen surface of the lake.

I can't see the main campus building from here, but it's out there. And in a few short hours, I'll be inside the academy's walls.

The familiar nervous pang begins in my gut as I start mulling over what my first day will be like. All the usual worries flash through my mind.

Will I know anyone in my classes? What if I'm still too far behind to understand what they teach? How will I find my way around?

Then my thoughts take a dark turn. What if I see the Winter Prince? We've been holed up inside our dorm for two days, long enough to nearly forget the possessive way he claimed me.

But now . . . well now the thought of being near him fills me with anxiety. The scrape of his sword from its scabbard when he nearly executed me echoes inside my skull. The way he looked at me earlier, the way he pervades my mind . . .

All at once, a dizziness washes over me. My thoughts go blank. My vision dark. I blink and suddenly I'm in someone else's room. A huge, opulent chamber ten times the size of my dorm room.

I'm not actually there, I realize. I'm in someone else's mind. A male someone. Seeing what they're seeing. Feeling what they're feeling.

Speaking of feeling . . . oh my God . . . he, whoever he is, is sitting in bed without a shred of clothes.

He looks to his right, and I recognize the royal blue hair spilled over the pillow. The blue lips, smeared slightly and swollen, like they've been kissed hard.

AUDREY GREY

Inara.

She looks up at him, her big dewy white eyes full of adoration. But all he feels is disgust. I can sense the dark emotion swirling around him. Whoever this is, he's awash in darkness. Beyond that, there's a cold indifference inside him.

Layers and layers of it, like a shield.

He slips from bed, still fully naked, and saunters over to the fireplace. I can feel the warmth of the flames kissing his bare skin. Can feel the cold lurking beneath his flesh.

"I don't know why you insist on that stupid fire," Inara says. "Doesn't the heat bother you?"

"I like looking at it," he answers in a distorted voice. Being inside his head, his words sound like they come from underwater.

"You like looking at it?" The derision in her tone annoys him, but she sounds oblivious. "You're so weird sometimes."

"Get out."

"Excuse me?"

"Leave."

Inara huffs as she hunts around the bed for her clothes. When she's zipped back into her dress—a silver, sequined thing that looks gorgeous on her—she glides over to him, making sure he notices the way the slippery fabric hugs her hips.

He does. I can feel his desire rise along with his disgust.

"Didn't you like what we did earlier?" she purrs, stroking a hand down his shoulder.

"I did," he admits coldly. "And now I would like for you to leave."

Anger flashes in her eyes, and she bares her teeth at him. "You're a dick."

He turns and stares into the fire as she leaves. I can feel his mind calm as he watches the flames dance and shiver, even as the heat repulses him. There's a mirror just above the mantle, and I desperately try to will him to move into a position where I can make out who's head I'm in.

Instead, he reaches up and retrieves something hidden inside a silver heart-shaped box. Little foxes and deer are engraved on the sides, the inside red velvet.

As he peers down at what he took, I see it's a picture. Of a girl . . .

I gasp when I make out the long, wavy blonde-white hair tumbling over one shoulder. The hazel eyes that can't quite hide their sadness. The wide nose I hate and lips one might call kissable. A little scar indents the skin just above my mouth.

Me. He's looking at a picture of me. A school portrait taken my sophomore year. My heart spikes into my throat as I recall how it just went missing one day. I looked everywhere for it because my hair actually cooperated, for once, and my skin was clear. Making it my best school photo ever.

That was over two years ago.

My suspicions are further confirmed when I see the condition of the photo. It looks worn. Fingerprints dull the surface. The edges are curled, the lacquer from one side peeling back.

Whoever this is, he's looked at my picture a lot. I stare at the two hands he uses to hold the photo, careful to only touch the edges. Soft white half-moons ridge his slender, neat fingernails.

Emotions slam through him as he stares at me. Darkness. Confusion. Rage. Despair. And something else. Something so powerful it eats at him. But I can't decipher the emotion.

What the hell?

Then he calmly tilts the photo toward the fire until one of the edges erupts in flames. A surge of loss rises up inside him, followed by relief as my face burns away to nothing.

Only when the heat blisters his thumb does he finally

release my photo. The moment my image disappears inside the licking orange flames, a ragged sigh escapes his lips.

Flicking his hand toward the fire, he sends a howling wind of ice and snow to snuff out the flames.

When he glances at himself in the mirror, I nearly scream.

The Winter Prince stares back at me, and it feels like those mournful eyes are looking straight into my soul.

It feels like he can see me.

I don't know if it's the pure terror hurtling through my veins, but whatever connection I have to him severs. I'm no longer in his room, but back in mine. Standing right where I was before, by the window, my hands pressed against the cold pane.

Only now it's freezing inside our room, and when I turn around to flee back to my bed and its mound of covers, I see why.

The magical fire that never extinguishes has died.

I 'm a bundle of nervous energy as Mack and I walk to class through a wooded path, shadowed by one very angry sprite. Her name is Ruby, but I've learned little else about her. It's hard to make conversation when she's continuously rattling off what have to be curses in a totally different language while darting around our heads.

I also watched her chug a tiny thimbleful of brambleberry liquor earlier and then give the world's largest belch.

Mack's sprite, on the other hand, is actually helpful. Thornilia delivered Mack a flaky raspberry tart this morning, and she must have hustled because it was still warm, steam curling from the paper sleeve around it. Then Thornilia helped Mack pick out an outfit, steamed it, and braided her hair, weaving tiny winter roses through her dark strands.

She even did some cleaning spell on my hoodie and jeans.

Of course, she got the go-getting, hair-braiding, sober sprite while I got the tiny trash-talking lush.

A large group of human shadows from the second Seelie dorm walk up ahead. When Mack and her sprite hurry to join them, I slow down, enjoying the moment to myself.

My sprite wandered off a moment ago—I actually think she may have passed out beneath a tree. Normally I'd be worried, but the path from our dorms to the main campus has a warm shell of magic around it, and most of the snow has been cleared.

Aside from the crunch of my boots on the gravel trail, the forest is quiet.

With the sudden silence, last night's events flicker across my mind. The entire ordeal seems like a dream. So much so that I'm starting to wonder if it was one. Only the fire did, in fact, go out, and the dorm monitor said he'd never seen that happen before.

That can't be a coincidence. Right?

Inside the main academy, we cut through the commons to grab breakfast. Other than a few humans, the wood-paneled halls are empty. It's nearly noon—Fae don't rise until late—and my stomach has been growling for hours.

After wolfing down two hard rolls, a strange yet heavenly winter fruit called a pink-melon, and an odd assortment of nuts and cheese, I glare at the spread of tea packets and hot water, beyond disappointed in the lack of coffee.

Of course the Fae drink watered down varieties of tea. Most I've never even heard of.

My caffeine addiction aside, I'm starting to relax. They're actually feeding us. And no one has tried to freeze me in place and part my head from my body. So there's that.

Once we make it to the lower levels where the mortal studies take place and I see that the hall is packed with humans but very few Fae, the knot of unease that's been tightening with every step deeper into the academy loosens.

Maybe I won't have to see the Winter Prince today.

Maybe he's forgotten all about me and the Nocturus, and I can just avoid him for the rest of my life. Although that's going to be hard if I keep falling into his mind.

I still can't get over how weird that was, even if, when it happened, it felt so normal. Like I had done it hundreds of times before. Like it was . . . natural to slip inside the mind of the most terrifying Fae on campus while he's naked and in bed with another girl.

And, holy Fae balls. If Inara knew I somehow jumped inside her boyfriend's head and witnessed her march of shame as he kicked her out—well, I'm pretty sure she'd claw out my eyes.

"Hey. You okay?" Mack asks as she smooths an already perfect strand of chocolate-brown hair behind her ear.

Biting my lip, I shift the backpack across my shoulders. The books weighing down my new, hunter green backpack came this morning, along with the bill for said items, and a schedule.

I haven't even had time to freak out about the debt yet. The moment I laid eyes on my courses, the reality of the next four years all came crashing down.

The paper hasn't left my sweat-stained hands ever since.

For the hundredth time, I glance down at it, trying to read through sweat-smeared print even though I know my schedule now by heart.

1st Period Faerie Courts and History
2nd Period Gaelic Language Studies
3rd Period Faerie Anatomy and Physiology
4th Period Combat Theory
Lunch
5th Period Understanding the Modern Mortal World
6th Period Mythological Creatures
7th Period Potions and Poisons
8th Period Properties of Magic: Elemental and Soulmancy
9th Period Combat Skills

I've also been assigned three extra shadow training sessions a week. The one-and-a-half hour sessions are before regular classes. Thank God the Fae don't wake up until around noon, which is when school starts, or I'd be condemned to a year of early-morning sparring sessions.

Mack smooths the cute cream jumper she wears and then flashes me a smile. "You'll do great. Just don't punch anyone or call anyone a bitch."

I cringe, wishing I hadn't eaten the rolls as a wave of nausea crashes over me.

When she sees my look, she grabs me by the shoulders. "You'll slay your classes. Just take as many notes as possible and I can help later with anything you don't understand. Okay? See you in Combat Theory."

Fourth period is our only class together before lunch. I watch her go and then search for my locker. After finally finding it—no thanks to Ruby, who I last saw frolicking in a tray of oatmeal—I run to my class on the second floor.

And, of course, I'm the last one to walk in. Right before class starts.

According to the name scrawled over the chalkboard, my teacher is Professor Hawthorn. She peers at me behind thick, wire-rimmed glasses. She's tall with prominent ears longer than most Fae, bright red hair pulled into a french-braid, and jade skin. "Glad you could make it . . . ?"

"Summer," I say as I slide into the only empty seat in the front and begin taking my books out of my backpack. Two girls snicker behind me.

Someone mutters, "Trailer Park."

I glance back to discover Reina at a desk whispering with another girl I don't recognize. A white bandage covers Reina's nose, the skin around the bandage purple and swollen, and she sports two black eyes.

I'd almost forgotten a broken nose did that.

"Wow," I say. "That looks painful. You should probably put some ice on that."

Someone laughs, and then Mrs. Hawthorn calls out, "Enough! Any student who speaks out of turn will be glamoured into silence. Do it again and you'll find yourself in Headmistress Lepidonis's office. Understood?"

The girl beside Reina frowns at Mrs. Hawthorn. "I thought you were only allowed to glamour us if we try to escape or harm ourselves?"

The smugness of her tone grates on my nerves. Apparently, it does the same to Hawthorn's because she marches toward the girl, looming over her.

"Lily Wright, this is my classroom and I can do whatever I want to you."

"I would tell someone," Lily insists quietly.

"Would you now?" Pushing up her glasses, Mrs. Hawthorn leans down, causing the girl to shrink low in her seat. "How would you do that when I've glamoured you into silence?"

The class goes completely still. Lily suddenly clutches at her throat. Her mouth opens . . . but not a word comes out.

Grinning, Mrs. Hawthorn breezes up the aisle and waves her hand, causing one word to appear over the chalkboard: power.

"The first lesson is this," she calls out. "In Fae society, power is everything. We rise and fall with our ability to create it, wield it, and retain it. What are the three main components of power?" When no one says a word, she adds, "Anyone? Or is this entire class suddenly glamoured into silence too?"

"Magic?" someone calls out.

She nods. "Yes, magic in our society is very important to retaining power. That is why the Evermore, the highest ranking Fae in each court, do what?"

"They make rules allowing only their kind to perform a renewal ceremony," Reina proudly answers. "Every time an Evermore renews, their power increases, while the magic of the lesser Fae has been slowly weakening over generations as it dies out with them."

"Yes," Mrs. Hawthorn says. "Controlled renewal is a controversial yet very effective rule that's been in place for centuries."

Renewal? I open my textbook and quickly search the glossary in the back until I find the word.

Renewal: When a Faerie's soul enters a new body. The soul retains any magic from previous lives, and, over time, can generate powerful magic. The Faerie lifespan typically runs around a thousand years, so renewal ceremonies are held every millennium.

That explains the name, at least. Evermore. Because they will literally live ever-freaking-more, body hopping like the characters in a bad science fiction movie. The idea weirds me out.

Someone calls my name, bringing me back to reality.

Mrs. Hawthorn stares at me expectantly. "Are you with us now, Summer? Good. I asked what the second rule of power is. The rest of the class doesn't know. Do you?"

Accordingly, my mind goes blank. I pinch my leg beneath my desk to refocus my thoughts. Who do I know that has power . . . ? Cal and his father immediately come to mind. I'd never wondered how, exactly, they came into such power.

They didn't have magic. They had money, of course. But it was more than that . . .

"Influence?" I say.

She raises an eyebrow. "It that a question or an answer? If you want me to believe what you say, perhaps you should learn to influence me."

Someone snickers, but she holds up a hand. "The delivery needs work, but Summer is right; influence is the second component of power. With enough magic, anyone can make someone do something. But if you can learn to influence them instead, to make them think your goal is what they desire most, you are one step closer to ultimate power. Strong magic and the skill of influence is a dangerous combination."

"And the third component of power?" Reina asks, pencil poised over her notebook, ready to scribble down the answer and learn world domination. God help us all.

Mrs. Hawthorn's lips curve into a grin that doesn't quite reach her eyes. "The first student who answers that correctly will receive an automatic A in this class. But"—she raises a hand in protest as the class tries to throw out answers—"answer carefully because you only get one opportunity."

The voices go quiet as she adds the first two components of power—magic and influence—on the chalkboard. Number three goes just below.

As she has us open our books to chapter one, I stare at the empty number three spot, wondering what the third component could be.

If surviving the Fae requires power, then I should probably learn the answer. And, judging by the way Reina and her friend not-so-quietly whisper about me, I should find it soon.

19

"I've seen zombie movies with less gore," Mack declares, her nose scrunched. "The darkling just munched on the poor Fae girl's face like it was a deep-dish supreme pizza."

The girl sitting with us, Evelyn, a Summer Court shadow, groans and shoves her orange lunch tray across the table. "Thanks for that. I'd finally just managed to scrub that image from my brain."

I pluck the uneaten apple off her tray without even thinking. Hoarding food becomes an instinct when you've spent years starving. But the video seriously dampened my appetite, and I pocket the fruit for later.

Watching a human monster rip someone's face off has that effect.

I glance over at Evelyn. So far, she's the only shadow who will dare sit with us. Honestly, she's sweet but not incredibly bright, and I think she truly has no idea I'm the equivalent of social kryptonite. Mack said Evelyn comes from a long line of legacies and that her parents infused the school with a huge sum to get her admitted.

I don't doubt that for a moment. Everything she wears— from her sparkling diamond earrings to her immaculately fitted black pantsuit—looks expensive. Her vibrant red hair hangs just past her shoulders, the silky-smooth strands curling under. Not a split end in sight.

I finger the broken ends of my own wild, wavy hair, suddenly all too aware of its deficiencies.

Mack slurps her milk. "Half the class puked, but I thought it was cool."

I raise an eyebrow. "How was that cool?"

She shrugs. "It shows how important our jobs are. Why the Fae need us. They might treat us like dirt, but at the end of the day, they know we're the only ones who can protect them from those things."

She sounds like the combat teacher, Mr. Crayburn, who said we needed to understand what we're up against, and why protecting our Fae partners is so important.

Still, I wasn't expecting that level of violence from the darklings. Nor the speed. They moved so fast at times that they became blurs on video. The Fae were formidable, their magic splashing bursts of light into the camera. A few had weapons and they wielded them with expert skill.

But it wasn't enough. Not even close. The darklings seemed unaffected by the Fae's magic, and their speed allowed them to dodge the Fae's weapons with ease. Even when their weapons did hit their mark, the darklings seemed impervious to the steel blades.

The footage was taken inside a restaurant in an unnamed Everwilde city. None of the Fae had shadows.

It was a slaughter.

Evelyn shudders. "I saw a darkling once."

"Where?" Mack demands.

The charm bracelet on Evelyn's wrist tinkles as she makes a sweeping gesture with her hand. "Right here."

My eyes go wide. "One broke into the school? I thought the new wards were impenetrable." At least, according to our teacher, Professor Crayburn. Although the guy wears tweed suits so I'm not sure I trust his judgement.

"She was a student, and I was here touring with my parents." Evelyn stares at the double doors behind us as if the darkling is still here. "I think she had just turned because her eyes looked almost human, and she wasn't all deformed. Just . . . different. With horns and stuff. Before she could hurt anyone, a group of fourth years burst in and shot her with rowan-berry laced darts. Then they took her away, to be killed, I'm sure." She inhales deeply before releasing a long sigh. "If I became that . . . monster, I'd want to die too."

After lunch, I go to meet Rhaegar on the upper floors for fifth period. I'm so busy searching the halls for half-turned darkling humans that I fail to notice how many Fae there are. Right up until the point I nearly crash into Inara and her friends.

Reina is already with her, and it looks like they've been waiting for me. Crap.

Shifting my backpack on my shoulder, I glance back, looking for Mack. But she had to run by her locker after lunch. I'm alone.

Inara laughs as she glides toward me, all smiles and teeth. She wears a striking shimmery-blue ensemble that I could never pull off with my complexion.

"Excuse me," I say, trying to slide past her.

She grabs my shoulder and squeezes hard. Anyone looking from the outside might think the shoulder touch is friendly. But the terrifying strength pouring from her fingers is anything but, and I grit my teeth to keep from crying out in pain.

By now, a crowd has gathered. All Unseelie by the look of them. I'm surprised they're not wearing evil-and-proud T-shirts.

"Where are you going?" she asks, still smiling.

A pit of dread opens inside me. Inara wouldn't make the effort if she didn't plan to do something horrible to me.

"To class," I answer. I try to slip away, but her fingers grip tighter, so hard I think they'll rip my shoulder out of place.

Her cruel gaze slides to my bag. "But how can you go to class without any books? We all know you can't afford them."

My jaw clenches as I recall the bill that showed up along with my new things. A bill I have no idea how to pay. Thanks, Winter Prince.

"I have my books," I growl, "now, move."

"Check." There's something in her voice. A command. I shiver as the order repeats inside my head, and then I find myself sliding my backpack down my arm and unzipping it.

"Pull one out," she orders in a silky-smooth voice.

Suddenly I want to retrieve one of my textbooks. Not just want to, I have to. I slip my hand inside the bag and feel something soft brush my fingers. Soft and sticky. Not a book. Something heavy and familiar.

And there's an alarming metallic, coppery scent coming from inside. My body recoils from it. I don't want to reveal what I'm holding. There's a sick dread in my stomach. A terrible, gnawing ache.

But I have no choice. My body isn't my own. Slowly, I pull out whatever this is . . .

It's a head. A bloody, severed head inside my backpack. Red pig-tails. Freckles. Blood and other horrifying things drip from the neck. But worst of all—worst of all, I recognize the face.

Jane.

With a wail, I fling the head away and fall to my knees as a pang of grief splits open inside me. The pain is unreal. I gag, warm vomit tickling my throat. My thoughts ping-pong all over the place.

Do Aunt Vi and Z know yet? When did this happen? Why? How?

Laughter echoes around me. Cruel, cold, unending laughter. A few Unseelie whip out cell phones and shoot videos. Someone jumps in and takes a selfie with me.

I hardly notice them. I clutch my chest. Unable to breathe. To focus on my surroundings. My heart. My heart is tearing in half.

"What's happening here?" a deep voice booms.

A male professor stands just outside the classroom, frowning at the whole affair. I point at where I tossed Jane's head . . . except now there's only a book. And the blood staining my hands and the floor has disappeared.

It was a . . . trick. A spiteful, brutal, callous trick.

The professor sees Inara and then his face goes slack with fear. Still, he seems about to help me, taking a step forward, despite Inara's terrifying presence. Then his gaze slides to my right and he freezes. The blood in his face drains until his skin is the same hue as snow.

With a quick, apologetic glance at me, he disappears into his classroom.

Coward.

I follow his gaze, wondering who could be more intimidating than Inara, and my eyes snag on the Winter Prince. He's leaned against a locker watching Inara, his gaze avoiding me completely. He wears his usual lazy smirk, the one that makes me want to throat-punch him. His blue-black hair is artfully messy and falls around his slender, pointed ears, the white collar of his tunic unbuttoned and open to the top of his chest.

He looks like he just fell out of bed. He probably did.

My skin tingles with fear as I remember last night. Does he know I trespassed inside his mind?

"Keep your filthy trailer park eyes off him," Inara hisses. "He's off limits."

I'm still on my knees as she leans down and takes my chin between her fingers, forcing my focus away from her mate. One of her pack of sociopaths moves in to video the encounter.

I should stand, but I'm afraid if I move, I'll hurl. The sight of Jane's head is still too fresh. The horror of her fake death still too raw. My body hasn't recovered from the influx of grief, fake or not.

"That was just a taste of what I can do." Cold emanates from Inara's fingertips. She yanks my head up by the jaw, tweaking my spine and forcing me unsteadily to my feet.

My hand curls as I prepare to deck her, but the homicidal look in her eyes says she'll snap my neck if I try.

Instead, I grin, fighting back with the only thing I have available: words. "I'm curious. Why did you make my book look like an adorable puppy?"

Confusion flickers across her face. "That's not what you saw."

"Yeah. He had the cutest nose—"

"I saw you fling it away."

I shrug. "It was cuteness overload. I panicked."

The dark blue vein snaking down her forehead throbs. She can't puzzle me out. Why I'm not afraid of her. It's either a really smart—or really stupid—play.

"Whatever," she says. "Leave, Trailer Park. This school isn't for you."

That nickname is really getting old. "You're wrong," I

somehow manage as her fingers dig deeper into my jaw. "I don't even . . . live in a trailer."

I swear in my periphery I catch the prince's lips quirking.

She tilts her head to the side, her eyes narrowed like she's trying to figure me out. Somehow I manage not to flinch as she leans down and sniffs me—sniffs me, for Fae's sake.

A cruel smile bares her snow-white teeth, complete with a set of fangs. She must be half-shifting, but I'm too nervous to remember what her animal shifter form is.

"Joke all you want," she says, "but you can't hide the stench of your fear."

"Fuck you." The words just tumble out. Maybe she is getting to me.

Something dark and dangerous flashes across her face. A shot of cold pierces my chest—

"I'm bored, Inara. Let's go." The Winter Prince is standing next to Inara, his hand resting on her shoulder. I recognize the long, delicate fingers from my vision last night, the fingernails kept neat and clean.

Her eyes brighten at the contact, and the icy dagger I felt spearing my flesh disappears as she makes doe eyes at the prince. Gag me.

Someone's obviously been forgiven.

The hatred pouring from her dissipates, but she's not totally done with me yet. "Where's your Summer Court now? What about your friends?" She glances around, pretending to look for them, while panning for the camera. Someone laughs. She slides her dark gaze back to me. "I rule this school, and no one, not even the teachers, can help you. Stay, and I'll discover your deepest fear and make it happen."

She releases my jaw, and I rub the tender spot where her fingers gouged. That'll leave a bruise.

"See you in class, Trailer Park," she calls. "Unless you know what's good for you."

She turns on her heel and struts down the hall with her minions in tow. Reina flashes me a smug look before trailing after them with her two boy toys. The Winter Prince is the last to leave.

"You shouldn't antagonize her," he admonishes.

I grit my teeth. "It's not in my nature to roll over and play dead."

"I can see that." His eyes linger on me. There's a darkness in his look.

I stare back, letting my frustration and anger over Inara's trick leak out until it fills the air between us. Our seemingly mutual hatred. The air between us crackles with the raw emotion, so real it could drown us.

The memory of being trapped in his head last night surfaces. The intimacy of seeing his most private moments. I feel his confusion, his anger and need. I see the way he looked at my picture and realize it's the same way he looks at me now.

Only, maybe it's not hatred in his stare, but something else. Something I don't quite understand. Something dark and ragged and . . . yearning.

And then it happens again. A burst of icy warmth blooms between us. For a moment, a breath, I feel drawn to him. Tugged along an inescapable chain of familiarity and desire.

Suddenly he shoves off the locker and stalks away, leaving me confused and disoriented.

What the frick was that?

By the time Mack and Evelyn find me, I've collected myself enough to pick up the book I tossed. *Properties of Elemental Magic.*

I'll never look at it the same.

"Oh, God, Summer," Mack cries. Her mouth falls open as she takes in the look on my face. "What happened?"

"Inara happened," I mutter. "She glamoured me and then

did some trick and I saw . . ." I choke on the actual description as the image of the severed head pops in my mind. Bile stings my throat, my stomach clenching. "It looked so . . . real."

"That's one of her powers," Mack reminds me. "She can make you see your worst fears. It's a hundred times stronger than glamouring. But whatever you experienced, she couldn't see it."

She doesn't know about Jane. I release a frayed breath, my need to barf decreasing to a tolerable level. I assumed . . . but knowing for sure gives me strength.

Mack toys with the belt buckle at her waist. "You can miss class, if you need to? I'm sure Rhaegar will understand."

"Hell, no. Then she wins. And that will never, ever happen."

Using Jane to intimidate me into leaving did the opposite; it pissed me off, and in doing so, gave me a reason to fight. A reason to stay.

I'll never let a bully like Inara Winterspell win.

20

Never in a million years did I imagine I would be in a class full of beautiful immortal beings, staring at pictures of the Mall of America. An escalator pops onto the screen and Professor Lochlan turns to the class, her dark hooves clopping against the wood floor.

"Who can tell me what this is?" she asks. She's a centaur, her sleek gray body dappled with white spots to match the lustrous white hair she wears in a french-braid. I haven't stopped staring since I arrived thirty minutes ago . . . late, of course.

I shift on my feet next to Rhaegar's desk. As his shadow, I have to be ready for emergencies. Things like retrieving his charger if his laptop has a low battery, or refilling his gold hydro-flask if he's parched.

Important life and death stuff.

Just my luck, Inara and her sociopathic friends are in this class too. But with Rhaegar here, they mostly ignore me. The class is a mix of Seelie and Unseelie, and they're just as divided on technology. The Unseelie use real books and notepads to write on; the Seelie have laptops and iPads to follow from and take notes.

I recall Mack saying the Seelie have adapted to our technology a lot faster than the Unseelie. Although the Unseelie crowd was more than happy to break out their cell phones earlier to record my humiliation.

The class is stumped. Rhaegar cuts a quick glance at me, and I mouth, *escalator.* So far, that's been my most important job of all in this class: giving him answers.

I'm an expert in this course. The class, Understanding the Modern Mortal World, teaches the Evermore students all about our culture. That way, if and when they decide to travel to the Untouched Zone, they'll be ready to blend in.

The thought makes me sick. Apparently it annoys Inara too, because she raises her hand and then speaks without waiting for the professor to call on her. "Why do we need to know what that contraption is called, exactly?"

Professor Lochlan regards her with a mixture of contempt and fear. "Do you not plan to visit the mortal world, Miss Winterspell?"

"Oh, I do," she answers. "I just don't plan on visiting the Mall of America."

The room erupts in laughter. The only Fae not laughing, it seems, is the Winter Prince. I have my head tilted so I can make out his face in my periphery. So far, all he's done is stare straight ahead. Ignoring everyone, including me.

Inara made sure to sit next to him. With last night's memory still floating around my head, it was almost painful to watch her eyes light up as she glanced his way. Then watch that spark extinguish as he regarded her with apathy.

Doubling down, she'd offered her shadow, Reina, to take notes for him. When that didn't work, she placed a hand on his thigh and started moving it up. Because, when all else fails, a mid-class hand-job might do the trick.

Gross.

For a moment, he seems caught in some internal struggle. Jaw clenched, eyes narrowed, muscles in his neck tight. Then our eyes lock—much to my absolute embarrassment—and he breaks free from whatever invisible force he fought against.

He guides her hand back down his thigh, his face donning that icy mask. After a second of awkwardness, she retrieves her hand, crestfallen.

If she wasn't the devil incarnate, I might actually feel sorry for her.

After the Mall of America, the professor visits other interesting "human" traditions like football, ping-pong, and rollerblading.

I almost choke on my suppressed laughter as Professor Lochlan explains football. "In this bizarre and violent sport, the ball represents a human baby," she says, cradling a Nike football in between her large, furry hands. "The males on the field must prove they can protect this baby to entice women to be their mates."

Well, then. Who knew? All of the shadows in the class are smart enough not to laugh at Lochlan as she continues her humorous interpretation of our world.

The rest of the lesson is on the differences between human and Fae virtues. As Lochlan explains, humans don't outwardly appreciate cunning and cruelty in the same ways the Fae do. "Don't get me wrong," Professor Lochlan adds, her tail twitching. "In my experience, mortals have the same capacity for cruelty, they simply hide it better."

Jeez, it's almost like she knows Cal Miller.

After that class, I fall into rhythm as Rhaegar's shadow. I hold his books, type in his notes, and follow him through the hallways as he makes conversation with every Seelie student in existence. He doesn't talk to me much, but I don't mind, using the time instead to take in this new world.

Rhaegar moves within the Seelie circle, and he seems to know a little something about everyone. He asks a pixie boy who comes up to my waist about his sick mother. He flirts with a girl from the Autumn court, peppering her with compliments until the flesh of her cheeks goes from turquoise to pink.

It's almost like he's campaigning, although I have no idea for what. Perhaps all Fae are constantly maneuvering like this. Forming alliances.

Either way, it's exhausting. By the time we make it to our last class, Properties of Magic, every step down the auditorium stairs sends my head spinning. When was the last time I drank water?

Ironically, I still have to pee. Crossing my legs, I carefully interrupt Rhaegar mid-conversation. He rips his gaze away from the four female fauns he was talking to, but the moment he recognizes me, his annoyed expression changes back to his pleasant mask.

"Do you need something?" he asks in a honey-sweet voice.

"I . . . can I use the restroom?" I ask, hating that I have to get his permission.

He frowns before sliding his lips into a tight smile. "Class is about to start, but tell you what . . . I need my tablet charger out of my locker. Grab it for me, will you? And if you have time, you can do the other thing."

I flee before he can change his mind as the Fauns praise him for being so kind to me.

I'm not sure letting me answer the call of nature deserves sainthood, but who am I to judge?

My boots pound the wooden floor as I race down the corridors, desperate to unload my bladder. His white charger is in his locker just like he said. With the cord firmly in hand, I sprint to the bathroom.

The old clock above the wall says one minute till 6:30 p.m. Shit.

I make it just in time. *Ah, sweet God in heaven.*

When my bladder is gloriously empty and my hands are washed and smell of the school's verbena and lavender soap, I dart out the door and jog for the stairs.

Please don't be late. Please don't be late. Please—

Voices snag my attention. I halt next to a stairwell, where the voices emanate, and press against the wall. From where I stand, whoever is speaking can't see me.

"You were supposed to make sure she was yours," an agitated male voice says.

"And she would have been, if you hadn't jumped in," a sultry female voice counters. "Rhaegar would have conceded to me. He was only doing it to get a rise out of the Unseelie. But once you entered the equation, he'd rather die than give her up."

"Well, he'll get the chance soon enough." The smarmy voice sounds familiar, and I still my breathing as I strain to listen.

I grin as an *oof* sound—like the girl hitting the boy— makes its way to me.

"I still think bringing her here was wrong," the girl snaps.

"I didn't have a choice. Not with tracker wolves so close."

The girl sighs. "She's not ready for this—for any of it."

"Then you have to *make* her ready."

They must lower their voices because all I can hear are muffled whispers.

Then the girl says, "You're sure about her?"

I lean closer, only to be disappointed when I can't hear his reply. More garbled words follow, then, "Prince, promise you'll stay away from her."

Prince? Curiosity overrides my survival instinct as I peek around the corner, unable to help myself. I barely hold back a gasp as I recognize Eclipsa. She leans against a marble post on the first landing, her silver eyebrows bunched together.

And the Fae male talking to her . . .

Even with his back to me, I would recognize that haughty stance and blue-black hair anywhere. His hair is cut short, tempering what I imagine would be curls into unruly ends that fall against the creamy skin of his neck. The tips of his sharp ears poke through his messy hair like daggers.

What would it be like to touch them? As soon as the thought comes, I shove it down deep. *What the Fae is wrong with me?*

As if he can feel my stare, he begins to turn around, revealing the severe line of his jaw . . .

The air sucks from my chest as I dart for the nearest door —a janitor's closet. The lemon and vinegar tang of all-natural cleaners slaps me in the face and makes my eyes water. When I've waited at least five minutes—long enough for my heart to slow into an even pace—I leave my hiding place and hurry to class . . .

Late, of course.

The professor, Mr. Lambert, pins me with a stern stare as I stand in the aisle next to Rhaegar. I would sit in the chair next to him, but his backpack and headphones occupies that seat, and he doesn't offer to move them. Heat rushes up my neck and pools in my cheeks. Rhaegar says nothing as I hand him the charger, but his disappointment is clear in the downturn of his lips.

And four rows behind me, the Winter Prince's chilly stare bores into my back like icepicks.

21

Once class is over, we follow the crowd to the lower courtyards. My legs feel like Jell-O from standing, and my arms shake from holding Rhaegar's stuff. Well that and the negative wind chill.

Groups of students congregate around orbs floating above pedestals, the warmth barely making a dent in the cold. Mack is there with Basil, and she looks just as worn out as I feel. But her fur-lined gloves and winter coat keep her warm, at least, and Basil thought to bring her a mug of hot cocoa with marshmallows . . . freaking marshmallows.

Meanwhile, Rhaegar hasn't looked my way in an hour. He's engrossed in a discussion with a group of fauns about their treatment in the courts. I don't blame him; it's not his fault his shadow can't afford proper clothes or isn't used to standing all day.

I bite my cheek, using the jolt of pain to focus on staying upright. I think the combination of not eating lunch—thanks, gory face-eating video—not sleeping, and more physical exertion than I've done in years, has caught up to me. And my sweatshirt just isn't made for this type of cold.

All at once, a wave of dizziness crashes over me, and my vision pirouettes in jarring circles. I try to hold onto Rhaegar's books, which he brings along just in case his tech isn't working. The last thing I want to do is drop them in the snow.

Suddenly the weight lifts from my hands. Blinking away the shadows, I see the one person I was hoping not to: the Winter Prince.

He holds the books in one arm, an elegant midnight blue eyebrow arched. "You okay, Princess?"

Princess? "Of course," I lie through gritted teeth. "Although I'd be better if you gave us some sunlight."

With a scoff, he marches over to Rhaegar, who's still deep in conversation with a faun, and shoves the books into his surprised arms.

"If you're going to have a mortal shadow, Rhaegar, you might remember that she is *mortal*."

Annoyance darkens Rhaegar's normally gorgeous face as he takes in the prince. "What do you care?"

"She's on loan to you," the Winter Prince points out, the smarmy dickwad. "But in a few moon cycles, she's mine. Perhaps I don't want you to break her before it's my turn."

Bastard.

A snarl rips from Rhaegar's chest. "You're the one with a track record of killing those you love."

At those words, the prince goes still . . . but it's a predatory stillness. He watches Rhaegar without blinking. Without breathing. Every ounce of his focus is on the Summer Fae as giant snowflakes begin to fall.

The trickle quickly becoming a blizzard.

Adrenaline surges through my frozen veins. Any moment now I expect the prince to strike.

It's almost comical how fast the Fae students scatter to

form a circle around us. Then it's just Rhaegar, the Winter Prince, and me.

Through the dwindling visibility, I spot Inara with her flunkies by the nearest frozen fountain, watching everything unfold with rapt attention. In fact, the entire courtyard stares, entranced, as the snow rages around us.

Once again, I'm the focus of attention. Fabulous.

Someone laughs, and I turn to see Eclipsa Skywell saunter over and clap the prince on the shoulder. "Oberon's beard. If you're going to kick off a war between Seelie and Unseelie, I want to be invited."

I tense, expecting the prince to react badly to Eclipsa's touch. So does everyone else, apparently, because the silence turns into palpable fear. Every eye is riveted to the Winter Prince, and that's when I truly realize just how powerful he must be.

But instead of agitation, Eclipsa's presence seems to calm him. His muscles uncoil as he flashes a boyish grin at her. "Trust me. If the Winter Court wages war, you'll be the first to know, Eclipsa."

Well, now I know what it sounds like when an entire crowd sighs with relief. Just like that, the blizzard stops. With the threat of a fight gone, murmurs break the silence as students stop holding their breath and begin to whisper.

"Oh, good." Eclipsa rolls out her shoulders before sliding a pointed glance at the prince. "For a moment I thought you two idiots were about to fight. But it's just a testosterone-fueled stare down. Gotcha."

Despite my annoyance at the situation, her sarcasm makes me smile.

Rhaegar opens his mouth to speak then seems to think better of it. Instead, he switches his focus to me.

Whatever he sees, it must not be good because pity flashes across his handsome countenance, his green eyes widening.

God, I hate that emotion.

"Summer, I'm sorry. I didn't know . . . and why in the scourge aren't you wearing a coat?"

"Because she can't afford one," the prince reminds him. "She came from the Tainted Zone, remember? And in case you aren't familiar with humans, they aren't like the lesser Fae slaves your father keeps. They do need sustenance and the occasional rest. Even the poor ones."

"You would know," Rhaegar growls. "Considering all the human slaves *your* father forces to work at his clubs."

Anger warms my cheeks. I'm tired of being used by both of them as a pawn to piss each other off. "I'm *fine*."

The Winter Prince scowls at me as if my human frailty is a mortal sin. Unfortunately, his fierceness only makes him more beautiful. Especially the way his wavy blue-black hair falls around his forehead. And his lips curl at the edges, a small dimple forming on one side of his face . . .

I shake my head, trying to dispel my random musing about my former tormentor's looks. What in the Shimmer is wrong with me? Rhaegar is just as handsome as the prince, but I'm not losing my mind over Rhaegar's kissable lips.

The Winter Prince's scowl rips me from my thoughts. "Fine?" he counters. "You were swaying on your feet, and your lips have turned a disconcerting shade of blue."

I hate that he's right. I also hate the way Rhaegar is now looking at me like some wilting flower. What if he decides not to fight for me now? That I'm not worth it?

Pushing past the prince, I plead with Rhaegar. "I was dizzy. I'm not used to this much standing. That's all. I'll find a way to buy a coat. I—"

"No." Rhaegar's jaw is set. "I'm releasing you from your shadow duties early. See you at combat class."

His voice leaves no room for argument. It also makes his

disappointment impossible to overlook. "Wait? You'll be there?"

"Yeah. We train as a team. Now, go and warm up."

The Winter Prince smirks at Rhaegar before stalking away, and Rhaegar frowns in return. It's obvious he doesn't appreciate having my perceived mistreatment pointed out by an Unseelie.

22

O nce I'm back in our dorm room with Mack, glued in front of the fire, I realize he was right to let me out early. I'm exhausted. Mentally and physically. And we still have fight training in an hour.

I barely have time to eat the apple I stole earlier, down a glorious cup of coffee, and pull my hair into a high ponytail before we head off to training.

A huge gym awaits with several different arenas. We follow a bunch of first years to a locker room where we change into stretchy black athletic gear that melds to our bodies, leaving very little to the imagination.

Then our instructor, Mrs. Richter, a former shadow guardian with long black hair restrained in a loose braid and the buffest arms I've ever seen, leads us into the largest arena.

Other than Mr. Willis, she's the first human instructor I've seen at Evermore Academy, but by the tight set of her lips and serious expression, I very much doubt she'll have sympathy on us.

The room stinks of years' worth of sweat and old socks, but the equipment shines like new. Black punching bags line the far wall and red wrestling mats are positioned around the area. The door to another smaller padded room is open, where students with little crossbows on their wrists shoot at targets along the wall.

Evelyn raises her hand. "Instructor Richter, when do we get to train for *that*?"

Our instructor follows Evelyn's gaze to the other room and then purses her lips. "Shadows aren't taught how to use class three weapons until second year."

"Then how are we supposed to kill darklings?" a boy with spiky blond hair and acne jokes.

"With your hands," Richter says dryly.

The boy snorts and mutters under his breath, "I'd rather have a wrist-mounted crossbow. They're so freaking cool."

Richter regards him with narrowed eyes. Then she retrieves a small wrist-mounted crossbow from the other room and hands the weapon to the boy. The class goes quiet, the only sound a dull thud as the bolts hit their targets.

"What do I do with this?" he asks, his eyes huge as they go from the weapon to the instructor.

"What's your name, shadow?" Richter asks.

"Be—Ben."

"Well, Ben. You said you wanted a wrist-mounted crossbow. Now you have one."

He flicks a nervous glance at the weapon. "I've never—"

"Used one? I think not. This particular weapon is a semi-automatic wrist-mounted, laser guided crossbow, to be exact." She closes the distance between them until the sharp end of the bolt is inches from her heart. "Pretend I'm a darkling and *shoot* me."

"No, I . . . I can't. Right?"

"If you want to stay in this academy, Ben, you can and you will."

The crossbow shakes as he fastens it to his wrist. His finger moves to the trigger . . .

Right before the bolt releases, Richter side steps. At the same time, she brings her right hand down on his elbow. Her other hand lifts the weapon from the bottom and thrusts up, stripping it from his grip.

She tosses the crossbow away, and it clatters near Evelyn's feet. Richter grins. "Now your *freaking cool* weapon is gone. What do you do?"

I'm pretty sure Ben is about to piss his pants. When he can't come up with a solution, Richter holds up her hands, a clever look on her face. "Weapons have their place. But these"—she wiggles her fingers—"will always be with you, and they should be your most honed weapon."

After that very convincing display, she sends us to do laps around the gym. We end the session with pushups and burpees, and I'm not entirely sure how I don't vomit. My head spins. My stomach churns. I assume we're done until Richter leads us through a small padded room into another even larger gym.

There's no equipment here other than mats. Mirrors line the far wall. Our keepers wait on a large mat, stretching. They all wear similar tight black workout gear and are sweaty like they've been here a while. Except their *sweaty* and ours is entirely different.

They're like the models on sports magazines who have been sprayed with droplets of water to get a picture. Gorgeous. Every hair in place. Not breathing hard at all. Skin all dewy and crap.

The Elite Six are off in a group by themselves. All except Eclipsa, who stretches over in the corner. Inara and her twin brother, Bane, whisper as they watch me. Meanwhile, Lyra, Bane's lycan girlfriend, shoots daggers at me from his side.

I glance over at the wall of mirrors. Patchy red spots dot

my chest, the hair from my ponytail pasted all over my head and neck like limp noodles. My tight black outfit reveals every angle of my body, highlighting my thin arms, sharp hip bones, and starved muscles.

Rhaegar calls me over. As I take my place beside him, I feel the Winter Prince's cold gaze scouring my flesh. Inara notices too and a near-imperceptible frown tugs her lips. Bane flicks a quick look my way and frowns with her.

Something about him creeps me out . . . even more than Inara does.

Mack hip checks me, bringing me back to the now. "Stop staring at them."

She stands next to Basil, who's wearing special shoes to keep his hooves from damaging the mat.

"I think they're the ones staring at *me*," I counter.

She chuckles. "They have that right; you don't. If you want to survive this class, keep your head down and try not to grab their attention."

Good point.

I tear my focus from the Six to the Seelie Fae next to us. Now that we're close to our keepers, I notice how big both men are. Their black uniforms, stretched comically over swollen muscles, could be painted on. Rhaegar has taken out the jewelry that usually adorns his ears, his thick mane of gold hair twisted into a man bun.

Take away his impossibly good looks and godly body, he could almost pass for human.

A broad grin plays over Rhaegar's lips as he notices me checking him out. "Feeling better?"

"Yep," I lie, trying super hard not to sound out of breath from earlier. I rip my gaze away from his perfect physique and swallow repeatedly, trying to draw moisture back into my dry mouth.

The Winter Prince walks to the other end of the mat, one

hand held behind his back. In contrast to the Summer Court males, he's all lithe muscles and broad shoulders, his waist tapering to a beautiful ass. Unlike Rhaegar's raw power, he glides gracefully across the mat, his every movement controlled yet rippling with an undercurrent of explosive power.

I'm used to the prince's presence drawing my attention. The tug of familiarity and longing I feel around him that I've chalked up to some weird form of Stockholm syndrome.

Rhaegar's grin melts into a scowl as he notices me checking out the prince. "All that power, all that promise . . . wasted."

"What do you mean?" I ask, never taking my eyes off the prince. He has a way of doing that when in a room; demanding undivided attention just by being.

Rhaegar lets out a soft breath. "Nothing. Just that it's a shame the most powerful Fae in centuries is Unseelie and couldn't care less for furthering our race."

Basil grunts. "The Six wouldn't dare rule without him. With him gone . . . the academy would be a better place."

For solidarity, I try to look as annoyed as Rhaegar. But as I watch the prince, I find my traitorous lips tugging upward.

By the graceful, proud way he moves, he knows every eye is on him.

Eclipsa saunters over to stand next to him and then faces us, arms crossed, a fierce grin brightening her face. Asher Grayscale follows. I haven't seen much of the prince's dragon-shifting best friend, but the dark look he graces us with lives up to his Elite Six status.

"Attention, shadows," the Winter Prince calls, his icy gaze sweeping over us. "If you haven't heard, I run this part of the class, and Eclipsa and Asher are my assistants." Both Eclipsa and Asher frown a bit at that. "We'll be helping you learn to work as a team with your guardian."

Holy Fae ears. Who the heck would put this psychopath in charge? I scour the room for Richter, but she's already left. Beside me, Rhaegar's jaw goes taut.

I have the distinct feeling this won't end well for either of us.

"How is he our instructor?" I whisper to Mack.

Mack finishes readjusting her high ponytail; half her hair is too short to reach and it falls to her shoulders. "He may seem like a jerkoff, but when it comes to fighting, the Winter Prince is a god. I hear he trained directly under his grandfather, the Darken."

I shiver, the name dredging up memories from school. We didn't learn much in high school about the Fae, but my history class did cover the Lightmare. There was only one page on the terrifying Unseelie king who ruled over all Fae-kind, King Oberon. He was responsible for unleashing the catastrophic dark magic on the world during the war—before both sides decided he was too evil even for them and slaughtered him.

For both Seelie and Unseelie to turn against him, he must have been horrible.

"The Winter Prince actually trained with King Oberon?" I mutter, refusing to use his creepy nickname. "That explains so much."

The Winter Prince stops talking and glares at us. "Something you want to add, Princess?"

"Nope." I shake my head to emphasize my point.

"Good. Because you're first. Get up here."

23

S cowling at the prince, I slowly make my way through the crowd to the front of the mat where he stands. A nervous energy chokes the room. Whatever I'm going first for, it's probably not good.

He takes a step toward me, sending my heart into a tailspin. His eyes flicker—enough that I know he can hear my rapid heartbeat—and then he leans forward and whispers, "I just need to put this on you. Okay?"

After days of his disdainful tone, the sudden gentleness of his voice is jarring. He's so near I can smell him—balsam and cedar and the air right after fresh snowfall.

I blink. *Yes, Summer. You just sniffed the Winter Prince in front of everyone.*

Someone laughs.

"Yes?" he prods.

Oh, right. Answer him. I nod as my wide gaze rivets to the black vest he carries, right before he slips it over my head. Three red targets cover the vest; one in front where my heart is, one just over my liver, and the last on the back, dead center where my skull meets my spine.

When he calls Reina up next, my body becomes a live wire of adrenaline. Reina's eyes are locked onto mine as she moves into position across from me. Eclipsa fits her with a vest. Twin fish-braids carve down either side of Reina's head. A few dots of old blood stain the strips over her nose.

Someone came to play.

"Summer," the Winter Prince calls, and I glance over my shoulder at him, just in time to spot the baton he tossed—hurtling end over end at my face.

On instinct, my hand flies up, and, for once, my fingers aren't clumsy as they flex around the cold bar and I manage to catch it.

Yes!

I'm incredibly pleased with myself . . . until Eclipsa tosses a baton to Reina, who snags it without breaking eye contact with me. Inara grins behind her.

Crap.

Cold sweat crops on my temples as I take in her predatory stance—legs spread, one leg forward like she's ready to pounce—and the lethal gleam in her dark eyes. Mack said all the other shadows have trained in mixed martial arts their entire life in preparation for the academy.

I caught her by surprise the other day. That won't happen again.

The Winter Prince crosses his arms over his chest and sweeps a dark gaze over both of us. "The rules are simple: if Reina touches me, she wins. If Summer touches Inara, Summer wins. Your job"—he glances at Reina before letting his icy blue eyes settle on me—"is to protect your keeper. Anyone who lights up the other's vest three times wins by default."

Rhaegar grunts in annoyance at the Winter Prince's implication that I'm his shadow, but my focus doesn't deviate from Reina. The moment I look away, she'll strike.

We circle each other. The room goes quiet, highlighting the thrum of my heart pounding in my skull. I can't quite catch my breath. Can't blink for fear—

One second Reina is in front of me. The next, she's hurtling for me at lightning speed. I throw up my baton, barely blocking the end of hers from striking the target above my heart. The impact of our batons colliding splits the air and reverberates in my forearm like electricity.

I might have knocked her baton aside, but her body keeps coming. She pivots, her shoulder slamming into my chest.

My arms spin as I fly back on my ass. The mat does little to soften the blow, pain shooting up my tailbone. With me out of the way, she lunges for the prince.

Hell, no. I pop to my feet and rush her. Seconds before she reaches the prince, I slam my baton into the red target at her neck, sending her sprawling. The red light flickers, filling me with hope that I can win.

From my periphery, I swear the prince's eyes crinkle with amusement.

Rhaegar and Mack cheer, along with a few of the Seelie. I find myself grinning, my dry lips practically pasted to my teeth.

Reina fell to her hands and knees, but she explodes back to her feet with a grunt. When she turns around, I flinch at the fury inside her eyes. Nostrils flared, she glances over at Inara, who gives her a little nod.

Wiping her mouth, Reina stalks toward me, mouthing, *you'll pay for that, bitch.*

I'm ready this time when she attacks. I might not know martial arts, but I'm fast, and I manage to dodge her advances. But each charge, she gets closer.

Meanwhile, I'm slowing down. My arms ache; my head spins wildly from the exertion.

Then her baton catches me in the mouth. My bottom lip splits open as blood splatters.

Mother trucker, it hurts.

My adrenaline turns the pain into a dull ache, and I prod the area with my tongue, ensuring I still have teeth left. After that, she catches me on the temple, knocking me dizzy. Blood drips from my forehead into my eye. My fingers and hands are next. She strikes over and over with lethal speed—too fast to be human.

Every time she makes contact with me, the crowd gasps.

The next few minutes are a blur of metal flashing and throbbing pain. She lands blows everywhere. At first, she's not even trying to hit my targets. She's going for my exposed flesh. My face. My head. My hands. Anywhere there's breakable bone.

Anywhere that will cause excruciating pain.

At some point, Eclipsa begins to rush over, but the Winter Prince holds up his hand to stop her. They argue and then Eclipsa storms to the corner, arms crossed.

Is he enjoying this? Watching me slowly get beaten to a pulp? Rage and betrayal surge inside my veins, forcing me to keep going.

Before I can switch my attention back to Reina, her weapon connects with my shoulder. I hardly feel the blow, even as the force slams through my body.

I stumble.

A few seconds later, a pulse of red flashes from my vest. Another. I didn't even see her strike. The pain and adrenaline form a fuzzy cloud around my vision. I'm gasping for breath, not even caring how winded I sound. My bare feet slip on the puddles wetting the mat, a mixture of my sweat and blood.

A stinging blow to my abdomen nearly drops me to my knees. The air flees my lungs. I can't breathe.

For a split second, I lose sight of the prince.

And then Reina switches the baton from her right hand to her left. I follow the movement as she swings the baton at my head, barely ducking as the baton glances off my skull. Waves of dizziness crash over me until I'm drowning in darkness.

Blinking, I claw my way to the surface just in time to catch sight of her bare foot inches from my face.

The roundhouse kick feels like being hit by a sledge-hammer to the face. Next thing I know, I'm on my back, staring at the metal ceiling fan whirring above. As the room erupts in cheers, she steps over me and touches the Winter Prince with her baton.

A light, gleeful touch.

Damn.

Get up, I order my body. But it just lays there, broken and sad, in flagrant disregard to my order.

Traitor.

On her way to her cheering fan club, Reina smirks down at me. "Might want to put some ice on that."

Ouch.

Mack rushes over with a towel for my face. "Is anything broken?"

"Just my ego," I moan as I press the towel to my lip; the white fabric comes away soaked in blood.

Mack helps me up to a sitting position.

I wince, tears of pain and humiliation stinging my eyes. "Everything hurts and I'm dying."

She snorts. "You might wish you were dead right now; I saw Bane filming the entire thing."

"Wonderful." I'm scared to even touch my face and assess the damage. "How bad is it?"

Mack snags her bottom lip between her teeth. "Imagine if a psychopath took a metal baton and smacked you in the face repeatedly. You look like that."

I groan as throbbing fire prods my brain. How many times

did she hit me? Gathering all my courage, I run my fingers over my face and head. The examination reveals two lumps on my left side, a swollen lip, and a bloodied eyebrow the size of a golf ball.

Eclipsa bounds over to me, an infirmary kit in her hands. "You lasted way longer than I thought you would."

I pull the towel away from my lip, frowning at the blood. "Thanks. I think."

As Eclipsa procures a butterfly bandage for my eyebrow, Mack stares in awe at the Unseelie assassin. But I'm too tired and beaten up to care that one of the Six is talking to me.

"She was . . . fast," I mutter. "Freakishly fast."

Eclipsa glances at Asher as he strides over carrying a bucket of water and rags. Mack looks like she might pass out at the sight of another of the Six, but she collects herself enough to gape idiotically at them.

Asher clicks his tongue as he drops to one knee beside us, his bulky body taking up a ton of space. "Prince should have called it. Reina was definitely using a speed spell."

"She cheated?" Mack demands, forgetting her awe over their presence. In her world, cheating is the worst sin possible.

Asher is bent over, flashing a beam of light into my eyes. He glances up through a curtain of dark hair to appraise Mack.

For a moment, his gaze lingers, and I swear sparks alight in his exotic green eyes.

Whoa. Dragon boy definitely checked her out.

Then he drops his gaze and growls, "Of course she cheated. She's Inara's shadow. I'd expect nothing less."

The Winter Prince scowls at Eclipsa as he joins us. "Don't fill her head with nonsense. Cheat or not, that was embarrassing. If Summer wants to be my shadow, she has to actually protect me."

Ugh, the nerve of this guy. I try to glare at him, but furrowing my brows sends a fresh wave of agony into my skull. "I *don't* want to be your shadow. And I certainly wouldn't ever protect you if it came down to it."

Eclipsa's mouth falls open, and she and Asher exchange glances. The dragon shifter suddenly goes from barely looking at me to studying me with a deeply curious half-grin. He must like what he sees because the other side of his lips curve upward into an impressed smile.

"Don't listen to her," Asher says, still grinning. "She has a pretty severe concussion. I'm surprised she didn't pass out."

The prince ignores both of us, his face schooled into a serious mask as he runs his fingers over my body, checking for broken bones. Every brush of his fingertips sends little bursts of pleasure rippling through my core.

When he's done with his assessment, he yanks his hands up to my head, pressing his cold fingers into my temples.

I try very hard not to notice the way his palms graze the tops of my cheeks—or the way my heart flutters at the contact. I need help. Mental help. Finding him attractive when he's the reason I'm here is madness.

He touches a tender spot and I flinch.

"Be still," he barks. "I'm trying to heal your concussion."

A shot of cold surges from his fingertips. I cry out, but a second later, the pain in my head dissipates.

The moment he's done, he jerks his hands away like my flesh burns him and shakes them out. Then he shifts his gaze from me to Eclipsa. "Who's doing her extra combat sessions?"

Eclipsa tugs on the end of a silver braid. "I think Richter assigned—"

"No," he interrupts. "Whoever she assigned, they won't be good enough. Can you take over her training?"

"I . . ." Her gaze slides to me, back to him. I can see she wants to refuse. But then she nods. "Fine. I'll do what I can."

Not exactly a vote of confidence, but I don't blame her after my shameful beat down.

An awkward silence falls. Mack suddenly brightens. "Wait. You healed Summer's head, which means you can heal the rest of her, right?"

Everyone stares expectantly at the prince, even me. With the pain gone, I might be able to forget the whole humiliating experience. And my lip stings something awful.

But he rewards us with a deep scowl. "Only her concussion, not the rest. She needs to feel every bruise. It will motivate her to pay attention in her first session tomorrow with Eclipsa."

Jerk. I frown, sending a fresh wave of agony through the tender, swollen flesh of my lip.

"You get off on this, don't you?" I snap, the pain adding fuel to my already short temper. "You could have called anyone up there, but you chose me, knowing I wasn't ready. Why?"

A muscle jumps just above the razor-edge line of his jaw. "Just be ready tomorrow for Eclipsa's sessions."

When we arrive at the dorms, I shower in a daze and then collapse onto my bed. I stopped by the healing center on the way back, but the Advil and bitter herbal capsule the nurse insisted I take did little to soften my throbbing bruises.

Bruises the Winter Prince could have easily healed—if he wasn't a sadistic dickwad who enjoys making me suffer.

Mack settles in beside me, and then we stare at the upper bunk and try to come up with a solution to food that doesn't involve going to the dining hall. No way can I face anyone now.

Before either of us can find an answer, a knock sounds and then a school employee drops two trays brimming with food on the coffee table.

The offering is a mixture of human comfort food—hamburgers and pizza—and the Fae rabbit food I'm beginning to expect, like fruits, nuts, and vegetables.

Mack squeals and grabs the note, reading it in a male voice. "You haven't bothered attending the dining hall much since you arrived, so I'm sending the food to you." She flips the card over and frowns. "It's not signed . . . but it has to be Rhaegar. Have I mentioned how you totally lucked out landing him?"

"Agreed," I admit as I snag the burger, delighted to see American cheese curling over the edges of the thick meat. God, is there any better kind? There are even packets of both mayo and ketchup, and a little ramekin of pickles.

Jackpot. The only thing better would be tacos. But beggars can't be choosers.

"Oh, wait." Mack holds up something . . . a Charm lollipop. "There's a whole box of these here too."

My breath hitches. Rhaegar has no idea I love Charm lollipops, but the prince does. He stole them from me the night we met. The same night he took my fate and stomped it to smithereens.

The bite of cheeseburger turns to dirt in my mouth. I force it down, push my cheeseburger aside, and take a lollipop.

Whatever sick game the prince is playing, I want nothing to do with it.

"**A**gain!" Eclipsa orders. I'm lying on a weight bench while she stands over me, arms crossed, a frown tugging her lips. She's glaring at the two shaking weights in my hand. I'm supposed to be pressing them toward the ceiling, but my muscles refuse. Sweat drenches my temples, and a stripe of my blonde hair is pasted across my forehead.

I'm only on my second rep. Lord save me.

When I showed up this morning at 10:00 a.m. she was waiting for me in the weight room wearing cute silver leggings and a jet-black racerback tank that showed off her toned arms. Her silver hair was wreathed around her head in a complex set of french-braids, and silver half-moon barrettes held everything together.

"Hoping I didn't show and you'd get stuck with Richter?" she had asked.

"No, of course not," I said. "I just . . . it's hard to get used to students as instructors."

She'd grinned at that. "Summer, how old do you think I am?"

I stared at her poreless face, not a saggy bit of skin or wrinkle anywhere, and shrugged.

"Five hundred and seven." She waited until the shock registered on my face and then added, "We mature slower than humans. And most Evermore don't receive the full extent of their powers until around half a millennium, so that's when we attend the academy. But I promise you, I've had hundreds of years to hone this beautiful body into a weapon of mass murder."

"Huh." It was the smartest thing I could think to say.

"Richter's good . . . for a human," she added. "But she's like a blunt force instrument. All brute and no finesse. Wouldn't you like to know the exact spot between the ribs to stick a dagger to stop someone's heart before they can make a sound?"

My mouth fell open.

Taking that as a yes, she continued, "The Unseelie side values the Winter Prince. He harbors the most powers and promise of any Evermore student in over five thousand years, maybe even more than the Darken. Seeing as he insists on you being his shadow, I'm now tasked with making you competent."

"And if I end up with Rhaegar?" I had asked.

She smiled that sanguine smile. "You won't. Trust me. What the Winter Prince wants . . . he gets."

Not if I can help it.

I barely had time to suppress an eye roll before she was putting me through round after round of weight lifting and stretches until my heartbeat felt like one giant throb pulsing pain to every bruise on my body.

Now, an hour of torture later, my body is in full-scale revolt, my lip has started bleeding again, my tights have wedged into every crack I possess, and the cut above my eye needs another butterfly bandage.

I'm falling apart at the seams.

But the prince was right. My humiliation from last night's epic smackdown fuels my workout, and I've pushed way beyond what I ever thought I could do physically. It's kind of exhilarating.

"Breathe through your nose and into your belly," Eclipsa commands, ripping me from my daydream and back to the very painful present.

"I *am*," I promise.

"No, you're sucking mouthfuls of air through your lips like you're drowning. It's the most inefficient way to get oxygen to your body . . . and you look like a dying fish."

Well, she doesn't mince words.

Lifting the weights from me like they weigh nothing, she gives me a second to breathe.

"Let me ask you a question," she begins. "For a human, you have what could be a strong, athletic body. Why are you so weak? Does your kind not have training to keep you in shape?"

Her words sting, and I glance over my too-thin body. It's hard to remember what I looked like with muscle and curves in all the right places. "We have sports, but . . ." Anger, hot and unexpected, surges through me, and I have to forcibly unclench my fists. "We're starving where I live. Hard to build muscle without food, you know?"

Surprise flickers across her face before she can school her expression into a neutral mask.

My heart clenches. Talking about my life on the other side conjures a wave of sadness as I realize how much I miss my aunts and the others, especially Jane. Are they okay? Do they have enough to eat? Are they safe?

An ache forms in the back of my throat. I can't think about them. Not now. Not until the day I walk out of this academy.

Grunting, I open my hands and motion to the weights,

hoping the grind of pushing my body to its limits will remove the hollow grief that's settled deep inside me.

Eclipsa is looking at me different now, but she hands them over, and I finally manage to lift the dumbbells halfway. She coaxes a few more reps from me and then allows a water break.

I tell myself it's not because she feels sorry for me. The idea she might pity me now is unbearable.

When I've downed five cups of water from a metal tumbler, I casually start to ask questions, hoping to distract her from our torture session. "So . . . what's the deal between Rhaegar and the Winter Prince?"

She's in the middle of some ridiculous yoga pose, and she slowly untwists her lithe body and meets my eyes. "Oh, you noticed that, did you?"

"Kind of hard to miss. I feel like a tennis ball being smacked back and forth."

"A what?"

"Never mind. So . . . they have history?"

She switches to a one-legged pose, her arms unfurling above her head as her eyes shut. "They both loved the same girl."

Drawing my knee up to stand on one leg, I try to emulate her pose and nearly fall over for my effort.

"That sounds . . . tragic," I tease, righting myself. But then I see her face and wish I hadn't joked.

Her lips are pressed tightly together, her eyes dark with emotion. She slides a careful look over to me. "It was, actually. She died." She grabs a towel and tosses it at me. "We're done for the day."

Thank the Shimmer. Sopping the sweat from my tired body, I grab my clothes and limp for the locker room. A hot shower and change of clothes later, I at least don't feel like roadkill.

On my way out, Eclipsa pulls me aside. "Word of advice? Don't ever mention what I just told you. It will be a miracle if we can keep Rhaegar and the prince from starting another war."

"The mother of all surprises," I grumble.

Eclipsa laughs, a real laugh that shakes her entire body, and I'm suddenly thankful I can speak my mind around her without fear of reprisal.

"You and the prince seem . . . close," I begin, struggling with how to phrase my words.

She stiffens. "Most of my early years were spent as a hostage living at the Winter Court. The Unseelie King learned I'm stealthy and possess a great memory, so he employed me as a spy. And when he discovered my skill with weapons . . ." She lifts her fine-boned shoulders in a shrug. "The prince is like a brother to me, and his father's influence is the only reason I have a spot in this school."

The prince. I can't get over how everyone calls him that. "Do *you* know his name?"

"No," she says, staring in the mirror as she re-clips one of her barrettes. "And he'll never tell anyone, even me. As the most powerful Evermore to ever grace these halls, he's a target. If anyone had his true name . . . well, anyway." She shakes her head, the half-moon jewels curving her forehead shimmering. "That will never happen. He's not a fool, and only his mother knew his given name."

Debatable about the fool part. "Knew?"

"Yeah. She died too."

It doesn't escape me that the important women in the prince's life are dead. Coincidence? Doubtful. Either way, the new information only makes me surer than ever of one thing: I cannot let myself become his shadow.

After the Winter Prince embarrassed Rhaegar by pointing out my fatigue, he pays a lot more attention to me. He stashes his books in his locker so I don't have to carry them, and he's more attentive to my human needs. Things like having to pee, consuming the occasional nourishment, and staying hydrated.

There was even a beautiful, fur-lined baby-blue coat delivered to our dorm room a few nights ago. Bags of dried rowan berries are sewn into the hem, and steel-blue leather gloves with creamy opal fur trim were stashed in the pockets.

Considering their color, the items are probably from the Winter Prince and not Rhaegar, but my ego won't get in the way of staying warm and *unfrozen*.

Basic human rights for the win. I'm feeling very spoiled.

Which is all a good thing since the weather has only seemed to worsen, my bladder is the size of a walnut, and my muscles feel like goo after my morning sessions with Eclipsa. Along with running laps until I collapse, we've moved on from strict weight lifting to fifteen minutes of martial arts.

Turns out, that's just as strenuous on your body, and I finish every session close to puking.

Rhaegar also has other Seelie—usually Magus or Basil—meet me in the hallway when he can't be there. I'm assuming the videos of Inara glamouring me and her shadow kicking my ass have already made the rounds, which explains why he's taking extra precautions.

And why the other students snicker and stare when I pass. But after a few weeks of ignoring them and avoiding the spotlight, things start to die down. After classes, Mack and I mostly stay in our dorm to study. Sometimes Evelyn joins us, although she's not one for "books and stuff."

Boring, but it helps people forget I punched another student, called the Winter Prince a bitch, caught the attention of the most terrifying mean girl in school, and then got my butt kicked by her shadow.

I've also managed to stay out of the prince's head, and that strange episode begins to feel like a bad dream. My bruises have even healed, the only reminder of that humiliating episode a tiny scar intersecting my blonde eyebrow.

Things are definitely looking up.

I'm lying on my bed, deep into a book on *Elemental Magic and Its Many Uses*, when Mack breezes into our dorm, followed by Evelyn. They're both grinning like maniacs. I was so entrenched in reading that I didn't even know Mack left.

"Find anything?" Mack asks, her gaze sliding to the book.

I shake my head. "There's almost nothing on the Nocturus in this book or any of the history books."

"Maybe try one of the old tomes in the library tomorrow? I think they're open on the weekends." She shrugs. "The Fae are methodical historians. There has to be something somewhere that can help you."

Evelyn plops on the bed beside me. Bright swirls of green and gold paint decorate her cheeks—they must be doing face painting outside. The entire campus has exploded in excitement over the Samhain celebration tomorrow.

I, on the other hand, feel sick just thinking about it. Samhain means the day my fate is juggled by two blood-thirsty maniacs.

"What time do they fight tomorrow?" Evelyn asks, toying with a silky strand of her fiery red hair.

I sink my teeth into my lower lip. "I don't know . . . maybe midnight? We're not allowed to attend."

I glare at the flyer I set on the desk stating all mortals have to be in by dusk for Samhain. It goes on to explain the Fae students' magic will be heightened, along with their base desires. The words NOT SAFE are printed everywhere in bold, capital letters.

"I know of a fourth year boy who died during Samhain," Evelyn says darkly. "They found him eviscerated."

"Lovely." I shut my book and stretch, wondering why Evelyn always has the macabre stories. My movement makes Ruby stir on my pillow. Her wings flutter, and she moans, flipping onto her side.

I found her earlier surrounded by empty Charm wrappers, white sticks, and puke.

She ate them all. The gum that didn't make it to her stomach found its way into her lovely magenta locks.

Mack wiggles her eyebrows suggestively. "My parents said Samhain is really just a giant orgy."

"Oh, good. Another reason I'm not leaving this dorm until Monday," I mutter.

"You can't hide here forever."

"Watch me." I glance out our little window. Darkness fell an hour ago, the snow a slow drizzle. By now I can tell the difference between the dirty gray half-light that means it's daytime, and the full, foreboding darkness of night.

Lights flicker in the distance. There's a bonfire near the

lake of sorrows that rages Friday and Saturday for the festival, and twinkly lights are strung through the evergreens and oaks. Through the frosty windowpane trickle sounds of celebration.

Of *fun*. Whatever the hell that is. I've literally forgotten.

Laughter draws my attention to the open door. A group of human girls pass in the hallway carrying streamers of green and gold—Summer Court colors. Usually on the weekends the campus and dorm clear out, but everyone is here for Samhain.

Mack lifts up on her tiptoes, a thing she does when she's excited. "We're going out tonight. You should come."

"It's not the bonfire, is it?" I ask warily. "Because the answer is a hard no."

I'm not in the mood to be stared at and whispered about. Everyone knows about the Nocturus tomorrow, and I'm suddenly back in the spotlight.

"Ick, no." Mack makes a face. "Only first years and dweebs go to school sanctioned functions." I refrain from adding that we are first years. "All the cool students go to the Ice District in Everbrite. They usually only let fourth years shadows in . . . but Rhaegar told Basil we could come."

"What's the Ice District?" I ask as Evelyn flings open the closet door and starts rummaging around Mack's clothes.

"The row of bars along Pixie Street in Everbrite? You've never heard of that?" Evelyn glances over her shoulder as I shake my head. "It's famous . . . and basically the coolest place in Everwilde. The who's who of Fae are spotted there all the time."

"Why's it called the Ice District?"

Mack finishes zipping herself into a skintight red dress that highlights her tawny complexion and hourglass figure. "The bars are all owned by the Winter King."

"Count me out." They try to change my mind, but I refuse

to leave my bed. The idea of visiting a club owned by the Winter Prince's family makes me physically ill.

"Suit yourself." Mack leans down and tweaks my ear. "But, for Fae's sake, get your head out of that book and do something. It's Friday night. Walk the grounds. Watch a movie in the commons with the other first years. Make out with some nameless—but hot—fourth year boy toy. But you need to leave this room."

I cringe. If Mack, the most studious girl in our academy, is telling me to get out and do something, I probably should.

But the only thing I want to do is find something, anything, that will help Rhaegar win me tomorrow for good.

Once they're gone, I throw on my jeans and my old Dallas Cowboys hoodie.

I'm pretty sure when Mack suggested I get out and have fun, she didn't mean going to the library. But that's exactly what I plan to do as I summon poor Ruby and slip out the front door. The frigid wind assaults me the moment I shove open the heavy mahogany door.

With a yelp, Ruby dives into my hood.

"I think . . . I might be . . . sick," she moans.

"Maybe next time don't steal my candy and gorge yourself on it," I scold.

She gives an aggrieved scoff. "You left it out. Right in front of me. What was I supposed to do?"

Rolling my eyes, I start down the path toward the main academy building. A deep, unsettling cold has taken hold of the campus grounds, and I shove my hands into my jeans. If the cold becomes too unbearable, I'll slip into my gloves.

By the time I make it to the main campus, I've lost all feeling in my nose. It's not much better inside. Like most weekends, the fires are low, the corridors dark and empty. A chilly draft permeates the halls.

"Ruby," I say. When she doesn't answer, I call louder. "Ruby!"

She jerks awake from where she curls, snoring, in my hood.

"Find the library."

She drunkenly swirls around my head, her arms crossed over her chest and tiny face twisted in annoyance. "*Hmph*. Do I look like the Fae version of Alexa?"

"Please?" When she refuses to help me, I sigh and add, "In addition to my eternal gratitude, I'll throw in a thimble-full of brambleberry wine."

Her eyes brighten, and I know I've won.

My footsteps ring hollow against the wood-paneled walls as I follow her through the corridors to a stairwell. After plunging ten stories, at least, we're greeted by a locked gate. She waves her fingers over the lock and it springs open.

Man, that lock-picking magic would have come in handy in my other life.

On the other side of the gate is a collection of the oldest books I've ever seen, housed in rows of tall metal bookshelves that look like they haven't been touched in a thousand years. A copper chandelier resembling the clawing branches of a tree, complete with leaves of orange and red, hangs from the domed ceiling, providing a pittance of sputtering amber light.

Cobwebs and dust cover everything.

"Why would the library be down here?" I say, holding back a sneeze.

"This isn't the student library," answers Ruby. "This is the library for forbidden books."

My gaze slides from the broken lock to Ruby. "We're not supposed to be here, are we?"

She snorts. "My, aren't you a clever one? What gave it away? The locked gate or the word 'forbidden?'"

"Ruby, I need the library. You know, the place where we won't get expelled for entering."

"No," she corrects smugly. "You need here. Assuming you still want to discover a way for Rhaegar to win the Nocturus?"

My eyes widen. How did she know that?

With a maniacal grin, she adds, "Unless you're too scared to break a few rules, human?"

"Pfft." I roll my eyes. "Where do we start?"

She swirls her hand in the air and a bright golden orb appears, floating just above her.

With my sprite lit up like a living flashlight, I search for the section labeled, *Ceremonial Magic*. A part of me wants to laugh at how different my life is now.

Three months ago, I was dead broke, desperate, and breaking into warehouses . . . now I'm still dead broke, desperate, and breaking into a library while using a tiny person as a flashlight.

I guess some things stay the same, after all.

When *Ceremonial Magic* proves to be a dead end—and also incredibly boring—I move on to *Enhancing Your Power the Natural Way*. Another dead end. The next section, *The Forbidden Arts*, is interesting only because I wonder why they don't teach it in class—but it's not helpful.

Ruby yawns above me, her little light bobbing as she wavers in the air. Afraid she'll fall asleep midair and plummet to her death, I settle her on my shoulder and move on to the very last section.

A half hour later, with my sprite's snores serenading me, I find a book without a spine covering. Curious, I pull the leather-bound tome from the shelf and search for a title. The front cover is missing, and the parchment feels as if it will crumble at the touch.

My heart leaps when I read the title page.

Histories of the Nocturus, from the Winter Wars until the Dark War.

"Gotcha." I'm so excited that I fist pump the air, waking my sprite.

"What in the Fae hells?" she screeches. She nestles back on my shoulder, her eyes drifting closed . . . when they pop back open.

Alarm flickers across her face. "Do you smell that?"

The moment she mentions smell, my nose begins to pick up something. A fetid, dying odor. Like something dead is trapped beneath the floorboard. Except the rank odor is only growing stronger.

Ruby zips above my head, still sniffing the air. Then she hisses, "Deamhan," and whips out a miniature dagger with a jeweled hilt. "Come meet your fate, deamhan!"

"Ruby, what's a deamhan?" I demand just as the sound of something heavy stomps outside the library. Heavy and dragging. Each ominous thud shakes the floorboards and sends dust flying off shelves. A low, gravely bellow splits the air, and my gut clenches.

Ruby's lilac eyes are big as peas. "Orc!"

By the loud noises, I was expecting the orc to be big, but not can't-fit-through-the-freaking-door big. Ruby and I are watching from behind a bookshelf as the orc tries to duck under the doorway into the forbidden library. But it's not just a matter of his looming height.

There's no way his enormous frame will fit.

"Nothing in here for you, big guy," I whisper. "Move along."

The ropy muscles of the orc's neck strain as he literally tries to cram his way through.

Not the brightest bulb, are you, bud?

He's even more hideous than I imagined. Beady, all-black eyes blink from beneath a huge, overhanging brow, and an underbite sends his lower fangs curling all the way to his upper lip. Pointed ears shorter and more jagged than a Fae's stick out from a bald head. His flesh looks rotten, all ashy and green-tinged.

With a frustrated howl, his head disappears from the doorway.

Ruby shoots into the air, waving her dagger. "That's right, you hideous, wart-faced orc! You don't want a piece of *this*."

And then a huge *boom* shreds the air as the orc smashes into the doorway in a burst of dust and debris. I flinch as jagged chunks of stone zoom by my head. His stench floods the room.

Gag me.

When I peer back into the library, I see the doorway is now a giant, gaping hole. The orc's enormous body stands near the first bookshelf, dust swirling around him. Tilting his giant head, he begins to sniff the air.

"Oberon's luck," Ruby mutters. "I thought for sure I scared him off."

Add overconfidence to my sprite's ever-growing list of negative attributes.

We both duck low as quiet descends. My heart rams my ribcage, my fingertips numb as adrenaline funnels all my blood to my main organs.

The orc roars, and my heart flip-flops. Shivering, I peek through a hole in the books just in time to see the orc lift a club the size of a full-grown adult human. Spikes longer than my hand poke out from its wooden surface.

Spikes, for Fae's sake.

We're so dead.

I hold my breath as he smashes the weapon into the book-shelf on the end of the row. The impact is so big I feel it in my bones. Books and wood splinters fly all around us. My mouth goes paper-dry.

One thought flashes in my head: We need to get out of here.

Afraid any noise will alert the orc to our location, I motion Ruby to run toward the door, using the bookshelves as cover.

"What?" she whisper-yells. "You need to pee?"

"No!" I whisper, throwing up my hands. I shake my head

while planting a finger over my lips. But it's too late. The parquet wood floor trembles and creaks as the orc approaches, sniffing and making animalistic grunts.

A quick glance and I nearly die from fright. The orc is on the other side of the shelf, close enough I can make out the black dots flecking his green skin, the frayed leather pants he wears. Each desperate breath sends noxious odors funneling down my throat.

The sound of a deep inhalation fills the air. *Crap.*

I grab a wood splinter—the only weapon I can find—and motion to Ruby to split up. *Run on the count of three,* I mouth. *One, two—*

Ruby darts away before three, a war cry screaming from her lips. She makes it five feet before a hand the size of a basketball shoots through the top shelf, sending books flying, and snatches her.

Dammit.

Her curses flood the air. My legs urge me to run. To flee. I imagine shooting down the aisle to safety. He's distracted. It's not like he's going to eat her—

"Tasty thing," a deep, booming voice comments, the sound like two boulders smashing together. "I will crush your head like a grape and crunch your tiny bones between my teeth."

Oh, hell.

Mustering the remnants of my courage, I jump out into the open. "Hey, Ugly! Let her go."

The orc's olive-green brow furrows, deep lines converging. "You." He sniffs again as if confirming something. "You," he repeats.

With a growl, he tosses Ruby aside and lunges for me. I dart left and make a break for the door.

I make it two whole freaking feet before fingers like stone wrap around my waist. The ground disappears—he's lifting me! I twist in his hand enough to face him. Hot, rancid air blows over my face as he appraises me with a hungry look. "Can't eat. Must take to him. Can't eat, but want to eat."

Oh, God.

Ruby appears, Shimmer bless her. She buzzes around his head, pricking him with her toothpick-sized blade. He bellows and swats at her. She ducks his blows, sending balls of magic into his beady black eyes.

The world careens around me as he fights with Ruby. The stench and the swirling and the fingers vising my stomach make puke surge up my throat. Then I remember the splinter of wood in my hand. It's only four inches long, but the end is sharp . . .

The orc swings again, his fist finally connecting with Ruby. I scream as I watch her arc through the air and slam into the stone wall near the gaping hole that used to be the door.

"Hideous bastard!" I scream.

The orc glances at me, his eyes wide as if he forgot I was still here. A slow, stupid grin reveals a mouthful of daggerish teeth. "The Dominus will give me shiny things for you. So many shiny things."

With a wild roar of anger, I lift the makeshift stake and then plunge it into his right eye.

A deep bellow spills from his chest. The grip around my waist loosens and then I'm falling, my stomach somersaulting. The floor smashes into me so hard I swear my soul leaves my body along with every bit of air in my chest.

Pain rips through my leg until I welcome the darkness circling my mind. Then nothing.

I come to a moment later, my head ringing and chest tight, just in time to see the orc stumble into a bookshelf. The entire thing careens over and lands with a huge boom. A rage-filled screech surges from his mouth as he yanks out the splinter in his eye and flings it to the floor.

One giant hand covering his injured eye, he focuses his good eye on me. His lips twist into a hateful sneer. Large teeth honed down to needlepoints and dripping with saliva flash in the low light.

I try to stand, but daggers of pain sink deep into my calf the moment I put any pressure on my right leg. I'm ninety-nine percent sure it's broken. I'm also ninety-nine percent sure the orc isn't going to take me to the Dominus anymore—whoever that is.

By the hatred inside his remaining eye as he stumbles toward me, he's going to kill me. Or eat me alive first and then kill me.

Both options suck.

A second before he reaches where I lay, bright blue jags of light flash and strike the orc mid-chest. A cold blast of air draws goosebumps over my flesh, the room suddenly ten degrees cooler.

The orc goes still. Frozen with his arm raised above me, mouth open wide, a millisecond before he would have pounded in my skull. Frost creeps over his ashy-green skin, crackling and popping, until a thick layer covers him. His uninjured eye is the last to freeze. My stomach churns as I watch it turn opaque white.

All I can do is stare as my savior struts out of the shadows. I know that swagger. That predatory smoothness. That icy disdain for everything around him. His collar is askew, his hair messy and rumpled, as if he took a stroll out of bed.

My heart lurches at the sight of the prince. *Where the hell did you come from?*

He doesn't even glance at me as he squares up to the orc, one arm behind his back. Then he waves his hand like he's flicking water off his fingers and, with a thunderous crack, the frozen orc shatters into a million tiny shards of ice. Frozen bits pepper my hair and face and oh God . . .

I'm covered in orc pieces.

"My sprite," I call, my voice raspy with pain. "I think she's near the desk over there."

Once he's collected her, he moves on to me. His dark blue eyebrows meet above a frown as he scoops me into his cold arms. "You hurt?"

"No," I mutter through gritted teeth as a spasm of pain consumes my lower leg. "My leg always sticks out at a ninety-degree angle."

I swear to God an actual smile twitches the corner of his lips.

A moan slips from my throat and he shifts me in his arms so his one hand is free. *Yes, he's totally holding me with one arm like I'm nothing.* A flash of icy pain shoots up my leg. The sensation is so startling I can't even manage to cry out as my breath gets caught in my throat. Then the fiery agony of my leg melts away.

"I didn't have time to heal it," he says as he begins taking the stairs two at a time. "I need to get you out of here in case there's more orcs. But I used a spell to mask the pain." His breath is cool on my neck, his voice soothing and not at all winded.

Now that my pain is gone, the aftereffects of the orc and adrenaline dump hit me. I'm sinking fast into darkness.

"You have to stop doing this," I mutter.

He's quiet for a beat. "What?"

"Acting like you care about me at random times. You send me food. You give me expensive coats. You save my life. It's confusing and you have to stop."

Cold wind envelops me as he begins stalking across the lawn. As luck would have it, the campus is packed with Fae. I ignore the stares, the shocked faces and whispers that fill the night.

"Would you rather I left you to die down there?" he asks, sounding genuinely curious.

Closing my eyes, I relax my head, letting it fall gently against his chest. He smells of juniper and balsam and cedar. It's intoxicating.

I nuzzle into his neck, inhale his scent deeper, and whisper, "I'd rather have never met you at all."

27

I'm not sure if I'm awake or dreaming. I know I'm in bed because I can feel cold, starched sheets lightly fitted over my legs and waist. But it's like I'm underwater, in a pocket of space between sleep and reality.

I can't open my eyes, can't speak or move.

The first voice I hear is Eclipsa's. "Are you sure you didn't heal her? Because a healing of that nature . . ."

"I think I would know if I did," the male voice answers.

Oh, I know that voice. The confident, sultry tone practically runs through my head on repeat. The prince.

"You have to be careful," Eclipsa warns. "If it takes hold—"

"It won't. Believe me. She hates me."

Who hates him? What are they talking about?

They continue speaking but it's far away now, muffled voices from the end of a long tunnel. And then I plunge into a warm, velvety darkness.

"Why do I have to stay here even though I'm healed?" I ask, sitting up in bed. The healing center is on the main campus, a good-sized three-story white brick building with large windows and flowers in every room.

My nurse, a blue Fae girl with a huge nose and black eyes, glances at the clock and sighs. "Twenty more minutes and you're released. Some humans have reactions to the healing magic."

Right. I remember reading about that in class. Humans who have adverse reactions usually do so within twelve hours. Which means I've been stuck in this room for the entire morning.

"Pfft, she's fine," Ruby yells from where she sits on my headboard. "Look at her."

The nurse shoots Ruby a dark look before handing me two herbal drinks to help with any residual pain; one reeks of swampy mud and is lumpy and gray, the other has a verbena and lavender scent.

Ick.

Ruby flits over and snatches the verbena tumbler. "You gonna drink this, kid?"

"All yours." I throw the covers off, antsy to find a way back to the library and grab that book. Hopefully it's still a crime scene, or whatever, and I can somehow slip by and find it.

Mack and Evelyn sit in the faded blue loveseat in the corner, pretending to read human magazines. They burst in here a few minutes ago when nurse killjoy decided I could have visitors.

The moment the nurse finishes with me and leaves the room, they rush to my side.

"We heard what happened," Mack squeals. "A Cave Orc? Really, Summer?"

"Yeah, the whole school is talking about how it almost ate you," Evelyn adds.

Mack grins. "Did it stink? Cave Orcs are supposed to smell the worst."

Evelyn's face drains of color. "Oh . . . God. I think I'm going to be sick."

Mack rolls her eyes and jerks her shoulder at Evelyn. "Someone had way too much Faerie wine last night."

"Nope, not gonna puke. It passed." She flashes a bright smile, as if not puking is an achievement. "And I can't help if Rhaegar kept handing me drinks. He asked where you were, Summer, by the way."

Rhaegar? He seems like the last person who'd be plying a first year with alcohol.

"That's why we didn't show up until now," Mack adds, frowning at her feet. "If I had known what happened . . . well, anyway. Thank the Fae the school's shadow guardians heard the noise and came."

I cringe at the lie. The prince left almost as soon as he brought me here. But not before making me promise to stick to that story. I wouldn't be surprised if he glamoured all the Fae witnesses to forget, too.

Can't have his bad boy image tarnished. Not that I mistake him saving me as kindness—he obviously doesn't want me to die before he gets to torment me as his shadow.

"Yes," a female voice says. Headmistress Lepidonis strides through the room, her moth wings tucked low into her back. "Thank the Fae."

She flashes a tight smile at Mack and Evelyn as Mr. Willis enters the room. The girls look from the headmistress to Mr. Willis, their mouths hanging open.

My focus immediately hones in on the variety of weapons strapped to his person. I might not actively want to be a shadow, but wearing enough blades to arm a small gang?

Totally cool.

"Girls, I hear you had a late night," Lepidonis says with a smile that doesn't quite reach her dark eyes. "I would think you'd be very tired after such an eventful evening. Shouldn't you be getting back?"

A red flush creeps over Mack's cheeks, and she flashes me a see-you-later look before disappearing with Evelyn.

The moment they're gone, Lepidonis turns to me. "Miss Solstice, we've already suffered one human death this term and we cannot have another. The Council for the Mistreatment of Humans has already opened an inquiry into Miss Turner's death. Another death would be very bad for us, especially this close to winning the vote."

"What vote?" I ask, twisting the white sheets between my fingers. I haven't watched the news since I arrived.

"The vote to allow permanent residence for the Fae in the Untouched Zone, of course."

I swallow, my mouth suddenly dry. Currently, our laws allow the Fae visas for temporary living status. But if they became permanent residences . . . I can't even imagine such a thing.

She arches a severe eyebrow. "I take it you're not a supporter of integration, then?"

"You have a home," I point out, trying and failing to keep the anger from my voice. "Why come to ours?"

The furrows along her forehead deepen. "Because our lands are infested with darklings while our enemies, like the orc and the troll, grow stronger every day. Even with the human soldiers, the scourge continues to eat away at our homes, our territories. The court borders grow smaller, meaning more wars between themselves as they fight for land. Unless something changes, it is unsustainable."

Mr. Willis steps forward. His mouth is stern, but there's a kindness in his voice as he speaks. "The creature that nearly killed you was a Cave Orc from the scourge lands outside the wards. They're powerful but incredibly stupid. You were lucky. Had it been a darkling . . . "

"Pfft, nearly killed *us*?" Ruby shouts, darting from wherever spot she's been hiding. "You have that backwards, Mustache."

I cut my eyes to Ruby before meeting Mr. Willis's amused gaze.

"I thought the wards were strong enough to keep everything out," I say.

"They are," the headmistress promises. "We're still trying to determine how the orc got through our defenses . . . or who might have let it through. Only someone inside could have done a spell strong enough—" She stops mid-explanation, clicking her tongue. "All you need to know, Miss Solstice, is that we are investigating the matter."

"I hear the orc was missing an eye before he was killed," Mr. Willis adds, one side of his lips curved upward. "Impressive, Miss Solstice."

"That orc is lucky someone else *who isn't the prince* showed up," Ruby adds, winking in my direction like she's having an epileptic attack, "or we would have kicked his warty ass."

The headmistress and Mr. Willis exchange looks before they make to leave.

On the way out, the headmistress glances over her shoulder. "Miss Solstice, the prince says you were down there under his command. If I find out otherwise, you will be immediately expelled. Now, gather whatever you need from your dorm and then go to the gymnasium, and do not venture into the campus again until tomorrow morning."

"The gym?"

"Yes. Because of the intense . . . scrutiny our school is under, we have decided to make all mortal students sleep in the gym as an extra precaution. Professor Spreewell put a temporary ward on the building to keep any Fae from entering, and the building will be guarded by Mr. Willis's fourth year shadow guardians."

I should be grateful for the extra protection, but all I feel is bitter. The only reason the academy suddenly cares about human lives is because they want the human world to think they're kind and good. That they see us as equals.

But nothing could be further from the truth.

They have the first years set up in the upper room of the gymnasium overlooking the campus. The mats have been taken away and cots with white sheets line the floor. Evelyn, Mack, and I have the beds closest to the large floor-to-ceiling window.

Because the gym is normally chillier than the dorms, they've even cast a spell for warmth.

As luck would have it, we're right next to a group of Unseelie shadows. Reina's two boy toys from the first day, twins Drake and Vance Cartwright, sit on a cot beside Reina and her friend, Lily. This part of the gym is supposed to be girls only, but the twins must have snuck in.

"Hey, Trailer Park!" Reina calls, loud enough for the entire gym to hear. "I heard an orc picked up on your odor all the way from the scourge lands and sniffed his way here." Lifting her nose in the air, she inhales. "Yep. Smells like poor white trash to me."

Evelyn pushes her Gucci travel bag under her bed, ignoring them. "Pretend we don't hear them and they'll leave us alone."

"Screw that," Mack snaps. She drops her duffel to the ground with a thump and squares to face them. "Hey, Reina. Don't forget I have pictures of you from summer camp, before you discovered your love for bulimia, hair extensions, and plastic surgery. Be a shame if they found their way online."

"Whatever." Reina rolls her eyes. "You know, my dad said since you're adopted, you shouldn't even be considered a legacy."

My hands ball into hard fists, and I toss my paper sack full of stuff onto my bed and join Mack. Picking on me is par for the course. But Mack is off-limits.

Reina's barb hit its mark; a red blush creeps up Mack's neck.

Then Mack rallies. "What, the one time of year he comes to visit you? My parents might not be my birth parents, but at least they *enjoy* my company."

Mack's words must strike a nerve because it's Reina's turn to flush, anger brightening her pale skin. With a dramatic flip of her gorgeous curls, she turns her back on us.

"Bitch," Mack mutters. "I've known her since we were little and she just gets worse with time."

"I hear her mom became a darkling and they killed her right in front of Reina when she was, like, six or something," Evelyn whispers cheerily.

I slap a hand over my mouth. I might despise Reina, but no one deserves to see their mother become a monster and then be killed. "I thought . . . people in the Untouched Zones didn't turn."

Evelyn lifts her delicate shoulders, causing one red braid to slip over the side. "That was before they completely cut off contact to the Tainted Zone, thank the Shimmer."

My jaw clenches. Evelyn usually forgets I'm from the Tainted Zone, even though I've reminded her countless times.

"I remember," Mack says as she sits on her cot, a distant look softening her focus. "It was all over the news. Her dad was a prominent politician, so it was a big story."

After that pearl of happiness, we busy ourselves unpacking our stuff and settling in for the day. I try not to look at Reina where she holds court with her minions. Try not to let the sadness I feel for her seep inside my heart.

But it creeps in, anyway. Damn human emotions.

We spend the rest of the time hanging on Mack's cot gossiping and ignoring the Unseelie crew. As Mack puts little streaks of violet in my hair with hair chalk and then french-braids it, the nervous knot in my belly begins to soften.

I even find myself laughing along with Mack as Evelyn divulges all the campus secrets. Which shadows are sleeping with whom. The forbidden love triangle going on between a Dawn Court shadow and two Mortal Creatures Court shadows.

Apparently, even fraternizing with other shadows outside our keeper's Court is frowned upon.

Oh, goodie. Just another reason I can't become the prince's shadow.

I perk up even more when I learn the students are allowed to go into the basement where some of the mythological creatures are kept—the ones who can't stand the bitter cold in the outdoor menagerie.

My favorite beast ends up being the basilisk, a large venomous green snake with horns. His entire cage is coated with magical tint to prevent his gaze from turning anyone he looks at to stone.

Creepy, but rad.

As soon as night falls, a fourth year comes in dragging an old television on a cart and places the TV in the front of the room. The movie has just barely started when another fourth year comes in and says someone wants to talk with me outside.

The fact they can't come inside means they're Fae. The way the fourth year looks close to crapping his pants means they're important. And by his armband, the fourth year is an Unseelie shadow, meaning the Fae is probably Unseelie as well.

The prince. My heart wobbles in my chest.

Everyone's attention is on me as I stretch out my legs on the bed and shake my head. "Tell him I'm busy."

The fourth year, a tall boy with thin lips, big ears, and sandy blond hair, tugs at his shirt. "He said you'd say that, and to tell you that you owe him."

"Well tell him I don't want to distract him from his battle tonight."

Beads of sweat trickle down his temples, his eyes tight with fear. I almost feel sorry for the boy, but not enough to give in.

"He said you'd say that too, and to tell you if you want the book, you'll meet him."

My breath hitches. The book? As in the book I nearly died for?

Finally convinced, I ignore the stares of literally everyone as I throw my coat over my pajamas. I insist Mack and Ruby go too, and the fourth year nods, looking so relieved that he'd probably agree to anything at this point.

Technically, I don't need Ruby or Mack to face the prince. But I've learned the hard way that Ruby can't be left alone. I'd likely come back to her having started a brawl with the Unseelie sprites or stolen something.

And Mack . . . Mack is coming because a part of me no longer trusts myself around the prince.

Not when he saved me. Not when the parts of my skin where he touched still tingles. When my cheek still remembers the sensation of his flesh, cold and hard, as I rested my head against his chest.

There was so much pain and relief flooding my body that I hadn't thought about it then, but ever since, that's all I can think about.

Him. How I *want* to hate him—how I *should* hate him— but I can't.

Not after last night.

Not after discovering how being in his arms felt like the rightest thing in the world.

Somewhere deep down I know that my hatred is the only wall of defense I have against the magnetic pull he exudes. Once that defense is gone, I'll be powerless.

And that scares me.

Outside, two shadow guardians stand by the heavy metal doors. Weapons drip from their black and red uniforms, the sight reminding me of the dangers outside these doors. At first they try to stop us, but the fourth year whispers into their ears and they let us pass.

The bonfire must be twice the size of last night because it lights up the entire campus, an angry sun surrounded by dark shapes. A primal energy swells the frigid, smoky air, and strange, animalistic noises carry with the wind, sending Ruby diving into the breast pocket of my coat.

Beneath my layers of clothing, the hair on my arms stands erect.

The fourth year shadow leads us across the snow into a side courtyard walled in on three sides by a stone fence. A giant oak tree stands sentinel in the middle, its long, regal branches weighted with snow.

As soon as we step foot in the courtyard, the fourth year retreats.

A sudden howling wind draws my eye to a raging wall of

snow. It circles around the courtyard like a bubble, faster and faster and faster until we're trapped.

"What's happening?" Mack whispers, resituating her scarlet wool scarf around her neck.

"He wants privacy," I mutter. "Showoff."

"Who?" Her crystallized breath plumes across the courtyard.

I'd completely forgotten I haven't told them who we're meeting. Before I can answer, the Winter Prince emerges from a doorway on the other side, his owl perched on his shoulder. Asher trails beside him, arms crossed over his massive chest and a miserable look on his face. As a shifter, he might be Unseelie, but I learned in class that dragon shifters are cold-blooded by nature and need warmth.

Basically, the opposite of this place.

The moment Asher locks eyes on Mack, the big guy's face lights up.

My gaze slides to Mack beside me. A blush stains her tanned cheeks, a timid smile playing across her lips as she returns his stare.

The prince and I, on the other hand, glare at each other like opposing generals before a battle.

"Do you have my book?" I say in lieu of greeting, jutting out my hand palm up. I ignore the tiny jump my heart gave at the sight of him. At his stupid messy blue-black hair and perpetual smirk. The moonlight glimmers inside his irises, making them look more silver than blue.

He reaches inside his sable waistcoat and retrieves the leather-bound tome. "You mean, this old thing?"

My eyes narrow. I sense a trick. "Wait, why aren't you and Asher, you know . . ."

"Overcome by our primal urges?" He arches an infuriatingly sexy blue eyebrow. "Some of us can control our inner beasts . . . when we want to."

As if just to toy with me, his irises suddenly pulse azure-blue, making his appearance too inhuman for my comfort. Mack gives a little squeak and jumps back a step.

Asher snorts, casting an amused look at the prince. "It's midnight when you need to worry, little humans. Even the most controlled Fae won't be able to harness their urge then."

That's when the prince and Rhaegar will fight. A twinge of unease settles between my shoulder blades, and I sweep a heavy gaze over the book, held carefully inside the prince's long fingers. "Why are you giving the book to me if it might help Rhaegar win?"

An arrogant grin carves into his angular jaw. "Because there's absolutely nothing in this world that will make that happen."

"Have you read it?"

"Of course not."

Arrogant dickwad. I reach for the book but he jerks it just out of my reach.

"First," he says. "Some questions. What did the orc say to you?"

Shivering, I shove my gloved hands into my coat pockets. "That he wanted to eat me . . . but he couldn't."

"Why not?" Asher asks, too quickly.

"He wanted to bring me to his master—no, he called him something in another language. The Dom . . . something."

"Dominus?" the prince finishes softly.

I nod.

Mack gasps, and the muscles flex in Asher's jaw as he lobs the prince a worried look. Even Ruby begins to shiver inside my pocket.

"Who is the Dominus?" Part of me doesn't want to know. For some reason, everyone is looking at the prince.

"Every court has different names for him," Ruby offers. "My fellow sprites call him Blackheart."

"Who?" I press.

"The Darken," Mack whispers in a low voice, as if he might hear her.

"King Oberon?" I brush back a strand of my violet-streaked hair from my face. "I thought he was dead?"

"Never mind that," the prince growls, his expression dark. "Why didn't you tell me what the orc said when I found you?"

I shrug, hating how stupid I suddenly feel. "I thought it was an orc hierarchy thing, like, on How to Train Your Dragon . . ." My words trail away as his face goes blank with confusion. "You know the movie where the dragons took food to the master dragon?"

Yeah, keep digging yourself a hole of stupidity. Mack grinds her elbow into my ribs and I remember Asher is a real-life dragon.

"No offense, dragon boy," I add.

He gives me a panty-dropping wink. "None taken, human."

I almost smile . . . until my gaze wanders to the prince and his sour expression. I can't understand why he's so angry. Especially if King Oberon is dead.

"This isn't a joke," he finally says. "You need to take our world seriously if you're going to survive it."

Hot anger blooms over my cheeks. "I'm trying. All I do is study until my eyes cross. I've made A's on all my tests . . . I practice with Eclipsa until my body is black and blue. What more do you want from me?"

His nostrils flare. "I want you to be safe."

I wasn't expecting that, and for a heartbeat, I'm speechless.

How dare he claim the high ground. How dare he try to pretend that all of his cruelty is for my benefit.

Jaw clenched, I close the distance between us. "Safe? If

you wanted me safe you would have never brought me to Everwilde." I yank the sleeve of my coat up until his mark shows, moonlight sparkling inside the metallic lines. "And you would have never branded me like an animal."

Hot tears sting my throat. Tears I'd rather die than shed in front of him. I hate the control he has over me; I hate that his mark embeds my skin; and I especially hate the knowledge that all it would take is one kind smile, one apology, and my anger would melt away like snow beneath the sun.

Mack takes my gloved hand in hers. Asher finds a spot on the wall to stare at.

The prince and I meet eyes. My heart dances strangely in my chest the longer I hold his stare, that inexplicable pull between us growing stronger, the anger and confusion and frustration rising with it to form a chaotic spell of emotions I can't break free of.

"Why did you bring me here, Prince?" I will those words over the snow and into the black pit he calls a heart.

For the briefest of seconds, the defensive wall he keeps over his countenance lowers—just enough that I think he might finally open up. Might finally give an answer that indicates he's not the soulless Fae I suspect he is.

The one who loves to watch me hurt.

Instead, his jaw firms up and that infernal cold mask slips over his face, his eyes going hard and cruel.

He shoves the book into my open hand. "Go back to the gym and stay there until morning. By then, you'll be mine."

"Yours?" I hiss, but he's already stalking across the snow, his stupid cape slithering like a shadow behind him. If I wasn't afraid the book would disintegrate on impact, I would throw it at his miserable head.

Note to self: wear boots that come off easier.

Just like that, the wall of blinding snow disappears, and the fourth year escorts us back to the gym.

Inside, Mack settles in to watch the rest of the movie with a slice of pizza. The higher ups apparently thought a *Twilight* marathon and deep dish pies shuttled in from a famous pizzeria in Evernell would keep us content.

It works—for everyone but me. While the others stuff their faces and then nod off to Edward and Jacob fighting over Bella, I pore over the book the prince so pompously gave me.

I'm determined to help Rhaegar win no matter the cost.

At some point, Ruby flutters over to my bed and sits atop the book, her little bean pod shoes making scuffing sounds against the old parchment. I lean down to hear what she has to say.

"I can help you," she offers carefully. "If the prince wins you as his shadow, I can get you out of Everwilde and back to the human realm." I open my mouth to object and she adds, "I can do it, you know. I may be small, but I'm good with spells. I can make you invisible to sneak you past the guards. . . or make it so anytime the prince looks at you he develops violent diarrhea. Two weeks, tops, and he'll trade you."

Wow, that escalated fast. And what is it with her and bodily functions?

But her offer warms my bitter heart, and I make a little nest of covers by my pillow for her. "Thank you, Ruby, but as long as I bear his mark, he can find me anywhere."

Fae can't cross into the human world without a visa. But if a human bears a Fae slave mark, there are plenty of bounty hunters who would find me and bring me back. Not to mention, I'm absolutely positive the Winter Prince has a visa.

It's like this: the Winter King and his family undoubtedly have a monstrous townhouse in the major cities in the Untouched Zone, while my family can barely scrape by in a dying land.

Because life isn't kind to those without power.

Turning the page, I go back to my research. Deep in my gut I know the answer I need is inside these stories. And I'll be damned if I become the prince's shadow without a fight.

I find what I'm looking for on the very last chapter. *Breaking Dawn* is playing over the television, the meager bluish light just enough to read if I squint really hard. As far as I can tell, everyone is asleep. It must be near midnight.

I've blown through exactly thirty chapters of intense recountings of the Nocturus over the years. All of them interesting, intense, and gruesome.

How very, very Fae.

The prologue gives a small history of the Nocturus. The Faerie Courts are notoriously corrupt, so many disputes were decided by the Nocturus, a battle of cunning and magic. In ancient times, there might be one hundred Nocturi held on the two major holidays when Fae powers are at their height: Samhain and the Wild Hunt.

Over the years, the Nocturus fell out of favor. Mostly because the Fae justice system became streamlined once the prince's grandfather, Oberon, consolidated power to become ruler over all the courts.

The rules of a Nocturus are simple: Each opponent

chooses three weapons. Then they fight using said weapons and magic until one kills the other or one asks for mercy.

Most willingly die rather than shame their court.

The last chapter piques my interest for three reasons. One, the battle was held in secret, with only one witness per contestant. Two, the first opponent was a girl, the princess and heir to the Summer Court, Hyacinth Larkspur.

And, three, because the Winter Prince was the other player. I read his name twice, Prince Sylverfrost, just to be sure. There's also a fairly good illustration in the book of the entire scene.

The girl is strikingly beautiful with long, unruly red hair and a stunning display of iridescent wings, two on each side of her shoulder blades. She wears a crown of ivy weaved with poppies and bellflowers.

The Winter Prince is dressed in his usual pale blue cape and ice crown, his hair depicted bright royal blue.

My heart jackhammers so loud in my chest I think it'll wake the Spring Court shadow on the nearest cot as I read below the illustration. The girl was incredibly skilled in both swordplay and elemental magic, and the fight went on for nearly an hour until both their powers were reportedly low.

It was then the girl drew her last weapon—a whip threaded with snowdrops.

Something about the whip caused the prince to cower, stumbling to a knee, and she used a staff to knock his own blade from his hand. Weaponless and magicless, he bared his throat for her to cut, smiling . . . if the text is true.

Only she didn't kill him. Instead, for reasons not explained in the book, she claimed a truce that let both players keep their dignity, allowing the prince to live on to eventually torment me.

Excitement prickles my skin. I slam the book shut,

sending dust flying into my face. The whip . . . why would that have bothered the prince?

A memory bobs to the surface. A story I heard Evelyn tell once during one of her long tales regarding the Winter Prince's depravity.

She claimed King Oberon made him fight a soldier every evening when the prince was a boy. If he lost, if he showed a hint of emotion or mercy, the Darken tied him up in front of the entire court, stripped his shirt, and hit him with an iron whip until his skin cracked open.

According to Evelyn, wherever the prince's silver blood touched between the cracks of the cobblestones, snowdrops blossomed. And today an entire field of snowdrops fill the courtyard of the Winter Castle, beautifully sad reminders of his beatings.

Right until this moment, I chalked her story up to another fancy tale.

Not now.

Throwing on my coat and gloves, I shake Ruby awake. "I think I know how to help Rhaegar win!"

One tiny eye flutters open, and she stares at me dreamily. "You and your five brothers, huh?" She giggles. "I've always wanted my own harem of human men."

"What?"

Both eyes snap open and focus on me. "What?"

"Ruby, I need you," I whisper. "I know it's a lot to ask . . . but can you still do that invisibility spell?"

A wide grin brightens her face, and she flits into the air, giving a little bow. "Ruby Ricin, at your service."

The only problem with being invisible in winter is the tracks along the snow. Well, that and my breath, which wafts into the sky in milky bursts once it clears the invisibility bubble Ruby keeps around us.

"How much farther?" I whisper, the book clutched beneath my arm. At Ruby's suggestion, we cut through the forest to get to the ceremonial meadow where all Nocturi are held.

Ruby darts into the trees and then zips back down into the protective bubble. From inside, the shell looks much like an actual soap bubble, its delicate, clear surface tinged in faint rainbows of color. "It's just up ahead, but we need to hurry. Looks like it's about to start."

Through the gaps in the trees, fire sputters and dances from torches erected to form a circle. In between the torches, a magical boundary of some sort shimmers. To keep the fighters from running away, Ruby informs me.

A crowd of Fae surround the makeshift arena, blocking my view inside.

Leaving me to wait, Ruby zigzags through the trees toward the meadow. I lose sight of her in the crowd. Clutching the book to my chest, I wait, shivering and praying none of the nearby Fae smell me.

What feels like hours later, Rhaegar and Basil come up the path to meet me. Sleek gold armor is fitted to Rhaegar's chest, and varying shades of green kerchiefs hang from his shoulders, the little bells sewn into them tinkling.

A distrustful look darkens Rhaegar's normally handsome face. The moment Ruby lifts the invisibility spell and I appear, his eyes widen and he rushes to me.

"What the Fae hells are you doing here?" He shifts his gaze to scan the woods before returning his attention to me.

"If another Fae sees you, they could hurt you. *I* could hurt you. You shouldn't be here."

That's when I notice the green glow smoldering inside his golden eyes. The bulge of fangs beneath his lips. He retreats to keep a wide distance between us, but I make out his nostrils as they flare slightly at my scent.

"You shouldn't be here," he repeats in a gravelly tone I don't recognize. His eyes are now glowing as bright as the torches in the distance, and black talons sprout from his hands.

A twinge of fear spikes my blood, and I retreat a step. "I came to give you this." Slowly, I hold out the book. Basil takes it from my hands and delivers it to Rhaegar as I quickly explain what I learned.

While I talk, Rhaegar's face twists and morphs into more beast than Fae; long black muzzle, lupine eyes, and glittering fangs mask any trace of his humanity. The change is so slow I hardly notice until it's done, and then I can't stop staring.

Especially when he smiles at my newfound information, baring a row full of needle-sharp teeth perfectly capable of shredding flesh.

Even Basil seems nervous around him. His tail twitches behind him, his long goat ears pinned to his head and eyes rolled to the side to watch Rhaegar.

A whiny snarl trickles from Rhaegar's chest, and he touches his face, his predatory eyes locked on me. With a final growl, he flips on his heels and storms back to the arena.

"What is he?" I whisper, my entire body clenched to keep from shivering. I don't remember wolf shifter in his bio.

Basil watches him go, worry settling over his face. He hasn't changed much. His horns might be longer, his face a bit more goat-like. Otherwise, he seems normal enough.

"His shifter form recently became more lupine in nature."

His hooves stomp nervously in the snow until grass and soil peek through.

"Aren't you scared?" I ask, leaving the 'of him' part out.

"This is Everwilde; I'm always scared. As you should be, mortal." An inhuman wail comes from somewhere deep in the forest, and he shifts an anxious glance at the noise before lowering his eyebrows at me. "You need to leave. Now."

Ruby conjures the invisibility spell, and I make sure to start walking back down the path so my footprints show. Satisfied, Basil joins the others in the meadow just as a wild cheer reverberates the air.

It's starting. And my fate hangs in the balance. How can I go back to the gym and wait? My nerves and the not knowing will eat me alive. Just the idea twists my gut, sending hot bile lapping at the back of my throat.

Turning on my heel, I follow the path, stopping ten yards from the forest's edge. Then I find a passably climbable tree, take off my gloves, and shimmy my way up.

"What are you doing, human?" Ruby hisses, darting in nervous circles around my face.

"Climbing a tree. I thought that was obvious?"

"What's obvious," she replies, "is that you are a bigger idiot than I thought." She pokes me in the spot between my eyebrows, hard, and then settles onto a frosted branch close to my face. "And they call me unhinged."

"This is my future," I say, settling onto a limb I'm fairly confident will hold my weight. "Did you really think I would miss the opportunity to watch it be decided? Hell to the no."

"Titania save us," she mutters.

"Just keep that invisibility spell going and she won't have to."

In the arena, I spot a Fae with a ram's head cross to the center of the meadow. He holds up a white horn, curved into a spiral, and blows, sending a shimmer of sunset-orange dust into the air.

The sound echoes through the forest, the eerie, otherworldly melody prickling my spine. Silence descends. A horrifying silence one could drown in.

For a paralyzing moment, my heartbeat thunders louder than the horn—at least, inside my head. I don't think I can take the waiting. A hollow feeling carves out my belly, the strange moonlight and animalistic noises and threat of imminent death all too much.

An inner voice, the one that's kept me alive this long, whispers that I need to get down from this tree and run. That there are things in these woods more dangerous than the prince.

But I cannot turn away from the battle, not when the outcome will shape four years of my life. So I cling to the icy tree, hardly daring to breathe as a roar of bloodlust and excitement thrums the night.

And then two male Fae step into the ring.

Every nerve inside my body tingles as I hold the trunk for dear life, watching the battle unfold. I don't dare blink, don't dare move an inch. My vantage point is close to perfect, the entire arena splayed out before my prying eyes.

Rhaegar is half-shifted, his head wolfish and large—because that's not terrifying at all. Even stranger, he stands upright, a bow held at the ready. A collective gasp of awe stirs the air as Rhaegar lights the tip of the arrow with magical fire.

We are not in Kansas anymore, Toto.

Behind him, Basil stands on one side holding the weapons Rhaegar chose. I can't tell from here what they are, but surely one is a whip. A group of Seelie crowd around Basil, shouting encouragement at Rhaegar.

The prince has his back to me, but I would recognize that arrogant stance anywhere. He seems much the same. No shifting. No predatory beast form to instill fear and reverence in the crowd.

Just his normal, dickwad insolence. One arm held behind his back. Lithe, sexy body all loose and casual and stuff, like he isn't the center of attention. Like he isn't about to kill someone—or die himself.

I don't even have to see his face to know he's grinning.

A frown tugs at my half-frozen lips. Why wouldn't he shift?

Unless he thinks he's already won . . .

With a warrior's snarl, Rhaegar leaps into the air. At the same time, he looses his arrow of fire. The entire meadow erupts in yells as the fiery weapon streaks at the prince, sparks raining in its path . . . only to bounce off a shield of some sort.

The prince circles to the left enough that I can make out his face. Yep, grinning. The torches cast deep shadows that highlight the dimple in his cheek. The one that tempers his otherwise jagged features. Fangs tip his teeth, his eyes emanating a vibrant blue light.

He calls out for his first weapon, his voice casual, almost playful, and Asher tosses a longsword into the prince's outstretched hand. The rest of the Six pace behind the dragon shifter, obviously not as calm as the prince.

Blue flames run along his blade and illuminate the meadow, the play of orange and blue light creating an other-worldly sight. Rhaegar growls and shoots off countless arrows. Each time, the prince uses his sword to deflect them with ease.

He moves gracefully, effortlessly. As if unworried by the encounter.

His carefree attitude only serves to feed Rhaegar's frustration and rage. Rhaegar tosses his bow into the audience and retrieves another weapon. Firelight glimmers off the face of the double-sided axe. Growling deep and low, Rhaegar begins to circle the prince.

A swarm of sprites flock to the air for a better view. A few fights break out as the aggression spills into the circle of onlookers.

A predatory energy descends, choking the air and filling my body with alarm. More fights break out. Screams taint the night. Even the moon seems tinged with a dusky red as if the Fae control it.

Maybe they do. Nothing surprises me about their powers anymore.

The prince evades the axe as easily as he did the arrows. He still hasn't chosen his second weapon. Snow begins to drizzle, as teasing as its master. The prince ducks and weaves Rhaegar's advances, slipping through the air like smoke.

All at once, the prince lunges forward and catches Rhaegar's ear. The crowd goes wild. The tip of the sword strips the diamond earring from Rhaegar's ear. He howls in pain. Blood dots the snow.

Someone shrieks in excitement as the prince catches the diamond in his palm and holds it out to the throng of Fae. With a clever grin, he tosses it to a blue-skinned female pixie, serenaded by a mixture of boos and cheers.

Then he winks.

Showoff. He's toying with Rhaegar. Grinding his ego down one skillful maneuver at a time. He's not even using much magic—which is a shame since the extent of his powers are unknown. Perhaps that's why he doesn't access his magic.

Or perhaps he's just a maniacal jerkwad.

Either way, his strategy is working. Rhaegar's movements grow sloppy, his footwork slow and clumsy, like he's half drunk. His breath spews into the air as he works to breathe.

After swinging at the prince and missing—again—he throws the axe, nearly impaling a male Fae with monarch butterfly wings. A savage expression has taken hold of his normally handsome face, his golden eyes stretched wide inside his wolf's head, tongue lolling.

Black lupine lips curl in a snarl of sharp teeth; then he charges. The prince rebuffs the assault with a flick of his hand, sending a breeze to knock him back. He tumbles across the meadow like he weighs nothing.

The closest onlookers scatter, fear on their faces as they appraise Rhaegar.

Their fear spreads to me as I take him in. He's almost completely changed. His body now more wolf than Fae. His back is hunched, dark fur jutting from his arms and legs. His predatory eyes are unrecognizable.

Even from here I can feel his animalistic hatred, the deep-seated, almost instinctive need to kill.

I watch in horror as he charges the prince and a bloodier battle ensues. This time, the prince strikes flesh and bone with his blade. Rhaegar howls, a mixture of rage and pain.

The breeze carries the metallic odor of blood.

Rhaegar's shifter form weakens, and he starts to wildly throw balls of fire into the arena, sending the onlookers scrambling backward. Most miss the prince, but a few get close enough to burn. Only the moment they near the prince, the moment the orange of the fire tinges his high cheekbones, the flames sizzle and die, snuffed out by whatever he fancies.

Falling sleet. A wintry breeze. Buckets of snow. The world seems at his disposal, the icy landscape his to harness.

It's a slaughter. I close my eyes, force them back open. Rhaegar's last chance is the whip.

Pull it out!

A chaotic jumble of emotions spills through me. What if he loses? What if the prince kills him? What if he kills the prince? That can't happen. All of these options are crap.

No—I push the negative thoughts from my mind, squeezing the tree trunk so hard the bark gouges my frozen cheeks. The pain, numbed by the cold, works to extinguish the violent flurry of what-ifs raging inside me.

A rush of unease hits me as the mood changes. The crowd's cries for blood grows louder, more insistent. The air becomes charged with energy and magic and the promise of death. So strong, so *real* I can almost see it, like a beastly shadow creeping closer.

I shouldn't be here. The thought hits me like a sledgehammer. Once the battle is over, whatever the result, these woods will be full of Fae turned savage by bloodlust.

But my gaze rivets to the two Fae in the arena, mesmerized by their fierce fight to the death. By their contrast. Winter and Summer. Ice and Fire. Brute force and cunning skill.

The prince has finally decided to use his magic offensively, and his theatrics brighten the sky. Bursts of police-siren blue magic erupt repeatedly until, even with my eyes closed, the flares etch into my eyelids. Fireworks of ice detonate near Rhaegar, tiny frozen slivers peppering his flesh until it's slick with red.

But none of it really hurts him. The magic meant more to impress than injure.

What is the prince doing?

Limping, Rhaegar stumbles over to Basil. Rhaegar's body is tired, broken, the only trace left of his wolf form a few patches of fur and incisors. Basil tries to hide his worried expression as he hands over the last weapon.

Wrapping my arms around the tree trunk, I crane my head to see what it is. Did he take my advice? Anticipation wets my palms inside my gloves, the muscles between my shoulder blades tight as rocks.

The prince is too busy grandstanding to the crowd, his back to Rhaegar, to notice the new weapon. A hush falls as everyone watches to see what it might be.

"Hey, Ice Prince," Rhaegar calls. His voice is raspy and tired and whispers of pain, but there's a newfound hopefulness there too.

Beautiful face still wearing that clever smile, the Winter Prince turns back to his foe, slowly, driving the blade of carelessness deeper into Rhaegar and then twisting it for good measure. Saying he is nothing.

But Rhaegar has one last trick up his sleeve. As he jerks his hand back, I spy the long end of the whip. Little white clusters of something twine around its length. Snowdrops.

The crack of the whip snapping toward the prince is so loud that I gasp. The end strikes his cheek, opening up a layer of pale flesh. Surprise twitches across his lips as he watches the snowdrops scatter over the snow.

From his blood or the whip, I haven't a clue.

I wait for something to happen. For the prince to laugh at Rhaegar, or use his power. Instead, his posture changes, his strong shoulders drooping as he falters back. The insolence and conceit he's worn like armor for the entire bout fall away, replaced by a much more potent emotion: fear.

The prince is afraid. He cowers, falling to his knees. A look of absolute terror transforms his expression.

The change from powerful to vulnerable cuts deep inside me. I grip the tree, confused by my change in heart.

I want Rhaegar to win. I want to command my fate. I want to be paired with a keeper who doesn't hurt me and confuse me and send me spiraling out of control.

But I don't want the prince to die.

Stupid Fae rules. Stupid Fae everything. I hate them at this moment more than I've ever hated anyone. Rhaegar and the prince and the whole lot of them.

Inara screams for the prince to get up; Asher roars, featherless dragon wings snapping out behind him, smoke rumbling from his snarling mouth. But they can do nothing to help the prince as Rhaegar stalks toward him.

The prince tries to use his powers, but his palms are

barren; he depleted his magic during his dumb, showy display.

What have I done? My belly twists. Each step the Summer Fae takes toward the fallen prince is a stab to my heart. I feel sick.

Hollowness and terror sweep over me.

He's going to kill the prince and I helped and I'll never forgive myself. I don't know why I care but I do.

I *do*.

Rhaegar kicks the sword from the prince's hand and catches it midair. His eyes are black, murderous. He may not be a wolf anymore but his eyes are all beast. The Seelie crowd chants a single word, *marbhadh*, in Gaelic over and over and over until it seems to come from one god-like voice.

I don't need to speak Gaelic to know what the word means.

Kill.

From my vantage, the prince is on his knees partially facing me. Both their expressions are half-visible. Rhaegar holds the blade at an angle, tip pointed down at the prince's heart.

"Any last words, Sylverfrost?" Rhaegar asks, his gloating lips spitting the prince's surname like poison.

The prince's eyes grow pensive as he seems to contemplate Rhaegar's question. *Oh, Lord.* This is really it. I hold up my arm, prepared to throw it over my face at the killing blow.

Wait. I watch the slow, curling smile tug the prince's lips upward, confused as his fear morphs into something else. "Yeah, actually. If you don't mind." His gaze shifts from Rhaegar—to me.

Me, hiding in the tree invisible . . . except, actually, a quick look shows Ruby curled up in some evergreen foliage, asleep.

So I'm not invisible.

My heart spikes into my throat as the prince holds my stare. A surge of electricity zips up my spine.

Then he winks, his stupid, infernal lips mouthing, *thank you.*

What the everliving—

I don't even see the prince gesture, but an explosive boom shudders the forest. Ice and snow burst off the branches. Ruby wakes with a screech as an avalanche of snow and wind scour the trees, nearly knocking me from my perch.

Dark, ominous clouds blacken the sky and blot out the moon, veiling the meadow in layers of shadows.

His power—he didn't use it up. It's everywhere. Vibrating from the trees; swelling the air; roiling in the dark clouds above. A maelstrom of magic and death.

Tightening my hold, I turn my attention back to the meadow to see Rhaegar caught inside a tornado of ice and snow. The churning force lifts him into the sky, higher, higher . . . and then slams him down with a bone-cracking thud.

The scream of a Summer Fae in the crowd pierces the quiet and then abruptly dies.

No one speaks as we all focus on Rhaegar where he lies on his back. A universal question on everyone's lips. Is he dead?

He tries to lift his head—so hurt but alive.

Icy spikes larger than my forearm shoot from the storm clouds toward Rhaegar. Horrified, I force myself to look at the Summer Fae, sure he's been impaled. My mind readying itself for blood and horror.

But the spikes instead nail his clothing through the thick crust of snow and into the frozen ground, trapping him like a butterfly pinned to a board by its wings. Two spikes at his shoulders. Two at his waist. Countless more along the leather fabric of his pants. They even pin the top of his pine-green cape, spread out behind him like alien blood.

The snow beneath him becomes alive, white tendrils of ice

twisting over his body until he's practically entombed. Only his face remains uncovered.

And his fear, unlike the prince's, is absolutely real.

Whistling, the prince closes the distance between them in blood-chilling silence. He playfully twirls the sword that, moments ago, was ready to slice through bone and flesh into his heart, ending him.

When he stands directly over Rhaegar, any humor drains from his features, his jaw tight and eyes emotionless. "What will it be, Rhaegar? Death . . . or mercy?"

A collective gasp fills the cold air. Basil frowns, worrying his fingers. A few of the Unseelie boo at the option, obviously wanting the prince to kill Rhaegar and be done with it.

I look to Ruby, who's now wide awake, her mouth gaping at the events.

"What happens if he asks for mercy?" I whisper.

Ruby shakes her head, as if the idea is too impossible to fathom. "He would never . . . such a cowardly thing would make him an outcast from his court forever. He would never," she repeats.

But he does. The entire ring of onlookers goes quiet as Rhaegar's voice, broken and ashamed, spills into the meadow. "Mercy. I ask for . . . mercy."

The prince nods; the cage of ice melts away. The Unseelie side goes wild, a victorious cry rising from their ranks while the Seelie turn their backs on Rhaegar and quickly flee into the woods.

Half in shock, I slide down the tree, not caring that the bark tears at my face and clothes. Not caring that someone might see me. Not caring about anything in this moment but the horrifying truth.

He used me.

He *tricked* me.

The thought worms under my skin as I turn it over in my

mind. The way he gave me the book and let me believe, in his arrogance, he hadn't read it. That same arrogance was used in the arena to goad Rhaegar into thinking he'd used the last of his power.

In allowing Rhaegar to assume his power was gone, he lured the Summer Fae into letting his guard down. But it was more than that.

Any number of times, he could have ended Rhaegar.

Instead he destroyed the one thing that Rhaegar valued over all else: his honor.

Why? What twisted Faerie game is he playing? More importantly, what sort of person can wield their emotions so expertly, like a weapon honed to perfection?

A Fae prince. I should have expected as much.

The moment my boots crunch the snowy ground, I break into a sprint. Ruby dives into my pocket just in time. I crash blindly through the path, overwhelmed with emotion.

He used me. He played me. And I fell right into his trap. My stupidity ended in the one thing I didn't want to happen: I am the Winter Prince's slave *and* shadow.

We are intimately linked for the next four years.

And now that I know what he's really capable of . . . now that I know how he wields his emotions to make anyone see exactly what he wants . . .

There can't be a more dangerous Fae in all of Everwilde.

W hen I finally fall asleep, I tumble into a pit of nightmares. Each one worse than the last. In the first, Rhaegar has completely shifted into his wolf form. He's injured, curled on his side in the snow, his onyx fur contrasted deeply against the pure white. His voice is a half-howl as he calls for mercy, but the prince runs him through with a sword anyway.

In the other, I'm lost in a blizzard. Slowly freezing to death. The Winter Prince reaches for me but when I take his hand, he turns to ice, his fingers shattering inside mine.

Then I toss and turn on my cot, trapped in that ethereal dream state where I'm not quite sleeping and not fully awake. The fire has blown out and my breath spills from my lips like mist to join the others.

Everyone is asleep, but a slithering noise comes from beneath the metal beds. Like something slowly dragging itself along the floorboards of the gym.

Gathering my courage, I move my head to discover what's making the noise, but I'm paralyzed. Unable to look, to blink, to cry for help. The slithering grows closer. Closer. Now it's beneath my bed.

There's a hiss near my head.

In my periphery, I catch a long, slender nose gliding along my pillow. Dark green scales tipped black glitter in the half-light, a pink forked tongue flickering softly. Finger-length white horns crown a serpentine head.

The basilisk. A black shadowy mist leaks from his orange eyes, his vertical pupils blown wide. He hasn't looked at me yet . . . but the moment he does, I'll be turned to stone.

His body crushes mine as he slides over my waist, his heaviness forcing the air from my lungs. He begins to turn. I remember the info on his cage explaining that he pins his victims before forcing them to look into his eyes.

All at once, a bright red warmth pulses at my chest. The snake hisses, flinching from the glow, and then its heavy body thumps the floorboards as it drops. The horrible weight lifts from my chest. Then the rustling noise of its scales scraping wood grow fainter.

When I wake up, Mack sits at the end of my cot, one hand over her mouth. Tears clump in the dark brown eyelashes framing her blue eyes. I follow her gaze to the next cot over, where a crowd of students gather. One of them shifts enough that I can see what they're looking at.

It's the Spring Court shadow from last night. Her eyes are shut, the soft pink hush of dawn streaming through the windows and falling over her face.

She could be asleep, but deep in my heart I know she's not. Not with her ashen skin, pebbly and coarse. The way her mouth contorts as if still gasping for breath. Lips rigid and stormy-blue. Beneath the white sheet, one bare arm hangs to the side, gray and hard as . . . stone.

It's as if someone stole a statue from outside and placed it in the bed as a joke. But it's not a joke.

My pulse jumps erratically in my wrist as I quickly dress. My dream felt so real. What if it wasn't a dream after all?

Professor Balefire, the Mythological Creatures professor, arrives with some fourth years. He orders us to leave so he can begin the search for the basilisk. Under his breath, I hear him muttering over and over.

"Don't know how he got out," he says, tugging at one of his tufted ears. "The cage was locked. I checked myself. Don't know how . . ."

Snickering draws my attention to Reina and her friends. They're laughing and taking photos with their cell phones, for Shimmer's sake. When Reina notices my glare, she turns the camera on me.

"Aren't you sad, Summer?" she asks sweetly. "You are literally so hideous that you turned an innocent girl to stone."

Mack grabs me before I can react. "Not worth it," she whispers.

Furious, I storm from the gym. For the first time ever, I'm looking forward to my Sunday training with Eclipsa.

Evelyn and Mack try to cheer me up, but all I can think about is the poor girl who died. Rumors are swirling about what happened. Theories range from a spurned Fae lover spelling the basilisk to the Mythological Creatures instructor, Professor Balefire, being to blame. After my training with Eclipsa, the headmistress called me in for a statement.

She was not happy, and I had to give two statements: one to Mr. Willis, and one to a representative from the Council for the Mistreatment of Humans.

Mack gets up from the lower bunk and rifles in her closet. "Enough of this pity party. We're taking you out."

"Where?" Normally I would argue, but I need something to wash this horrible weekend from my memory permanently.

I duck just in time to miss the black blouse she tosses at my head. "Get dressed and brush your teeth. I have a surprise."

The top is meant for her curvier chest and is a little big, but I knot it at the bottom and it looks cute. My jeans are the same frumpy ones I arrived with. Only now, thanks to a steady diet of food and some new muscles, I actually fill them out.

My new coat goes on last. I've learned to assume that wherever we go, it'll be freezing.

I glance in the mirror right before we leave. My hair is the same train-wreck as always, but it's kinda sexy knotted high on my head. And I notice my face is glowing, my sunken cheekbones filled out and eyes bright.

Fresh food and exercise for the win.

The surprise ends up being a secret portal in the basement that takes us to another city. Apparently when Mack's parents were here, they discovered the portal, and only a handful of people know about its existence.

Also, apparently Mack doesn't play around when it comes to surprises.

The portal shoots us out onto pavement next to buildings —tall, modern skyscrapers, I discover. The snowfall here is less and I can actually see the stars.

Steam curls up from iced-over sidewalks and over our boots.

"Where are we?" I ask, following Mack and Evelyn around the corner.

Mack smiles. "Welcome to Evernell, capital city of the new Everwilde. This is where all the students go to relax." She nods her head to the sleek high-rises. "Many of the Evermore students have weekend homes here. Your boy the Winter Prince has the penthouse to that monstrosity ahead. It belongs to his dad, but only the prince uses it."

I follow her nod to the tallest building in the city, a metallic all-glass building two blocks down. The top floor is huge, and I study the tinted windows as if I can see the Winter Prince from here.

"I'm guessing by the weather he's not here?" I say.

"Or," she offers, cutting her dark eyes at me. "You bring out the worst in him. I mean, I may be wrong, but calling him a bitch in public was probably a little triggering. You should probably stop doing that if you want nicer weather."

"Well, the truth hurts."

Laughing, we follow a group of students across the street as I stare around in wonder. For some reason, I thought all of Everwilde would be forest and meadows . . . not *this*.

Bright neon signs glow from tall buildings, and in the distance, a fountain shoots water into the air to a strange Fae song. Something about this place seems so familiar.

"Wait . . . is this . . . ?"

"The City of Lights?" she finishes. "Yeah. Welcome to the old Las Vegas, baby."

That's right. When the Lightmare happened, I assumed all the cities had been destroyed. But I guess they were just repurposed. It was the human beings living here that got the short end of that stick.

Mack doesn't notice my anger as she grabs her phone and begins texting. "I'll shoot Callum a message to have an emotion potion ready for us."

"A what?" I ask.

She grins. "Just wait."

Callum is the third year mentor our hall is assigned to. Any questions, Mack said, and we ask Callum. I haven't met him yet, but the third and fourth year trials are supposedly almost impossible to pass, and he's been crazy busy.

I can barely keep from gawking at everything as we exit an alleyway into a side street. A row of bars with names like *The Black Cauldron* and *The Iron Centaur* spill patrons into the street. I gawk at them, too, overwhelmed by their strangeness.

A swarm of sprites flutter out from a door to our left below a sign that reads, *The Pink Pixie*.

Mack guides me away. "Don't ever go in that bar unless you want to end up drugged and wake up somewhere deep in Everwilde, enslaved to a woodland nymph or worse, a troll. The sprites think selling us into a thousand years of slavery is an entertaining sport."

That sounds exactly like something Ruby would do.

When we near the end of the street, Mack leads me down crumbling stairs to a black steel door. There's no sign other than a symbol with rounded ears inside a circle that Mack explains means 'human friendly.'

The second we enter we're enveloped in bass-thumping music and strobe lights. My focus immediately goes to a row of cages near the stage. Half-naked girls dance inside the cages, and I'm shocked to see they're human. Fae males clamor around their cages, slipping money into the shreds of clothing they do wear.

But the dancers' unfocused eyes stare off into the distance, and they hardly seem aware of the customers.

Glamoured. A surge of anger washes over me, and I have to look away.

I duck out of my coat and tie it around my waist as Mack leads us past a packed dance floor, up a flight of stairs, and into a VIP lounge area bespeckled in mirrors and red leather.

The bouncer, a warty, green-skinned orc, tries to stop us, but Mack holds out her wrist, showing off her new cuff mark:

ram's horns inside a circle for Magus's Mythological Creatures Court.

We don't get tattooed with our keeper's mark until next year, but Basil must have given her that to use for occasions such as this.

When the bouncer's tiny flashlight beam rolls over my tattoo, he frowns, showing off a mean underbite and bottom fangs that stick out. But he moves to let us pass quickly.

At least this dumb mark comes with perks.

We settle onto a gold couch with cigarette holes and questionable sticky stains. From here, we have an unhindered view of the dance floor and stage.

"Do you see those slave-girls dancing near the stage?" Evelyn says, peering over the edge of the bannister.

"They're slaves?" I say, clenching my fists as another surge of rage barrels through me.

"Yep," Evelyn answers, oblivious to my anger. She points. "See that one there?"

I follow her gesture to a petite brunette to the far right. Her mind might be glamoured into oblivion, but her mascara smudges around red, swollen eyes. She's been crying.

"That's Ashley Hall, a second year student last year. Her parents live in the same building as mine. I heard the rumors, we all did . . ." She leans in close. "Supposedly Ashley slept with a third year Evermore. Why would she be so stupid? I mean, they're attractive, sure. But there are other things you can do that don't get you in trouble."

I glare at Evelyn. "So, what? She slept with him, and then they expelled her for it? What happened to him?"

"Nothing," Mack says, the low growl in her voice making it clear she doesn't approve. "But that's just the way it is."

"That is so backwards," I mutter. "But why not send her off to fight in the scourge?"

"Usually the students busted for hooking up with an

Evermore get sold to the clubs as . . . dancers, or worse. Once we sleep with an Evermore, we're marked forever as a Fae-whore."

I roll my eyes. "Sounds like my high school."

Evelyn tugs at her skirt, a mini leather thing that barely hides her goods. "I heard the Winter King himself bought her slave contract. I'd rather die than suffer that humiliation. Can you imagine belonging to the Winter Court? Being forced to work in their sleazy clubs and wear their brand?"

I don't point out that *we're* in one of those sleazy clubs, and *I* wear their brand. But her gaze flicks to my arm where the tattoo swirls over my flesh, and her eyes go wide as she realizes her mistake.

"Evelyn," Mack says, rolling her eyes, "insert foot in mouth."

Evelyn doesn't know why I have the prince's mark; only Mack knows that secret.

Before Evelyn can apologize, the door on the other side squeaks open and a boy around my age appears, carrying a metal tray that holds four flutes full of fizzing liquid.

"Finally," Mack groans.

His back is to us as he sets the tray down on the desk. *Wow. He's a big one.* I start to make a joke just as he turns around—

And then I gasp. My body physically recoiling from him. Without thinking, I leap to my feet, searching for a weapon as adrenaline floods my body.

33

"**S**ummer!" Mack yells, her eyes wide. "What's wrong?" She and Evelyn crowd around me, only adding to my discomfort.

I'm breathing hard as I look from them to our mentor, Callum. Or, as he's called on the other side, Cal.

"I know him," I growl, jerking my chin at Cal.

To his credit, he's putting on a good show of being surprised. He's pressed against the door, hands held high, a shocked look on his face.

"You know . . . Callum?" Mack asks, looking from me to him.

"Yeah, and I refuse to be anywhere near him." I cross my arms over my chest to drive home the point.

Cal actually has the audacity to look hurt, his bushy eyebrows mashing together above a frown. If I didn't know what sort of a-hole he was, I would have been convinced I truly hurt his feelings.

Mack's eyes narrow, and I can see her brain whirring behind her dark hair. "How would you know . . ." Suddenly the wrinkle trenched across her forehead smooths out. "Oh."

She marches over to where Cal presses into the wall and lifts his big hand up, exposing his wrist. The Winter Court mark, similar to the one inside my tattoo, flares against his flesh just below his palm. "Cal is a changeling," Mack says as if I know what the hell she's talking about.

"A change-what?" I say.

"Oh, right. We haven't covered that yet." She drops his wrist and then pats his arm. "It's okay, she'll calm down once I explain. Here"—she grabs the flute brimming with pink potion and offers it to me—"let's down these, since you obviously need to chill, and then I'll explain."

Normally, I wouldn't chug a mysterious, magical liquid, even if Mack promises I'll adore it, but after the shock of seeing Cal in Everwilde, I desperately need something.

The liquid fizzes all the way down my throat and into my stomach. When every ounce of liquid has been drained from the flute, a pink wisp of smoke trickles from the rim and dances around my head in the shape of a dragon.

Mack's becomes a smoky teal sprite that giggles before evanescing. Callum's is a centaur that gallops around the room shooting arrows of smoke. Evelyn's becomes a mermaid that circles her head, splashing smoke-water at her.

"Wow," I say, clutching my belly. "That was . . . intense."

For a moment, it feels as if a swarm of feathery butterflies have been let loose in my stomach. Then a wave of complete joy washes over me.

This is nice. So nice. Cal is nice. Everyone is nice.

"I love everyone," I purr.

I sit on my butt beside Mack and Evelyn, both girls matching my silly grin with smiles of their own. I have no idea why we're on the floor instead of the couch.

"See," Mack says, petting my face. "Now, ready for more truth about Callum?"

I nod happily.

"So Callum is a changeling," Mack begins. Callum plops his giant form beside us as he watches Mack explain. "He was taken as a baby and replaced by an *other*—a lookalike Fae child."

Despite my relaxed state, I shudder. "Do his parents know?"

I've never met his mom, or even seen her for that matter. But his dad and this other, this changeling, are together all the time.

"No," Callum answers for Mack. His big head rests in his hand, and his face looks crestfallen as he discusses his parents. "My dad made a deal with the Winter Court when I was seven, and then he couldn't pay. So they took me, put a changeling in my place, and glamoured my dad to forget he ever owed the Evermore. Since then, I've been a servant for the Winterspell family."

Winterspell . . . that's Inara's surname.

My head spins. "So . . . the Cal I went to high school with, the all-American boy who could be the poster child for rednecks everywhere, is a secret Fae? Why?"

"We don't know," Mack says. "There are changelings all over the mortal world, but who knows why they do it?"

"Are there other changeling humans at Evermore Academy?" I ask, trying not to sound too hopeful. If there are others here who haven't been groomed from practically birth for the academy, then maybe I won't stick out so much.

"No," Callum says, shaking his head. "I'm only here because I tricked Inara's uncle into wagering a spot here for me during a game of farvane."

Farvane is a dice game played by some of the Evermore students in the commons. The rules seem incredibly complicated, and some magic is involved.

Mack grins. "It hasn't exactly made him popular with Inara."

I sigh. "She has a new person to hate, so you're probably safe now. You're welcome."

Callum suddenly looks around. "Wait, why are we sitting on the floor?"

Mack giggles. "Actually, why are we inside this room? Let's go show those Fae pricks how dancing is supposed to look."

Dancing? I have as much rhythm as a praying mantis, but the others leave before I can protest. So I blow out a breath and follow them down to the dance floor. The floor is packed with bodies, all Fae.

There are so many horns and wings and tails and flashing lights that I can almost convince myself we're at a Halloween party back home. Except the creatures writhing on the dance floor won't peel off their costumes at the end of the night.

And to them, we're the freaks.

The thought of being the only humans here isn't comforting, but Mack, Callum, and Evelyn don't seem to mind as they immediately begin grinding on each other.

Ick.

I'm about to join them when a surge of Fae bodies surrounds them and they're swallowed by the crowd.

Just like that, I'm alone. A fruitless search ensues where I bump into every Fae possible, gathering annoyed scowls and more than a few offers to dance. But I'm not a fan of the hungry way the male Fae look at me like I'm something to be conquered and devoured.

Especially after we just had the reasons-not-to-sleep-with-the-Fae talk.

Plus, I need at least five more of those pink drinks before I can find a shred of rhythm, so I push and shove my way to the bar. The bartender belongs to the Court of Mortal Beasts. Black eyes stare at me from a bloodless face, and when he smiles, two long fangs flash.

Vampire. I shiver. Members of the Mortal Beasts look like mortals, for the most part. With a few major differences. Vampires drink blood and don't sleep, Lycanthropes shift into werewolves, and shifters, well, shift into animals.

The vampire lifts his overly-plucked brows, which also happen to be studded with piercings. "Going to order anything, little shadow, or are you just here to offer that delicious blood I smell charging through your fragile veins?"

Shit. Panicked at the mention of him drinking my blood, I say, "I'll have . . . the pink drink."

His grin is terrifying. "Coming right up."

When he hands me the champagne flute full of sparkling liquid, it looks way different than the other fizzy drinks from before. It's not even pink, but a rich, sparkly purple.

Before I can ask exactly what this is, he asks for payment.

"Excuse me?" I say stupidly. Of course money is a thing here in Everwilde. It's a thing *everywhere*.

He's about to reply when his eyes shift behind me. A whisper of terror flickers across his countenance, and then he hisses, "The drink is free," before escaping to a back room.

Before I turn, I know from the prickling cold feeling raking my back who's behind me. When I turn, I'm prepared to see the Winter Prince.

But I'm not prepared to see the three Fae girls from the Court of Mythological Creatures surrounding him. They have snowy-white wings and pale horns. Two hang on his arms. A third leans in and tips a glass of something to his lips.

Because he can't just hold his own damn drink.

Even with his mini flying harem attending to his thirst—and other things, by the look of it—his eyes never leave mine. I happen to have the misfortune of noticing how gorgeous he is, how big and full and kissable his stupid lips are.

But how can I find him attractive after he tricked me?

After he humiliated Rhaegar and claimed me like a car won in some poker game.

I'm not a car. I'm not a possession. And I will never let him own me.

As if he knows my thoughts, those lips slowly tug into a saccharine grin, and a pit of desire opens up inside me.

What the Fae?

I rip my gaze from his stupid, pretty face and grab my drink, toasting an imaginary glass. "Here's to being the worst shadow in history."

I slam back the sparkling concoction before I can change my mind.

The second it hits my throat, I know I've made a huge mistake. Of the *I'm-screwed* kind.

A wave of pleasure flashes over me, so overwhelming that I nearly fall off my barstool. At the same time, a pulse of fire ignites between my legs, a puff of air escaping my lips. I tamp down a moan as liquid fire smolders across my flesh. When I glance down over my skin I see that it's all dewy and glowing.

Across the dance floor, I catch sight of Bane, Inara, Kimber, and the whole homicidal crew laughing hysterically as they point at me and whisper. One of them holds up a cellphone to video the scene.

Shit. My body is on fire. I need to dance, to grind up against someone. To do more . . . so much more with someone. A male.

What the hell was in that drink?

34

Gripping the bar with sweaty fingers, I turn toward the dance floor. . . only to see I'm fenced in by a wall of male Fae. My body rejoices but my mind is freaked. A blue-skinned Fae with long, twisty horns grins at me. Another male slides into the barstool next to mine, his yellow eyes flashing. Lycan.

His fingers are like iron bars as they wrap around my wrist, hard enough to make me wince. With minimal effort, he tugs me into his lap. My heart spikes into my throat.

"What's your name?" he growls.

Part of me wants to throw my arms around his neck and then go somewhere dark, private. *Ew.* Gritting my teeth, I jump from his grasp before his arms can slide around my waist.

I'm not in control and the thought is terrifying.

Relief cuts through my panic as I spy Mack and Callum rushing toward us. Callum pushes through my muscled-up admirers, making a path for Mack.

She glares at the Fae males. "Get back, idiots!"

None of them move. An orc and a Fae male with feathery

wings get too close to one another and a fight breaks out. Someone grabs my hand and tries to pull me into the fray, and it takes all my strength to fight out of their grip. I can't breathe. Too many people. I'm closed in, trapped.

They're going to rip me apart.

Sweat dampens my temples. One of the males leans in and . . . what the Fae? He sniffs me, inhaling my sweaty scent like an alcoholic guzzling mouthwash.

This is getting so out of hand.

Mack's eyes are wide as she touches my face with the back of her hand, then her dark brows bunch together and her mouth pinches. "What did you take?"

Afraid if I speak a weird giggle will come out instead of words, I point at Inara and her friends. They burst into another round of laughter.

"Was the drink purple and glittery?"

I nod.

"Oh no." The panic in her voice makes me nervous. "We need to get you out of here, fast. That was a pheromone shot. Something about mortals makes it a hundred times more potent. Right now, you're irresistible to every Fae male in this place. Callum, start making us a path!"

Callum smashes his body into a tall vampire. As soon as the vampire goes flying, I dart through the space and run. Hands grab my flesh. I cry out as panic worms deep into my bones. Someone knocks into me. Then a Fae grabs me by the waist and another by the legs and they start to drag me off.

All at once, an ear-splitting roar rumbles the room. The hands around my body disappear, and I'm dumped onto the ground, landing hard on my shoulder.

Someone lifts me into their arms. I stiffen, prepared to fight.

"Don't move," a voice growls.

The Winter Prince glares down at me with wild, animal-istic eyes.

"Be very, very still."

Before I can so much as protest, he flicks his fingers. I tear my gaze from his face to the portal opening in front of us.

Without a word, he slips through, closes it, and then dumps me onto my feet as if my flesh burns his. My boots crunch snow. Trees rise around us, the glowing disc of the moon visible through their canopy of branches.

My body sags as I make out the wrought iron fence surrounding my mortal dorm.

After the noise of the club, the sudden silence feels . . . strange.

"How could you be so rash?"

The anger in his voice relights my own fury, and I round on him, fists clenched. "Rash? I was trying to finally have fun in this horrible, godforsaken, freezing place."

He flicks up an ink-blue eyebrow. "You call *that* fun?"

"I didn't know what was in that drink."

His mouth twists into dark grin. "Just assume everything in Everwilde can and will kill you, or worse."

"Charming," I seethe. "So glad someone had the fore-thought to bring me here against my will."

He swallows, his jaw softening. "Summer, if I hadn't been there—"

"But you were," I finish. "Because you're always there. Scowling and looking all hot and pissed."

A flicker of surprise animates his otherwise livid expres-sion. His lips press together, and then he murmurs, "Hot?"

Shit.

His gaze falls to my mouth, which has parted slightly. I become acutely aware of how near he is to me. Close enough that I could reach out and run my fingertips over the jagged cliffs of his cheeks.

Close enough that I could kiss him—if he wasn't a Fae and I wasn't a human and we didn't despise one another.

He jerks his focus from my lips, almost violently, and schools his face into a disdainful scowl. "You should go inside, Princess. Your body reeks of the pheromone drink."

His cruel nickname drives the dagger of his loathing even deeper. You don't call someone who shops at the Salvation Army *princess* unless you want to wound them deeply.

I'm about to tell him as much when Mack, Evelyn, and Callum come rushing from the front doors, dragging my attention to them.

Evelyn sees me first and shouts, "She's alive . . . and alone."

Alone? I glance back, but the prince is gone.

Mack throws her arms around me. "Where did you go? We thought someone took you."

"I'm . . . someone had the decency to bring me home," I half explain.

"Someone?" Mack says, reluctantly releasing me. "Who?"

"Just some Fae," I insist. "Thankfully, he's immune to my druggy charms." I can't help but wonder how much you have to despise someone to *not* react to a massive dose of pheromones.

"We should go," Callum insists. He's posted in front of me, arms crossed over his massive chest, staring down imaginary threats. "Until the drug leaves your system, you're not safe."

Callum decides to spend the night outside our room, in case any Fae follow my intoxicating scent here, while Mack gives me a talk about not drinking anything without first knowing what it does.

Then I take the world's hottest shower, scrubbing hard to try to rinse any residual pheromones from my body, and hop into bed.

Mack gave me a pajama set to wear, but the silk shorts barely cover my butt, the cami ending above my navel. Still, it's better than sleeping naked, and I sink into my sheets, grateful for a soft bed and roommate who's legit awesome.

Things could have turned out much worse.

Sleep drags my eyelids down, but my mind keeps going over tonight.

Why can't I just hate the prince? I don't even have a thing for dickhead bad boys.

"Mack," I whisper.

The top bunk shakes and then she's peering down at me with a tired, grumpy expression. "What?"

"Have you ever liked someone who was bad for you?"

Silence. When it stretches out into minutes, I assume she must have fallen asleep. But then the bed frame above wiggles and she says, "Sure. I once thought I liked my dad's personal trainer. He had full sleeve tats, rode a Ducati, and smoked weed."

"How'd you make it go away?"

She yawns. "I slept with him and realized his bad boy persona compensated for a dull personality and tiny dick."

I snort. I'm fairly certain that's not the case with the prince. "It doesn't matter, he hates me anyway." I stretch under the covers, yawning, "Good . . . night."

I fall into a restless sleep, and everywhere I turn, every new dream I spin, the Winter Prince is there. Haunting me with his cruel smile.

My first day back at school as the prince's shadow, my stomach is in knots. I spent all morning agonizing over what it will be like today. The hundreds of ways the prince will torment and tease me. Mack left early to finish an assignment, and I stayed an extra hour after my lesson with Eclipsa at the gym doing squats, deadlifts, and timed sprints.

At first I stayed because I didn't want to go back to an empty dorm before school. Then, as my physical exhaustion took over, I stayed because when I'm working out so hard I'm close to puking, nothing else matters.

It was a sweet release, but I'm paying for the exertion now. The continual slide of my backpack over my shoulders makes me groan, and my thighs cry with every step I take.

And I still have to make it through the second half of the day with the prince. What torturous things will he have me do?

You can do this.

Students whisper and point as I pass. The entire student body must have heard about the Nocturus by now. Or maybe

AUDREY GREY

the videos of me being practically mauled to death last night has made the rounds.

Really, it's a toss-up.

It's even worse in the lecture hall of our Gaelic Studies class. I sit with Mack and Evelyn and a boy named Jace. Reina sits two rows back, not even bothering to whisper as she trickles poison in everyone's ear.

"She's sleeping with both of them," Reina asserts to the large group of Unseelie shadows surrounding her. Our teacher, Professor Spellwart, left the class for a moment, and Reina's taking the opportunity to spew lies. "That's the only reason they would both fight over her. You should have seen her last night, trying to grab every male's attention with a pheromone elixir. It's pathetic."

I glare back at them in time to see her sidekick, Lily, add, "I hear she got pregnant with Rhaegar's baby and that's why the prince destroyed him."

Anger heats my face. But Mack shakes her head and I let it slide.

"They'll forget about it soon," she promises me.

I'm not sure that's true, but the incident with the basilisk takes some of the focus off of me. Lunch is worse. The minute Mack and I take our usual table by the windows, the room goes quiet. Evelyn stops before she gets to our table, looking like she might, for once, realize I'm a social pariah and abandon ship. In class our seats are assigned, but here, she has a choice.

To her credit, she scoots beside Mack and weathers the storm of whispers and stares.

Fae ears, I hate being the center of attention.

By the time my Modern World class rolls around, I'm ready for anything. I manage to march down the Evermore corridor to my class with my shoulders back and head held high. Inside, I'm freaking out.

All I can think about is the power the prince wielded, the way it rocked the world and spun Rhaegar like a toy.

And then, when he protected me at the club . . . correction. That wasn't protection. That was a dog guarding its favorite chew toy.

The class goes silent as I pass through the doorway. Professor Lochlan slides a quick glance over me. I cringe, ready for a lecture on tardiness followed by whispers.

Only none of those things happen.

Instead, the professor nods and the students—Evermore and human alike—look away.

On habit, I go to stand next to Rhaegar's seat—

It's empty. I let out a relieved breath, unaware until now how much I was not looking forward to seeing him. What if he hates me for giving him the book? Worse, what if he blames me for losing?

That's when I feel it. The cold presence of the prince. He sits near the back, long arms slung behind his head, legs crossed at the knee. His midnight blue hair is tousled, the top of his tunic unbuttoned and a bit wrinkled.

As always, he wears a lazy, amused grin.

For the billionth time, that invisible string between us jerks taut. He has to feel it too, right?

Hard to tell when he hasn't graced me with a single look. But I'm not buying his carefree, couldn't give a flying frack attitude. Not anymore. Not after watching him play everyone like a fool, including me.

No. Everything he does is to distract. To hide. I know that now—although I have no idea yet what he's hiding.

Clearing my throat, I flick my eyebrows up, impatient for a command. I'm used to Rhaegar being very clear about where I'm supposed to stand or what I need to hold. But the prince barely meets my eyes before gesturing with a jerk of his chin toward the closest chair.

The breath catches in my throat as I slide into the desk chair and set down my stuff. After that, it only gets weirder. I was expecting horribleness. Mistreatment. To have to stand by his side and fetch him meaningless stuff while everyone secretly laughs at me.

But none of that happens. Instead, I'm largely left . . . alone.

All the classes are like that. Not that I'm complaining. It's just disconcerting. Like waiting for the punchline to an awful joke I know is coming. If he said cruel things, if he mocked me or abused me, that would almost have been better than *this*.

When I ask to run to the restroom—thanks, tiny bladder— he gives me a weird look and then explains I never have to ask permission for such things. He carries his own stuff, makes sure I have my own chair in every class, and never, not once, says anything unkind.

The jerk.

When he's not going out of his way to prove he's decent, he ignores my presence. As does everyone else. It's not hard to determine he's protecting me.

The moment the bell rings and school is over, I go to follow him, expecting to shadow his every move like I did Rhaegar's. But he stops me, his eyes never truly meeting mine. "Go. You're free."

"Forever?" I joke.

"For the rest of the day," he amends. Is that amusement I see in his eyes?

"Just checking," I call as I dart down the stairs to the doors.

Two whole hours. That's how long I have to myself before combat class. Mack and I celebrate by spending the entire one hundred and twenty minutes—not that I'm counting—cramming Cheetos and Sour Patch Kids into our mouths and talking.

Ruby, who's just awakened from one of her twenty-seven naps she takes a day, grabs a green sour patch before Mack can swat her away.

The topic eventually veers to Rhaegar and the Nocturus. "They say Rhaegar is on probation with the Summer Court. That he might leave school." Mack frowns. "The whole thing just feels . . . wrong."

"I'm glad he didn't die, but someone as proud as Rhaegar shouldn't have to ask the Winter Prince for mercy." I shiver, remembering the awful events. "And then the thing with the basilisk."

Evelyn pops into the room and says cheerfully, "I heard they took Sky Sutton in for questioning today." She waggles her red eyebrows. "Apparently Sky and the dead girl had a fight right before they went to bed, and they think Sky released the basilisk. Professor Balefire is on suspension until they can figure out the whole mess."

"Where do you get all this information?" Mack asks. "They don't tell first years anything."

She shrugs, a cryptic smile lighting up her face. "I have my sources."

"Do you know how Rhaegar is doing?" I blurt, hope tinging my voice.

"What? Of course not." She pops to her feet, brushing sour patch sugar from her dark pants. "Shouldn't you guys be in combat uniform? Class starts soon."

"What got up her butt?" Mack grumbles as we dress for combat class in silence. I roll my eyes. With Evelyn, there's no telling. Before we leave, Mack shoves the remaining junk food in a safe and locks it.

While she resets the password, I fix Ruby with a stern glare. "Ruby, this is Mack's food. *Mack's*. Not mine."

It's important to establish that last part; Ruby swears there's a Fae law that makes anything mine also hers by right, since she's technically on loan from the academy to me as a slave.

Ick. Another reason to despise the Fae way of doing things.

Ruby puffs out her purple lips in mock affront. I'm hoping the safe does the trick, because Mack is ready to kick Ruby out of our dorm for good.

Despite being the most defective, crass sprite in Everwilde, she's grown on me. And I really don't want her gone.

When we pass through the gym doors to begin training with Richter, a nervous pang starts beneath my sternum. I'm sure that the prince will embarrass me in the second half of training. Sure there's some catch to his sudden inattention.

But it's my best combat class yet. I'm paired against Lily, Reina's friend. Although I don't mop the floor with her, I hold my own. When I'm done, a few of the Seelie shadows even clap me on the back and mutter praises.

The rest of the week goes just as well, and I settle into my new role as the Winter Prince's shadow. Rhaegar still doesn't attend classes, and slowly, the gossip over the Nocturus dies down.

But despite the relief I feel at the sudden turn toward normalcy in my life, a small part of me can't let it go.

By now, all the other shadows have begun to form bonds with their keepers. Mack and Basil have already progressed to fighting as a team in combat class, and he constantly checks on her to make sure she's not struggling with anything in school.

Even Evelyn and her keeper, a female Dawn Court Fae with fiery auburn hair and dark skin, text each other constantly.

"Easy there, Summer," Eclipsa says from behind the bag she holds. "Whose face are you imagining right now? Hopefully not mine."

I glance over the Evermore girl, my eyes lingering on the blue and silver tiger-striped leggings she's rocking. A loose black cropped tank top printed with her favorite metal band, *The Orcs of Darkbriar*, shows off a six-pack and a belly piercing. Several half-moon tats darken her ribcage, and the lunar cycle crests her stomach.

Pretty sure I could work out for years and never look that awesome. Refocusing on the bag, I work a few more jab hook combos and then transition to switch kicks. The bag shutters with each impact, the chain holding it jangling.

"It's okay if you don't want to talk about it." She releases the bag and grabs her steel water tumbler. The Unseelie sigil, a snake eating its tail entwined around a sword, decorates the metal sides. "I was there on the night of the Nocturus, so I can pretty much guess."

"We're not done, are we?" I ask, frowning at the bag.

She takes a long drink and then sets the tumbler down. "We've been here over an hour and your form is shit."

"Thanks." I drag my forearm across my forehead, collecting sweat.

"I mean, I can let you kick the bag's ass a few more hours, but that won't make you any more adept at killing darklings. You're too angry to get in any good skill work."

"Damn right, I'm angry. The prince tricked me into destroying a Fae that was decent and kind to me. And, for what? Some pissing contest? And now that the prince has what he wants . . . never mind. It doesn't matter."

"Has he . . . mistreated you?"

I shake my head, the thought sending a fresh surge of frustration crashing through my veins. Bouncing on my toes, I move on to the speed bag, hitting it until the black teardrop becomes a blur and my shoulders ache.

I'm totally going to pay for this tomorrow.

Eclipsa pads softly across the mat behind me. "I don't agree with the way the prince handled Rhaegar, or even the way he's dealing with you, but he has his reasons." A silver eyebrow arches devilishly. "If it were me, I would have lopped off Rhaegar's wolfie little head. Put him out of his misery."

That gives me pause. It's hard to get used to the cruel savagery of the Fae. Even harder to become accustomed to casually discussing decapitation with the one Fae I actually like.

I flash a dark grin between a series of jab crosses. "Eclipsa Skywell, your benevolence knows no bounds."

She snorts. "I speak sarcasm, you know." Her silver eyebrows crash together, and she flicks her tiny moon tongue piercing against her teeth. "I'm sure you think we're ruthless, barbaric, even. But there is so much you don't understand."

Done taking out my rage on the bags, I grab my hydroflask from my duffel. "You're right. I don't understand any of this. Maybe if someone, say, a Lunar Court Fae, helped me understand?"

"That's not how our world works. Here in Everwilde, on the Island especially, secrets are weapons. I can't just give you what could hurt me and my friends most."

My eyebrows flick up in anger. "Thanks for the vote of confidence. Who do you think I'd tell?"

"I don't know. Perhaps a gorgeous Seelie in the Summer Court?" My expression must show my outrage because she adds, "Rhaegar is incredibly influential, when he wants to be. He may not have Inara's gift with persuasion but he's not beneath glamouring, despite the new rules."

"How is persuasion different?" I ask, curiosity making me forget I'm angry. I assumed the day Inara tricked me that she'd used a glamour.

Eclipsa blows a few errant silver hairs from her face. "Besides being incredibly powerful? It's different than glamouring in that she can control Fae too."

"How does it work?" I ask.

"She can put things in your mind. Can make you think you want something, or see something. Her brother has a similar gift, but he's honed his gift differently. His favorite ruse is changing his face so you see someone else when you look at him. Oberon knows how many Fae females he's tricked into sleeping with him that way."

Bane? I'd almost forgotten about her twin brother. Compared to Inara's love of the spotlight, he seemed content creeping in the shadows. "That's . . . that's horrible."

She shrugs, her expression darkening. "How do you think

Inara's been able to control the prince? Keep him coming back to her again and again?"

I swallow, the memory of that night I was inside his head floating to the surface. Then there was his tense struggle in the classroom that day when Inara tried to service him.

Ugh. If what Eclipsa says is true, that's basically sexual harassment, if not rape.

His conflicting emotions toward her suddenly make a bit more sense.

"Look," I say, holding out my red Everlast boxing gloves for her to unstrap. "I'm just tired of having no control over my life."

She nods as she slips off my gloves. "I get it, I do. But control doesn't always mean safety. I'm sure that poor shadow had no idea she'd wake up in a few hours to an escaped basilisk. Now"—she points to the adjacent black mat near a wall covered in mirrors—"Less talking, more stretching."

I follow her lead to the smaller mat, contorting my body into the Lord of the Dance pose. The concentration needed to keep from falling on my face is almost enough to still my mind. Almost.

But the images of my next-door bedmate turned to stone, her mouth spasmed wide with fear, won't leave. After a few more poses, I break the silence with a question. "What if her death wasn't an accident?"

Eclipsa unfolds her graceful body, canting her head so that her silver braided ponytail falls over one dark eye. "What do you mean?"

I give a detailed account of my dream, how the basilisk seemed interested in me, at first. Plus I mention the selkie that wasn't drugged at the Selection, in case they're somehow related. "Both incidents led to someone around me dying," I point out, half in realization. "And the orc." I tuck an errant strand of sweat-damp hair behind my ear. "That can't be a coincidence, right? What if, in both instances, I was meant to die, but something protected me?"

My fingers itch to stroke the pendant hidden between my breasts, but I busy my hands retying the silver band around my braid instead.

Eclipsa isn't the only one who's allowed secrets.

She doesn't say much, but her demeanor changes after that. Her gaze sweeps the gym, body rigid and alert. And when I shower, she stands guard near the gross plastic curtain instead of washing off.

After I change and towel dry my hair, she takes me aside. "Go pack your bags."

My heart freefalls into my stomach. This is it. I'm being expelled. Maybe the deaths are my fault for some reason. Maybe Eclipsa knows about my pendant and that's somehow attracting the creatures. Whatever it is, I feel sick.

The walk back to my dorm seems like miles instead of a few hundred feet.

Inside, I silently pack my bag (singular). Totally dejected.

Everything I own—a few borrowed clothes and toiletries —fits easily in the black Nike duffel Mack gave me. Ruby rouses from where she passed out on the safe, flies drunkenly toward me, and opens her mouth to no doubt yell something obnoxious.

But when she spots Eclipsa, posted stoically against the door frame, Ruby's lips slam shut and her eyes go wide.

"Why is there a Winter Court assassin in our room?" Ruby whisper-yells next to my ear. The pungent scent of brambleberry wine nearly bowls me over.

"She can hear you," I whisper-yell back.

Tears sting my throat. Mack isn't here, and when I passed Evelyn's open door on the way here it showed her room empty too.

I won't even get to say goodbye to my two friends, the entirety of the people in this academy who will actually care that I'm gone.

Now that I'm faced with the reality of leaving, I understand a quiet truth: I want to stay here.

Sure, it's dangerous, and we're treated like dirt. But I like my friends. I like the academics. I even like being a shadow and the purpose it provides me. And the idea of becoming a weapon, of taking back the power I've never had . . . intoxicating.

Only all of that is gone now.

We traipse across the snow. As a whisper of warmth settles over my cheeks, I crane my head up to see the ghost of a sun. I mean, it's buried behind a curtain of dirty gray winter clouds, but it's there. Its fiery outline visible.

Just my luck, the day I get kicked out is the day the sun returns.

My chest clenches as I follow Eclipsa through the snow to a stone manor hidden behind the lake. When we get to the massive arched double doors and I see the prince's crest, an owl over two daggers, I halt, shifting the duffel higher on my shoulder.

Leaning sleepily against the door, holding a steaming cup of tea, is the Winter Prince. His tunic hangs wide open, giving me full privy to his god-like abs. Each ridge is so well defined I contemplate running my fingers over them. Black leather pants end in bare feet, the toenails just as neat and manicured as his fingernails.

Bare feet—in the freezing cold. Must be nice.

Ruby is buried in a hot-pink infinity scarf Mack gave me, and she lifts her head. "Dayuum, kid. I could do laundry on those abs."

I blink, unable to tear my gaze from his perfect form. Tats adorn his chest, all Unseelie symbols, from the look of them—

Holy hell.

His expression is a mixture of annoyance and concern as he eyes Eclipsa then me. "You said it was an emergency, Eclipsa. Care to explain?"

I raise my hand. "I'd like an explanation too. Am I not getting kicked out?"

Ruby leans forward on my shoulder, her little face agleam with mischief. If she had popcorn she'd be eating it about now.

Crossing her arms, Eclipsa turns to me. "Kicked out? You're not getting expelled, Summer. How could you even think that?"

I shift on my feet, the porch's warped wooden boards groaning softly. "Sorry, I have a bad habit of expecting the worst."

That's what happens when your parents are murdered . . . but I don't add that last part.

"Well this isn't the worst-case scenario. In fact, I think you'll like this new arrangement."

"What arrangement?"

"I'm relocating you."

"You're what?" the prince and I say together.

Her lips curve into a grim smile. "I think you're onto something about the accidents, Summer. And if I'm right, whoever is trying to kill you will keep trying. From now until I deem it safe, you stay here."

"I don't understand. Is this . . . another dorm?" My breath comes in ragged spurts.

I should be worrying about someone trying to kill me. If Eclipsa takes it seriously, then there's a real possibility I'm on to something. But all I can think is how the prince is here, looking like he just fell out of bed. Which means he probably did just fall out of bed.

Which also means he lives here. Sleeps here. Naked—as

my memory serves. Not a scrap of clothing on that wonderful body . . .

Blinking, I refocus on reality. Eclipsa is watching me with an amused look. Oh, crap. Have I been staring at the Winter Prince and his abs the entire time?

Yes, Summer—yes, you have.

And he's glaring at me, his silver-blue eyes narrowed and lips sullen. Wheeling around, he shoulders open the oak door and stalks inside, letting the door slam in my face.

Well, this is going to be fun.

Propping open the door, I turn to Eclipsa. "At least the prince and I finally agree on something. This arrangement blows."

Behind me, Eclipsa groans, muttering a prayer to Titania.

As my wet boots squeak over the dark wood floor, and I take in the luxuries—marble paneling, expensive couches, crystal vases with imported summer dahlias, and more windows than walls—a new thought emerges.

True, the prince's on-campus house might be the safest place for me . . . physically.

But the same can't be said for my heart.

The blazing fire in my room barely touches the chill. Throwing the sateen duvet over my head, I squeeze my eyes shut. I've been thrashing in the king-sized four poster bed for hours trying to find sleep. But the icy cold seeps through the five layers of covers and into my bones.

I think Eclipsa said there are more covers in the closet downstairs. She stays here, too, a guest of the prince. Gathering the top blanket over my body, I slide to the wood floor. A gasp shoots from my lips as the painful cold meets my feet.

I forgot to close the heavy damask curtains framing the large dormer window, and moonlight trickles into the room, falling over the furniture. A cream loveseat near the foot of the bed. Twin nightstands made of sandalwood. Matching dresser and wardrobe.

The soft white bear rug spread across the large floor feels wonderful on my toes as I cross to the door.

Voices trickle from downstairs. I pause at the top of the landing to listen.

"I had no place else to take her," Eclipsa is saying. Sliding down the wall, I peek my head just enough to make her out.

She's lounged on one side of an enormous white couch, clad in a cute unicorn onesie and thick rainbow socks. On the other side, spread out like a lion sunning itself, is the prince. He's shirtless . . . because of course he is.

"Believe me," Eclipsa continues, "if I thought there was any other place that could keep her safe, I would have taken her there instead. But the wards on this place make it the most protected spot on the Island."

"I don't want her here."

Ouch. Even though I shouldn't be surprised, his outburst cuts to my core.

The muscles of his abdomen and arms shift and flex as he inhales sharply. "You know what could happen."

"How far along is it?" she asks softly.

"I feel it every waking second. My dreams are worse. And now—I don't know how much longer I can hold it off."

"Can we stop it somehow?"

He shakes his head. "If anyone discovers . . ." He shoves his hand through his ruffled hair, tugging at the ends. "Look, just make sure the moment it's safe, she's gone. Okay?"

Hurt twists my belly, and I slink quietly back to my room. He doesn't want me here. I mean, duh. That was obvious. But him saying it, aloud, drives it home.

It's stupid to let the prince wound me, but I can't help it. Years of being judged for where I lived, what I wore, or how much money I had comes roaring to the surface. Of being indiscriminately hated for reasons outside my control.

I flop into the feather mattress and hug my pillow. But now that I know in my heart I want to be here, my entire game plan has shifted. Perhaps it's time I move away from my scorched earth policy to one that will make my life on the Island better in the long run.

The prince hates me because of my humanness, so maybe it's time to show him how great we humans can be.

Starting with me.

I wake up an hour before noon, the sun's muffled warmth dappling through pale clouds. Perhaps it's my imagination, but the world outside seems lighter today. The sunlight just a bit warmer.

My gaze follows the path of the soft light across my room. While I slept, someone delivered a bunch of clothes for me to wear. They line the far closet doors. Each luxurious outfit dangling from a metal hanger is varying shades of silver, white, and blue.

Lest anyone forget I now belong to the Winter Court.

Happy face, Summer. Remembering my new mission to charm the prince, I pad cheerfully downstairs to the dining room where Eclipsa and the prince wait.

Eclipsa gives a little shout of glee. "I knew you'd pick the gray leather pants. They're killer, right? And that blue blouse is perfect for your complexion."

I worry the hem of my shirt between my fingers as I sit. Like always, for a moment, before my mind grows accustomed to being around the Fae, adrenaline burns my veins. Something about their sharp ears and exotic, not-quite-human features this early in the day is disconcerting.

"You just missed Headmistress Lepidonis," Eclipsa says. She takes a bite of some kind of Fae fruit that looks like a cross between a nectarine and an apple.

I grab a stainless steel carafe and a teacup, praying to every god in existence there's coffee inside. Dark liquid sloshes into my cup.

As the nutty, acidic smell of coffee swirls inside my nose, everything in the world rights itself.

"What did she want?" I ask between sips. The coffee is perfectly heated—probably by magic.

"To express her immense displeasure at my decision to kidnap a first year without the headmistress's permission," the prince answers, sliding an accusatory gaze to Eclipsa.

Eclipsa rolls her eyes. "She didn't say we had to return her."

"No, but at some point she'll need answers as to *why*. Any progress on that end?"

Stabbing a square of cheese with a disconcertingly big steak knife, Eclipsa shakes her head. "Still working on it. They tested the basilisk for residual persuasion magic, but so far nothing. And they've released the girl's friend who they suspected. She had an alibi." She gives a shrug meant to make her seem less worried than she is. "Speaking of friends, Summer, one of yours came by today. A Mackenzie Fairchild?"

"Mack?" I scour the dining room as if she might still be here. "When?"

"Right before you woke up." A smile lifts her cheeks. "I could tell she was scared; it took her ten minutes to knock on the door. But she did, and then she demanded to know if you're okay."

Crap, why didn't I think to get word to her?

"What did you tell her?"

"That you were fine, but sleeping. You'd had a late night."

My cheeks burn. Does Eclipsa know I eavesdropped last night?

After that, a heavy silence descends. The prince is doing his best to ignore me. Surprise, surprise.

I reach across the table, butter some toast, and slather it with some fig jam. Time for step one of my plan: kill him with kindness. "Sleep well, Prince?"

His gaze darts to me and back to stare solemnly into his

honeydew-green tea. "Fine." Eclipsa clears her throat and he adds, "You?"

"Great," I lie. "Ready for today?"

His silver-blue eyes are almost the same color as the clouds outside as they regard me beneath ink-blue eyebrows. "Always."

"Good." I snatch the rest of the toast from the table, ignoring the disapproving scowl from a lesser Fae servant, and shoulder into my coat. "See you after lunch."

The minute the door shuts behind me, I sag against it, not sure whether to laugh or cry. I have no idea if my plan will reach beneath that icy surface—or if there's anything there to even reach—but damn if it won't be fun trying.

38

Two whole months. That's how long I've been trying to crack the prince's icy facade. And so far, it's been a total failure.

I've been the perfect shadow. I greet him every morning like he's my favorite person on earth. I'm helpful during classes, grab him items before he asks, and go the extra mile by making sure all his pencils are sharpened and his electronics charged. I've improved in combat class, the extra lessons with Eclipsa finally paying off.

But none of it has gotten me any closer to him; in fact, some days I think it's the opposite. The nicer I am, the more I present myself as a human being, the more he resents me. He's gone most nights now, so I never see him at the house.

Rumor has it he's back with Inara, not that I give a flying frick.

Exhaling, I breathe out my frustrations as I lean my head back, taking in the rare sun. All the first year students are sitting on blankets in the snowy grounds near the lake, enjoying a picnic before our excursion begins.

The combined field trip is put on every year by our Mythological Creatures and Potions and Poisons classes.

All around me, students try to guess where we're going.

"Somewhere in the Spring Court, hopefully," Evelyn says, tossing her hair over her shoulder.

In this light, the gold filaments between the red are visible. Man, I would kill for hair like that.

"I couldn't care less," Mack says. She's dressed in khaki shorts and knee-high riding boots, Ray Ban aviator sunglasses hiding her eyes. "As long as the tacos keep coming, I'm happy."

Our food is catered by the students' top choice, and this year the restaurant just happened to be my favorite taco truck stand in existence, *Locos Tacos*.

The purple-and-gold checkered blanket we sit on is soft against my legs. Wherever we're going on this mysterious field trip, we were told to be ready for warmer weather, and I've rolled my jeans up as high as they go.

But it's unseasonably warm on the Island too. Despite being early December, the sun's kiss breaches my thin powder-blue sweater.

I could have worn shorts, I suppose. The prince provides me with an endless supply of clothes for every occasion, even though I only ever go with the leather pants, loose sweatshirts, and hoodies.

But then I'd have to ask him for a razor, and I'm tired of him giving me things to make up for his callousness.

A shadow draws lazy circles around our blanket. The prince's owl. He follows me when Eclipsa or the prince aren't with me.

Nothing has happened since the basilisk; I'm starting to think I overreacted. After all, Everwilde is a dangerous place. Despite the headmistress's concerns, mortals are bound to die.

It's the Fae way.

"Gonna eat that or eye screw it?" Mack asks, jerking her chin at the basket of tacos in my lap. I take a bite and pure heaven glides over my taste buds.

"Fae ears," I moan through a mouthful of green chili pork taco. "I can die happy now."

Mack wipes her hands on a napkin and grabs another soft taco, the corn tortilla breaking apart between her fingers. Tomatillo sauce smears her cheek, her dark hair pulled into a messy bun. Purple and teal streak the chocolate brown, her newest colors.

"This is better than sex," she declares like someone who's had a ton of sex. Which I'm pretty sure she hasn't.

"Whoa, ladies." Jace is a first year shadow who, if the rumors are true, has more experience in his pinky than Mack and I have put together. His parents own a bunch of Fae condos in Florida. "You must not have found the right partners yet."

Mack arches an eyebrow. "And what would you know about that, Jace?"

Everyone knows Jace bats for the other team. Grinning, he gives a careless shrug. "Enough to know if you think a taco is better, you're doing it wrong."

"No," I say, finishing the last bit of mine. "You just haven't met the right taco." I wink. "Try the green chili pork; they'll blow your mind."

Dusting the shredded cheese from my hands, I get to my feet. On the other side of the grouping, near a cliff overlooking the frozen lake, lounge the Six. Unlike the rest of the Evermore, they refuse to eat with their shadows.

And, of course, they don't lower themselves to eat our human fare.

A veritable feast of summer fruits and vegetables brought in from Summer Court territories mound little silver trays, and they pick from them lazily beneath a royal-blue pavilion.

Inhaling a lungful of courage, I grab a cardboard boat with two soft tacos and march uphill toward them. As I walk, I catch sight of Rhaegar sitting off near the woods with Basil. Both Evermore look dejected.

My breath catches in my chest, and I quickly look away.

Rhaegar returned to class a few weeks ago. His temporary probation was lifted, and he's once again a member of the Summer Court. But, despite being a member on paper, he's ostracized. He eats mainly alone or with Basil, he sits in the back of his classes and doesn't participate, and he hasn't taken on a new shadow.

Pushing Rhaegar from my mind, I top the hill with my offerings. Bane is the first one who notices me. He tenses where he sits with Lyra, a silver goblet of Faerie wine between them.

Kimber, the vampire, hisses, "Lost, little shadow?"

Ignoring them, I search for the prince. As I drag my gaze over the lounging bodies, it snags on his hair, a deep sapphire blue in this delicate light. That same tiny shock I get when first seeing him zips through me, the invisible thread between us tugging softly just behind my breastbone.

He's lying on his back, his head resting in Inara's lap. Her fingers tangle in his dark locks, and a whisper of jealousy trills through me.

His eyes are closed, but he must sense the change in the air because they snap open and focus on me. He stiffens before carefully extracting Inara's hands.

"What do you want?" he asks coldly as he gets to his feet. Eclipsa is there by one of the tent poles; she watches our interaction carefully.

My mouth goes dry. Why did I think this was a good idea? But if I'm going to get through his thick shell, this is as good a time as any. Plus, everyone loves tacos. "I just thought you might like to try some . . . tacos."

Bane snorts, and the rest of the girls follow suit.

"Aw," Lyra purrs. "Your shadow brought you some of her disgusting human food to try."

Correction: Fae hate tacos. Of course they do. Heat prickles my face. I hold up the bowl, my stupid stubborn side refusing to leave. "They're really good."

The muscles in my body go rigid as Kimber glides over. She moves so fast and gracefully that I blink and she's here. Her eyes are more red than golden. Crap. I know from my books that means she needs to feed.

Baring the tips of her fangs, she leans close as if to smell my offering.

Only she ignores the tacos, sniffing me instead.

I grit my teeth, trying to ignore the rumors swirling around the dorms that she glamours her shadow into letting her drink from her.

"Hmm," Kimber purrs, her lips now inches from my throat. "You're right. It smells delicious."

The prince strides over, his face impossible to read. Kimber senses his presence and immediately backs off. The others all watch to see what he'll do.

The prince looks down to the tacos, back to me. "We have enough food here, but thanks."

I should leave; this is not going as planned at all. But my frustration from all these weeks spent being mannerly and nice, fetching him every single thing in existence and trying to connect with his stupid, infernal black heart suddenly catch up to me. "You know, it wouldn't kill you to try something human. We're not that bad."

His cold laugh feels like a thousand tiny knives shredding what's left of my ego. "Aren't you?"

My fingers tighten on the taco boat. All I'm trying to do is be nice and bless him with the best freaking tacos in Texas. And his lips—they're smirking. Crushing my soul with every smarmy twinge.

A surge of rage bursts inside me. My mind blanks.

When it comes to, I'm lifting the tacos and dumping them on the prince's wicked head. Shredded cheese, greasy ground meat, diced tomatoes, and green chili sauce cascade over him in slow motion. The ingredients that don't catch in his beautiful hair settle in his shirt collar and shoulders.

A string of lettuce hangs from his nose.

"See," I snarl, surprised at how unafraid I sound considering I feel like puking. "Delicious."

Then I march down the hill, sure every step I take will be my last. But, for once, the universe aligns in my favor, and the two professors take that moment to announce the field trip.

Professor Balefire gathers us around. I flock to the front before the members of the Six can reach me, my arms shaking.

A flash of dark hair draws my eye to the right. Kimber. Flat, normal teeth flash as her lips draw into a grin. "That was awesome."

By the time Eclipsa rushes to me, Kimber has already left to join the Six on the outside of the crowd.

The Mythological Creatures instructor, Professor Balefire, and Potions and Poisons instructor, Professor Spreewell, stand around a wooden chest.

Professor Spreewell is the first to speak. "Inside this chest, we have class two weapons taken from the forbidden vault below the school. Every shadow will choose a weapon and two items they deem helpful."

"What are the weapons for?" a lycan boy with golden eyes asks.

A Lunar Court Fae girl with one side of her head shaved adds, "And where are we going?"

Professor Balefire holds up a gloved hand. I try to focus on what he has to say rather than the large horns that curve around in spirals over his ears.

"We will be traveling to the Hemlock swamps situated deep in the Summer Court," Balefire says as murmurs fill the air. "Shadows and their keepers will be paired together in duos. The first duo to come back through the portal with the white venom of a raverous snake wins the very special potions and creatures cup for their Court."

Spreewell takes a golden cup trophy out of a purple bag. "Autumn Court was the last court to win. Let's see who will take the cup this year."

"One more thing," Balefire calls, the crowd going quiet. "The Evermore are not allowed to use any magic. So, shadows, choose your weapon carefully. If you get into life-threatening trouble, say the words *eros sanctum* and a portal back here will appear."

After that, Spreewell casts some sort of lottery spell, and our names are called in the order they're drawn. I cringe when Reina's named as the first shadow to select her weapon. She chooses the sword of flames. Its edge can cut through anything.

Her next two items are predictable: a net and a rat to entice the snake.

More names are called. A few Evermore like Eclipsa and Asher don't have shadows, so they're paired together for the challenge. Mack finds me just as Asher draws out a giant magical axe, a lovesick grin carved into his square jaw as he appraises his weapon.

"Is he going to chop off the snake's head with that thing or sleep with it?" Mack teases, her gaze lingering on the dragon shifter.

I chuckle, but something weighs on my mind. "Hey,

Mack. I thought the raverous snake was only found in a tiny swamp in the Spring Court?"

I clearly remember reading how rare the raverous snake is, their white venom harvested for powerful spells. My textbook said the only surviving wild snakes were in the northern region of the Spring Court.

Mack worries her bottom lip between her teeth. "It does seem strange."

Evelyn gives a bored sigh. "Who cares? They obviously brought them in for the contest. Or maybe the snakes migrated."

But I can't get the thought out of my mind, and when my name is called, I think I've puzzled it out. Still, I don't share my suspicions with the others as I peer into the chest. The chest has been spelled to have room for hundreds of weapons and items, each one visible when I look inside.

But, if I'm right about the snake, only one weapon will work. It's hard to breathe as I reach for the small golden flute, nearly lost among the glint of steel blades.

If I'm wrong, the prince and I are totally screwed.

The moment the flute leaves the chest, Inara, who stands nearby with Bane and Reina, lets out a tittering laugh. "Someone tell her that's a Leonidas flute; it only works on warm-blooded beasts like wolves."

"Or lions," I mutter, grabbing my last two items: a map, and a vial for the venom.

Reina sees the map clutched in my fingers and shakes her head. "A map? Everyone knows the raverous snake loves water, and we're going to a swamp. Water will be everywhere."

Mack is in line a few people down, and she sends me a supportive thumbs up. I can't tell if she has the same thought I do, or is just being a good bestie, but I don't have time to talk to her before Spreewell shoos me toward my keeper.

I find the prince waiting for me with a group of Unseelie Evermore. He lifts his eyebrows at my choice. "A flute? Are we going to kill the snake with terrible music?"

Waves of heat crash over me as I see bits of the taco filling I dumped on him still cresting his shoulders. But he hasn't killed me yet, so that's progress, right? Unfortunately, he now smells like a friggin' taco, making him even more irresistible.

It takes all my willpower not to lean close and sniff him.

Eclipsa frowns at my choices. She herself holds a little cage with a gray rat inside. "What will you lure the snake with?"

I shrug. "Maybe they like tacos too."

The prince frowns and picks at a shred of cheese on his lapel.

When all of the pairs have their weapons, we line up. The professors walk down the line, opening portals for every pair.

Spreewell stops in front of the prince and I, his dark purple cloak bright against the white snow. "*Eros sanctum.*"

At his words, a dark spot opens. The spot is pea-sized, at first, but quickly grows to the size of a basketball. A chair. When it's big enough to accommodate a large person, Spreewell motions us toward the portal.

I peer through the rippling veil to the world on the other side. Trees so tall they block the sun sprout from mossy, wet earth. Beyond, waterfalls cascade over cliffs. Warm, moist air scented with pine and stagnant water wash over my cheeks.

This is really happening. No matter how normal portals seem to the Fae, I'll never get used to them. Never.

The prince smiles at me. "After you, Princess."

39

The second I lunge through the portal, a wet blanket of humidity slaps me in the face. My boots sink up to the top laces in green mud. Ugh. Pocketing the flute, I pull out the map and try to get my bearings as the prince appears.

His nose crinkles at the heat, and then he glowers at me as if I'm the cause of the unbearable weather. "I hate to admit it, but Reina was right. We don't need a map. We can walk ten feet in any direction and find swamp. And where there's water, there's raverous snakes."

"Hmm, yeah. About that." I glance up from my map. "We're not looking for a raverous snake."

He peers at me through his dark blue lashes. "No?"

"Nope." I have what I'm looking for so I fold the map, shove it into the back pocket of my jeans, and take off toward the cliffs in the distance. Ferns slap against my thighs, the mud squelching beneath my boots. Tiny creatures similar to sprites but smaller flutter up from the dense foliage. The hum of mosquitoes three times the normal size stirs the air.

Of course this place would have smaller sprites and bigger mosquitoes.

The prince catches up to me. "Care to share this plan of yours, Princess?"

I flash a mischievous grin. Let him see how it feels to have no idea what's going on for a change.

I duck beneath a curtain of hanging moss and trudge straight through a shallow swamp, water sloshing around my boots. A sulfurous, muddy smell clogs my nose. Green algae and lily pads float on the surface of the brackish water.

Flashes of movement catch my eye below.

He grabs my arm, the cold from his fingers breaching the thin fabric of my sweater. A zip of electricity shoots through my flesh, like static electricity but more powerful. "You are aware there are creatures in these woods who would love to feast on a human?"

Yanking my arm away, I push forward, boots splashing loudly.

"Yes, splash," he mutters. "Maybe they'll hear you. Good plan."

"Afraid, Prince?"

"Afraid, no. Why would I be? This swamp only hosts at least ninety-nine things that can kill you, yet we're armed with a . . . flute."

When he puts it that way . . .

Yep, this place sucks.

I quicken my pace. The weight of his dark gaze falls heavy over my back, but he follows quietly. When we get to the first waterfall, I pull out my map again. Satisfied, I nod to a high cluster of mountainous ridges in front of us. They're dark gray quartz, nearly black, spotted with trees and thorny bushes.

The climb to the top is a lesson in pain. By the time I

scramble over the side, panting, sweat burns my eyeballs and pastes my shirt to my back.

The prince waits for me on a rock, his entire beautiful body stretched out as he lazily swats at two persistent mosquitoes the size of apples.

"You know," he says with a dark grin. "If your plan is to throw me off the cliff, there's a problem."

"What's that?"

"I can fly."

Ignoring the urge to lie face down on the rocky ground, I struggle to my feet. "Holy Fae ears, Prince. Was that a . . . joke?"

"I do make them, on occasion."

"What, in between being a giant asshole?"

His jaw clenches. "Okay, I deserve that."

"No, you deserve being thrown off a mountain naked into a swarm of fire ants."

He flicks up an eyebrow. "Well that's mildly worse than being bathed in taco innards."

"Is that another joke?" I say. "Two jokes in a day. Someone call a healer, there's something wrong with you."

Turning my back on him, I take stock of our position. We're on a large, flat area of the ridge overlooking the swamps below, which from here look like a blanket of bushy green treetops. Above us, waterfalls feed into a small basin of clear blue water, their spray forming countless mini rainbows. Without the cover of trees, the sun's glare scorches our skin.

Sprawling out on a flat outcropping, I close my eyes, enjoying every minute of the sun.

When I open my eyes again, the prince sits beside me, his knees splayed wide. He's wearing ridiculous riding pants with the leather cut-outs for the knee.

"What's wrong with your rock?" I ask.

He backhands a mosquito near the pointed tip of his ear.

"I'm hoping these bloodsucking bastards will notice you and leave me alone."

A laugh spills from my lips. His discomfort here gives me great pleasure, and I don't bother hiding it.

His eyes narrow. "This game has gone on long enough, Princess. What are we doing here?"

"Enjoying the sun." I grin wide as I say this; I'm pretty sure he hates the sun. "Also, I hate that nickname."

One side of his lips quirk up. "The nickname stays." He leans close, his arm brushing mine, and peers into my eyes. "So, *Princess*, what's to stop me from glamouring you into telling me this secret plan of yours?"

"What's to stop you from glamouring me into doing a lot of things?" Holy crap, why does that sound so dirty?

He settles his hands on his splayed knees and glares at the forest below. "Fine. We'll stay here and fail. It's not like my father expects me to win the cup anyway."

There's something in his voice that gives me pause. My heart skips a beat. Never once has he mentioned his father in any of our stilted, two word conversations. Curious, I try to get more out of him. Carefully, of course.

"He doesn't care how you do at the academy?" I ask.

"Oh, he cares. But only when it comes to certain areas."

"The combat side?"

His razor-edged jaw goes taut. "Anything that requires the use of power to win, I had better win."

"Like the Wild Hunt?" I say, referring to the end of year test. We've just started the training and everyone is freaking out about it.

He peers into the horizon. "Exactly."

"And if you don't win?" I ask.

"That never happens."

Arrogant much? But I don't roll my eyes like I want to. Arrogance aside, he's actually opening up. "So that's why you had to follow through on the Nocturus with Rhaegar? Some sort of power trip?"

He regards me through his dark lashes, a muscle twitching in his temple. "That was different. I was protecting you from Rhaegar. He's dangerous."

I'm too stunned at first to say much. Rhaegar, dangerous? Besides, the prince makes it clear on a daily basis he despises me. Why would he care if I was hurt?

"What if I don't need your protection?"

He chuckles, the sound low and throaty. "Like with the orc?"

Touché. "Okay, fine. But can I ask you something?"

He pauses from picking bits of dried mud from his no doubt outrageously expensive black boots. "Haven't you been for the last five minutes?"

"How did you know I was in trouble? In the forbidden library?"

He sighs, his bowed lips pressing together as he straightens. "I felt it—your fear."

"Felt it?" Adrenaline floods my senses as I remember being inside his head, feeling his emotions. Was it like that for him too?

Oh my God. What if he could see inside my head?

"What else do you feel when you're around me?" I ask, digging for the truth. "Anything . . . weird?"

What I really want to ask hovers on the tip of my tongue: Do you experience an inexplicable sense of familiarity when we're together, Prince? Does your heart feel close to exploding whenever I'm near? Do you ever dive straight into my head on accident—or on purpose?

But I don't say any of those things, for obvious reasons. He stares at me, the fading sun highlighting the indigos in his hair, the hint of steel-blue in his eyes. His Adam's apple bobs low as he swallows.

Then he jerks to his feet and stares into the setting sun. "We should probably head back now. The others will all be done."

I sigh. "You haven't been listening at all, have you? There is no raverous snake. At least, not here."

His eyes narrow. "This game grows old, Princess."

The sharp edge in his voice tells me it's time to explain. That plus it's almost dusk. "We need the venom from a raverous snake," I begin, hoping it sounds more logical aloud than it does in my head. "But the raverous snake can only be found in a tiny region of the Spring Court."

"So . . . there is no raverous snake?"

I glance down at the hemlock swamp below, a grin lifting my cheeks. "It's like this game they play where I live called snipe hunting. They take the fool into the woods looking for the snipe, but the snipe doesn't exist. It's a fool's errand."

The way his eyebrows gather says he's not convinced. "Then where do we get the venom? It must be possible since there have been prior winners."

A roar comes from near the waterfall, the sound making every hair on my body stick straight up.

"From him," I say, grabbing the flute from my pocket. "The chimera. He comes out at dusk to hunt."

Wow. Saying that aloud sounds way worse than in my head. Comes out to hunt . . . and there's only one thing here to hunt currently.

Us.

I can see the wheels turning behind the prince's eyes. When the truth hits him, he smiles, the first true smile I've seen from him. "Chimeras are made up of a lion, a goat . . . and a snake for its tail."

I could swear his voice sounds impressed.

"Yep. The textbook doesn't say what kind of snake, but

there's mention of the serpent's milky white venom being used for powerful spells . . . just like the raverous snake."

"So, you brought us to the den of a chimera, the most dangerous mythological creature in the Summer Court, armed with only a flute?"

Okay, maybe I was getting ahead of myself when I thought he sounded impressed. There's definitely anger in his voice now, and major judgement.

Another ear-splitting roar cracks the air. It's closer than before. Probably only ten feet away.

Technically, the prince can't use his powers, but that doesn't stop him from pushing me behind him as the largest lion I've ever seen comes prowling around the trees. He's the size of a horse, with a mane of shaggy wheat colored hair two shades darker than his pelt.

I thought I was prepared for the chimera. But there's nothing that could have readied me for his immense size, the predatory power oozing from his graceful body. Muscles ripple beneath his golden fur like living things trying to escape.

From his back, a white goat's head bleats at us.

As the beast pads lazily toward us, his tail whips back and forth behind him, hissing. I spot the snake head at the end, the retreating sunlight glancing off the dark green and yellow scales.

"There's our snake," I whisper, shoving my way to the front. I retrieve the vial from my pocket and slip it into his hand.

Before the prince can stop me, I approach the creature, the golden flute pressed to my lips. My heart spirals into my belly. The sound of my gasping breaths drowns out every-thing else.

"Hey, kitty-cat," I coo. "Listen to this pretty song and don't eat me, okay?"

In my head, I walk up to the chimera playing the flute like the badass I am, and he falls asleep at my feet. It's supposed to be the defining moment of my life, a cool story to brag about for eternity.

But that's not what happens at all.

40

The chimera growls, and I can feel the vibrations from that low rumble inside my bones. Closing my lips around the flute, I blow—

I don't see the chimera's paw until it's too late. Claws snag the flesh of my shoulder, the force of his swat sending me tumbling toward the cliff. The flute jerks from my fingers. The prince calls my name.

Grabbing onto whatever I can hold, I stop my body a foot before the edge of the cliff. Fire rushes up my shoulder; a quick glance shows my sweater is shredded, furrows dug into my skin. Blood darkens the blue sleeve, turning it a soft purple.

"Run," the prince orders. He stands between the chimera and me, one hand held up like a lion tamer. "Summer, get out of here."

Ignoring him, I search for the flute. It must have rolled over the side of the cliff, and I find it on a ledge three feet down. Without hesitation, I leap below to grab it.

Don't look down don't look down . . .

Once the flute is safely in my hands, I glue myself to the side of the cliff. Rocks dislodged by my boots clatter ten stories below. Nausea clenches my stomach, my hands sweaty and clammy as I drag myself back up the cliff. Thankfully, adrenaline numbs the pain in my shoulder.

At the sight of me, surprise flickers across the prince's face. The chimera must notice the prince's focus shift, and he lunges.

A scream sparks in my chest. I shove the flute into my mouth and blow. The first two times nothing happens. Finger holes! Hands shaking, I adjust my sweat-slick grip so my fingers cover the holes and try again.

The moment I blow into the instrument, a sound fills the air. The most angelic, comforting tune I've ever heard. I almost stop, sure there's no way my lips are making something so enchanting. The lion's body grows rigid and then, slowly, sluggishly, he sits back on his hindquarters.

His bright honey-gold eyes are half-slits, a strange green glow emanating from them. Even though I know lions can't smile, his feline lips are curved upward, his floppy pink tongue lolling to the side.

It's working!

I draw closer as the prince glides around to his hind end. The raverous snake tail slides back and forth on the ground, but it too seems lulled by the music.

Drawing the vial out, he carefully secures the snake by its neck. The snake hisses, he slides the vial beneath its curved fang, and it's done.

When he joins me, I notice the claw marks across his chest where the beast raked him. I try not to stare at the metallic silver blood dripping from his wounds. The sight nearly makes me stop playing the flute, but I keep my breaths coming despite my shock.

"The moment you stop playing," he whispers, "we need

to scale back down the cliff." His gaze darts to my injured shoulder. "Can you climb?"

I nod.

His eyes narrow like he doesn't believe me. There's something strange about them, the silver band of iris tinged green —like the chimera's.

His voice is soft as he begins to count.

One, two, three . . .

I pocket the flute and dive for the side of the cliff where we ascended earlier. The chimera snarls, awakened from its magical stupor. And it sounds pissed about the entire ordeal.

Right as I slide toward the edge, ready to flip around and start scaling back down, arms slide around my waist. Cold, strong, capable arms.

"This will be faster," he murmurs. My stomach lurches as he picks me up with inhuman strength and dives toward the forest below.

The feeling of the earth leaving my feet sends a wave of panic crashing over me. A carpet of green trees grows closer with every breath. The sun is nearly set, only a sliver of fiery orange burning through the top of the forest canopy, dusky pink and red shafts spearing the air.

Midnight blue wings the same color as his hair beat the air in my periphery.

I'm not going to die because he has wings. The realization is followed by another. *He has really cool, really sexy wings.*

Once the thought settles into my brain, I relax in his arms. My fear melts away as I focus on the prince's body touching mine. His cheek pressed against my cheek. His fingers splayed over my stomach.

Does he notice the way my new abs (thanks, Eclipsa) tremble at his touch? Does his body sing with excitement at being so close to me?

Oberon's beard, I need to get a grip.

All too soon, the swampy mud squelches beneath my boots. But he doesn't let go. If anything, his arms tighten.

Whoa.

My body responds, pushing into him. The feel of his cool, muscular form like a drug sizzling through my veins.

Oh, God. I *like* this feeling.

The pulse in my wrist throbs. My head spins as a hollow ache opens up inside my belly. The prince turns me to face him, or perhaps I do that on my own. It's all jumbled. My name forms on his lips, is whispered so softly I think I imagined it.

Then he's pressing me into the rocky cliff base. His wings —Holy Fae his beautiful midnight blue wings—spread wide behind him, encapsulating us. There's something feral and raw about his expression that should scare me.

It really should.

But it doesn't. Quite the opposite.

"Summer." His voice is raspy and low, his breath a cold wind. His nostrils flare as he inhales me, his pupils enlarging at whatever he smells.

Knowing what he can do, I should be terrified this close to him. At the very least, I should despise him for the way he's treated me. The secrets I know he keeps. But I'm not in control of my body or the way it reacts to him.

I reach up, capture his inky locks inside my fingers. He watches me while I tug softly, marveling at its silkiness.

A memory nibbles the surface of my mind.

"Why do you feel so familiar?" I whisper.

"Because I am." His fingers trail over my cheek, my lips. I gasp as their iciness leach into the flesh of my neck. Down my throat. Over my collarbone. Despite his frigid skin, the goosebumps his touch conjures, my insides warm and puddle.

Everything feels so out of control.

This is madness; it makes zero sense. I've never felt this way about anyone. Or maybe I have . . . but when? Why do I get the feeling it was with him?

His lips skim my ear and I nearly collapse in his arms. A part of me knows he's affected somehow by the flute. Knows I might be too. Knows—and doesn't care.

This is right; so very right.

"You asked me earlier what I felt around you." His lips drag down my neck, tasting me. His arms slide around my waist and pull me tight. "Every moment I'm around you, every time I hear your laugh, all I can think about is this. Touching you, holding you. The way you taste. I want to be near you always, Princess."

A low, groaning sound slips from his mouth.

I want to ask him how that's possible, when he so clearly hates me. But not right now.

Later.

Now I want his lips on mine. Reaching out, I touch his jaw. I shudder at the feeling of the sharp edge pressed into my palm. The way his bottom lip curls as the pad of my thumb grazes it. First on accident—then curiosity.

And all the while as I touch his face and breathe him in, one thought eclipses all others: I've done this before. A hundred times. A thousand. More.

But how is that possible?

His eyes smolder, but some of the ethereal glow has faded from their depths. Before we can claw back to reality, before the flames of this madness can be snuffed out, I guide his lips to claim mine.

My heart hammers at the contact, his tongue parting my lips—

He jerks away suddenly, shaking his head as if to dislodge something. "No. This is wrong, we can't . . ." His chest heaves. Stumbling backward, he stares at me in horror. "This should have never happened."

I flinch like I've been gut-punched. "Wait, I don't understand. Why?"

"Summer, look at me." His voice has taken on a beautiful, hypnotic quality as he forces me to stare into his eyes. There's magic in his voice, ancient Fae magic. I'm powerless against it; I can't refuse. Can't look away even as I know what he's doing.

"Don't," I whisper.

"I have no choice," he says, quietly, almost to himself. Then he finishes the glamour. "Summer Solstice, by Titania's light, I order you to forget everything that was said and done in the last five minutes. I flew you down here, nothing more."

Nothing. More.

I blink, a warm tear sliding from the corner of my eye as my memories start to float away. The feel of flying in his embrace. His arms wrapped around me. The swell of his lips as they brushed mine.

He's taking all of it back.

But then something happens right as my mind goes blank; a flash of energy surges, and suddenly the memories snap back into place, clearer than before. The ruby pendant resting between my breasts pulses with heat, just like all the times before.

The Winter Prince has no idea his glamour didn't work. I can tell by the tragic look in his eyes, the sad tug of his lips. And I don't tell him.

Assured my memory is erased, the prince sets to healing my wound. But this time when he touches me, his fingers are missing the intimacy from before.

Darkness has fallen completely, and the forest stirs with the sound of exotic creatures I'd rather not encounter. We hurry to the portal in silence.

As we both jump through, I try very hard not to shudder when his cool hand brushes my warm one. When his palm presses into the small of my back. The moment he's sure I'm steady, he jerks his hand away like my flesh is molten lava.

"It's too bad the cup goes to the Unseelie side under the Winter Court banner," Mack says, eyeing the Six from her chair next to me. We're in the Properties of Magic lecture hall, sitting a row behind the Six.

Rhaegar has claimed his usual spot with Basil away from the rest of the class at the very top.

A part of me grieves, remembering how different Rhaegar used to be. Sometimes, more than I care to think about, the weight of his stare presses into me.

I nod without making eye contact; I'm half listening. The lecture, for once, is interesting. We've moved on from elemental magic to properties of soulmancy.

Eclipsa stands on the stage, preparing to demonstrate the elusive, ancient magic. She looks fierce in dark leathers, her silver hair combed into a lustrous sheet. Curved daggers drip from her hips.

"Should have used your newfound fame to ask for a spot back at the dorm," Mack says. She knows I'm there for my protection, but nothing more. She's also figured out by now something changed in the Hemlock Swamp between the prince and me.

He's seven feet away, keeping his distance like he has since we returned from the Summer Court field trip. But his eyes are always on me. I can feel his heavy gaze whenever I'm not looking. Can feel he keeps track of me in a room.

And that invisible thread between us has become a thick, insistent rope of electricity. Tugging and tugging, even while I sleep. Especially with only walls to separate us.

Since we won the cup, he hasn't been to visit Inara at night once. It feels like a tiny victory. But I can't celebrate because I'm overwhelmed with my own emotions. And when I close my door at night and lay down, it takes every single bit of willpower I possess not to go to the prince.

After awakening a few nights ago standing outside his room, where I must have sleepwalked like some horny hooker, I've even taken to locking my door.

But that doesn't stop the dreams. I squirm in my seat as I remember last night's tawdry vision. So real I'm still not totally sure it didn't happen. My cheeks inflame, and a spark of warmth opens between my legs.

Holy hell.

The prince goes still, lifts his nose in the air, and inhales. Then he jerks his head to me. Our eyes meet and a wave of fire crashes over me. Can he smell my desire for him?

I remember his taste, the same bittersweet sensation tingling my tongue even now. I remember what he did to me in my dream last night and a wild ache fills me until I think I'll burst.

I rip my gaze away and try to catch my breath.

"Summer," Evelyn is calling. She snaps her fingers in front of me. "Earth to Summer. You okay?"

"Yeah . . ." I clear my throat, certain everything I feel is painted over my face.

"I was saying, I wish I had a video of Reina and Inara when they saw you and the prince emerge with the venom."

Our victory is all the school can talk about. I'll admit, if it wasn't for the crazy mix of feelings overwhelming me since we returned, I'd be stoked about the change in my status. Earlier at lunch today, five Seelie shadows joined Evelyn, Mack, and me.

That would have been unheard of before my trick with the chimera.

I force a smile. "It was pretty awesome."

"Awesome?" Mack scoffs. "They haven't had anyone actually obtain the venom in over a decade."

"Girls," Professor Lambert calls, his stern voice echoing inside the high ceiling of the lecture hall. "I expect total silence during Miss Skywell's demonstration."

We all nod, and thank God, the attention of the room quickly shifts back to Eclipsa. Soulmancy is an ancient art, and once forbidden. The little I do know about it so far is fascinating. The Evermore, the elite and powerful Fae from the most prominent families, use soulmancy exclusively to live forever.

"As you may know," Eclipsa says, her voice carrying from her spot on the stage. "Soulmancy can be very dangerous when done wrong. But when done right . . . it's an absolute miracle to watch. Notice that when the spell is complete, the new body transforms to look like the old one. That doesn't always happen, and it requires total focus, but that is the goal. To restore the Evermore to their former self completely."

Apparently, Eclipsa has already declared her specialty in soulmancy, even though the Evermore students don't have to declare until the beginning of the third year.

She motions toward the back of the stage at a Fae with donkey ears and a tufted tail. At her invitation, he joins her, carrying a cage with something inside. Soft black fur. Long, floppy ears.

They take the poor bunny out, his body limp and unmoving. Then Eclipsa unwraps a dark green linen napkin, revealing a light brown ball of fluff.

"This is third year Evermore Milken and his familiar, Bramble. Unfortunately, Bramble died three days ago of old age. A preservation spell was used to keep him fresh and his spirit close until another vessel presented itself. This"—she holds up the smaller brown baby rabbit—"is a baby rabbit born in Professor Balefire's menagerie. He died shortly after birth today."

Mack makes cooing noises along with half the girls in class.

Eclipsa sets the baby bunny down beside the older one. Then she places her hands palm down above the two rabbits. Behind her, Milken watches the ordeal with a stricken look, his hands tugging at his shirt.

From here, I can see Eclipsa's lips moving as she speaks the incantation, but I can't hear what she says.

Anticipation charges the room as we wait for something to happen. Then someone gasps.

At first, I don't see what's causing the class to react. Leaning forward, I spot the glow swelling beneath Eclipsa's left palm. More light begins to seep from the older bunny. I watch, speechless, as shimmering fingers of sentient mist unfurl. They give a languid stretch and begin prodding the air.

They're searching for . . . something.

When the tendrils of light reach the baby bunny, they hesitate, cautiously running along its brown fur. All at once, the light surges, pouring into the poor little guy. A sense of awe falls over all of us as we train our eyes on this tiny, furry thing. Willing him to awaken.

His foot jerks. I don't blink, afraid I'll miss what happens next.

With a startled squeak, the baby bunny begins to kick and thrash. But his fur is changing, darkening. When he's completely black, he seems to calm, his frenetic movements ceasing. He hops to his feet and begins to chew on some grass Eclipsa hands him.

"Milken," Eclipsa says, motioning him over.

Milken trembles as he approaches the bunny. "Bramble?"

The rabbit stops chewing and glances up. When he sees his familiar, he hops into his arms. It's basically the cutest thing I've seen in years—or the creepiest. I'm still not decided.

The room erupts in applause, and Eclipsa performs a bow. "The transfer of the soul is complete."

For the first time ever, I wonder how many times the prince has completed the soul transfer thingy-majig, and how old that makes him. Being attracted against my will to a rein-carnated Fae thousands of years older than me was never part of my life goals.

Then again, I'm starting to question everything I ever thought I wanted. Six months ago, I would have told you my biggest ambition in life was finding enough food to feed my family. Six months ago, I would have laughed in your face if you told me I would be secretly attracted to a Fae Ice prince.

Six months ago, the idea that I would attend an academy and find not only friends, but a home, would have been ridiculous.

For whatever reason, the thought that I might love this place terrifies me more than anything. Because if life has taught me anything, it's that the moment you love something, the universe rips it away.

After Properties of Magic class, we meet our Combat Theory instructor, Crenshaw, in the great hall. Most of the students lounge on the wide marble stairs that split into separate stairwells on either side of the mahogany paneled walls.

A stained glass window at the top of the stairs depicts deer and foxes playing in the snow together near a lake. It's actually quite beautiful, like most Fae art, the light shining through the glass coloring the students orange and teal.

Professor Crenshaw has to call out three times to get the group's attention. Today is Friday, and the Fae Yule holiday, meaning many of the students will be going home for the weekend. I try not to be bitter that I'm stuck here, telling myself I wouldn't know what to say to my family, anyway.

The lie almost sticks.

Mack babbles on about her plans to visit her parents as the entire group follows the professor down a low-lit corridor to a dank set of stairs. We trudge single file for what feels like thirty minutes into a dingy basement. Cold, damp air settles around us, the scent of magic everywhere.

The professor waves his hand and orbs light from the overhanging chandeliers. That's when I realize how big this place is. Glass cases line the worn wood floor, jewelry and chalices and other oddities inside. Beautiful, worn armor made of silver and gold hang off wooden mannequins. Gorgeous jewel-toned ball gowns fit for a Fae queen sparkle beneath the magical light.

"This is the hall of antiquities," Professor Crenshaw says, his voice trembling in awe. "Some of these items are ten thousand years old. If you experience an overwhelming sensation of magic, that is the preservation spell you feel."

Someone gasps and points to the ceiling. I follow their gaze.

At first, I'm not sure what I'm seeing. It looks as if a girl is suspended in the air above, her long vibrant red hair hanging far below. The peaks of her high, pointed ears are just visible. The train of the emerald green and gold brocade velvet gown she wears tumbles a good fifteen feet below, the delicate silken fabric putting every dress in the room to shame.

I blink as my brain tries to process why a Fae girl would be preserved above this place like some sort of prize. A living art sculpture on full display.

"Who is she?" Evelyn asks. For once, she doesn't know something.

The professor's face turns grim, and he takes off his hat. "No, they wouldn't teach this story in your history books, would they?" His dark eyes turn watery, and he makes the mark of Titania, a touch to his heart and then a touch between his eyes. "She was the Summer King's only daughter and heir. But when she fell in love with a member of the Unseelie, the king killed his only child, Titania's favorite, to prevent her wondrous magic from falling into the Unseelie's hands."

"Why is she displayed?" Mack asks quietly.

Crenshaw twists his hands together. "A reminder of the

new edict: No Seelie or Unseelie may fall in love or ever marry."

After that, he makes another mark and refuses to say more. As the group wanders to other oddities, I have the sudden, overwhelming feeling that if I don't get out of this room, I'll suffocate.

When the professor beckons us to a red door with strange markings covering the surface, I tear my gaze from the dead princess and run to join the others.

"The forbidden Vault of the Darken. These weapons were used by the fallen king during the war, and their warped magic is partially responsible for the fallout that tore our worlds apart."

Silence descends, heavy and ominous. His eyes narrow. "Before we enter, you should know, the weapons on the other side are outlawed weapons forged from dark, forbidden soul-magic. Touch anything, and I do mean anything, on the forbidden side, and you will be immediately expelled."

He gestures and Magus appears, his hooves clopping loudly against the wood as he nears. "Only Magus can access this room. Anyone else, even with the keys, and the unlaggin that guards it will bash in your skull."

"What's an unlaggin?" I whisper to Mack.

She grins darkly. "A type of orc with one eye."

Lovely. A cyclops orc. Fae monsters can't just be regular ones, after all.

Everyone moves aside to let the centaur access the lock. I watch him fiddle with a key ring. The door pops open with a creak. As I pass, he nods kindly at me.

"Not going inside, Magus?" I ask.

His ears twitch. "If you knew what lurked inside, you wouldn't either."

A burst of magic comes from the next room, but it's laced

with something different than the usual lilies and copper smell.

Something closer to dust, blood, and decay.

An ominous sensation permeates the room, a dark, musty chamber that must be huge by the way our footsteps echo. Here, there's no glorious chandelier, only small torches hanging from stone columns, making it hard to determine the exact size of the vault.

As we trickle into the room, I can't shake the image of the dead princess. I must have read about her somewhere.

Could she have been the one who fought the prince in the Nocturus?

But, as I follow my classmates, my thoughts quickly shift to the row after row of deadly instruments displayed in the middle of the chamber.

Longbows with strange markings similar to the door. Ornate leather quivers brimming with arrows made of bone and iron heads. Iron axes that give off dark, curling shadows. Iron forged swords and daggers still smeared with old, black blood and gore, huge magical stones embedded inside their fancy guards.

Crenshaw explains that these are class six through ten weapons. Below our very feet, in a vault guarded by six beasts, are the few class eleven and twelve weapons confiscated during the war.

"They're all iron," someone remarks.

The professor nods, a strange look on his face. "The forbidden magic melded into the weapons made it possible for the Fae who created the weapon to wield it against another Fae. Does anyone know how forbidden dark magic is created?"

Reina, who's standing near the axe looking for all the world like she might lift it when no one's looking, raises her hand. "Forbidden magic is created when a soulmancer takes a Fae soul and drains its essence to use in a spell."

"Very good, Miss Rinehart," Professor Crenshaw says.

Reina shoots me an arrogant smirk.

"Some of these weapons may have been forged with dark magic using up to one hundred souls." The professor sucks in his cheeks as if the very thought gives him a bad taste. "They are sentient, in a fashion. The guards outside say sometimes they can hear them calling to their masters."

"What would happen if you touch, say, the bow over there?" Jace asks.

The professor draws near to the longbow and quiver in question, a bright gleam in his eyes. "Why it would kill me dead, boy. This bow gives its master speed and unrivaled marksmanship."

"Were they all used in battles against other Fae?" I ask, mesmerized.

"Some. But just as many were used against darklings."

"Even back then?" Reina asks, her love for the dark weapons matching my own.

"Oh, yes. Darklings in some form have always existed in our lands—although not to the degree they infest it now. During the ancient battles between troll and Fae, the troll created darklings using the same forbidden magic that permeates these weapons. In fact," the professor reaches out his fingers as if to touch the tassel hanging from the quiver, then smartly thinks better of it, "a Fae princess once used this bow to kill a hundred darklings in less than a minute."

I stare in wonder at the seemingly simple longbow, bands of iron and turquoise embedded in the ironwood. An inscription is gilded at the bottom of the leather quiver.

May every arrow find its mark the way you did my heart.

I hardly breathe as I stare at the weapon, wondering who the inscription could be for.

"You are lovely, aren't you?" I hear myself purr before Mack grabs my arm and drags me over to a crossbow that's supposedly haunted.

Forget the Winter Prince. I need to find a boyfriend who dedicates a forbidden weapon to me.

"**A**re you sure you don't want to come home with me?" Mack asks. She tries to hide the worry in her voice but it's there, along with two lines that crinkle between her dark brows whenever she's uneasy.

I shake my head. "I'll be fine. It might be nice to be alone for a few days, and I have to catch up on reading for Potions and Poisons class."

She snorts. "You've aced every single test so far in that class. In all our classes. I think you've even surpassed me for highest grade in our class. Surely you can relax for a few days?"

Sighing, I give her a huge hug. How I lucked out in landing Mackenzie Fairchild as my BFF, I'll never know. But I can't tell her that being at her house, watching her family celebrate Christmas, will remind me too much of my family. Not without ruining her holiday, too.

And no way I'm doing that.

"Go. And I'm expecting something fancy and expensive as a present when you get back," I say, my voice sounding cheerful despite the sudden flood of loneliness. "Mack," I call as she walks away.

She flips around. I can tell by her hopeful smile she thinks I might change my mind.

"Merry Christmas." Tears sting the back of my throat, and I blink to keep from shedding them.

"Happy Yule, Summer."

Once she's out of sight, I trudge across campus to the prince's tiny mansion. The setting sun colors the frozen surface of the lake rosy pink and tinges the sky tangerine. Sunlight. I'd almost forgotten what it felt like on my skin.

Come to think of it, the weather has been better lately. The prince's mood has improved, I suppose. I'd kill to know what —or who—is responsible for that shift.

My gaze wanders the rest of the grounds.

If not for the pointy-eared inhabitants and the bitter, numbing cold, this place would be beautiful beyond anything I've ever known.

Especially now with the campus decorated for Yule. Large clusters of silver bells hang from evergreen trees, their tinkling a constant song. Streamers waft around totem poles for each court, placed all over the campus by the second years. They also strung our dormitories with strings of colorful orbs. The magical glow lights the dusky sky.

In the distance, candlelight flickers inside the arched windows of Queen Titania's temple. Shadow students aren't allowed to participate in any of the temple celebrations until second year, but I've heard rumors of Fae and humans alike offering sacrifices during the Winter Solstice.

I glance at the sky above the prince's house. Pale smoke drifts from the tall stone chimney. He's home. Surprising, since most of the Fae have already left to join their families for the long holiday weekend.

I can't tell from my chaos of emotions whether I'm happy or disappointed he's here.

More like terrified, since I saw Eclipsa leave for her family's palace in the Lunar Court half an hour ago.

Here, alone. Together.

I want to be near you always, Summer. I tremble as his voice replays inside my head. My lips press together as I remember how he brushed his mouth over mine.

Holding my breath, I enter as noiselessly as possible. Which is impossible with his heightened Fae senses.

Heart racing, I sneak a quick glance up the stairs. He must be in his room, but I can *feel* his presence as if he's right next to me. The stupid magical rope between us tugging low and insistent in my belly. Trying to pull me up toward him. To close the distance between us.

At the same time, I have this overwhelming urge to smell him like some weirdo. To hear his snarky voice and see one of his rare smiles and feel the weight of his intense, penetrating gaze on my flesh.

Like that's not annoying at all. Particularly when I know deep down how irrational this is. I'm supposed to hate him, not want to rip off his clothes and sniff him like a candle at Target.

I pad up the stairs, cursing each creak. When I pass the prince's room, I hesitate, caught in his orbit. I can feel him on the other side, waiting.

For me to come inside? Screw that. He tried to glamour me, to erase my memories. I might be caught in a wave of undeniable attraction for him, but that's a betrayal I can't just forget.

"Summer?"

I startle at his voice. Its velvety smoothness settling deep inside me. A voice shouldn't possess that power, especially when attached to a face like his.

"Come in," he orders.

Orders.

Shit. My stubborn side surfaces, and I contemplate stomping down the hall to my room. But of course I don't do that.

I slip inside but leave the door open. It's dumb. There's no one here but Ruby, and odds are high she's passed out somewhere. But maybe if I pretend Eclipsa is just down the hall blaring her heavy metal pixie music, I won't do anything stupid.

I pause near his door, my eyes wide as I take in his room. It's furnished for royalty. A king-sized bed of marble takes up the right side. Ice-blue silk drapes frame the huge windows. A white fur rug, similar to the one in my bedroom but a million times bigger, spreads across the floor.

The Winter Prince lounges on his bed, propped up on pillows. And he isn't wearing a shirt. Thankfully he *is* wearing the same dark sweatpants from the night on the roof, his bare feet giving him a strange, almost boyish look that clashes with the savage beauty of his features.

"Hey, you called?" Somehow my voice comes out disinterested. *Summer for the win.*

"You didn't go with Mack?" he asks softly.

I shrug, keeping the pain from my face. "I never really liked Christmas anyway."

His inky brows gather. "You know, for a human, you're a terrible liar."

I sigh. "What would you have me say? Of course I love Christmas. There's pies and presents and hot cocoa, and everyone is nicer than normal. It's like the most magical time on earth. But none of that matters when I'm not with *my* family."

He frowns at the tablet in his lap.

That's when I notice something white in his pointed ear. "Is that . . . an AirPod?"

He nods. "Don't tell my father. He's very much against anything modern. Although I think if he heard the Faerie Haunts play, he might change his mind." He plucks the AirPod from his ear. "Want to listen?"

I take the device and settle on the side of the bed, making sure not to sit too close to him. Once I saw he wasn't wearing a shirt, I should have left immediately, but I'm curious to what kind of music the prince likes.

As the ethereal voices fill my ear, all the emotions I've been holding back rush to the surface. A spasm clenches my throat, and tears prickle my eyes.

I wrench the AirPod away and toss it back to him.

"You okay?" Beneath his smart-ass tone, I catch a hint of worry.

"No, I . . . it's just been a long day and I'm tired." The thought of him seeing me cry fills me with horror. Hiding my face, I flee from the room, making up some excuse neither of us believe.

Only once my door is firmly shut, the covers tucked around me in bed, do I let the tears release. I force my face into my pillow, the tears quickly soaking the soft cotton. I cry so hard I don't make a sound.

The creak of a door jolts me from my pity party. The prince stands just outside the threshold of my room, and he has the audacity to look concerned. His arms are lifted, his hands clenched into the top of the doorframe so hard I think the wood will break.

He doesn't enter. He won't let himself. As if he's afraid of what will happen when he does.

Anger floods my cheeks in a fiery wave.

"Summer—"

"No," I say, swiping at my cheeks. "You do not get to

come in here and act concerned. It's too confusing. You hate me. You like me. You want nothing to do with me. Then you come in here without a shirt looking concerned and—just enough. *Enough.* I can't take it anymore."

His nostrils flare, his jaw flexing as he just stares at me. Then he nods, reaches for the door handle, and leaves.

As soon as my door quietly shuts, I cry and cry until the flood of emotions washes me into my dreams.

"I killed her." The words I wake up screaming echo off my bedroom walls. I thrash in my bed. Sheets tangled around my legs. Hair pasted with sweat to my forehead.

"I killed her I killed her I killed her." I can't stop saying that as the nightmare I just wrenched from invades my mind. Oh, God.

For some reason, I'm not surprised to see the prince in my room. His eyes glow faintly silver, their depths impossible to read. "It's a nightmare, Summer. Just a nightmare."

I pull my knees to my chest as tears pour freely down my face. "I was back at the farmhouse and the children were there. It was Christmas Eve. We were all gathered around the tree when . . . I looked outside." My voice catches. "My mom was out there. My real mom. But she was different. I knew immediately she had changed. Become one of . . . *them.*"

"A darkling?" he asks softly. His voice is still heavy with sleep, but there's a gentleness to it I can't ignore.

"Yes. She—she tried to get inside. Clawing at the doors with her fingernails. Then she called my name and . . ." I wipe at my face. "I took a knife from the kitchen, the one we use to carve meat, and I killed her. She didn't even try to stop me."

He watches as I try to pull myself together. As I slowly force my brain to accept that it isn't real. I didn't kill my mother. I would never kill my mother. I may not have memories of her and I, but I know we loved each other deeply.

"I would never kill her," I say. "Never."

Through my wet, clumpy lashes, I search his face for disdain. For cruelty. For all the emotions I imagined he would feel if he saw weakness on my part.

But the only thing I catch inside his eyes is sorrow. A sorrow so deep it could fill an ocean.

"What time is it?" I whisper, if for no other reason than to take his intense focus off of me and my red, crumpled face.

"Nearly dawn." He reaches for me, hesitates, then brushes his knuckles over my wet cheek. "Go back to sleep. I'll stay here and if you have another nightmare, I'll wake you."

I blink through bloodshot eyes at him, unsure leaving him in my room while I sleep is a good idea. He must think I'm scared of him because he retreats a few steps. "Trust that I won't hurt you, Summer."

"Won't you?" I whisper.

He gets my meaning immediately. I can see that by the way his mouth tightens at the corners. He shoves a hand through his hair and takes a final step back to rest against the side of the wall.

Then he fixes me with a long, piercing stare. "Go to sleep, Summer. You're safe with me."

As I lay back on the pillow and close my eyes, I'm sure I'll never fall asleep with the most powerful Fae in existence watching over me. But I do.

Not only that, but it's the most peaceful sleep I've had in weeks.

W hen I wake up, the prince is gone. But there's a note. Scrawled across the cream stationery in elegant penmanship are four words:

Be ready by dusk.

~W.P.

Okay, that's a bit bossy. I exhale and then stare at the paper. What could he be planning?

But as much as I hate surprises, I find myself counting down the clock. I try to study but I can't concentrate. I take a shower but end up using conditioner instead of shampoo, twice.

I spend two hours of my life I'll never get back playing a Fae card game version of Go Fish with Ruby. Usually I catch her cheating, but this time I'm too consumed by anticipation to notice until I've lost all of the Twizzlers Mack sent me.

Damn.

By the time five rolls around, I'm practically coming out of my skin. The moment I feel the tugging sensation I know means the prince is close, I jump from the couch downstairs and run out the door.

He meets me on the porch, his eyes hard to read. "Grab a coat."

I t takes until we're almost to the winter orchard where I first met the prince for me to realize where we're going. My heart lurches. "Wait, are we going . . . ?"

I can't finish that sentence. The words carry too much hope.

The Winter Prince smiles softly. "You can't speak to them or get near your house. But I thought, maybe, if you could see they're safe . . ."

Now it's his turn to let his words trail away.

Excitement builds inside my chest as we weave through the trees. Once we cross the Shimmer, the trees grow smaller and less dense. I find one of my old paths, the familiarity eating at me as my boots trace a line toward home.

Home.

He follows behind, hesitant. Or maybe that's not the right word. Perhaps he can feel the difference in this world and it bothers him.

My gaze falls on the snow. It's nearly dark, the merciless Texas sun I remember a shadow of itself.

Can it already be winter here? But of course it is. Being in Everwilde made me lose all track of time.

I've been gone over six months.

Noises give me pause. Laughter, high and squealing.

The kids.

My heart clenches. I leave the trail and use the denser parts of the forest for cover. Ten feet from the edge of the forest, I stop. The prince pauses next to me. Through the cracks between the thin sycamore trees, I catch movement.

I see the twins first, Juliana and Gabe. They're building a

snowman. A really sad imitation of one with a lumpy middle and no head. They're both wearing mismatched mittens with holes, their faces hidden by threadbare scarves and woolen hats too big for their heads.

I'm reminded of how hard the winters here are. The way the cold seeps into every crack and pore of the old farmhouse. How we never have enough coats and boots for everyone, nor enough food to sustain our shivering bodies.

"Come inside and warm up for a bit, tiny heathens," Aunt Zinnia calls. At the sound of her high voice, the breath catches in my chest.

I spot Jane sitting on the rickety porch swing, her braids sticking out beneath a green and red striped hat. She's pretending not to watch the younger kids play in the snow, even though she wants to join them. Chatty Cat sits on her lap, looking like he might attack anyone who comes near. I can hear his weird purr-growl from here.

My stomach clenches at the sight of everything. The normalcy of it all. Even the old farmhouse tugs at me. With its sagging porch, the siding in desperate need of a good painting, the flickering porchlight.

I glance up at my bedroom window and immediately wish I hadn't. It's dark, the curtains drawn.

It feels like a thousand years ago that I snuck out onto that sloping roof and changed my life forever.

Only the lawn wasn't full of snow then. I frown. "I don't think it's ever snowed this early here."

"How else could I get them out here?" he says, staring at the children playing. "You humans are so fragile when it comes to the cold."

"You did this?"

"It was nothing."

I wonder what's going on inside his head. Does he think

I'm silly for needing this? Needing to witness them alive and safe and okay?

"Would you like to see more snow, Princess?" he asks, watching me carefully.

"Yes."

Snow begins to fall. I peer up at the sky and watch the fat snowflakes twirl down between the trees. In this moment, I'm not sure I've ever experienced a more beautiful sight. I feel like I'm staring into a recently shaken snow globe, only I'm on the outside of this magical world looking in.

Across the lawn, the kids whoop with joy. They've ignored Aunt Zinnia completely. *Shocker.*

I smile. She'll come out two more times, then she'll enlist the help of Aunt Vi.

A few minutes later, I watch Vi herd them inside. The sound of Christmas songs fills the night. Without looking, I know they'll be gathered around the tree opening presents.

Aunt Zinnia will sing along with the holiday tunes, and Aunt Vi will roll her eyes, a steaming mug of hard cider spiked with moonshine in her hand. The twins will argue over their presents while Jane pouts in the corner. And they'll all act incredibly surprised and grateful when they unwrap their gifts and see their hand-me-down clothes.

I let out a ragged breath. God I miss this. So very, very much.

"They're nice," the prince offers, his eyes squinted in the house's direction. "For mortals."

"They're not nice, but . . . they're mine." Thinking about my family leads to a question. "Why aren't you, you know, off doing stupid Faerie holiday traditions with your family?"

He pulls at a wavy strand of hair that's fallen over his sharp ear. "My father remarried. For the fifth time. He's spending the Winter Solstice with *her.*"

"I'm sorry," I say, unsure how to weave this new layer into what I know about the prince. "I'm sure that's tough."

He chuckles, but it's a raspy, bitter sound. "When you live as long as we do, you learn that disappointment is a way of life."

"And how long *have* you lived, exactly?"

There's a long pause. "Three-thousand-five-hundred years."

He grins darkly, obviously enjoying the way my jaw drops. Then he reaches into his shirt and pulls out something —a necklace. The silver emblem is shaped like an owl's head holding a sapphire in its beak. A soft blue glow emanates from the stone.

"My soulstone," he says, his fingers reverently stroking the sapphire. "All Evermore get one for their renewal ceremony. It's sacred."

My hands twitch to go to the necklace around my neck. The one that's almost exactly like the prince's, right down to the delicate silver chain and infinity clasp. The only thing different is his is shaped into an owl and mine is a wolf.

If soulstones truly are sacred then why would the half-blood Fae give me one?

I refocus on the prince, only to see he's watching me with a still, penetrating gaze.

"My glamour didn't work, did it?" he asks softly.

"How could you tell?" I ask.

His eyes darken. "By the way you stare at me."

Oh my God. "How, exactly, do I *stare* at you?"

Hopefully not like I want to jump his bones.

A rakish smile carves his jaw, and it takes all my willpower to force my gaze up to his eyes. But that's a mistake too, because the intention inside his feral gaze nearly brings me to my knees. "You look at me like you are right this very moment. Like you could give yourself to me completely."

I scowl, trying to hide the truth in his words. "I don't know what I'm capable of when I'm with you," I admit. "Just like I don't know why you tried to glamour away what happened between us in the Summer Court . . . when I'm beginning to think you enjoyed it too."

"Of course I did." His voice is gravelly, close to a growl. "There are so many things you don't understand. We can't—" He scrapes a hand through his midnight blue hair. "Everything I do is to keep you safe, princess."

"Liar," I accuse. "If that were true you wouldn't continue breaking my heart."

"Better a broken heart than dead."

I release a frustrated sigh. "What does that even mean?" When he doesn't answer, I throw up my hands. "Fine. More cryptic bullshit. Just tell me this, Winter Prince. What do you feel when you're with me?"

Such a simple question. I hold his gaze, daring him to look away. Daring him to spout another cryptic answer so I can be done with him.

Instead, he looks me straight in the face and says, "When I'm with you, Summer, I feel like I'm drowning."

"I'm thinking of winter jasmine and primrose for the Winter Formal," Evelyn says. She somehow managed to grab the student position of event coordinator. Unfortunately for everyone around her, she takes the role very seriously.

Mack yawns. "Evelyn, if you put half as much effort into your grades, your parents wouldn't spend their fortune paying for all your after-school tutors."

We're sitting outside for lunch in the courtyard, enjoying the unseasonably warm day. At the stone picnic table we're joined by Jace and two Dawn Court shadows, Layla and Richard.

Some of the snow has melted, revealing patches of green grass and the beautiful black and white mosaic of the courtyard. Thin, stringy clouds drift in the sky above.

Jace grins. "Honey, no one cares about the flowers. Just make sure the punch is spiked with Faerie wine and the music is fast enough we can all grind our bodies together and you'll be fine."

His gaze slides to the table by the fountain and lands on

Basil. The poor Faun looks miserable sitting next to Rhaegar. Mack said Basil stays with him out of loyalty, but after that night, he seems more afraid of Rhaegar than anything.

I don't blame Basil. Rhaegar has changed, although I can't exactly say how. And I catch him watching me at odd times when he thinks I don't notice. The other night, on the way home from a late night studying session for finals, I felt someone following me.

The next morning, there were footprints below my window.

I push the chilling thought away and focus on reality, just in time to see Basil look up from his plate of fruit. When he spots Jace watching him, he grins softly.

Meanwhile, the Dawn Court girl, Layla, keeps trying to make conversation with Richard, who's more interested in Evelyn. And Mack keeps shifting her gaze to the picnic table where the Elite Six sit, along with a certain dragon shifter.

This entire Island is one big cesspool of love. Ick.

"Richard promised to pick me up for the dance in a chariot flown by a pegasus," Evelyn is saying. "Right, Richard? Oh my God, and you guys *have* to see my dress. I had it portaled in from the best dressmaker in Everwilde. Mack, have you gotten your gown yet?"

Mack and I share an annoyed look. Then she gives Evelyn the side eye. "No, I've been too busy studying for finals. You know, that massive test we have to pass to come back in the Fall?"

Evelyn makes a face at that, and a knot suddenly forms in my gut. The tests will be tough, but I'm prepared.

It's the Wild Hunt at the end that scares me. We partner with our keeper for that. Just the thought of the prince warms my cheeks. As if he can feel me thinking of him, I suddenly recognize the heavy, prickling feeling that means he's close.

At the same time, Mack gives a near imperceptible jerk of

her head behind me. I turn just in time to see the Winter Prince stop by our table. Eclipsa and Asher stand on either side of him. I'm pretty sure the entire courtyard stops what they're doing to stare.

Terrified silence falls at the table. I always forget how scared the others are of the Six.

"Can we sit?" Eclipsa asks in an amused tone, one side of her mouth quirked.

"Yes, of course," Evelyn gushes, shoving her tray into Richard's as she tries to make room. I hold back a grin as Asher tries to fit between Mack and Jace. I'm sitting on the end next to Richard. The prince locks eyes with me as he glides around to our side and stands behind Richard.

Richard's face turns three shades of red, and he jerks to his feet. "I'm done anyway." He sweeps one more longing look at Evelyn before picking up his full tray. "See you guys later?"

I watch him go before scowling at the prince.

His eyes glitter as he takes the place beside me. "Didn't mean to frighten him."

"Didn't you?" Eclipsa drawls through a devilish grin.

He smirks. "Says the Fae assassin wearing *seven* blades. I mean, surely one will do, Eclipsa. Do you really need seven?"

"Eight," she corrects. "I have one stashed in my boot." Eclipsa turns and winks at Layla and the girl almost passes out.

The prince hasn't addressed me, hasn't even looked my way, but I feel my traitorous body rejoice at his nearness. Ever since Christmas, when he told me he felt like he was *drowning* around me, I've taken to ignoring him.

And by that, I mean I dream about him every night and can barely breathe when he's near and turn bright pink when he touches me.

Like right *now*. Beneath the table, his thigh presses into mine, and I've never been so aware of anything in my life.

How am I supposed to concentrate on finals when my body reacts to his presence like a drug?

Thank the Shimmer, I talked Eclipsa into allowing me back to my dorm with Mack. We all agreed I'm probably safe, and that everything was a coincidence.

I still see him after lunch and combat class. Each time I leave the encounter feeling like I'm drowning. Like he's an itch I can't scratch. A smarmy, arrogant, beautiful pointy-eared dickwad rash I can't get rid of.

It's torture.

"Ready to start extra training this week?" Eclipsa asks before biting into an apple. I watch her eat for a moment, the small, quick movements almost predatory. As if the apple is a heart she's just plucked from an enemy's chest.

I refrain from saying something cheesy like *I was born ready*, and nod. But I'm excited. Our training sessions have become my favorite part of the day.

"Good, because the Wild Hunt is coming up in a few months. You'll need all the help you can get to pass." Her gaze shifts to the prince. "And you? Ready to get up early to train with Summer?"

What the frick?

"Why does *he* need training?" I blurt.

He grins, the act somehow wanton. "Eclipsa thinks we need to *gel* as a team."

Bastard. He knows exactly why that's a bad idea.

I swallow, picking at the initials someone carved into the table. How will I survive four days a week with him in tight clothes that showcase every single hard angle and plane of his gorgeous body?

"Scared?" he teases.

Yes, I want to say. *Terrified.* That's what happens when you have no control.

Instead, I glare beneath my brows at him. *"Puh-lease."*

My bragging isn't all hot air. It's been three months since the prince and I sat in front of my house in the snow, and I've put every bit of pent up attraction toward my training. I haven't gone against Reina since the last time, but I'm confident I would smoke her now.

Speaking of. Inara and the rest of the Six watch us from their table. Reina and her two boy toys are there, along with Lyra, Bane, and Kimber, who wears a black veil over her face to counter the bright sun. Her shadow, a timid, pale girl with short auburn hair, holds a pink Hello Kitty umbrella over the vampire Fae.

From what I've read, Kimber won't burn to cinders or anything, but her skin suffers a poisonous reaction to the sunlight. Even ten minutes in full sun could be crippling. A full hour and she could die.

Kimber winks at me, and I decide to pretend the gesture is friendly. After the taco incident, she treats me like a monkey here for her amusement. But I don't have any illusions about our relationship.

If the situation called for it, she'd rip out my throat in a heartbeat.

The rest, however, glare without even trying to hide their loathing. If not for the prince, I have no doubt they'd be over here torturing us right now.

Inara and I lock gazes, and the hatred in her eyes sends a chill down my spine. I'm starting to wonder if there are cracks in the Six. More importantly, I'm beginning to question what could cause a rift between the most powerful group in school.

And I'm praying it has nothing to do with me.

"**A**gain," Eclipsa commands. It's the Thursday before the Winter Formal, and classes are out early for Ostara, yet another Fae holiday. So, instead of combat class, I get my own personal private lesson.

I spring forward, my baton held high, blocking the Lunar Fae's advance. Her sword flashes as it arcs through the air. It connects with my baton, the impact rattling my bones.

"No," the prince says, coming up behind me. I freeze as his hands glide around my waist, repositioning me. Then his fingers brush the underside of my arm as he lifts my reach an inch higher. "There. Better form."

He jerks away quickly, and Eclipsa notices. Her sharp gaze shifts from the prince's fingers to my face.

Crap. My stomach flip-flops. *She totally knows.*

The door to the gym crashes open, and a worried student rushes to Eclipsa. "Professor Spreewell said I need to find you. There's an incident with one of the soulmancy spells."

Eclipsa glances over at us, her brow furrowed. "Can you work with Summer the last thirty minutes without me?"

The prince stiffens.

Taking his silence as an answer, she follows the student out the door.

The moment she's gone, I feel our aloneness acutely. The air becomes heavier, swollen with expectation.

He glances after Eclipsa. "We can cut practice short . . ." His words trail away as he see me rounding on him. "What are you doing?"

I slip on a pair of fingerless striking gloves and grin. "I'm practicing."

I toss a pair of gloves at him. He catches them without breaking eye contact. "This is a bad idea, Princess."

"Why?" I counter, circling to his left. "Because Eclipsa isn't here to save you?"

His eyes narrow. "You know why."

"No, actually, I don't."

Then I lunge for him. Surprise widens his eyes, but he manages to recover in time to leap back before my round-house connects with his head. Prowling closer, I follow that up with a jab uppercut combo.

A sweep of my leg would have tripped him—if not for his freakishly fast Fae speed. He falls into a defensive stance, easily maneuvering out of my grasp. He refuses to fight back, instead using his quickness to avoid me.

"Coward," I snarl. "Fight back."

He may be taking it easy, but I try to take his head off with every strike.

Who's drowning now?

I even manage to land a few. Each time my flesh connects with his, his eyes gleam brighter.

He might have protested, but he's definitely enjoying this. Then again, so am I. If he's going to be in pain when I'm around, might as well make it physical.

I surprise him with a flurry of rib punches before catching

him on the chin. "Summer," he growls in warning. His eyes are practically on fire.

"You said you feel like you're drowning when I'm around," I snap, ignoring the plea in his voice. Another round of jab cross combos push him back on his heels. "Drowning, prince. Do you know how that feels?"

Wow. Up until right this moment, I had no idea all the pent-up anger raging inside me.

His chest heaves. "Princess, you have no idea what you're doing—"

I strike again, forcing him to duck.

"Stop talking and fight back," I order.

"Once I do, once I let go . . . I won't be able to stop."

"What? Hurting me?"

A smile twitches his lips. "No, Princess. Not hurting you."

Oh. Beneath my thick sheen of sweat, my skin flushes bright red.

Something inside him reacts to that. His stance widens, his jaw sets. Grabbing the bottom of his shirt, he hoists it over his head.

I don't even bother hiding my interest as I stare at his body. The shadows trapping in the muscles of his abdomen. The way the Unseelie tattoos seem to writhe against his flesh with every single movement.

Instinctively, I tug off my over shirt, leaving a thin ribbed black tank. His eyes go to my own tattoo. The one cresting my forearm and winding up my elbow.

The one that says I'm his.

His nostrils flare, and he lets his gaze slide to my body, every single curve evident beneath my shiny black leggings and tank. The newly fleshed out hips. My athletic thighs, hard and lean from my time spent here.

He inhales sharply as he trails his focus slowly upward to meet my stare.

His eyes are wild, predatory. I don't flinch from their intention. He begins to circle me, and I work to keep space between us as my heart jackhammers into my ribs. A little smile finds his face.

He can hear it.

We fall into a dance of attacks and defensive maneuvers. But this time the rules have changed. I know it and he knows it. He stalks me across the mat and it's all I can do to evade him. When he gets too close, I catch him on the cheek. A light, playfully blow.

His eyes go wide with excitement.

After that, I know I can't get away. The moment he draws near, my foot shoots out, landing against his thigh. He doesn't even flinch. With lightning speed, he hooks a hand under my knee, trapping my leg under his armpit.

For a breath, he holds me there. Hopping on one leg. Captive to whatever he desires. No amount of yanking or cursing can break me free.

He wants me to know I can't stop whatever comes next. My breaths come in rapid spurts; my head spins with excitement and anticipation.

Then he sweeps my other leg and gently lowers me to the mat.

"Princess," he says, his gaze practically a weapon as it scrapes up and down my captive body. He braces his hands on either side of my head. "Say the word and I'll leave right now. We can both walk away from this."

He says this almost pleadingly, like we're poised over a dangerously high precipice, about to jump to our deaths. If that's true, I'm already in freefall.

I shake my head. "No."

My legs wrap around his waist. At this point, my body has a mind of its own, and it wants to feel him. Every part of him.

I try to use my thighs to pull him closer, but he hesitates. Lowering to his elbows, he stares down at me. Sweat darkens his hair at the temples and brings out the waviness. His pupils are huge, his irises slivers of bluish-silver. His lips part suggestively.

My body is freaking out. His presence so close. His sweat everywhere.

He leans closer until I can feel the cool energy coming off his bare flesh, the sweat slicking his chest wetting my clothes.

My body rejoices, a sensation of everything righting itself descending. But I also remember Mack's words about not ever falling for a Fae. And that's exactly what I'm doing. Not just falling for a Fae, but tumbling headfirst for the most powerful Fae in the academy.

I reach up and touch one of his ears, stroking the inside. I have no idea how I knew to do that, but he moans, hardening between my legs.

Holy crap. Evelyn once made a joke about Fae males being larger than human males—not that I know the difference—but damn.

One more flick of my finger and his full weight presses into me. His lips are just as soft as I remember as they graze mine. Gently, slowly, his tongue slides against my lips and into my mouth. His kiss becomes more desperate.

I moan, three months' worth of pent-up need coming to a head.

I lose myself in him. His scent. His power. The exotic coldness of his flesh, the way the sweat around us freezes into frost with his excitement. Snow forms from the rafters above and dusts the mats. Our breath curls around us in ivory wisps.

Loud voices stir the night. They come from somewhere outside, but it's enough to break the spell. The prince stiffens and then rolls off me, and I'm thrust back into this startling new reality. I kissed the Winter Prince. The Fae responsible for all my misery.

And I liked it.

And I'm fairly certain he liked it too.

He brushes a finger over my lips. Then he helps me to my feet. As I stand, his eyes drag over my body once more.

I think he might say he made a mistake, and my heart is prepared to be hurt. But he just stares at me for longer than any man ever would.

Then he says, "I've been meaning to ask you something."

Anything. I would say anything at this point.

"Are you going to the dance?"

I'm not sure what I was expecting, but not that. "No."

"No? I thought all mortal girls liked music and dancing?"

"I . . . I don't have a dress." Or a date.

Not true, exactly. Mack promised we could go together. She offered to lend me one of her old bubble gum pink mermaid prom gowns from high school. I still haven't committed one way or the other.

He frowns. "Go to any Faerie shop in Everwilde or the mortal world, give them my name, and they'll put it on my account."

I pause, suspicious of his offer. "No, I can't."

"No?" His eyes widen like someone who isn't told no very often.

"I can't pay you back," I remind him. "And I'd rather not owe you or anyone else at this school. Lord knows I already have to find some way to take care of my bill for food and books."

"Get the dress, Princess."

I swallow, all kinds of thoughts running through my head. Mainly that I can't dance, and he's going to be there to witness that. But also that this is the second time he's done something nice for me and I'm not sure how that feels.

My throat clenches. "I'll find a way to pay you back."

"Seeing you in a dress will be payment enough."

We clean the mats and lock up the gym. On the way out, I happen to glance to my left. The sun has gone down, but there's enough moonlight to make out the snow-packed ground. The white crust is pristine, untouched.

All except by the window, where two large footprints sink deep into the snow.

"You have a footman?" I ask, my gaze ricocheting from the marble walls veined with gold to the huge fountain in the center of the lobby. We're in Manhattan, inside the first floor of the Woolworth Tower where Mack's parents live. The plan is to stop by to say hello and then go dress shopping. Evelyn, who already has her dress, is here to help us make the *right decisions*, whatever that means.

"Wait," Mack says, "we just traveled through a portal to Manhattan from Everwilde, and your mind is blown over a footman?"

It's true. If anything should have blown my mind, it's the charm on her bracelet that, when pressed where portals are allowed, forms a portal to her house in the Untouched Zone. It's a recent gift from her parents for passing midterms.

But I'm already accustomed to magic and its many, many conveniences. We can set the temperature in our dorm just by telling the magical fire what degree we want the room kept, we can find our place in the academy books just by saying, "*nerum lantius*," which means find last page read.

And today, in the commons, I discovered a magical coffee

mug that fills to the brim with hot, delicious lattes whenever I ask.

I'm a little annoyed that it took me this long to find that party trick, but, yeah, magic has lost its wowing abilities. On the other hand, the Upper East Side of Manhattan is blowing my mind.

I tug on the hem of my tight blouse, trying to pull it down to cover my navel. "He was wearing livery, for Fae's sake!"

The charm on her bracelet was supposed to take us into the lobby of her apartment, but apparently it needs tweaking because it spat us onto the street outside the Gothic skyscraper.

She sighs as we enter an elevator with an operator—because rich people can't punch their own buttons, apparently. The operator hardly glances at the two sprites fluttering about our heads.

He must see this stuff all the time.

According to Mack, this building was one of the first to allow integration, and they have a least twelve Fae families who split their time between here and Everwilde.

Just like the footman, the operator gives Mack a curt nod. "Penthouse floor, Miss Fairchild?"

"Yes, please, Mr. Phillips," Mack says before throwing me a sheepish grin. "What?"

The Penthouse? I mouth.

She shrugs. "Go big or go home, right?"

Mr. Phillips—an older gentleman with a gray handlebar mustache—and I exchange a look. The kind of look between two people who will never own an apartment in *any* floor of this building.

As soon as we exit, I follow Mack and Evelyn down a mirrored hallway. Soft cream rugs line the white marble floor. I frown at myself in the mirror. My jeans—Mack's jeans —are stained from overuse, and the sleeves of the gold jacket she gave me to finish off the ensemble hits just below my elbow.

I refused to take any of the clothes from the prince's manor, but now I regret my stubbornness. I'm meeting Mack's parents. By now, after hearing all of Mack's stories, I practically love them, even though I've never met them. I want to make a good impression.

"Stop fussing, you look great," she orders as she drags me to the dark gray door. "Tell her, Evelyn."

Evelyn gives a feeble nod. This is the least I've ever heard her talk.

The moment the bell rings, an excited cry comes from the other side and the door swings open. Two men wrap Mack in an embrace.

Startled by the unannounced hugging, I retreat a step as I study them. Both men are handsome, in their mid-forties, and in good shape. But that's where the similarities end. The one who practically lifted Mack off her feet has soft green eyes, cropped red hair that's thinning on top, and thick muscles that scream CrossFit at least twice a day.

The other man is dark skinned and wears a dinner jacket with fashionably distressed jeans. He's slender and tall, with a shaved head and impeccable eyebrows. I have him pegged as more of an elliptical/hot yoga kind of guy.

As if just remembering me, Mack ducks from the red-haired man's grasp and shoots me a smile. "Summer Solstice, meet my dads, Nick"—she nods to the red-haired dude—"and Sebastian."

Dads? Both men are beaming their picket-fence straight teeth at me. Then Nick grabs me in a vise-like hug. "So this is the girl we've already heard so much about."

I lock eyes with Mack, wondering exactly what she told them about me.

"I might have texted them about the Shadow Selection,

and the bar incident with the Winter Prince." She flashes an apologetic smile. "And possibly about winning the cup."

"Honey," Sebastian says, waggling his perfect eyebrows at me, "Evermore gossip spreads like wildfire. Just assume we know *everything*."

My unease must show because Nick laughs. "Yes, I've heard the prince is quite enamored with you. Is he as delicious as they say?"

Sebastian *tsks* at Nick. "First, of course he is—he's the Winter Prince. Second, give the girl some space. You're smothering the poor dear."

"Darling you know you love my smothering," Nick amends, but he does, indeed, give me space.

I flash Sebastian a relieved smile. After they both shower Evelyn with hugs and questions about her family, we all trail inside as Nick and Sebastian take turns gabbing. Apparently I'm the talk of their tiny circle. Poor Tainted Zone girl gets into the academy and becomes shadow to the Winter Prince.

"It's like a fairytale," Nick proclaims.

"They're talking about making one spot available each year for underprivileged students from the Tainted Zone," Sebastian adds. "Wouldn't that be wonderful?"

I nod dully, praying my true feelings don't show in my face.

High up in their fantasy world penthouse, with its flying buttresses and terracotta gargoyles, Mack's dads have no idea what the borderlands are really like. Most kids in the Tainted Zone don't want a scholarship to the Fae academy; they just want clean water and enough food to last the winter.

We all trickle into the kitchen. A stunning dining table set for twenty spreads across the room, but my eyes go to the people filling it.

"Mack," I whisper-yell as I tug on the sleeve of her ivory leather jacket. "You didn't say there'd be other people here."

I glance over the gilded sideboard buffet to see Ruby taking bites out of blocks of undoubtedly expensive cheese. She loads her arms up with yellow sugared candies the size of her head, ignoring the shocked looks from the guests.

Shimmer help me.

"Oh," Nick says, flicking his hand at the table. "That's just one of Sebastian's casual lunch parties."

"Lunch?"

Mack twirls a strand of indigo hair around her finger. "They host them on Fae time."

Right. Most Fae eat lunch around five o'clock, and dinner around eleven. But at the academy lunch is closer to three o'clock.

Evelyn's eyes brighten. "I love Fae lunch, and I'm starving. Do we have time to join them?"

I almost hug Mack when she shakes her head. "Nope, we're on a mission. Look hot as frack at the Winter Formal, remember?"

After a round of informal introductions, we grab some Fae delicacies—candied fig and a type of soft, tart cheese rolled in a layer of pastry so light it crumbles in your fingers—and catch a cab to the dress shop.

The store appears tiny from the outside. The brick studio has no signage and is tucked between a bakery and a tattoo shop. But inside is another story entirely. Rack upon rack of the most beautiful custom gowns I've ever seen grace the walls. Each piece exquisite.

A dress with a skirt made entirely of dandelions spelled not to blow away. A flowy ensemble that looks created from giant pink rose petals. A sleek black dress plated with metallic black scales.

Definitely not in Amarillo anymore, Summer.

As soon as we entered and the bell above the door tinkles, a pixie Fae comes out from the back room carrying an armful of buttery-gold silk. Glasses perch on his nose, his skin a light shade of moss.

He takes one look at our human features, frowns, and says, "Can I help you?"

Before I can utter a word, Ruby rises above us, arms crossed over her chest. "You are looking at the shadow of the Winter Prince. Show some respect, pix."

The Pixie pushes up his glasses to study me. I lift my eyebrows. I'll never get used to the shrewd way the Fae stare. Whatever he finds, it must be passable because he snaps his fingers and a swarm of sprites descend with measuring tape.

"I know the perfect color for you," he says, leading us into a private room. A sprite with clear wings flies over and offers us the Fae version of champagne from a vineyard in the Winter Court territories.

Mack takes one of the bubbling flutes, and when Evelyn waves hers away, mumbling about suddenly not feeling well, Mack snatches Evelyn's as well.

"Do you have any food here?" Evelyn asks. "I'm really hungry. I think that's why I have such a headache."

As the sprite flutters off to find Evelyn some crackers, I stare at Evelyn and try not to frown. She's been quiet the last couple of days. I think, despite her assurances to the contrary, that she's worried about finals. She didn't even comment when I casually mentioned the prince offered to buy me a dress.

I push the thought aside and down a swallow of the sweet, fizzy drink. Then I set the glass champagne flute on a metal side table and hold out my arms. I'm actually relieved to have someone make all the decisions for me. I wouldn't have the first clue about picking a dress, or what colors flatter my skin tone; I've always worn whatever was available.

When all my measurements are taken, the pixie brings

over a fold of fabric. I stare at the amethyst-purple silk. "I'm not sure—"

My words trail away the moment he brings the material up to my face and I catch my reflection in the mirror. A gasp tumbles from my lips. The color brings out the gold in my hazel eyes and makes my skin look radiant. Mack and Evelyn murmur their approval, and then Mack holds out her two drinks and clinks them together.

"To kicking this fancy ball's ass," Mack says.

"I'll drink to that," I mutter, finishing my glass.

Ruby waggles her eyebrows. "The prince won't know what hit him."

I hang my dress on the closet door and stare at it, afraid if I blink, it will disappear. Or perhaps the magic used to meld all the pieces into a seamless gown will fade away and the dress will fall apart.

Mack sighs. "I'm not sure I've ever seen anything so beautiful." She sinks her teeth into her lower lip. "Summer, you'll be careful, won't you?"

"Careful?" I laugh, not sure where's she going with this.

"I mean, I'm glad the prince bought you a nice gown. You deserve it, truly. But . . ." She hesitates, worrying her hands. "I've seen the way you look at each other. Just remember, whatever happens, you cannot fall in love with him."

"Love has nothing to do with it." My voice comes out way more defensive than I planned.

I tug my lip between my teeth. That's not what this is, right? But as soon as I tell myself that, I know it's a lie.

Oh, God. I think I *am* falling for him.

How is that possible?

I've never believed in love at first sight. I've never even thought much about love at all, other than the knowledge it wasn't in my cards. At least, not for a long time. And I would have never guessed someone like the prince could be the one.

Love is supposed to be this beautiful thing. It's supposed to happen after you get to know a person. It's supposed to feel inevitable, something you see coming.

But there it is.

Unexplainable.

Undesirable.

Undeniable.

I am falling in love with him . . . and I hardly know him.

Fuck. I'm falling in love with a Fae prince, and I think he's falling for me too, and none of it makes any sense.

The horrifying realization must show on my face because Mack says, "Oh, no." Her hand flutters over her mouth, the breath she releases rushing through her fingers. "I have to go to the ceremony. Just . . . we'll talk about it later."

"Wait?" I tilt my head. "What ceremony?"

That's when I notice she's wearing makeup—a lot of makeup. And her dark chocolate hair is shiny and curled into loose spirals that show off her new silver and indigo highlights.

"Didn't the prince tell you?" she calls over her shoulder as she plucks a black sheath dress from her closet. "There's a banquet tonight for the Evermore and their families. Shadows are supposed to attend. It starts in like twenty . . ." Her gaze flicks to her watch. "Oh, shit, like five minutes."

Five minutes? My heart stutters into a frenzy. Crap. The prince failed to mention a banquet tonight, but he must have been busy preparing for his father's visit. I glance in the mirror and sigh. I need a shower and a come-to-Jesus with Mack's makeup palette before I can do anything.

Especially since the prince's father is here. The prince's father, King of the Unseelie.

Definitely not ready for that. Definitely not ready for any of this.

Anxiety settles squarely between my shoulder blades. Grabbing Mack's pink shower caddy, I rush for the communal showers with the promise to meet them at the banquet.

Thirty minutes later, my hair is wrangled into a wet bun on top of my head, and I've managed to dab on lipstick and mascara. None of Mack's dresses will fit me, so I run barefoot to Evelyn's room, praying she has a dress I can wear and maybe some shoes.

Not that I won't rock my Salvation Army combat boots if I have to.

Buried deep in a pile of clothes on the floor is a slinky coral mini-dress that barely covers my butt. I glance at the clock, a frustrated breath rushing out.

Tiny stripper dress it is.

I shimmy into the dress, nearly break my arm trying to zip it, then slip into some black three-inch heels a half size too small. Right before I run outside, I check my reflection in the mirror.

The dress might be short, but it hugs my curves in all the right places.

My gaze travels down and snags on something inside Evelyn's small metal trash can. I drop to a knee and peer into the pile of tissues, sifting through a few cans of Diet Coke her parents must send her.

There's a box with a pregnant woman on the front . . .

Oh, no. No. No. No. I dig deeper into the tissues and my fingers catch on something long and hard. I hold up the pregnancy test, my heart in my throat.

I stare at the results. Then I grab the box to see which mark means pregnant, even though I'm already pretty sure.

Once I've confirmed what the two lines mean, I drop the box back into the trash and let out a deep breath.

No. She can't be . . . she can't be.

My brain whirls with questions like who and how far along, but I'm already late to the ceremony, and I want to make a good impression on the prince's father.

Shit. Shit. *Shit.*

I'm torn between finding Evelyn and going to the banquet, but she should be there. If not, I'll make up some excuse and go find her. The prince and his father will just have to deal with it.

As I rush from Evelyn's room and take the stairs two at a time, I pray Evelyn is there tonight. I can only imagine how scared and alone she feels.

The commons have been transformed for the Winter Formal. Blue and silver streamers hang from the walls along with stringed lights. Giant crystalized snowflakes descend from the high cathedral ceilings, and what looks like real snow covers the ground, paths carved through the pristine white.

I'm rushing so I don't have time to appreciate all the decorations, but Evelyn must be proud.

My heart sinks a little at that, but it's hard to focus on her when my nerves have now twisted into a giant knot in my stomach. The idea of talking to the Unseelie King is terrifying. And a tiny part of me wonders why the prince didn't tell me about tonight.

What if . . . what if he doesn't want me here.

Swallowing, I place a clammy hand on the curved door handle to the great hall, and pause. My hand is surprisingly slick. Through the pounding of my heart, I hear muffled noises from the other side.

The door opens easier than I expected, meaning I practically slam it open. *Awesome.*

As soon as the heavy oak door slides shut behind me, I freeze. The room is full of Fae dressed in gorgeous attire. The long banquet tables are grouped by court. Before I can flee—which is exactly what I plan to do—an attendant appears and takes my elbow, guiding me through the rows of tables.

I can feel every eye following me, the weight pressing down on my shoulders. I fight the urge to stare at my feet, or to cross my arms over my chest. When we near the prince's table, I see an empty spot by the prince. His father, the king, sits with what must be his new wife, a petite, pretty girl with thick black hair and empty eyes.

But she's a mere shadow in the Winter King's presence. Unlike the silvers and blues his son prefers, this king wears all white. From his armored breastplate to his tunic embellished in silver to the cape flowing from his wide, imposing shoulders. Even his hair is white, falling well past his shoulders. Deep-set pale eyes blanched of color watch me above thin, cruel lips.

I lock eyes with the prince, and a shock goes through me. He's annoyed. His mouth pressed into a grim line. Eyes tight. The muscles of his neck are corded with anger.

Oh, hell. As the realization hits home, I feel my cheeks flare with heat.

He doesn't want me here.

But it's too late. Too late to run. Too late to hide. They're all staring at me as I slide into the spot beside him.

The prince is on my right, the king on the other side. He hasn't stopped staring at me. I don't want to look, but with the way he's watching me, it would be awkward not to. Gathering my strength, I drag my eyes to meet the Winter King.

A tiny puff of air escapes my lips. My reaction to his face uncontrollable. There's something about him, a familiarity, that I can't deny. And not in a good way.

I fight down a rush of nausea, my body instinctively recoiling from him. Pinching my fingers inside my inner thigh, I squeeze so hard my hand trembles.

Once I focus on the pain, my body forgets everything else, and I manage to wrangle my face into a smile.

The king doesn't smile. He just stares at me with that terrifyingly unreadable expression until I'm forced to look away.

My focus flickers to Cronus as he walks to the center of the dais at the end of the chamber. He pinches a microphone between his fingers and leans into it. "Evermore, the most important ceremony of the year has arrived. The Three Seers have declared they have three bonded pairs of souls."

I look around, trying to recall this ceremony from my studies. But I draw a blank.

Three hunched figures draped in black, frayed robes make their way slowly to Cronus. When they stop and face the crowd, a wave of applause crashes over the room. Deep cowls shroud their faces in shadow, but I have no doubt that's for our sake.

The cacophony of cheers is so loud it almost feels like I'm drowning in the sound.

Together the crones lift their hands, twisted and gnarled with age, and hold up a swirling ball of fire. It's so bright that I can't look directly into it, like they've carved out a piece of the sun. "Three have the eternal fire found bonded together," they chant. "Three has it claimed for its purposes."

I feel someone grab my arm, the force of the act startling. The prince brushes his lips over my ear, his breath cool as he orders, "Leave. Right now, Summer."

"What?" I say, twisting my arm away. Why would he want me to leave, unless . . .

Oh. Bonded souls. Like mates. I suddenly recall all those times Inara claimed he was her mate. That's what this is. A mating ceremony. And he doesn't want me to see him and Inara formally claimed.

A surge of anger ripples through me. Anger and shame. I'm angry because the thought of the prince and Inara being bonded for life makes me sick. And I'm ashamed because I shouldn't care. If he truly is Inara's mate, then I'm an idiot and a fool.

The crones chant something in Faerie-tongue. Then six creatures of light spring from the fire inside their wrinkled palms. Beautiful wings of shimmery iridescent mist open and close as the magical butterflies flutter toward the tables.

Two muted orange ones seemingly made from autumnal leaves break off in search of their choices. Two vibrant iris-purple butterflies swirl and dive.

But the last two . . . they're completely different. One has wings of silver, like strings of ice weaved into a delicate tapestry, tiny snowflakes raining in its path. The other is a vibrant green, its gossamer wings longer and more graceful than all the others.

I have no idea what the colors mean—if anything at all. I'm pinned to the spot as I watch the sparkly creatures bob and dance over everyone's heads. The first two matching pairs choose their students quickly.

No surprise, two Autumn Court mates are selected by the orange butterflies, and two Spring Court mates are picked by the purple ones.

So the colors do mean something.

A hand touches my shoulder. I look up to see Eclipsa frowning down at me. "Come with me," she growls, ignoring the looks she gets from the crowd.

My chest clenches. I didn't think Eclipsa would try to hide the truth from me too. I glance once more over at the prince, who won't even look at me. His hands are splayed in front of him. I've never seen him so tense.

I slip from my seat, relieved that I don't have to witness the act. This is a good thing, I tell myself as I follow after Eclipsa, rushing to keep up. The lie almost sticks.

When we get to the door, the attendant takes one look at Eclipsa's expression and moves. She opens the door so hard it smashes into the wall. I take a step—

"Wait." Cronus's voice booms over the banquet.

Somehow, I know he's talking to me. And that turning around will change everything.

The panic in Eclipsa's eyes sets me on edge. I've never seen her even mildly upset.

That's when I notice the total silence. Not like before, when the room was quiet but there was still the normal background symphony of tinkling silverware and murmurs and chairs squeaking over the parquet floor.

This is the kind of silence that permeates every cell of your being. The kind you remember for years to come.

Slowly, I turn to face Cronus. My heart is battering against my breastbone like a scared rabbit trying to escape its cage. If only I could let it out. Maybe then the chaos of emotions ravaging my insides would quiet.

Cronus has left the stage and stands a few feet away. His face looks as confused as mine. But there's also terror in his expression.

"No," he whispers, more to himself than anyone.

What is happening? My gaze darts around the room. Mack sits to my left at a table with Basil. Her hand is slapped over her mouth. Inara has lurched to her feet, her chair knocked violently back behind her. Her face is flushed with rage, her nostrils flared and chest heaving for each breath.

Her perfect face looks seconds from crumpling, like a puffed up pastry just out of the oven.

Her parents are there, two gorgeous Winter Fae dressed in ivory furs and weighed down in silver jewelry. Their faces are twin expressions of rage, and her father trains his outrage on the Winter King.

Inara's mother whispers something in her husband's ear, and then they slowly all turn their rage on me.

If not for the crowd, I'm fairly certain they would murder me where I stand.

But why? And why is everyone staring at me?

No, not at me. *Above* me.

I force my eyes up, knowing what I will see.

Please no. Please no. Please—

When I spot the gorgeous green butterfly hovering just above my head, my mind goes blank. Literally just stops functioning for a hot second.

Cronus turns his head to face the crones. "There has been a mistake."

A mistake. Yes, a mistake!

The crones hiss and moan. "The eternal fire never lies," they chant. "Never. Never. She has been soulbound."

The headmistress appears to my right. She's walking toward me, her forehead wrinkled and mouth stern. But my attention slides to the Winter Court section, to the prince's table . . . and the crystalline butterfly perched on one of the sharp peaks of his icy crown.

"We're . . . mates?" I whisper.

The prince locks eyes with me. Gone is the angry, dismissive expression. The total apathy. I startle at the emotions there. The vulnerability and pain.

We're . . . mates. Soulbonded, whatever the frack that is. Suddenly, it all makes sense. Complete, total sense. The way I feel about him. The way my body reacts when he's around. My insane attraction to him.

I'm not falling in love with him. I'm bonded to him . . . against my will. There's nothing between us, nothing but some stupid Fae magic that gives me no choice.

And he lied to me about it. He knew.

I feel the attention shift from me to the prince's table. The Winter King stands. He's tall, taller than the prince, and every bit of him exudes power. From the way he commands utter silence to the way he wields his gaze like a weapon.

Cronus flinches beneath the king's stare, and the head-mistress's hand flutters to her face, as if she can hide behind it somehow.

"Tell me, how is this possible?" the king says. The quiet tone of his voice scrapes down every knob of my spine. "How has my son, heir to the Unseelie Courts, been soulbonded to a . . . human?"

His lips curl at the last word, human, like it's distasteful.

"There must be some rational explanation," the head-mistress whispers. "There has to be," she repeats, as if saying it twice will make the statement true.

The king's penetrating gaze slides to me, and suddenly I can't move, can't draw enough air into my lungs. My hand goes to my throat, and I can feel my pulse hammering against my palm.

Screw this. I've never run from a fight. Never once fled something just because I was overwhelmed. But I'm not just scared. I feel cracked in half. Exposed. My mind drowning in a torrent of conflicting thoughts.

How could this happen? Why didn't the prince tell me? But more than anything, I feel betrayal deep in my core.

I didn't choose this. My parents were killed by the Fae. Aunt Vi and Aunt Zinnia's families all died because of the Fae. How can I face them if I'm mated to the creature that ruined their lives?

How can I face myself?

So I flee. I think Eclipsa calls my name as I dart past her, both shoes tumbling free. I even think she might chase after me. But all these months of running laps and cardio training has finally paid off, and I find myself alone, sprinting bare-foot through the snow.

"Oberon's beard," Mack growls as her cell phone lights up in the semi-darkness. "Can he not take a hint? You don't want to talk to him right now."

Ruby covers her ears with her hands. "Tell him to stop enraging that damnable device. It's torturous."

We're all huddled together on the bottom bunk, under multiple layers of covers. After I fled the banquet, the weather dropped like thirty degrees. Now a full-scale blizzard pours from the sky.

Whatever the prince is feeling, it's not good.

I ignore the phone and concentrate on the book in my lap. As soon as Ruby heard what happened, she disappeared. Ten minutes later, she reappeared with a textbook she swiped from a third year student.

I found what I needed on chapter twenty-seven, The Soulbonded. When a Fae is reborn, they take their powers with them. But sometimes, their connection to another Fae in their previous life is so strong that a magical bond transfers over.

That bond is sacred to the courts because it allows mates to share their powers through the bond. Soulbonded Fae mates usually end up in very important positions in each court because their combined magic is so strong. They've even been known to challenge kings.

But there's only one problem with all of this.

I'm not a Fae.

And I have no magic. Zilch. Not even a smidge. Nor can I use the prince's magic. I mean, I think I'd notice the ability to freeze people. In fact, that would really come in handy.

A loud smack against the windowpane draws my attention to a tiny form just outside. Eclipsa has been trying to reach me for hours. Her messenger, an obscenely happy sprite with teal wings and a rainbow mohawk, was chased away by Ruby.

Twice.

I feel a sense of pride in that. I might be a magicless human but my sprite is kick-ass.

Ruby lets out a war cry and zips through the air toward the other sprite. When Eclipsa's sprite sees the light golden orb of magic in Ruby's palm, she screeches and darts back into the night.

A part of me feels bad about Eclipsa, but I just can't deal with any of this right now. Nor can I overlook how Eclipsa knew the truth and kept it from me. They both did.

At the thought of the prince, I suck in my lower lip. I've been turning snippets of conversation over in my mind for hours, piecing everything together. He's known we were mates, maybe since the beginning. But he didn't want *me* to know.

And he tried keeping me from the ceremony tonight because he didn't want anyone else to know, either.

A thought occurs. What if his father is angry? The same father who had him whipped for showing any emotion. Could he be in danger?

A new round of nausea surges into my belly, and I groan.

"What did he say?" I whisper, hating myself for asking.

Mack lifts her eyebrows. "Sure you want to know?"

I nod, and she shoves her phone into my hands. I don't have a phone and neither does the prince, so the prince has been texting Mack's phone using Asher's.

I glance at the screen. I'm a bit surprised to see Asher's name at the top of the chat, already put in from another time. I'll have to ask Mack about that later.

Asher: The prince wants me to tell you to tell Summer that he's sorry, and to please meet him outside your dorm.

I grin. There are wards in the dorm that keep the Evermore out.

Me: Tell the prince she said not in a million years.

Asher: He told me to tell her stop being stubborn. And . . . another thing.

Little conversation dots flash at the bottom as he types, taking his sweet time.

Asher: You looked hot tonight in that tiny black dress.

I clap a hand over my mouth. Then I roll my eyes, my thumbs flying over the letters.

Me: Tell him she said screw yourself. Also. Thank you, Dragon Boy. I did look hot. Really freaking hot.

Sweet baby Jesus, Mack's going to murder me.

Mack leans over trying to read the text. "What's he saying?"

I pull the phone away and grin just as another text dings.

Asher: Damn right you did. You had better save a dance tomorrow for this dragon boy. Oh, and she can tell him herself. He found a way up, the maniac. Careful, he's in a mood.

Shit. My heart punches into my throat. I toss the phone and lunge for the door. The moment it opens and I see the prince's face, I slam it shut and slide the deadbolt.

"Oh God," I mutter. "He's here."

"How?" Mack screeches. She jumps from bed, sending the dark green covers sliding to the floor. "What about the wards?"

"I'm a Fae prince," a sultry voice says through the door. "I can break most wards on this campus." A long pause. "I can also open locked doors, Princess."

Of course he can. I release a ragged breath. "I don't want to see you right now."

"Are you sure about that? Because your breathing and your racing heart say otherwise."

Ruby takes a defensive position above my head. "Hey, ice bastard! Just try coming inside and I'll shrivel your balls to frozen little raisins."

"Sounds entertaining." Another pause. Then, "I'm unlocking the door now. Please refrain from shriveling anything until Summer hears me out."

I step back as the deadbolt unlocks itself, the telltale perfume of lilies and copper permeating the air. The door slides open with a *creak* and then the prince fills the doorway. His hair is disheveled as if he's run his hand through it a hundred times, his eyes dark and a little wild.

Cold surges from him in frigid waves.

"Well that's one way to open a locked door," I snap. "The other is to not fucking open it because it's locked."

His lips twitch into an amused grin. If he was within touching distance I would throat-punch the smirk from his stupid face.

"There's not enough magic in the world to force me to be your mate," I hiss. "Now get out."

His eyes darken, but instead of leaving, he takes a step in my direction.

I retreat until the far wall meets me back. The prince's eyes don't leave mine as he claims the space between us. His hands go on either side of me against the wall, pinning me between his arms. Ruby gives a war cry and rushes toward us—

He tilts his head and she freezes midair.

Without breaking eye contact, he says, "I need a moment with Summer."

Mack hesitates, her arms crossed.

But I nod without looking at her. "It's okay."

"Fine, but I'm right outside," she points out. "In case you need me."

When she's gone, he releases Ruby. "While I appreciate your concern for Summer," he says, "this is between me and my mate."

Mate. The word reverberates through me like a curse, even as something warm and electric opens inside my middle.

I hear Ruby cussing all the way down the hall. When she's

gone, he conjures a gust of wind to shut the door. I glance at the door, back to him. The knowledge that he could keep the door closed for as long as he wants settles in my core, along with the knowledge of what might happen if we're alone.

Already I can feel my body responding to his closeness. Changing. The anger and tension bleeding from my shoulders and neck. The need to feel his touch, to kiss him and more, so much *more*, consumes me.

He stares into my eyes for a long time. Then his focus shifts to my lips. He goes to drag a thumb over my bottom lip and I slap his hand away. He blinks, a growl stirring his chest, and then tries again.

I hate how my lips part for him. How I gasp as the rough pad of his thumb brushes the sensitive part of my bottom lip. A tremor shakes his shoulders. He's excited by my reaction. I can see it in his eyes.

And I like his excitement. Oh, God. This is all wrong. I was supposed to be mad at him. At the very least, I was supposed to get answers out of him.

If he doesn't leave this room right now, I'll lose control.

Ducking beneath his arms, I stride to the door and point. "Please leave."

He stares at me for three breaths. Then he nods. "You're right." He rubs his head, and for the first time I wonder if he's as conflicted inside as I am. "I'm going back to the Winter Court tonight with my father. I have to fix this before it gets out."

My heart lurches sideways. "Does that mean—did the eternal fire thing make a mistake?"

I'm supposed to feel hope at the idea, but all I experience is panic.

He walks up behind me and his arms slip around my waist. His fingers splay over my stomach, low and firm, his chin resting in the spot above my collarbone. The fabric of my dress is so thin that I might as well be naked, the cold of his fingers bleeding into my flesh.

His lips brush the sensitive shell of my ear. "Does this feel like a mistake to you?"

I sink into him, sighing as I do. Holy hell. Nothing should feel this good.

"No," I whisper.

"I'll be back as soon as I can. Eclipsa is going with me, but Asher will stay here with you. When I return, I'll explain everything."

"You're missing the dance?"

"Not if I can help it."

My body jerks as he pulls away. A rush of air hisses through my teeth. "Wait. I don't understand any of this. I don't even know . . . your name."

He stiffens. Outside, snow batters the windows in violent bursts. When he looks at me, there's such vulnerability in his face that I fight to avert my gaze. "I have enemies everywhere. Enemies who would use such information to destroy me."

I reach into my dress and tug out my pendant. "I have this. I think it's why I was immune to your glamour, which means no one can force me to reveal your name."

"Even so. Trusting isn't in my nature. Call it a result of my upbringing."

The dark sarcasm in his voice can't hide his pain.

"Prince, I'm not your enemy."

"Life has taught me that everyone is a potential opponent, even those close to me." A muscle flickers in his jaw. "*Especially* people close to me."

"I am not your enemy," I repeat softly. "If I can trust you not to hurt me, you can trust me with your name."

He hasn't stopped staring at me. Hasn't blinked. That raw vulnerability making him irresistible. I want to break down those walls. I want to destroy them and anyone responsible for their creation.

"Be careful looking at me that way," he says, his voice low and gravelly with warning.

"Or what?"

"Or I won't be able to leave."

"Then don't. If that's what it takes to get the name of my mate." What the hell am I saying?

But it's too late. He prowls toward me until we're inches apart. His hands slide over my waist, cool and claiming. His thumbs begin circling low on my belly. "Say it again."

"What?"

"My mate. Say it."

A rush of air escapes my lips. I hadn't meant to utter that phrase, but there it is. A wave of dizziness crashes over me as the words come to life on my tongue, heavy and terrifying and final.

The moment I release them, I won't be able to take them back. Not a second time. And I can see in his eyes what that means.

But I can't stop my rebellious mouth from parting. My traitorous lips from curling to form each syllable. My errant lungs from sending a surge of air to release the two words that will change my life forever.

"My *mate*."

His hands leave my hips and frame my face. Then his fingers slide over my jaw to cup the back of my head. Two of his fingers twine in my hair, gently controlling my head. His lips crush mine. The force startling. When his tongue enters my mouth, my eyelids snap shut, a soft moan rumbling in my throat.

Instinctively my hands go to his hair, fisting the silky strands.

He stiffens before growling into my mouth.

"Tell me you don't want this, Summer," he whispers. "Tell me to stop and I'll walk away." It's almost a plea. Maybe he feels as out of control as I do. But I couldn't stop this thing between us at this point even if I wanted to.

Everything after that is a blur. I'm in his arms. There's a flash. A portal. We're in his bedroom. Snow speckles the air like dust motes and fall over my feverish skin, tiny pinpricks of cold. My crystallized breath spills from my throat in milky bursts.

He settles me onto a pile of furs over his bed and then stares down at me with a predatory look that sets my insides ablaze. He drops to his knees and spreads my legs. I watch as his hand fists the hem of my dress. Watch as he tugs it up to my belly, his other hand stroking the inside of my exposed thighs. My newfound muscles respond to his touch, clenching and trembling.

All the nerves inside my body are melting down. I feel *everything*. The impossibly soft fur against the back of my bare thighs. His fingernails flicking over my skin. My silk dress as it slides up my stomach and over my head. His hungry gaze unapologetically raking over every inch of me.

I watch, mesmerized, as his slender hands move over me. Curling a finger beneath my panties, he tugs them off. My bra is next.

His eyes never once leave mine.

He wants me to see his intentions. To take in the full force of his desire. Every time I gasp, it ripples through him. Every time his fingers graze my flesh and I tremble, one corner of his mouth curls in amusement.

At one point, his gaze snags on my tattoo. His brand. He captures my wrist between his hands, holds the inside of my forearm up to his lips, and kisses the inky swirls, his mouth tracing up my arm.

There are no words between us. My rapid breathing creates a symphony in time with the wild hammering of my heart. I don't even have a chance to feel awkward at my lack of experience because he does everything.

I wish I could say when he lowers himself onto the bed that I protest a little. Wish I could say I hesitate, even for a moment, as he claims my body as his. That Mack's warning and Evelyn's predicament and my own misgivings give me pause. But nothing matters except satisfying the savage, primal urge raging through every cell in my body.

I have to quench the inferno or I'll die.

"Promise," I breathe as his teeth capture my earlobe.

"Anything," he pledges, his voice thick with excitement.

The chill of his cool breath against my ear makes me sigh. "Don't hurt me."

A long pause. "I promise to always protect you." He punctuates his answer first in the form of a languid, penetrating kiss. Then with his fingers as they glide between my breasts, across my stomach, between my thighs, and inside me.

"Always," he repeats. "No matter the price."

We don't have sex, but the acts we do are just as intimate. Maybe more. And through it all, he kisses me. My neck. My lips. My breasts. Other places. Until there isn't a spot on my body his lips haven't claimed.

That gentle act sprinkled between the passionate, almost desperate clash of our bodies is enough to undo me completely.

In this tiny sliver of time, I am his and he is mine.

Hours later, I fall asleep against his chest, so tired I couldn't move if my life depended on it. When I finally come to, the prince is whispering my name. "Summer."

"Sleepy." I bury my head in a pillow to avoid the silvery light trickling from the crack between his heavy blue drapes.

"I have to leave," he says. "Feel free to stay as long as you need."

With his voice comes reality. A startling, sobering reality.

I am naked and the room is freezing and . . . oh my God, the others must be so worried about me.

Fisting the plush duvet between my fingers, I drag the covers around my body and sit up. The prince sits in bed, naked, sipping some type of fragrant tea from a gilded teacup. But all his attention is on me.

I can't tell if the gleam in his eye is from amusement at my shyness or his memory of last night.

Holy hell, last night. A spark of desire rushes through my middle, and warmth blooms over my chest.

Without breaking my gaze, he sets the teacup down on his nightstand, leans forward, and kisses me.

The kiss isn't a morning-haven't-brushed-your-teeth-yet kiss. It's a full blown, sexy, third date kiss.

A knock on the door finally breaks us apart. Eclipsa peeks her head in the room. When she sees us in bed, her eyes narrow. "Time to go, Sylverfrost. I've been waiting hours for your ass."

"I'll be down in five," he promises. She gives me one last look before leaving.

As soon as the door shuts, he prowls across the wood floor, oblivious to the chill, or the fact he's completely nude, and dresses. He has to go to the Winter Court to speak with his father, he explains. Despite my newfound shyness, my body still burns with need for him. My throat is parched, my flesh feels feverish and tender, and my stomach aches with hunger.

I'm half sure I'm going to wake up and realize this has been another dream.

When he's dressed in his Winter Court finery, he approaches me. For a moment, he just stares. I can't read the emotions filtering through the mask he wears. Can't break through to the person I connected with last night.

Then he leans down, a few wavy locks of his hair brushing my cheek, and whispers, "Valerian. My name is . . . Valerian Sylverfrost."

I s it possible to become someone else in a single night? To transform so completely that you don't even recognize yourself in the mirror? That every breath you take, every step, every laugh feels as if it comes from a stranger?

I meet this stranger's eyes in the full-length antique mirror. Her face looks nothing like I remember: Mack's golden highlight shimmers across my full cheekbones, my gold-flecked hazel eyes bright and clear. The amethyst dress cascades from my tall frame, showing off my healthier figure. My arms are badass, rippled with lean muscle. Even my hair looks shinier, pulled into a plaited concoction atop my head by Ruby.

She even surprised me last minute with miniature silver peonies she weaved into the strands of my pale blonde hair and the folds of my dress. The magic that makes them hold imparts a soft lily scent.

I wave my arms, just to be sure this is me and not some magical mirror that shows you a better version of yourself or something equally dumb. But there's no denying it. The gaunt, sickly girl who entered the academy over nine months ago is gone.

Maybe I *am* a totally new person.

Ruby cat-calls from the corner of the room, giving her seal of approval the only way she knows how. "Kid, if you were a steak you'd be well done."

I laugh. "Are you . . . hitting on me, Ruby?"

"Just saying, kid. My lips are like skittles." She waggles her eyebrows. "Wanna taste the rainbow?"

"It's true," Mack confirms, coming up behind me. "You're practically glowing."

I meet her eyes in the mirror. The veiled accusation in her words matches her gathered eyebrows. She frowns, holding my stare a second longer than comfortable. I shift on my feet, digging the pointed heel of the amethyst pumps the pixie gave me into the wooden floor.

She exhales, her face softening into a smile, and touches my arm. Then she crosses the room and digs her Louboutin platform heels from the ever-growing clothes pile on the floor. They're studded with crystals and spikes.

I watch her slip the platforms on, my shoulders sagging. When I came home this morning, Mack darted across the floor and wrapped me in a tight hug. She and Ruby were so worried about me that they were about to report me missing.

Worse, still, the headmistress had come by to talk about the 'incident,' as she termed it. Being out of the dorms past curfew was bad enough, but I had no idea how to explain *where* I was last evening.

Selfishly, I had totally forgotten about them—or anything —the entire night. This thing between the prince and me is so all-consuming that when he's around, I lose track of every-thing else. Even those I care about deeply.

The thought makes my stomach clench with unease.

My guilt only multiplied as I fended off their questions

with an excuse about the prince wanting to make sure I was safe. After multiple assurances that he didn't kidnap me, I steered the topic away from the prince and to Evelyn. I didn't spill her secret, though.

That's not mine to share.

The others agreed that her recent moodiness was out of character. A quick search found her in her bed with the drapes closed. She said she was sick but was going to try to make it to the dance tonight.

If I didn't know the truth, I would have believed her; she looked ill. Her skin was pale, clammy, and splotched with red marks, her hair lifeless and greasy, and bruise-blue shadows pooled beneath her dull eyes. And skinny—she had dropped like ten pounds in a matter of days.

I wanted so badly to stay and tell her I knew she was pregnant, but I decided to wait until after the dance.

She needs to enjoy this night like everyone else. Tomorrow I'll go to her and we'll sort it out. Tomorrow I'll sort *everything* out.

I hear the music before anything else. Loud, rhythmic, Fae techno music that vibrates the walls of the commons. When we reach the great hall where the dance is set up, a quick flashback of last night hits me. I remember running from this place and all the hateful, angry stares.

And then . . . the prince and I . . .

A surge of prickly heat blooms over my cheeks as I follow the others into the hall. Asher wears a gorgeous ensemble over his massive body; green and gray scales converge over his chest in some type of ceremonial armor, his soft brown hair for once teased out of his green eyes. He has an arm slung around Mack's shoulders.

I've never seen her eyes so sparkly or her smile so big.

Evelyn, on the other hand, sags against Richard. Her gold empire dress is loose around the middle, but I swear I can see the outline of a bump. How far along is she?

The moment the doors swing shut behind us, I'm enveloped in a winter wonderland. Snow—real fricking snow —drizzles from the high ceilings and pools on the floor. The tiny snowflakes catch in our hair and the folds of our dress. But it doesn't melt.

They've been spelled to stay perfect.

The walls, too, have been spelled to look like a snowy forest surrounds us. But there are real trees too, scattered around the enormous room, owls swooping from their branches.

I touch Evelyn's arm, shocked at how cold she feels. "This is beautiful."

She regards me quietly with dull, uncomprehending eyes.

Richard looks at me and shrugs. "I'm going to grab us some drinks. That might pep her up."

I watch her stumble across the dance floor with Richard. Poor Evelyn. All this preparation, all this planning, and she can't even enjoy it.

The dance floor writhes with Fae and humans. Some of the Fae are half-shifted, and most wear outlandish clothes that I'm sure are the latest fashion. Small white moths with glittering wings flutter above the throng of students. Higher up, sprites dive and twirl in frenetic, choreographed moves.

The sprites' bodies have been spelled to glow; it's like watching the stars dance.

Mack and I stand by a crooked tree while we wait for Asher to bring us our drinks. Against my will, my gaze scours the dance floor for a certain prince. Part of me celebrates when I can't find him. But a much larger part of me mourns.

If anything, after last night, that tether between us has only grown stronger. More insistent. And now that I know his name . . .

Where are you, Valerian? I remember his father, how terrifying and imposing he was, and shiver.

Asher comes back with steel goblets brimming with a metallic silver liquid. Already his lips are stained with the stuff, making him look like he wears lipstick. His eyes drift to Mack, a little smile playing across his face. "Ready to dance?"

She looks at me, torn, but I gesture to the dance floor.

"Go," I say. "I'll be fine."

Minutes pass. I sip the drink, but whatever's inside makes my head spin and my pulse quicken dangerously fast, so I toss it. The students on the dance floor don't feel the same way. Their lips and chins are stained silver, the mercury-colored liquid glowing softly beneath the neon lights.

The music grows wilder. The dance floor pulses with charged energy. I see a few of our professors acting as chaperones, but they retreat as the party becomes crazier by the second.

A Dawn Court shadow from my Gaelic studies class runs by, tears melting her mascara down her cheeks. In place of her nose and mouth is a pig's snout, and her ears and feet have suffered the same fate. A coiled pink tail sticks out from her dress.

Two Summer Court Fae chase after her.

Thirty minutes later, Mack comes running up, her eyes frantic. Asher stands beside her looking bereft, his mouth tugged into a frown. A giant silver heart-shaped stain mars the front of her beautiful dress.

"I have to change. We have pictures in like half an hour!" She dabs at the stain with a stack of napkins, her eyebrows gathered. "Will you be okay? I'll be back as soon as possible and then you and I will dance. I promise."

I'm already uncomfortable, and the thought of standing here alone for another thirty minutes sucks. But I want her to look beautiful tonight, and there's still hours of the dance left.

So I plaster a smile on my face and shoo her away. "Don't worry about me, I'll be fine. And take dragon boy with you," I add. "Just in case."

I think about the Fae males chasing that poor girl. Tonight is not the night for humans to walk alone on campus.

Asher gives me a solemn nod, obviously taking his job of protecting my best friend very seriously.

As soon as they leave, I lean against the tree and drop my head back. This is going to be a long night.

5 3

I t feels like years since Mack left to change, and I'm relieved when someone approaches, asking for a dance.

Until I turn and see who it is.

Rhaegar grins at me. "Surprised to see me, Summer?"

His voice is soft and, yet it carries through the loud music. Basil stands a little ways off, frowning as he watches Rhaegar and me. But he doesn't intervene.

"No, I . . ." I smooth my hands down my dress, staining it with sweat. "I'm glad you're here."

"Are you now?" He's still smiling, but his grin doesn't reach his eyes. A stunning emerald waistcoat melds to his daunting figure, and a twisted crown of golden ivy twines around his head.

But there's something in his face that makes me recoil from him. I'm shocked to see he's half shifted. Dark fur runs along his arms, black talons curving over his fingertips. Bright silver paints his cruel lips.

And his eyes—

He grabs my arm, hard, the talons sinking into my flesh. "Let's dance."

No amount of jerking my arm or struggling against him can loosen his grip, and I'm dragged into a clump of bodies. When he finds a suitable spot near the middle, he yanks me close.

"Rhaegar, you're hurting me," I hiss. His body is hot, hard, a cage of flesh and bone.

His hand crushes mine as he forces my right arm out; with his free hand, he twists my wrist behind my back. Without any effort at all, he forces me into a stiff waltz.

He presses his cheek into mine. "Did you laugh at me?"

"What are you talking about?" I pant. He's whirling me so fast that I can barely breathe, or maybe that's just my panic.

"You and the prince. When you tricked me into losing. You humiliated me."

He throws me backward. I scream, but his arm slips behind my back before my body can slam into the floor. He leans down, his lips brushing against my ear. His breath feels like fire against my skin.

"Did you really think I wouldn't know?" He jerks me to my feet. My hand throbs with pain. "Do you know my father nearly disowned me?"

"Rhaegar, please, you're *hurting* me."

He seems not to hear me, his lips twisted with hatred. "Where is your Winter Prince now, hmm?"

I crane my head, searching the wall of bodies for a friendly face. But all I see are the Fae, their eyes wild, laughing and screeching as they dance and dance.

All at once, the music stops. After so much noise, the sudden silence feels wrong. I can hear my heartbeat hammering inside my skull, my breaths in tandem with my erratic pulse.

Rhaegar's hand slides up between my shoulder blades, soft, caressing, all the way to the back of my head. His fingers are so long that they reach both sides of my jaw. They dig into my flesh as he forces me to look at the stage.

Oh, no. Inara. Her beauty is overwhelming. Her eyelashes are frosted white, her lips painted a deep blue that contrasts against her ivory skin. A gown of frost shimmers around her body, the low-cut ensemble pooling along the floor like snow. Her cobalt blue hair is pulled high atop her head, held up by near-translucent moths.

The effect is mesmerizing.

"Beasties, fiends, and creatures, it's time to crown the Evermore royal couple."

A roar rises up from the crowd. My body begins to tremble.

"The queen of the Winter Formal this year is an . . . unusual choice," Inara purrs. "Before we announce her, I want to play a little slideshow."

I watch Reina walk to the stage and fiddle with a projector, then the white screen behind the stage lights up, and a video begins to play.

Of . . . *me*.

My unease surges to wild panic as I watch the video unfold. Every single incident this year plays over the wide screen. I watch myself, the feeling surreal, like watching another person.

Except the videos have been edited to only show certain parts. I'm on my knees in the hallway, arguing with Inara. Then I'm in the club, surrounded by male Fae. But from the angle of the camera, I look like I'm enjoying the attention.

Boos fill the air.

The video of me standing over the bed of the girl who was turned to stone comes next. I'm glaring at the camera, a snarky smirk on my face.

Of course Inara's comments have been edited out so it looks like I'm somehow responsible for the girl's death.

My heart sinks as more footage emerges. Moments between the prince and I that I didn't know were filmed. When the camera pans to a window and draws close, and I see the prince and I inside the gym, my heart sinks. He's on top of me, my legs wrapped around his waist.

"Fae-whore," someone yells.

I try to look away from what I know comes next, but Rhaegar's hand forces me to watch the final footage. I cringe as the girl in the video slinks from the prince's house, her white-blonde hair messy and matted.

"Yes," Inara purrs, "she's still wearing the same clothes from the night before. Classy." Her crystalline eyes meet mine, and a grin carves into her face. "Time to come up and claim your title, Summer Solstice."

Time seems to slow as Rhaegar forces me toward the stage. Boos and hisses assault me from all sides. Inara's lackeys mock me as I pass. Lyra performs a dramatic bow. Kimber doesn't bow, but she bares her fangs at me.

Reina winks at me and mouths, *you're so dead.* Her twin boy toys make vulgar gestures.

I climb the steps, my legs shaky. This will not end well.

Inara glides toward me like we're best friends. I should have known she wouldn't let the humiliation from last night stand. I should have been ready for something like this.

"This human thought she could come to our academy and spit on our traditions. She thinks she's better than us. That she can come here and use spells to trick the Winter Prince into thinking he's *mated* to her. First she tried to lure Rhaegar into her bed, and when that didn't work, she went after the prince."

A symphony of boos echo off the walls.

"She wants to become a Fae queen," Inara continues, "so let's make her one."

Panic swells behind my sternum. I scan the crowd for a friendly face. I can't breathe. Can't move.

"On your knees," she says pleasantly, still smiling. When I refuse, Inara motions to Reina. When I see what she holds, it takes all my willpower not to cry out.

Reina's hand squeezes around Ruby's body. Her other hand holds a pair of scissors.

"On your knees," Reina orders, "or I go snip snip."

"Don't do it, kid!" Ruby shrieks.

But what choice do I have? My ego isn't worth hurting my friend.

I force my head high and drop to my knees.

Reina releases Ruby, who takes to the air.

"I'm going to get help," Ruby promises.

My eyes are trained on her form until she disappears out a side door. I didn't have the heart to tell her it doesn't matter. The teachers are all lesser Fae, and the Evermore students have had thousands of years to amass their powers.

The professors are terrified of them. Which means they can do whatever they want to me.

"All hail the Queen of Everwilde," Inara says.

Raucous laughter vibrates the air. Tears wet my eyes, but I blink them back, my jaw grinding so hard my teeth ache.

"Every queen needs her king. Or in this instance, a prince."

My blood goes cold. I glance to the right where a figure begins slowly ascending the stage.

No, it can't be. I freeze as I take in the midnight-blue hair, for once combed neatly into submission. An ink-blue waistcoat so dark it appears black hugs his lithe form, and diamonds sparkle the length of his delicate pointed ears.

He lopes to the stage taking long, powerful strides, every movement screaming power.

A flicker of hope pierces my chest.

Inara beams as she settles a heavy silver crown over his head, just between his sharp ears.

Why is he playing along with this farce? *Look at me. Please look at me—*

"You never smiled for me that way," Rhaegar whispers. He's come up behind me. I guess he's sided with the Unseelie now. Their mutual hatred for me a glue that binds them all together.

And I am smiling, I realize. Because if Valerian is here, he'll put a stop to Inara and Rhaegar's cruel game.

My gaze slides to the prince. Despite the fear rushing through my veins, I feel a twinge of happiness at seeing him. Last night's events flash in my mind, so real I can almost feel his lips on mine, crushing me with his need. The sensation of those same lips dragging over my body is enough to make me blush.

Only now that mouth is mangled in a smirk.

Why won't he look at me? And why can't I feel the bond between us?

"Prince," Inara calls affectionately. "It's time to crown your queen."

My heart flutters as he walks this way. He takes the crown from Inara inside his strong, capable hands. Hands that have been all over my body.

Then he glances casually down at me, his face dark and unreadable, and offers to help me up. Rings glitter from his outstretched fingers. Rings I've never seen him wear before.

My palm is sweaty inside his as I stand. Thank God, he's going to explain this entire mess. His eyes rake over my dress, the one I wore for him. He smiles. Without warning, he leans forward and kisses me. A deep, probing, claiming kiss.

Except this time, it feels different. Shameful and gross. His teeth scrape mine; his mouth violent and bruising.

The great hall breaks into a cheer.

This is all wrong. I yank my head back, touching my swollen mouth. His lips are twisted into a hateful, cruel sneer.

His eyes gleam with excitement as he settles the crown onto my head. He forces it down hard enough that the edges dig into my forehead.

"Did you really think you could be my queen?" he whispers. "That you were my equal?"

Just like that—my heart shatters into a thousand shards of ice. And I remember Mack's warning.

The Fae males place bets on you. Whatever you do, don't fall for one.

"It was all . . . a trick?" I whisper.

"What else could it be? Did you truly think you, a slave-marked human, would stand beside me on my throne? That we could ever be anything but master and slave?"

The total disgust in his voice kills any doubts I had left. A slideshow of all the things we did last night flashes in my memory, just as real as the video Inara just played. The promise he made me becomes a taunting echo inside my head.

I feel sick. Used. An idiot. I remember the feel of his lips as they traced the lines of his brand and I want to cry.

All of this . . . all of it was to break me. What did the prince say the first time I met him? That he would freeze me, chipping away at me until all that remained was my heart. And then he would crush that last piece of me to dust.

I would be broken, erased, and forgotten.

He warned me, but I didn't listen.

But I'm not completely shattered. I refuse to let him have that satisfaction. I force myself to look into his eyes as I wield the raw, consuming pain eating me alive into armor. He cannot hurt me anymore than he already has.

I am broken. I am heartless. I am untouchable.

My rage fills me until it feels like a real, living, breathing

thing between us. And then, almost as if my fury has actually transformed into a monster, a piercing alarm sounds over the loudspeakers.

Three loud, succinct wails.

Darkling.

The dance floor breaks into chaos. Shadow guardians file into the room, headed by Mr. Willis. Part of me wonders where they were when I was up here having my heart publicly crushed for fun. But then again, I guess it's only Fae they protect; we humans mean nothing to them.

I watch inebriated shadows run to find their keepers, and a dark smile finds my face. That duty no longer applies to me.

As everyone rushes around, trying to figure out the best place to hide, no one notices as I slip away, still wearing my crown.

The headmistress doesn't seem surprised when I walk into her office. I'm still in my dress, the long hem stained from being dragged over the floor after I slipped off my heels. The crown fits tightly to my head. She doesn't seem surprised by that, either.

"I'm here to ask that you expel me from school," I say. My voice comes out emotionless, robotic.

She lifts her eyebrows. "On what grounds?"

"I'm sure you've heard what happened." One hand goes to my throat, but I force it down. "I used a spell to make everyone think I was the prince's soulbonded mate. Oh, I also slept with both Rhaegar and the prince. Is that enough? Or do you need the cleverly edited slideshow to convince you?"

She regards me for a long time. Long enough that I notice the ticking of the clock in her office. Long enough that I know she's already seen the slideshow.

Then she steeples her long fingers together and releases a deep sigh. "Somehow, I think that is not what happened at all, Miss Solstice. But in this particular case, expulsion is best for everyone. Especially after what happened with your friend, Evelyn Cantrell."

For the first time since this all happened, I let emotion slip through the carefully constructed armor around my heart. I'd forgotten about her. I knew Mack was safe because I saw her with Asher being herded by a group of shadow guardians into the gym.

"Is Evelyn okay?"

Lepidonis glances down at the papers on her desk, back to me. "I'm sorry to inform you that your friend changed into a darkling sometime last night. She escaped the Island, but not before killing two shadows trying to protect their keepers and a Dawn Court Fae. I hear she was searching for you, almost like she was sent to find you."

I sink against the wall, too shocked to feel the pain of it all yet.

"Very few are aware that when a human is pregnant with a Fae child, that child's magic can turn its host mother into a kind of darkling. They are more sentient than regular darklings, and they look almost human."

"I—I didn't know that was a risk of carrying a Fae baby."

"But you knew she was pregnant." The disappointment in her voice is like a slap to the face. "If we had been aware, we might have been able to give her medicine to stall the transformation until the child was born but . . ." She waves her hand, an angry gesture, and fixes her stern gaze on me. "That is why our rules are so important."

I nod as guilt settles in my belly. I should have told someone. I should have done something.

"Do you have any things to gather before you leave?" she asks softly, and the almost kindness in her voice is enough to bring me to tears.

I shake my head. As soon as I left the dance, I rushed to the dorms for the picture of my parents. I have nothing else.

She nods as if that was expected. "Very well. I'll have Magus prepare to transport you back home."

It takes a moment for that last word to sink in. "Home?"

The word feels awkward in my mouth. Wrong.

Home. Until a few hours ago, I would have said that was here.

"Yes, didn't the prince tell you? He made a special exception for you that specified if you were ever expelled, you were to be sent back to your human house in the Tainted Zone. It may not have all the luxuries you're used to here, but I assure you the Tainted Zone is better than fighting the scourge. The prince did you a kindness."

At the mention of Valerian, a wave of bitterness washes over me. "He did, but not in the way you think. He taught me an important lesson."

Never love a Fae. Lesson learned.

"Indeed." She stands, her moth-like wings unfurling behind her. It's still dark outside, and moonlight filters in through the stained-glass window, coloring her wings green and red and blue. "Unfortunately, whatever lessons you might have learned will be glamoured away, along with any memory of what happens here. We cannot have you spilling secrets for the entire world to hear."

I smile, my hand twitching to go to the necklace burning against my sternum. "Of course. Can't have the things I know falling into the wrong hands."

Her eyes narrow.

"But first, I have to do something."

The headmistress follows me through the darkened corridors to my Faerie Courts classroom. The question is still there on the chalkboard, the third component to power.

A few hours ago I would have guessed the answer was fear.

Not now. Fear may be a component of power, but there's

something stronger and more dangerous than making people terrified of you.

Lepidonis watches with a curious expression as I take a piece of broken chalk and scrawl an answer on the board.

Love.

The third component to power is love. Trick a person into falling in love with you and you can make them do anything. Forget their morals. Their promises. Their friends. Their obligations.

Trick someone into falling in love with you and they will give up themselves entirely. Trick someone into falling in love with you and they are yours forever.

I pause for a moment, then scratch something below it so hard the chalkboard squeals and my chalk breaks twice.

Fuck love. And fuck the Evermore.

55

Two Months Later.

The sun shines down, scalding and angry, and I shield my eyes as I hang another shirt on the clothesline. It's only May but my cheeks are on fire and the flesh of my arms are tinged bright red. Even after two months back in my world, I don't take the sun for granted. Every morning when it lances through my window like the asshole it is, I feel thankful.

I still dream of the cold. I dream of snow that spears the air like shards of glass, of frost that invades my marrow, and a prince who weeps sleet and ice. Sometimes I dream he carves out my heart and packs the wound with snow, and I wake up screaming, my chest aching with cold.

Very rarely, I dream that he kisses me. Those mornings I wake up to a pillow soaked with tears.

I don't care what he says. Our connection was real, just like I know Valerian is his true name. Whatever game he was playing, whatever cruel kick he got from making me fall for him, a part of him fell for me, too. And giving me his name raised the stakes for him somehow.

He knows I could crush him with that truth. And, deep down, I know he likes the power I still wield.

Mostly, though, I've managed to forget him and the dangerous, intoxicating world on the other side of the Shimmer. For a while, Mack would email me updates about school and our friends.

Evelyn is still missing. The Council for the Mistreatment of Humans has started a formal investigation into the school. Because of the inquest, the academy has doubled the training for the end of year Wild Hunt. Rhaegar grows darker by the day, and Basil traded Mack to Asher rather than face her glaring looks. She still hasn't forgiven him for not stopping what happened to me.

Also, the prince is back with Inara.

Soon after that, I asked her to stop mentioning the prince at all.

A few weeks later a package arrived with a cell phone inside. Now we chat daily. Mostly she tells me she misses me and I say I miss her too. Sometimes we talk about Asher and their flirtatious—but platonic—relationship.

Between what happened to me and Evelyn, any potential romance between Mack and Dragon Boy is gone.

Occasionally we bring up Evelyn, but her disappearance is still too painful.

Currently, the conversation revolves around the Wild Hunt.

That's today, by the way.

My stomach has been in knots all morning knowing how nervous Mack is. She and the other first year shadows will be dropped into the Forest of Eyes just outside the scourge lands with their keepers. They'll be split into teams as they face off against trolls and other ancient monsters. Each team will be sent to find one hidden artifact.

"Summer, lunch is ready!" Aunt Zinnia calls. She stands

on the back porch, wearing an apron that says, 'It's always five o'clock somewhere,' over a pink robe and slippers. She watches me for a moment longer, shielding her eyes, before the porch screen slams shut behind her.

When I showed up on the front porch at the crack of dawn two months ago, wearing a Fae dress and a gold crown, my eyes rimmed from crying, Aunt Zinnia screamed. Then she wrapped me in a hug so warm it chased away any of the lingering cold from Everwilde.

She hugged me for a good five minutes. Then, like any good Southern woman who discovered a girl in tears on her porch, she fixed me grits and tea so sweet it made my teeth ache.

Aunt Vi's icy demeanor has taken a bit more time to thaw. But I catch her checking on me late at night when she thinks I'm asleep. We don't speak about what happened, but they've taken to running salt over the windowsills and doorways, and I've found extra rowan berry charms inside my clothes.

I don't have the heart to tell them none of that matters. If the Fae want to come back for me, very few things can stop them. The mark on my arm ensures that.

It's the only part of the prince I can't erase.

I finish hanging up a pair of jeans and then grab the blue plastic laundry basket. For a moment, my gaze wanders to the east, where the Shimmer glints softly in the late morning sky.

I wish I could say I was okay. That I didn't miss the academy and the purpose I'd found there. That I didn't think about my friends daily. I've taken to running again, usually in the mornings. But it's not the same as training with the best Fae assassin in Everwilde.

Hefting my empty basket, I stride toward the house. I make it to the front porch steps when I see him. Cal leans against the top step with two of his friends. He's laughing and slurring his words like he's already drunk. When he sees me, he waves them back to the trio of four wheelers parked in our driveway.

The moment they leave, his demeanor changes. Gone is the drunk, stupid bully. In his place is a very alert, cruel Fae. His ears don't change, but the Fae cunning glints inside his dark eyes.

"Wow," I say, holding the laundry basket up like a battering ram. "What makes me special enough that I get to see the real you?"

A clever smile reveals large white teeth. "I thought you might have met *him* over there. Tell me. What's my human changeling like?"

"Decent. Kind. Basically the opposite of you."

"Ouch. You hurt my feelings." He jerks his head toward the woods. "Come. I want to talk to you."

I set the basket down and begin to follow him.

What am I doing?

I will my legs to stop walking, my mouth to scream. In my head, I know I don't want to follow him, but I can't help it. The long grass scratches against my bare ankles as we near the woods.

He turns, grinning. "You know, I always wondered why I couldn't glamour you into doing things like the others."

My heart lurches. I reach for my necklace . . .

"Looking for this?" His thick fingers pinch the stolen pendant as he holds it up, sunlight catching inside the ruby.

"When did you take it?" I demand, rage swirling inside me. That necklace contains the memory of my parents inside.

He plunges the pendant into his pocket and takes a step closer. "Why, while you were sleeping, Summer."

A shiver wracks my body.

"It's so easy to get inside your window. You should really stop leaving it open at night. And the salt . . ." He *tsks.* "Salt can't hold out a powerful Fae like me. You know that."

"What do you want?"

"Well I already got what I need. What I *want* is a different story."

For some reason, my body begins to tremble. "Cal, what have you done?"

"So the Winter Prince has a name, after all," Cal continues amiably. "Valerian Sylverfrost. Catchy."

My blood runs cold. "Who have you told?"

"Do you know how many Fae want the prince dead? Man, that guy really isn't popular." He shrugs and then glances down at his gold watch. "He'll be dead in about, say, four hours, give or take. Isn't that what you want, Summer?"

Oh, God.

"You probably don't remember, but after I took your necklace and glamoured you last night into giving me your precious prince's name, I had you tell me all about your experience at the academy. Wow, that was entertaining. And that ending . . ." He laughs. "The irony is that it wasn't even the prince who broke your heart."

"What are you talking about?"

"Oberon's beard, you're adorable. You were so over your head at that school." He closes the distance between us. I try to back away but he says, "No, stay."

And I can't resist him.

"Now, where was I? Oh, right. Bane Winterspell. He's a nasty character. Did you know he can make his face look like anyone's?"

My brain whirs as I try to make sense of his words. Where did Bane come from? He wasn't even there that night . . .

He wasn't even *there* that night. But if Inara was finally going to get her revenge on me, Bane would have been front and center with a bowl of popcorn.

Unless he *was* there.

I play Cal's words over in my mind. He can make his face look like anyone's.

Even a prince's.

"You see the truth now, don't you? Clever girl." He reaches up, pushes a strand of hair from my forehead. "The prince wasn't even at the academy that night. He didn't betray you, after all. But you betrayed him. You gave up his name as easily as you let him kiss you."

"Screw you," I growl.

"Oh, I've always loved your fight. After the prince is dead, I'm going to visit you every night. We'll have so much fun, Summer."

"How?" I say, trying to drag out any details possible. "How will they kill him? Even with his name . . . he's too powerful."

His nostrils flare in anger. "Powerful? Let's see how powerful he is when he's faced with an army of darklings and his magic is bound. Did you know, there are ways to control darklings? To use them as assassins? All you need is a name and you can focus all that savage hunger on one single Fae prince."

An army of assassin darklings . . . all trained on Valerian. I shudder. Still, after the last darkling attack, they reinforced the wards over the Island and the academy. They wouldn't be able to get that many darklings past those defenses.

But off campus . . .

"The Wild Hunt," I whisper.

"Ding ding ding." He beams at me. "Stop frowning, Summer. You don't need to worry about him anymore. You have me. In fact, why don't you come back with me for a little while. We'll have a party."

"They'll notice I'm gone." Panic constricts my chest. I

can't leave with him; I have to warn Mack somehow. She'll be with Asher and the prince . . . she could get hurt.

She could *die*.

"So what if they do?"

He reaches for me. At the same time, a blur catches my eye. A thunk, like a hammer hitting raw meat, fills the forest. Cal's face changes, his smirk twitching into surprise. He cries out, collapsing to one knee.

An arrow sticks from his shoulder, silver blood sticky around the entry wound.

Jane walks up with another arrow nocked and ready. They're not iron-tipped so they can't kill him. But they can hurt like the devil.

"She isn't going anywhere, dickwad," Jane shouts.

While he's still trying to process the situation, I slam my palm upward into his nose with a satisfying crack. He flails backward onto his back.

My heart is in my throat as I lean down and fish my pendant from his pocket. Then I grab Jane and we run. We don't stop until we're in my room. I watch from my window as his friends help him to their four wheelers. The same window he came inside last night.

How did I not know?

I don't stop watching until they disappear into the forest.

Then I run to my new cell phone and message Mack.

She doesn't respond, and the message remains unseen.

Crap.

"Summer?" Jane says. She's shaking, but her voice is steady.

"It's okay." I wrap her in a hug and then begin throwing on warm clothes. "You did good, Jane. Cal won't retaliate against you. It's me he wants."

"He's one of them, isn't he?" she asks, her voice way too calm for having just shot a Fae with an arrow.

I nod. "They call them changelings. How much did you hear?"

She tugs at one of her braids. "Enough."

I pull her close. "Thank you for saving me. But now, I have to go back to save someone else."

"The prince he mentioned?"

"Yes, but also my friends." Her hazel eyes narrow and I add, "They're human, and they're innocent bystanders."

She nods as if she understands that part of my speech, at least. But tears glisten her eyes. Tears she's too old and too stubborn to spill.

"Don't promise me, this time," she says, her eyes harder than any fourteen-year-old's should be. "Don't promise you'll come back. Not unless you will."

I squeeze my arms around her one last time, my throat clenched. "I'll see you again, Jane. Who else can keep you from running wild?"

Then I rush down the stairs toward the Shimmer before she can see the hesitation in my eyes.

56

M agus balks when I ask him to open the forbidden vault. He didn't hesitate when I stood in the Faerie ring and called him over using the Gaelic words he gave me two months ago, after he returned me home. Words only to be used in an emergency. And he didn't so much as blink when I demanded transport to the academy. But now, he finally seems to realize what I plan to do, and his large mossy eyes go wide.

Turns out stealing a forbidden weapon imbued with a hundred Fae souls using dark magic is where he draws the line.

He tries to talk me out of it. Tries to make me go to the headmistress instead. But by the time I find her, it might be too late for my friends. And even then, she might not believe me. Not with our history.

After a heated argument, I finally win him over. As the vault door grates open with a whoosh and the tang of dark magic washes over me, I nearly hesitate, everything becoming real.

But then I remember the video of the darkling attack

inside the restaurant. An army of darklings will decimate everyone in the forest today. *Everyone.*

And I cannot let that happen.

Magus grunts behind me, his hooves stamping the damp stone floor. "Hurry and choose your weapon, human. And let's hope it does not kill you."

"Not necessary," I say, pressing into the shadows. "It's already chosen me."

I find Ruby asleep in Mack's dorm room, surrounded by Kit Kat wrappers. She screeches when she wakes, and immediately pledges her services to me. Outside, we discover the portals the first years used near the Lake of Sorrows.

I send Magus off to alert Mr. Willis and then Ruby sniffs each portal before pointing at the farthest one down the line. "The prince and your friend went through that one."

"Are you sure?" I ask. We only get one chance at this.

She flashes an impish grin. "Kid, I'd know that Fae hunk of meat's scent anywhere."

"Which one? Asher or the prince's?"

"Both."

Okay, then. That's not creepy at all. I drag in an anxious breath, steadying my nerves. Then we count to three and cross over.

The second we step foot on the other side, a gray, lifeless world envelops us. Dead trees wend and tangle into a canopy of gnarled branches strangling the sky. There's no life anywhere. No budding foliage or grass or insects. The air is laced with the stench of decay, and snowflakes float around our heads.

No, not snow. Ashes.

"This has to be a mistake," I say. "This portal lead directly *into* the scourge lands."

"Um, kid, we have a problem," Ruby whispers. I glance behind me and my body goes cold. The portal is gone.

"No mistake," I growl. "Whoever wants the prince dead must have messed with the portal so it spit them out in the wrong spot and then wouldn't let them back in."

Earlier, I stuffed the forbidden weapon inside a bright pink backpack I stole from the commons room, and I sling the bag higher onto my shoulder. Ruby uses her abnormal sense of smell to track the group through the woods, leading us deeper and deeper into the Forest of Eyes.

I see immediately where the name came from. Eyes snap open along the tree trunks as we pass, their eerie gaze following us wherever we go. They're all different colors, each pair of eyes unique and too human for my liking.

Ugh.

An hour passes, and I'm sure Ruby has lost the scent, when I hear voices. Frantic voices.

I sprint toward the sounds, sure it's already started. A small clearing opens up. I see figures moving through the dead grass, and my heart leaps at the sight.

Mack and Asher stand side-by-side, holding up swords that glint in the muddled gray light. Eclipsa is near them, legs spread wide in a fighting stance. She wears all black leathers, her silver hair pulled into a simple ponytail that swings well past her shoulders.

A twig snaps beneath my boot, and Eclipsa's head swivels my direction. Her forehead wrinkles slightly in confusion, but then she smiles and rushes toward me. Her hug nearly crushes the life from me.

"What are you doing here?" she demands, pulling back to examine me.

Behind Eclipsa, I see Mack and Asher both turn our way.

Then Mack is screeching and running toward us. She slams into me, hard, and joins the hug.

"What the Fae hells is this?" Asher booms, lumbering over. "A love fest in the middle of the Wild Hunt? This isn't a slumber party, girls."

Eclipsa glares at Asher. "Pipe down, smoke-breath. We're having a moment."

"Well, have that moment somewhere else. That medusa spider is still out there."

Medusa spider? Yep, not even asking about that one.

Curiosity dances in his green eyes as they shift to me. "Summer, it's not that I'm *not* happy you're here. But . . . if you've come to talk to the prince, it's really not the best time."

Eclipsa's face darkens. "It's true. The portal was spelled with forbidden magic and the prince's powers have been bound. He's in a mood. We think it was a rival court, but we still can't figure out how—"

Suddenly, Eclipsa stiffens beside me. Asher glances over his shoulder, releases a long breath, as if shit's about to hit the fan, and then moves.

I knew Valerian would be here, but I wasn't prepared for the way my heart leaps when I lock eyes with him. Nor was I prepared for the look that flashes across his face.

Anger.

"What are you doing here, Princess?" he demands. "It's not safe."

The nerve of this guy. "Yeah, I'm aware."

His gaze scours my body as if scanning for an injury, something to explain my presence. The hard edge of his jaw softens. "Are you . . . in trouble?"

The protective tone in his voice pisses me off. He doesn't get to be that person anymore. The one who uses super annoying nicknames and pretends to care about me.

"No," I snap, "but you are, which means my friends are in trouble by association. I'm here to save *their* lives."

A muscle jumps in Valerian's temple. "Explain."

Ugh. I hate the coldness in his voice. His demanding tone. He might not have participated in Inara's cruel trick, but he let two months pass without telling me the truth. Two whole months where my heart felt cracked in half. Where he let my feelings for him burn into a sick, twisted hatred.

My sudden fury propels me toward him. I slam a finger into his chest—probably hurting myself more than anyone—and glare up at him. "No, you explain." I poke him again. "Explain why you never told me the truth. Why you let me drown in hurt when you promised to always protect me."

His hand reaches up, his cool fingers circling my forearm, where his brand scrolls over my flesh. Gently, his fingers slide to my wrist and he tugs my hand down. "I promised to keep you safe from harm. To protect you no matter the price. That's exactly what I did."

His stoic answer only serves to piss me off.

"Safe from harm?" I snap. "You broke my fucking heart."

The silence that follows is almost worse than the apathy in his voice.

Ruby flutters above the prince's head. "Kid," she says. "As much as I enjoy watching this public flaying, and I do—I really, *really* do. I have to wonder if we really have time for this?"

"You're right." Crossing my arms, I glance up at her and then to the others. "But when this is over, if we survive, I need to know the truth. All of it."

Valerian goes very still. He looks to Eclipsa then back to me. "Fair enough. Now, why are you here?"

The darklings arrive with the rain. I've told the others everything I learned, along with the changeling glamouring me into revealing Valerian's name. Eclipsa raised an eyebrow at that but didn't say a word.

I glance at the dark shapes flickering through the dead trees like shadows. Their hisses mix with the soft pattering of rain to form an eerie chorus. The thought that they were once humans weighs heavy on my mind.

Could Aunt Zinnia's daughter be here? Aunt Vi's family?

There are so many missing humans, any one of which could be the deranged creatures lurking in the trees beyond.

We're spread out in a circle, Ruby above. Only the prince's magic has been bound, but you'd never know it by the confident way he holds his broadsword.

Mack is to my right. I've never been more proud of my friend as she grips her rapier with unshaking hands. Ready to die to protect her keeper and her friends. But my bow has to be the coolest weapon of all. The wood is baby-smooth inside my palms as I retrieve an arrow from my quiver, pinch the shaft between my thumb and pointer finger, and pull the string taut.

Through the crashing roar of my heart, I swear distant whispers pulse from the weapon.

The darklings descend all at once. Almost as if on a command. They streak across the meadow so fast they're mere flickers. I release an arrow. Nerves throw off my aim, but the magic inside the arrow veers it into my target. Grinning, I release another. Then another. My movements impossibly fast.

Each arrow hits its mark effortlessly.

The other's fight just as hard. Mack's rapier cleaves the air as she pushes back the attack. Despite the darkling's speed, Mack makes contact again and again. But her sword is steel, not iron, and the darklings she hits rise over and over.

It's like some horrible dream where the bad guy doesn't die, just grows stronger.

Ruby uses some sort of confusion spell to make the darklings spin in circles like dogs chasing their tails. But that spell doesn't last long. Next, she sends a swarm of magical butterflies into the group. The darklings hiss and swat at the insects before refocusing on us.

A huge explosion of flame bursts across the meadow, illuminating the hundreds of darklings on the field.

Asher! A quick glance and . . . holy freaking crap. He's shifted into his dragon form.

Gasping, I barely rip my gaze from the sight of the enormous gray and green scaled dragon, his black-tipped gray wings outspread as they flap once, twice, propelling him into the sky. The gusts from his wings send darklings flying.

I watch, both petrified and in awe, as roiling swathes of fire surge from his mouth, the gray smoke choking the air.

Countless darklings catch on fire. They screech in pain. But even as living torches, they keep coming.

Only iron can kill them. Only *I* can kill them.

A group of darklings rush toward the prince. With a wild yell, Eclipsa and her twin blades fall on the writhing mass of creatures. Bright stars of magic bloom between the fray as she hits them with her powers, sending the wave receding.

At first, I don't think the prince is doing anything. Then I realize he's simply moving too fast. At some point, he's in the middle of a pack of darklings, the steel of his broadsword flashing the only thing I can make out, when a darkling sneaks up behind him.

No! Panic constricts my throat. I have an arrow in my hands and it's flying toward the creature before I can blink. It sinks to the fletching in the darkling's back. The moment the iron meets its flesh, the monster falls dead. The prince flips around just in time to see the darkling's body erupt in red flames from the inside out.

His gaze flicks to me.

I grin.

But when I glance back to the forest, my smile fades. There's just too many darklings. They spill from the trees like ants, a never-ending wave of death and destruction. And they're smarter than I gave them credit for, seeming to work in tandem to outflank us.

In fact, one of the darklings seems to lead the others.

Which, from everything I know about the creatures, is impossible.

I aim my arrows at the darkling leader, but the creature is just too quick. My arm is tiring. The bow quivering inside my aching fingers.

Ruby drops to my shoulder. "This is the end, kid. It's been fun. And by fun I mean screw this entire meadow and the Fae zombie humans who don't die."

I release another arrow, hitting a darkling a few feet away. "I'm not giving up yet, Ruby."

Eclipsa and Mack press close. I share a look with my best friend, surprised by how fierce she looks. A fiery look gleams in her eyes, her nose scrunched and jaw clenched in determination.

She truly would die protecting her keeper.

Valerian joins us as we're forced tightly together. "On the count of three, I'm going to run toward the woods." He nods to his right. "The darklings will follow me."

Eclipsa shoots him a savage scowl. "Hell, no. If you think for a moment I'm going to let you steal all this glory—"

"I'm ordering you," Valerian says. His focus shifts to me. "I made a promise to keep someone safe from harm, and I won't break that promise."

My stomach clenches. I feel queasy. I shake my head as Eclipsa gives a dutiful nod.

Before I can protest, before I can tell Valerian that despite everything he's done, I would never let him die alone, bright UV lights flood the field.

The darklings freeze. Then they begin wailing and tearing at their flesh. I follow the light to the group of shadow guardians rushing from the woods, and my body sags with relief.

Mr. Willis leads the guardians. They have guns and swords and weapons I've never seen before, all imbued with iron. A group of shadows hold a hose and a blast of silver liquid shoots onto the meadow, taking down scores of darklings. They make sure to direct the iron imbued liquid away from our group.

Mr. Willis runs over to us, a pistol held low and pointed at the ground. His wide-eyed gaze goes from Asher still in the sky, to Ruby, to Mack and Eclipsa, Valerian, and finally, the forbidden weapon in my hands.

"I thought for sure we would find you already dead." His voice is gruff, but I can tell by his smile he's impressed. He meets my eyes and holds out a gloved hand. "The weapon, Miss Solstice."

A growl rumbles in my chest. My fingers tighten over the longbow. Voices whisper into my ear, begging me to keep it.

We belong to you. Only you.

Mr. Willis holds out his hand. "Hand it over now, Miss Solstice. That's a very dangerous weapon, and you could hurt yourself or someone else."

I can barely open my fingers, every cell in my body urging me to resist. But I do. Finally.

A strange smile twitches his lips. "We won't tell Lepidonis about this, will we?"

I shake my head.

"Good. Now go before the iron cast off makes the Fae students sick. We have a portal close to this spot that will take you to safety."

A group of fourth year guardians have come to help, and they escort us away from the battle. The guardians flinch as Asher lands to the left, knocking over dead trees with a crack, and transforms back into his Fae form.

I'd always read shifters shifted back naked, so I'm a little disappointed when he's fully clothed.

Ruby curses beside me. "Stupid re-clothing spell."

Eclipsa laughs. "Trust me, it's not *that* impressive."

"Lies," Asher asserts, catching up with us. "Every part of me is impressive." He grabs the arm of one of the shadow guardians. "Hey, why are we leaving? I was just getting started frying those bastards."

Valerian snorts, pulling him off the poor fourth year. "Easy there, big guy. And you wouldn't be saying that if you were on the ground with those things."

I smile, but I can't help but remember how close the prince was to sacrificing everything for us.

For me.

We're nearing the edge of the woods when I glance over my shoulder. The shadows have pushed the darklings back, and some have started fleeing into the forest. One darkling, the one who lead the others, has broken off and follows along the forest line, shadowing us.

There's too many guardians for it to attack, but it follows anyway.

Not it. She. Unlike the other darklings, she walks upright, and she still has her hair and clothes. I can make out the tangled matted mess of red from here. A gold dress shredded and stained beyond recognition hangs in tatters around her emaciated form. Her features are still more human than monster, her ears jagged, deformed spikes.

Diamond earrings flash from them.

She grins at me, and something about the smile and the dress and the earrings pulls it all together.

Evelyn.

Before I can tell the others, she disappears into the cover of the woods.

As soon as we come out on the other side of the portal, the entire school cheers. When the headmistress learned of the attack, she cancelled the rest of the Wild Hunt, just to be on the safe side. Everyone has been waiting here to see if we survived.

The crowd quiets as the headmistress approaches us, her skin pale, almost bloodless. Her gaze flits over Valerian, then the others, assessing the damage. I can only imagine she expected more dead humans. Or worse. The death of the Winter King's heir.

I imagine that wouldn't be great for her career.

She regains some of her color as she realizes that everyone survived. Then she settles her focus on me. Her eyes narrow, her wings curling tight to her back.

She hesitates before saying, "Thank you, for saving the Winter Prince."

Ruby scoffs. "That's all Summer gets? A lame thank you? If Summer hadn't come back to warn you, that attack would have been a bloodbath. Fae and human body parts everywhere." Ruby flits over to stare the headmistress in the face.

"She didn't have to come back here. Hell, with the way this school has treated her, she should have let everything burn."

Eclipsa raises an eyebrow in offense, but doesn't say a word.

Lepidonis settles her firm gaze on me once more. "We owe Miss Solstice a great debt. What would you like in return?"

I don't even hesitate. "I want to come back next year."

Her eyes widen in surprise, and it takes a few moments before she answers. "As you wish. You are now enrolled for year two at Evermore Academy. At your own peril, might I add."

Mack and the others cheer along with half the school. The Seelie side, at least. But Inara and her friends don't even bother to hide their boos.

And Valerian . . . Valerian has donned his icy mask once again, his reaction totally unreadable.

Valerian stays true to his word. After all of us are assessed at the healing center to ensure we weren't bitten or otherwise injured, he leads me silently down to the vaults. Eclipsa follows at a distance. Probably because of the wary, hurt way I still look at Valerian. Even though the prince who humiliated me in front of the entire school wasn't actually him, he still hurt me.

Deeply.

"What are we doing here?" I ask. We're in the hall of antiquities where the beautiful gowns float around the room like specters.

"You'll understand soon." He stands there for a heartbeat, almost as if unsure where to start. Then his focus moves upward and catches on something.

I do the same. When I see what he's staring at, the

Summer Princess suspended midair, a puzzled frown finds my face. "Did you . . . know her?"

His eyebrows gather as something dark shifts inside his eyes. "I loved her."

Oh—*oh*. I stare at the Summer Princess with renewed interest, a pang of jealousy worming into my heart.

"But you and Princess Hyacinth fought each other in the Nocturus." I remember now the story of how the princess bested him with the whip and then spared his life.

A wry smile quirks his lips. "Yes. I knew I loved her way before she ever felt the same about me." He drags his eyes away from the floating Fae girl and settles his gaze on me. "Did you really think a whip with snowdrops would best me?"

"So the story about your father having you whipped isn't true?"

"Oh, it's true. But I let her win."

"Why?"

"Because I had to know if she loved me back."

"She could have killed you," I snap, trying and failing not to sound petty as another round of jealousy burns across my cheeks.

"Yes, but once you love someone the way I did her—let's just say, if she didn't return my love, I would have preferred death."

"But she did. Love you, I mean."

"Yes. We were soul bound."

I blink, wrestling with my emotions. Part of me hates her.

No, *all* of me hates her.

"When her father found out we were mates, he locked her up. You see, they had been hiding her rare magic from the world. It was stronger than even my own. With us soul-bound, my own magic would have been limitless. But her father couldn't stand the thought of all that power going to the Winter Court. He was afraid my grandfather, Oberon, would use it to finally destroy the Seelie Courts."

I take a breath. Why does this sound so familiar?

"She tried to escape. She nearly made it to me. I was waiting just outside the palace walls. We were going to run away together. But"—his hands flex into fists—"her father discovered her moments before she made it out the gates. And he killed her right there while I watched through the bars. He murdered his own daughter to keep her powers away from my court."

A sob bubbles up my throat and I barely swallow it down. I can't imagine a father killing his daughter. I can't imagine any of this.

"She was an Evermore, but the king refused to let a soul-mancer perform the proper rites. He knew every court would track her new soul down for the power it harbors. But her mother snuck into the burial chamber and performed the rites in secret. She was interrupted before she could fully complete the act."

I glance up at the girl again. "So, her soul is just . . . out there wandering around?"

He shakes his head slowly. "No, *Princess*. Her soul found a body. A human baby who had just died in childbirth."

"Where? Who?"

Only, at this very moment, I hear his nickname for me, Princess. Really hear it.

Like it slaps me upside my oblivious face.

Princess. How many times has he called me that? I thought he was just being cruel.

He lifts a hand to my face, seems to think better of it, and then curls his fingers into a fist at his side. "All the courts have been searching for her ever since then. I have spies in every court, and when I learned one of the Darken's followers had dispatched tracker wolves to a small town in the Tainted Zone . . ."

My heart skips a beat.

"I didn't know it was her, not for sure. Imagine loving someone and then they become someone else overnight. A stranger. They look different, their laugh has changed. Their nose crinkles when they're amused. They eat with their fingers instead of using utensils, and smile when they're sleeping, and cry when they're mad. They're starving, yet their heart is too kind to kill what they hunt. And anything they do bring home, stolen or otherwise, they selflessly give to their family."

Me. There's no doubt now he's talking about me. For some reason, I recall how he had my picture. How he had obviously stared at it for hours at a time.

Now I know why.

"I watched her for over a year. When I couldn't be there I had my familiar stay to protect her."

The owl.

"But then, the wolves found her farm. I knew any day they would discover her and inform their master."

The animal tracks around our house.

"So I made an excuse to send her to the academy, knowing the wards there would hide her from the tracker wolves. But I didn't realize the mating bond had already been activated by that one chance encounter."

I take a step back. I can't breathe. Can't think of a single thing to say.

"If anyone realized we were mates, they would know her secret. So I had to be cruel to her. Had to fight off my feelings every second of every day. I didn't expect her to feel the bond too. I hoped she would hate me, but when she didn't . . . I was too weak to fight the bond anymore.

"And then something happened that changed everything.

By then, the tracker wolves had moved on and she was safe again in her farmhouse. I knew going to her would only put her in danger, so I let her hate me . . . despite how it hurt me."

I remember the night we spent together. That was a moment of weakness for him, I see now. And in his mind, when Inara and Bane tricked me into hating him once again, he let me feel that way.

To protect me no matter the price.

"She did hate you," I whisper. "She burned with it."

"And now?" he asks. He watches me without blinking. He's so very, very still.

"Now, I don't know. I need time to process this. What you're saying . . ." I blow out a breath, sending blonde hair flying from my face.

How does one go about convincing oneself she's a murdered Fae princess?

"You can have all the time you need," he answers softly. "I'll be here, waiting."

I swallow. "I do know one thing."

He runs a hand through his dark blue hair, his eyes wide and expectant and a little afraid.

"I can never go back to my life before," I say. "This academy, this world, it's my home. I don't care if I'm not safe here. I refuse to cower and be afraid. Who knows? Maybe I can graduate and actually do some good. Change the way the Fae treat humans. That kind of stuff."

He stares at me for a long time. Then he dons his mask, becoming the cruel, heartless prince everyone knows him to be.

As he walks away, he glances over his shoulder, lips quirked in a dark grin. "Of that, I have no doubt. See you around . . . *Princess*."

"Chew with your mouth closed, jerk," Jane chides, glaring at Tanner. Chatty Cat purrs in her lap, his lime-green eyes trained on her hand as she slips him bits of honeyed-ham.

Tanner rolls his eyes and chews even louder. Aunt Vi scowls at the two before turning her attention on the twins. "Forks, children. Use them. Or are we a family of heathens?"

Aunt Zinnia rushes into the dining room. Her face is red and flustered, her golden curls sticking out at all angles. She holds out a pan of cornbread between two mismatched oven mitts. "It's here, I only burned it a little."

"Oh, goodie," Aunt Vi says before taking a long, careful sip of her spiked tea. I'm impressed she managed to hold back the barrage of sarcastic comments I know are loaded and ready on her sharp tongue.

Thanks to our guest, Vi's on her best behavior.

Mack sits beside me at the table, a grin brightening her face as she takes it all in. She's staying with me for the weekend. Technically, she's not supposed to enter the Tainted Zone, but her dads found a way to make it happen. I know they're worried about her because they call every couple of hours.

But after learning how I saved her life, they kinda love me. And with all that calling, Nick and Aunt Zinnia have become fast friends.

Despite Aunt Zinnia and Nick's opposing views on the Fae, they get along gloriously. They gab for hours on the cordless phone while Aunt Vi sits at the table and glares, pretending she's not listening in on their conversation.

"More rolls, Mackenzie?" Jane asks Mack.

Jane hasn't stopped staring at Mack since she arrived. They don't make girls like Mack in Amarillo, that's for sure. Already, Jane has talked Mack into painting her nails and putting streaks of black in her red hair tonight—black, for frick's sake.

I've never seen Jane so happy. I've never seen *any* of them so happy. It took a while after announcing I was attending the academy in the fall for things to return to normal, but eventually, we fell back into our dysfunctional rhythm.

It helps that I used the gold crown from the dance to buy enough food to last until winter. Turns out some people will pay a hefty price for a real gold crown from Everwilde.

"Oh!" Vi says. She throws a hand over her mouth. "We forgot to say the prayer." With a horrified expression, Vi turns to Mack. "We aren't normally so uncouth."

Mack and I share an amused look, and then she smiles, putting Vi at ease. "Aunt Violet, I've been to dinner parties that were the toast of the Upper East Side, but hands down, this has been my favorite."

After we're all thoroughly stuffed, we gather the china and take turns washing and drying everything. At some point, I hear Chatty Cat mewling to go outside. He likes to watch the birds in a patch of sun right before nightfall.

The iron plated door is heavy and cold against my palm.

All the windows and doors have been reinforced with the highly toxic metal, and a new box of shotgun shells containing iron pellets rests on the entryway table. Not that Cal would try coming here again.

I'm fuzzy on the details, but a few days after I returned home, I found a note on my pillow from Eclipsa. She's staying at the academy during the break to help Professor Spreewell with some soulmancy spells.

Hey, beotch,

I miss your mortal face. Please come back soon before I murder your sprite. Oh, and that changeling won't bother you anymore. The prince and I had a nice little chat with him. You're welcome.

Love and light,

~E

I have no idea what they did to him, but he hasn't shown his face since.

I push the door open, the hinges creaking. "Don't you dare kill any birds," I warn Chatty, "or you won't be long for this world. Got it?"

He growls in understanding and then, tail swishing, saunters to a puddle of sun on the porch and flops down.

Leaning against the doorframe, I peer out into the woods. A flicker of movement catches my eye. On instinct, I freeze. I know what lurks on the other side of the Shimmer, and I'll never look at our forest the same.

Through the tangerine shafts of dusk piercing the trees, delicate white specks spiral to the ground. They float slowly, almost trapped in the sunbeam, like snowdrops suspended in amber.

My breath hitches at the same time a light breeze stirs. It rustles the leaves and lightly lifts the ends of my hair.

Valerian.

I smile and watch the snowflakes filter through the

branches until they slowly fade away. The icy wind dies, the snow dusting the ground melts.

Anyone else would be surprised, or at the very least, impressed.

But once you've been to Everwilde, once you've seen the magic and the lethal beauty of the Fae, once you've met Lunar Court assassins, Fae who shift into massive fire-breathing dragons, and a prince with no name, anything seems possible.

Even snow in summer.

The End

AFTERWORD

Thank you so much for reading *Evermore Academy: Winter.* I hope you enjoyed getting to know Summer and her friends as much as I loved writing them.

Book two, *Evermore Academy: Spring,* should be up for preorder soon. Follow me on Facebook for updates!

www.facebook.com/audreygreybooks/

ABOUT THE AUTHOR

Audrey Grey lives in the charming state of Oklahoma surrounded by animals, books, and little people. You can usually find Audrey hiding out in her office, downing copious amounts of caffeine while dreaming of tacos and holding entire conversations with her friends using gifs. Audrey considers her ability to travel to fantastical worlds a superpower and loves nothing more than bringing her readers with her.

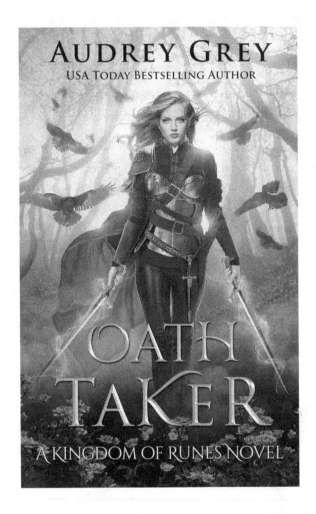

Light magic is forbidden.

Dark magic spells death.

Haven has both.

After the Prince of Penryth saved her from captivity, seventeen-year-old Haven Ashwood spends her days protecting the kind prince and her nights secretly fighting the monsters outside the castle walls.

When one of those monsters kidnaps Prince Bell, Haven must ally with Archeron Halfbane and his band of immortals to rescue her friend.

Her quest takes her deep into the domain of a warped and vicious queen where the rules are simple: break her curse or die.

Lost in a land of twisted magic and fabled creatures, Haven finds herself unprepared, not just for the feelings she develops for Archeron, but for the warring powers raging inside her.

Her rare and forbidden type of magic may be their only hope . . . but mixing light and dark comes with a steep price.

Haven's soul.

Faced with impossible love, heartbreaking betrayals, and a queen intent on destroying the realm, only one thing remains certain.

Haven must shatter the curse or it will devour everything she loves.

GRAB HERE: http://bit.ly/OathTakerBook

CPSIA information can be obtained
at www.ICGtesting.com
Printed in the USA
LVHW032016210221
679522LV00001B/49